# MIRROR OF OUR SORROWS

# Pierre Lemaitre

# MIRROR OF OUR SORROWS

*Translated from the French by*
*Frank Wynne*

MACLEHOSE PRESS
QUERCUS · LONDON

First published in the French language as *Miroir de nos peines*
by Éditions Albin Michel, 2020
First published in Great Britain in 2023 by MacLehose Press
This paperback edition published in 2024 by

MacLehose Press
An imprint of Quercus Publishing Ltd
Carmelite House
50 Victoria Embankment
London EC4Y 0DZ

An Hachette UK company

ISBN (MMP) 978 1 52941 691 6
ISBN (Ebook) 978 1 52941 693 0

Designed and typeset in Sabon by Libanus Press Ltd
Printed and bound in Great Britain by Clays Ltd, Elcograf S.p.A.

Papers used by MacLehose Press are from well-managed forests
and other responsible sources.

*To Pascaline,*

*For Catherine and Albert,*
*with my gratitude*
*and my affection.*

"For everything that happened, there was
someone else to blame"
William McIlvanney, *Laidlaw*

"Wherever man goes, he carries his novel with him"
Benito Pérez Galdós, *Fortunata and Jacinta*

"If it is powerfully to move, a play requires
great displeasures, injuries and deaths."
Corneille, *Horace*

April 6, 1940

# I

Those who thought the war would soon begin had long since grown weary, among them, Monsieur Jules. More than six months after the general mobilisation, the dispirited owner of La Petite Bohème café had ceased to believe that war would ever come. Indeed, as she worked her shift, Louise had even heard him remark "Truth be told, no-one ever really believed in this war". According to Monsieur Jules, the whole thing was little more than a vast diplomatic wrangling spanning the whole of Europe, punctuated by bombastic patriotic speeches, thunderous announcements: a continental chess game in which the general mobilisation was no more than histrionic posturing. Granted, there had been a few deaths here and there – "More than they've reported, no doubt" – the skirmish in the Sarre in September had claimed the lives of two or three hundred men but, "I wouldn't call that a war!" Monsieur Jules would say popping his head around the kitchen door. The gas masks that had arrived in autumn and now lay forgotten in some drawer had become the subject of ridicule in newspaper cartoons. People shuffled down to the air-raid shelters as if taking part in some pointless ritual; these were sirens without planes, and this was a war without battles that seemed to drag on interminably. The one thing that felt tangible was the enemy, the same sempiternal enemy the populace was vowing to exterminate for the third time in half a century, but an enemy that seemed no more inclined than they were to hurl itself into the fray. So much so that, by spring, the État-Major gave permission for soldiers at the front – here, Monsieur Jules would transfer his dish towel to his other hand and jab his finger at the heavens to underscore the enormity of the situation – to plant vegetable gardens! "I ask you . . . !" he would sigh heavily.

Little surprise, then, that the opening of hostilities – though it took place in northern Europe and was too far away for his taste – rekindled his enthusiasm. He would say to anyone who cared to listen, "When you see the drubbing the Allies gave Hitler at the Battle of Narvik, you know this war isn't going to last long," and, considering the matter closed, he could return to his customary causes for complaint: inflation, press censorship, the days he did not get to have an aperitif, the pen-pushers with their cushy jobs, the authoritarian antics of tin-pot governors (particularly that old fogey de Froberville), the curfews, the price of coal – nothing found favour in his eyes, excepting the military strategy of Général Gamelin, which Monsieur Jules considered peerless.

"If they come for us, they'll come through Belgium, that's self-evident. And let me tell you, we'll be waiting for them!"

Louise, who was carrying plates of *poireaux vinaigrette* and *pieds paquet*, overheard one diner muttering "Self-evident my backside . . ."

"For pity's sake!" roared Monsieur Jules returning to his rightful place behind the bar once more, "Where else are they going to come from?"

He seized the wire egg holder on the bar and set it down.

"There! That's the Ardennes: they're impassable!"

With the wet dishrag he drew a sweeping curve on the bar.

"That's the Maginot Line: also impassable! So, where else can they attack? The only possibility is Belgium."

Then, his tactical demonstration complete, he withdrew to the kitchen, muttering under his breath.

"Bloody fool . . . You don't need to be a général to work it out . . ."

Louise did not listen to the remainder of the conversation because her primary concern was not Monsieur Jules and his martial gesticulations, but the doctor.

This was how he had always been known; they had called him "the doctor" for twenty years, since he first began dining at the same table by the window every Saturday. He had never exchanged more than a handful of words with Louise: good day, good evening. He would arrive just before noon and settle himself with his newspaper. Though his invariable request was for the dessert of the day, every day Louise made it a point of honour to go over and take his order, uttered in a gentle, equable tone, "Clafoutis, oh yes," he would say, "clafoutis sounds perfect."

He would read his paper, stare out at the street, eat his dessert, drink a carafe of wine and, a little before two o'clock, as Louise was counting the money in the till, he would get to his feet, neatly fold his copy of *Paris-Soir* and leave it on the table, place a tip in the saucer, say his goodbyes and take his leave. Even the previous September, when the café-restaurant had been abuzz with news of the general mobilisation (Monsieur Jules had been so ebullient that one almost felt inclined to entrust him with running the État-Major), the doctor had not varied his routine one iota.

Then, suddenly, some weeks earlier, as Louise was setting down his crème brûlée à l'anis, he had smiled, leaned towards her, and made his proposition.

Had he suggested sleeping with her, Louise would have set down the dish, slapped him across the face, calmly returned to serving tables, and Monsieur Jules would have lost his longest-standing customer. But it had not been that. Yes, it had been a sexual proposition, but . . . how to put it . . .

"I would like to see you naked," he said placidly. "Just once. Just to look at you, nothing more."

Lost for words, Louise had not known how to respond; she had flushed crimson as though she were at fault, opened her mouth to speak, but no words came. The doctor had already resumed reading his newspaper, Louise wondered whether perhaps she had dreamed it.

She had spent the rest of her shift thinking about his proposition, vacillating between astonishment and anger, yet knowing that it was too late, that by rights she should have stood there with her hands on her hips and confronted him, shamed him in front of the other diners . . . She could feel black fury welling inside her. When a plate slipped from her fingers and shattered on the kitchen tiles, she snapped. She rushed back into the café.

The doctor had gone.

His folded newspaper lay on the empty table.

She snatched it up and tossed it into the wastepaper basket. "What on earth has got into you, Louise?" said Monsieur Jules, who considered the doctor's copies of *Paris-Soir* and customers' mislaid umbrellas to be the spoils of war.

He retrieved the newspaper, smoothed it out and stared at Louise perplexedly.

Louise had been an adolescent when she first began working the Saturday shift at La Petite Bohème and first encountered Monsieur Jules, sole proprietor and chief cook. He was a slow, heavyset man with a large nose, ears that sprouted thick tufts of hair and a salt-and-pepper walrus moustache. He invariably wore carpet slippers and a large black beret that completely covered his pate – no-one had ever seen him hatless. Every day, he cooked for some thirty diners – "Good honest Parisian food!" he would insist, jabbing an emphatic finger. The menu consisted of a single "plat du jour". "Just like at home – if customers want a choice, they've only to cross the street." What precisely Monsieur Jules did was shrouded in mystery. The clientele often wondered how this plump, slow-moving man who always seemed to be perched behind the bar somehow managed to cook so many meals of such high quality. The restaurant was always full; indeed, Monsieur Jules could have opened evenings and Sundays, even enlarged the dining room, but he always demurred. "If you open a door too wide, you never know who'll come in," he would say, then cryptically add: "Trust me, I know a thing or two . . ." The words would hang in the air like a prophecy.

Monsieur Jules had first asked Louise if she would help out in the restaurant the year that his wife, whom no-one now remembered, ran off with the son of the coal merchant from the rue Maracadet. What had begun as a favour for a neighbour carried on throughout Louise's studies at Teacher Training College. On graduation, she found a post at the local primary school on the rue Damrémont and so had no reason to change her habits. Monsieur Jules paid her under the counter, usually rounding up to the nearest ten francs, though always gruffly, as though she had asked and he were doing so reluctantly.

Louise felt as though she had always known the doctor. Consequently, she might not have considered his desire to see her naked so immoral had he not watched her grow up. His request felt somehow incestuous. Moreover, she had only recently lost her mother. What kind of proposition was this to make to an orphan? In fact, Madame Belmont had been dead for seven months, and Louise had not worn mourning for six of those. She winced at the weakness of her own argument.

She wondered why an old man should want to see her naked. Undressing herself later that evening, she stood in front of the full-length bedroom mirror. At thirty, she had a flat stomach and a tender pubis downed with light-brown hair. She turned sideways. She had never liked her breasts, which she thought too small, but she was proud of her arse. She had her mother's oval face, with high cheekbones, shimmering blue eyes and a pretty, slightly pouting mouth. Paradoxically, it was her thick lips that people first noticed, although she was neither smiling nor talkative, and never had been, not even as a child. In the neighbourhood, locals attributed her solemnity to the hardships she had endured: her father had died in 1916, her uncle a year later, and her mother had suffered from depression and spent much of her life standing at the window staring out into the courtyard. The first man to look at her as though she were beautiful was a *gueule cassée* – a soldier who had fought in the Great War and lost half his face in a burst of shrapnel. Talk about a childhood.

Louise was a pretty girl, though she refused to admit it, even in her thoughts. "There are hundreds of prettier girls out there," she told herself. She had many admirers, but "that doesn't mean anything, all girls have admirers". In her job as a teacher, she found herself constantly rebuffing overtures from colleagues and headmasters (and even the fathers of pupils) who would try to put a hand on her buttocks in the corridors, but that was hardly unusual, it happened everywhere. She had never lacked for suitors. Among them, Armand, who had courted her for five years. They were duly betrothed. Louise was not about to give her neighbours food for scandalmongering. Their wedding had been quite an affair. Madame Belmont had sagely allowed Armand's mother to take care of all the arrangements: the ceremony, the reception, the toast, the sixty guests including Monsieur Jules who showed wearing black tie and tails (Louise later discovered he had rented his suit from a theatrical costumier, which explained why everything was too small, except for the trousers, which he had to constantly hike up) and patent leather pumps that made his feet look as small as those of a Chinese empress, Monsieur Jules who insisted on playing master of ceremonies on the pretext that he had closed the restaurant so they could hold the reception there. Louise did not care, she was eager to go to bed with Armand, to have his baby. A baby that never came.

The engagement had dragged on for some time. The neighbours did not understand. They had begun to eye the couple suspiciously. What couple courted for three years without marrying? It was unheard of. It was Armand who had insisted on the wedding, meanwhile Louise deferred her decision every month until she stopped having her period. Most young women prayed heaven they would not fall pregnant before their wedding day; for Louise the reverse was true: no baby, no wedding. But still no baby came.

In desperation, Louise made one last attempt. Since they could not have a child of their own, they would go and get one from the orphanage – there was no shortage of babies who needed love and care. Armand saw this as an insult to his manhood. "Why not take in the dog that roots through the dustbins?" he said, "He needs love and care too!" These conversations would get out of hand, it happened constantly, and they bickered like an old married couple. On the day the subject of adoption was raised, Armand angrily stalked out, went home and did not return.

Louise felt relieved, believing that he was at fault. What a scandal the break-up caused in the neighbourhood. "For heaven's sake," roared Monsieur Jules, "if the girl doesn't want to marry, you can hardly force her into it!" But privately, he took Louise aside: "How old are you, Louise? Your Armand is a fine, upstanding young man, what more do you want?", then, in hushed, faltering tones, "A baby? A baby? The baby will come when it's ready, these things take time!" and he would retreat to his kitchen ". . . my bechamel sauce will be curdled, that's all I need . . ."

What Louise missed most about Armand was the baby she never gave him. And what, until that moment, had been an unmet desire slowly became an obsession. Louise longed for a child at all costs, at any price, even if it meant her ruin. She felt her heart break at the sight of a newborn in a perambulator. She cursed herself, reviled herself; she would wake with a start in the early hours, convinced she could hear a baby crying, scramble out of bed, bumping into the furniture, run down the corridor and open the door and her mother would say "It's just a dream, Louise," take her daughter in her arms and lead her back to bed as though she were a little girl.

The house was mournful as a graveyard. At first, she locked up the room she had planned to transform into a nursery. Later she would creep in on the sly and sleep on the floor with only a thin blanket, though her mother was not taken in.

Troubled by her daughter's fixation, Madame Belmont would hold her, stroke her hair, tell her she understood, that there was more to life than having babies – an easy thing for her to say, since she had one.

"I know it's not fair," Jeanne Belmont would say, "but maybe Mother Nature is trying to tell you that you should first find a father for your baby . . ."

It was a fatuous statement: Mother Nature, all that drivel that had infuriated her at school . . .

"Yes, yes, I know it upsets you. What I'm trying to say is . . .

Sometimes it's better to do things the right way round, that's all. Find the right man, and then . . ."

"I had a man!"

"Well, clearly he was not the right man."

And so, Louise took lovers. In secret. She slept with men from far-flung neighbourhoods, men from her school. If a man on the omnibus gave her the glad eye, she would respond as discreetly as morality allowed. Two days later, she would close her eyes, stare at the cracks in the ceiling, make little moans, then spend the next weeks waiting for her period to start. "I don't care how he behaves," she said to herself, thinking about her unborn child, as though accepting some future ordeal might hasten its arrival. This was a chronic madness, she knew it, yet it haunted her.

She began to go to church, light votive candles, confess imagined sins so that she might receive absolution. She dreamed of suckling a child. When lovers pressed their lips to her breast, she would weep; she longed to lash out at every one of them. She rescued a stray kitten, relishing the fact that it was filthy; she spent her days brushing, scouring, washing the animal as the cat quickly grew fat and needy, just what she needed to expiate the fault she felt she had committed by being barren. Jeanne Belmont said the cat was a catastrophe, but did nothing to deter its presence.

Wearied by her doomed attempts to conceive, Louise decided to consult a doctor. The verdict was categorical, she could not bear a child, a problem with her tubes, the result of several bouts of salpingitis, there was nothing to be done. As if in sympathy, that same night, the cat was run over outside La Petite Bohème. Good riddance, said Monsieur Jules.

Louise foreswore the company of men; she became surly and ill-tempered. At night, she would pound her head against the wall, she began to despise herself. When she looked at herself in the glass, she saw the imperceptible tics, that pinched, tense, prickly expression common to those women consumed by the disappointment of not having children. While some women she knew – her colleague Edmonde, or Madame Croizet who ran the tobacconist's – blithely accepted being childless. But for Louise, not being a mother felt like a humiliation.

Men were frightened by her repressed pent-up anger. Even café regulars, who had often taken serious liberties, no longer dared brush up against her as she moved between the tables. She seemed cold and distant. At school, she was nicknamed the "Mona Lisa", and it was not kindly meant. She had her hair cropped short to punish her femininity and appear more distant still. Ironically, the severe haircut succeeded only in making her look prettier. Sometimes, she feared she might take a dislike to her pupils, would end up like Madame Guénot, who would force timid boys to come to the front of the class where she would beat them and who, during playtime, would make naughty girls stand in the corner of the yard for so long they sometimes peed themselves.

These memories flooded back to Louise as she stood naked in front of the mirror. Perhaps because her relations with men were non-existent nowadays, she decided that, immoral though it might be, she felt flattered by the doctor's proposition.

Nonetheless, she had felt relieved the following Saturday when the doctor, doubtless realising the impropriety of his proposal, made no further mention of it. He smiled gently, thanked her for the carafe of wine and, as was his wont, engrossed himself in *Paris-Soir*. Louise, who had never paid the man much heed, made the most of his absorption to study him. If she had not instantly dismissed his proposition a week earlier, it was because there was nothing louche or unsettling about the doctor. His face was lined and haggard. She reckoned him to be about seventy, though she had little talent for such conjectures and was often mistaken. Much later, she would remember she had thought there was something Etruscan about his features. At the time, she had been struck by the word, since it was one she had never used. What she had actually meant was "Roman" because of his aquiline nose.

Meanwhile, Monsieur Jules, excited by rumours that communist propaganda would soon be punishable by death, suggested broadening the criteria ("If it was down to me, I'd have all the lawyers guillotined . . . I mean, wouldn't you?"). Louise was serving an adjacent table when the doctor got to his feet to leave.

"I would pay you, obviously, you need only tell me how much. And, to be clear, I only wish to look at you, nothing more, you need have no fear."

He buttoned his overcoat, donned his hat, smiled and walked out, giving a little wave to Monsieur Jules, who was now railing against Maurice Thorez ("He should be deported to Moscow, the animal. Or put in front of a firing squad!"). Caught unawares by the doctor's renewed suggestion, Louise almost dropped her tray. Monsieur Jules looked up.

"Are you alright, Louise?"

In the week that followed, she felt a black fury once again well up inside her; she would tell the old fart exactly what she thought of him. She waited impatiently for Saturday, but when she saw the doctor come through the door, he looked so old, so frail . . . As she went to serve him, she racked her brain to understand why her fury had so suddenly abated. It was because he was so self-assured. While she had been unsettled by his proposition, he seemed quietly confident that she would accept. The doctor smiled, ordered the dish of the day, read his newspaper, ate his lunch, paid his bill and, as he was about to leave:

"Have you considered the matter?" he said in a low voice. "How much do you want?"

Louise glanced at Monsieur Jules and felt a wave of shame that she was engaging in a whispered conversation with the doctor.

"Ten thousand francs." She spat the words, like an insult.

She blushed. The sum was exorbitant, unacceptable.

He nodded as though to say, I understand. Then buttoned his greatcoat and put on his hat.

"Agreed."

Then he walked out.

"You're not angry with the doctor, are you?" said Monsieur Jules.

"No. Why do you ask?"

A vague gesture. Nothing, nothing.

The sheer enormity of the sum was frightening. As Louise finished her shift, she tried to make a list of all the things that she could buy with ten thousand francs. She realised that she was prepared to allow this man to pay to see her naked. She was a whore. The thought appealed to her. It aligned with the image she had of herself. At other moments, she tried to reassure herself, reasoning that to reveal her nakedness was no different to visiting a doctor. One of her fellow waitresses, who posed for an art academy, confided that the only drawback was boredom, and the fear of catching a chill.

Then there were the ten thousand francs . . . No, it was ridiculous, the money must involve something more than taking off her clothes. For that price, he could insist . . . But Louise could not think of anything that a man might demand for such a sum.

Perhaps the doctor had had the same thought, because he no longer raised the subject. One Saturday passed. And another. And a third. Louise wondered whether she had asked for too much, whether he had sought out a more accommodating woman. She was fractious. She found herself setting his plate down a little brusquely, giving a little grunt whenever he addressed her, in short becoming the kind of waitress she would have loathed had she been the customer.

She had almost finished her shift. She was wiping down the doctor's table. Through the window, she could see her little house in the impasse Pers. She saw the doctor standing on the street corner, smoking a cigarette, the very image of a man waiting patiently.

She lingered for as long as possible, but regardless of the time one takes, sooner or later the task is done. She slipped on her coat and left. She vaguely hoped that the doctor might tire of waiting, but she knew that he would not.

She walked up to him. He smiled gently. He looked shorter than he did in the restaurant.

"Where would you like to do this, Louise? Your place? Or mine?"

There could be no question of going to his home, it was too risky.

Nor of inviting him into hers – what would the neighbours think? Not that she had many neighbours, but it was a matter of principle.

He suggested an hotel. It sounded like a bordello. She agreed.

He had clearly anticipated her response, because he gave her a slip of paper.

"Friday, if that is convenient? At about six o'clock? The room will be booked under the name Thirion, I've noted it on the paper."

He slipped his hands into his pockets.

"Thank you for agreeing to this," he said.

Louise stared at the scrap of paper in her hand, stuffed it into her back pocket and went home.

*

The whole week was an ordeal.

Would she go, would she not? She changed her mind ten times a day and twenty times a night. What if, after all, things turned sour? The place they were due to meet was in the fourteenth arrondissement, the Hôtel Aragon, so on Thursday evening she went there to survey the landscape. She was standing outside when the sirens began to wail – an air raid. She glanced around for somewhere she might shelter.

"Come with me . . ."

As the irritable guests emerged reluctantly from the hotel in single file, an elderly woman took Louise by the arm: it's just next door. A stairwell led down to the cellars. Candles were lit. No-one seemed surprised that Louise did not have a gas mask slung over her shoulder; barely half the residents had one. The hotel clearly had long-term residents, since the guests all knew each other. At first, they stared at Louise, but then a man with a pot belly that spilled over his belt took out a pack of cards, a young couple produced a checkerboard, and they lost interest in her. Only the hotel manager, a birdlike woman of uncertain age, with hair the doubtful coal-black of a wig, steel-grey eyes, and a mantilla wrapped about her skeletal frame – when she sat down, Louise noticed the bony knees beneath her dress – only the manager continued to stare at her, obviously unaccustomed to seeing new faces. The air raid was short-lived, and the assembled company trooped upstairs. "Ladies first!" said the fat man, and it was clear that he said this every time and in doing so felt like a gentleman. No-one had said a word to Louise. She thanked the hotel manager who watched her walk away; Louise could feel eyes burning into her, but when she turned, the street was empty.

*

The following day, the hours flew past. Louise had decided that she would not go, but after coming back from school, she had changed her clothes. And at 5.30 p.m., with fear gnawing at her belly, she left her house.

Barely had she stepped outside than she turned back, went into the kitchen, took a steak knife from the drawer and slipped it into her handbag.

When she approached the reception desk, the manager recognised her and her surprise was evident.

"Thirion," Louise said simply.

The elderly woman handed her a key and gestured to the staircase.

"Room 311. Third floor."

Louise felt the urge to vomit.

The place was calm and silent. Louise had never ventured into a hotel, it was not the sort of place the Belmont family frequented; hotels were for the rich, or at least for other people, for those who took holidays and lived on fresh air. The very word "hotel" was exotic, synonymous with "palace", or, when uttered in a certain tone, a synonym for "brothel", two places where no-one in the Belmont family had ever set foot. But now, Louise was here. The hallway carpet was threadbare but clean. Breathless from climbing the stairs, Louise stood outside the door for a long moment, summoning the courage to knock. There came a noise from somewhere and, affrighted, she grabbed the handle, turned it, and stepped into the room.

The doctor was sitting on the bed wearing his overcoat, as though in a waiting room. He was perfectly calm. He looked terribly old, and Louise realised that she would have no need of the knife.

"Good evening, Louise."

His voice was soft. The lump in her throat made it impossible for Louise to reply.

The room comprised a bed, a small table, a chair and a commode on which lay a thick envelope. The doctor allowed a benevolent smile to play on his lips, he tilted his head slightly as though to soothe her, but Louise was not afraid.

On her way here, she had made a number of decisions. Firstly, she planned to tell him that she would do only what had been agreed, on no account could he touch her; if that was his intention, she would leave straight away. Next, she would count the money; she had no intention of being short-changed . . . But now, standing in the cramped little room, she realised that her plans were irrelevant, that everything would play out simply and calmly.

She casually shifted her weight from one foot to the other, glanced at the envelope as though to marshal her courage, took off her coat and hung it on the hook on the back of the door, slipped off her shoes and, after a momentary hesitation, crossed her hands and pulled her dress over her head.

She would have liked him to help, to tell her what to do. The room was filled with an obscure, humming silence. For a second, she thought that she might faint. If she were indisposed, would he take advantage?

She was standing and he was seated, but her position afforded no advantage. His strength lay in his stillness.

He simply looked at her and waited.

Although it was she who had stripped to her underwear, it was the doctor, hands stuffed into the pockets of his greatcoat, who seemed cold.

To calm herself, she scanned his face for the familiar features of the customer she knew, but she did not find them.

After a momentary awkwardness, and because she had to do something, she reached behind her and unfastened her brassiere.

The man's gaze moved to her bosom, as though drawn by the light, and though there was not a flicker of movement, she thought she perceived some sort of emotion in his expression. She looked down at her breasts, at the pink areolae, it was faintly distressing.

She wanted this to be over. So she steeled herself, peeled off her drawers and stood with her hands behind her back.

Slowly, like a gentle caress, the old man's eyes moved down her body and stopped at her groin. Long seconds passed. It was impossible to tell what he was feeling. His face and his whole being were consumed by some emotion that was ineffable and infinitely sad.

Instinctively, she knew that she should turn around. Although perhaps she merely wanted to avoid this confrontation that was almost heart-wrenching.

She pirouetted on her left foot and stared at the nautical engraving that hung, slightly askew, on the wall above the chiffonier. She could almost feel his eye on her buttocks.

She felt a fleeting qualm, feared he might reach out to touch her, and whirled around again.

He had just taken a pistol from his pocket and shot himself in the head.

Louise was found naked, huddled on the floor, prostrate, her whole body trembling; meanwhile, on the bed, the old man lay on his side, his feet dangling inches above the floor, looking almost as though he had been overtaken by sleep. Almost; but in his surprise at seeing Louise turn back towards him, he had unthinkingly lowered the pistol just as he pulled the trigger. Half his face had been blown away, and a dark blood stain was spreading over the eiderdown.

Someone called the police. A guest in one of the adjoining rooms ran to help and, finding the young woman naked as the day she was born, did not know how to move her. By the arms? By the legs? The room smelled powerfully of gunpowder, but what most struck the man was the blood – the young woman was covered in it.

Trying his best not to look towards the bed, the guest crouched down next to Louise and laid a hand on her shoulder: she was cold, one might almost have thought she was carved from stone, but she trembled and shuddered like linen in the breeze.

"It's alright," he said. "Everything will be alright."

Grabbing her under the arms as best he could, he hauled her to her feet and strained every muscle so that she did not collapse again.

She stared down at the old man on the bed.

He was still breathing. His eyelids opened and closed, he was staring at the ceiling as though he had heard a strange noise and was wondering whence it came.

In that moment, Louise lost all reason. She let out a terrifying howl and began to struggle like a madwoman, like a witch trapped in a sack with a wildcat. She rushed out of the room and down the stairs.

On the ground floor, the gathering crowd of hotel guests and neighbours drawn by the sound of gunfire stared as Louise suddenly appeared, naked, shrieking as she elbowed her way through the throng.

She pushed open the door to the hotel.

A moment later, she was on the boulevard du Montparnasse, running as fast as she could.

What passers-by saw was not a naked woman, but an apparition, the blood-smeared body, the wild eyes, the contorted face.

Louise stumbled and zigzagged, drivers feared she might run into the street, throw herself under their wheels; the cars slowed, an omnibus braked sharply, the conductor on the rear platform blew his whistle, there was a cacophony of car horns, but Louise heard nothing, she carried on barefoot while those she passed stared at her in horror. She waved her arms wildly as though shooing swarms of imaginary insects, she weaved her way along the pavement, now pressing close to a shop window, now skirting around a bus stop, she stumbled, and everywhere she went, people stood aside. No-one knew what to do.

The whole boulevard was in uproar. Who is that? said someone. A madwoman, probably escaped from an asylum somewhere, someone should stop her . . . But by then, Louise had passed them and was heading towards the crossroads at Montparnasse. It was bitterly cold, and her skin was covered here and there with bluish patches. She looked like a woman possessed, it seemed as if, at any moment, her eyes would pop out of her head.

Further on, a gaunt elderly woman with a scarf knotted around her head like a concierge saw Louise approaching and immediately thought of her great-niece, a young woman of much the same age.

"She just stopped dead, like she was trying to work out which way to go. In a trice, I'd taken off my coat and thrown it over her shoulders. She stared at me, and she just dropped to the ground right there in front of me, fell like a sack of potatoes, I didn't know what to do to help her, but luckily there were some folk around who helped. The poor little thing was frozen . . ."

The milling crowd caught the attention of a mobile guard, who tossed his bicycle onto the pavement and elbowed his way through the little group of gawpers and onlookers to discover a young woman hunkered on the ground, clearly naked beneath her coat, who was wiping her face with a bloodstained forearm and panting as though she were in the throes of labour.

Louise looked up. The first thing she saw was the kepi, then the uniform.

She was a criminal; they had come to arrest her.

She glanced around frantically.

She felt a thunderbolt surge through her, once again she heard the shot, smelled the acrid stench of gunpowder. A curtain of blood fell from the heavens and cut her off from the world.

She reached out her arms and screamed.

Then she fainted.

## 2

Aligned in rows of twenty, the milk churns looked like vast stainless-steel barrels. Gabriel was far from reassured by the serried dairy ranks, which looked more like calcified sentinels than filters designed to protect against a mustard gas attack. When viewed up close, the Maginot Line, with its hundreds of infantry casemates and blockhouses conceived to repel a German invasion, seemed disquietingly vulnerable. Even the Mayenberg itself, one of the largest and most important "earthscraper" forts on the line, had its weaknesses: though sheltered from bullets and mortar shells, its entire military staff could easily be suffocated.

"That you, chief?" the sentry called mockingly.

Gabriel wiped his hands on his fatigues. He was thirty years old, dark-haired and with round eyes that made it look as though he were permanently astonished.

"I was just passing . . ."

"Yeah, of course you were . . ." said the sentry, moving off.

Every time he found himself on sentry duty, the young sergent-chef just happened to "pass by".

Gabriel could not stop himself coming to check on the filters, to make sure they were still there. Caporal-chef Landrade had explained that the system used to detect carbon monoxide and arsine was simple and rudimentary.

"The fact is, the whole system depends on the sentries' sense of smell. We just have to hope they don't catch a cold."

A born soldier, Raoul Landrade was an electrical engineer. He was a doom-monger and a peddler of pernicious rumours as specific as they were fatalistic. Knowing how much Gabriel worried about the prospect of a chemical attack, he never missed an opportunity to feed him the disquieting titbits he had learned. It was almost as though he did it deliberately. Indeed, the previous night:

"The filters are designed to be replaced as and when they become saturated, but I'll tell you something for free, they'll never be able to replace them fast enough to protect the whole installation . . . Guaranteed."

Landrade was a curious individual, with an unruly lock of hair that fell across his forehead like a strawberry-blond comma, a mouth that perpetually drooped at the corners, and lips as thin as a razor – Gabriel found him a little frightening. In the four months that they had been bunkmates, Landrade had come to personify the fear that Gabriel had felt the moment he first set eyes on the Mayenberg. This vast underground fortification had seemed like a subterranean monster whose gaping maw was ready to devour all those the État-Major sent as sacrificial victims.

More than nine hundred soldiers lived in the Mayenberg, moving through the winding galleries buried beneath millions of tonnes of concrete, amid the constant hum of generators, the steel panels that shrieked like the souls of the damned and the mingled stench of diesel and damp. Within metres of entering the Mayenberg, daylight guttered out to reveal a murky tunnel filled with the thunderous clatter of the train that serviced the retractable armoured turrets ready to fire 145mm shells over a twenty-five-kilometre radius if and when the age-old enemy dared show his face. In the meantime, crates of munitions were stacked, unpacked, inventoried, distributed and checked; there was little else to do. These days the subterranean train, affectionately dubbed *le métro*, served only to transport the "wonder ovens" used to heat soup. Though everyone still remembered the order stipulating that "all troops must remain in place with no thought of retreat, even if besieged or isolated without hope of imminent rescue until all munitions are exhausted", so much time had passed that no-one now could imagine a situation in which they would be forced to such extremes. While they waited to die for their country, they were bored to death.

Gabriel did not fear war – indeed, no-one here did, since the Maginot Line was reputed to be impregnable – but he found it difficult to live in this cramped, confined space that resembled a submarine, with its six-hour watches, the folding tables that lined the corridors, the tiny cabins, the tanks filled with drinking water.

He missed the daylight. Orders stipulated that he and the other soldiers were entitled to only three hours of daylight. Hours they spent pouring concrete, since work on the fortifications was not yet complete, or rolling out barbed wire to slow the advance of enemy tanks across miles of land, excepting areas where it would hinder the work of farmers or access to orchards (perhaps in the belief that a respect for agricultural labourers or a fondness for fruit would persuade the enemy to avoid these areas). They also drove railway sleepers vertically in the ground. Whenever the sole excavator was elsewhere, or the machine-for-driving-sleepers broke down again, they were forced to resort to mechanical shovels designed for digging sand: managing to drive in two railway sleepers during their shift was considered a good day's work.

In what spare time they had, they raised chickens and rabbits. A small drove of pigs had been honoured with a feature in a local newspaper.

For Gabriel, the worst moment was heading back: his heart

hammered at the very thought of descending into the bowels of the fort.

He was preoccupied by the idea of a chemical attack. Mustard gas, a toxic substance capable of seeping through clothes and masks, burned the eyes, the skin, the mucous membranes. He had mentioned his obsessive concern to the field doctor, a gaunt man, pale as a porcelain sink and grim as a gravedigger, who found it completely normal since nothing in this place was as it should be, neither the interminable wait for God-only-knew-what, nor the day-to-day routine in this anthill; no-one here is coping, he would mutter wearily, doling out fistfuls of aspirin; come back and see me, he would say, since he enjoyed company. Twice or three times a week, Gabriel would beat him at chess, which mattered little to the doctor, who liked to lose. The sergent-chef and the doctor had begun these bi-weekly games the previous summer when, though not actually ill, Gabriel had been finding the living conditions difficult and had gone to the infirmary in search of a little comfort. At the time, the humidity inside was almost one hundred per cent and Gabriel constantly felt as though he were suffocating. Temperatures inside the fortress were such that sweat could not evaporate, bodies were constantly sticky, bedsheets sodden and cold, uniforms heavy with moisture – since it was impossible to dry the laundry – and every berth smelled of mildew. Every room dripped with condensation. To make matters worse, the constant growl of the fans, which rumbled into life at 0400 hours every morning, echoed through the ventilation shafts. For Gabriel, who had always been a light sleeper, it was hell on earth.

Soldiers worried and fretted as they went about in fatigues, half-heartedly keeping an eye on the doors designed to absorb the shock of the enemy bombs, when they came, and since discipline had grown particularly lax, most spent the time between watches in the mess room (officers, who were not averse to joining the revels, turned a blind eye to the fact that it was open day and night). Men came from all around, squaddies from English and Scots regiments posted miles apart would show up at sundown, and, if they got too drunk, would summon field ambulances to take them home.

It was here in the mess room that Caporal-chef Raoul Landrade held court. Gabriel knew nothing about his life on civvy street, but here in the Mayenberg, Landrade quickly established himself as chief trafficker and the linchpin of every shady deal going. It was in his nature. To Landrade, life was a petri dish for his inexhaustible schemes and machinations.

He launched his dubious career in the Mayenberg as a master of the shell game. With only an upturned crate and three cups, he could make a nut, a ball, a pebble, appear and disappear at will. He had the rare talent, crucial to the thimblerigger, of inspiring such confidence in his mark that the urge to point to the hidden Queen or ball was all but irresistible. The daily monotony of life in the fort drew more and more gamblers to his game. His fame even spread to soldiers in other installations, despite the fact that they despised those stationed at the Mayenberg as a privileged elite. Everyone gave a warm welcome to the caporal, and his showmanship won admiration from officers and squaddies alike. His skill as a thimblerigger was facilitated by another factor: he insisted on playing only for the most derisory sums. Men could gamble a franc or two, lose gracefully and move on, but even at this rate, it was not unusual for Landrade to win three hundred francs a day. The rest of his time he devoted to orchestrating shady deals with nearby breweries, the NCOs in the Supply Corps and the staff in the mess hall. And skirt-chasing. Some claimed he had a sweetheart in town, others that he had visited the local brothel. Whatever the truth of the matter, he always returned with a beaming smile that no-one could gainsay.

Landrade often managed to palm off his sentry shifts at the power plant to comrades in greater financial need, and the authorities turned a blind eye. As a result, he had considerable free time in which to spend trafficking supplies to the mess hall, where he had negotiated a sophisticated yet impenetrable system regulating the purchase, sale and delivery of beer involving discounts, commissions and kickbacks, making a small fortune on the four hundred and fifty litres of beer consumed daily at the Mayenberg. Indeed there was no pie in which he did not have a tentative finger. He had discreetly insinuated himself into the kitchens, claiming that he alone could provide the produce that could not otherwise be procured, which was true. For officers, he sourced rare victuals, and for soldiers weary of eating beef twice a day, he provided something to spice up their fare. As the army settled into routine and the soldiers into idleness, he provided hammocks, crates, cutlery, mattresses, blankets, magazines, cameras – anything you needed, Raoul Landrade could find. The previous winter, he had shown up with a vast quantity of extra heaters and serrated knives (with everything frozen, daily wine rations had to be sawn off in chunks). Later in the year, he was hawking dehumidifiers, which were all but useless but sold like hot cakes. Confectionary – chocolate, marzipan, acid drops, etc. – were firm favourites, especially among the NCOs. The military authorities offered every man a tot of brandy with breakfast and a carafe of wine with every meal. Phenomenal quantities of wine and spirits were delivered to the fortress, with stocks being endlessly replenished. Landrade managed to discreetly siphon off a generous quantity which he sold off cheaply to neighbouring bars and restaurants, to local farmers and day-labourers. If war carried on for another year, Caporal-chef Landrade would have the wherewithal to buy the Mayenberg itself.

Gabriel checked that the shift change had gone smoothly. Being a mathematics teacher in civilian life, he had been posted to the Signals Corps, where he patched through calls from the outside world. Here, war was reduced to a handful of orders concerning site works and the allocation of furlough passes, which had reached a preposterous level. By Gabriel's reckoning, at one point more than half of the officers had simultaneously been on furlough. Had the Germans chosen that weekend to attack, they could have taken the Mayenberg in two days and been in Paris within three weeks . . .

Gabriel returned to his shared barracks room with its four bunks. He had a top bunk opposite that of Caporal-chef Landrade. In the bottom bunk was Ambresac, a guy with wild, menacing eyebrows and the large hands of a fieldworker, who was constantly complaining. Opposite him was Chabrier, whose thin, wiry frame and pointy face were reminiscent of a weasel. Whenever anyone talked to him, he would stare at them intently, as though waiting for them to react to a joke he had just told. This intense gaze was so unsettling that most soldiers would let out an embarrassed little laugh. As a result, Chabrier gained a reputation as a funny guy without ever actually telling a joke. Ambresac and Chabrier were Raoul Landrade's associates. This bunk room was the HQ of his criminal enterprise. Since Gabriel had never wanted to get involved in their nefarious schemes, whenever he walked into the room, the others fell silent; it was painfully awkward. This pernicious atmosphere was both the cause and result of the vicissitudes of barracks life. Some weeks earlier, one of the soldiers in their unit had complained about the theft of a signet ring engraved with his initials. Everyone treated it as a joke, since his name was Vincent Delestre, though it also brought home how living cheek by jowl led to arguments, annoyances and vice; there had not been many thefts, but a gold signet ring, now that was worth a pretty penny, to say nothing of the sentimental value.

When Gabriel stepped into the room, Raoul was sitting on his bunk totting up figures.

"Just the man," he said, "I'm trying to calculate airflow and volume, and I can't work it out . . ."

He was attempting to calculate the output of a number of compressors. Gabriel took the pencil. The result was 0.13.

"Shit!" growled Raoul. He looked shocked.

"What's the matter?"

"Uh . . . I just had a little niggle about the generators that are supposed to filter the air. If we come under a poison gas attack, you know?"

Faced with Gabriel's fretful silence, he continued:

"Thing is, these dumb bastards went with two-stroke compressors. And since they won't produce nearly enough power, they have to be supercharged. Which gives us the figure 0.13."

Gabriel felt the blood drain from his face.

He frantically recalculated. The result was still the same. In the event of an attack, the volume of air filtered by the main generator would barely be enough to decontaminate . . . the generator room. The rest of the fortress would be saturated.

Raoul folded the slip of paper with a fatalistic shrug.

"I mean, it's not exactly ideal, but still . . ."

Gabriel knew that there was no way now to replace the equipment. Whatever happened, they would have to fight the war with two-stroke compressors.

38

"We're alright, we can shelter in the Plant," said Raoul. "But you guys in the Signals Corps . . ."

The "Plant" referred to the power station. Gabriel felt his throat go dry. It was irrational. If fighting did break out, there was no reason to think that the Germans would launch a chemical attack. And yet, in Gabriel's mind it felt like a certainty.

"If there's a problem, I suppose you could always come join us . . ."

Gabriel looked up.

"We've got a secret code for the south door of the Plant. If you give the secret knock, we open it."

"What's the code?"

Raoul leaned back a little.

"There needs to be a little quid pro quo, old man."

Gabriel did not know what he could possibly offer in return.

"Information. In the Signals Corps, you know everything there is to know about the Supply Corps, the deliveries to the stores, everything the Mayenberg buys in from outside. If we had that information, it would make our lives easier . . . We could prepare."

Raoul was clearly proposing that Gabriel get involved in his various shady deals in exchange for a free pass to the south door of the Plant.

"I can't . . . it's . . . it's confidential."

He groped for a word.

"It would be treason."

This was preposterous. Raoul burst out laughing.

"Canned beef deliveries are a state secret? Well, well . . . military authorities clearly take things very seriously."

He unfolded the slip of paper on which he had made his calculations and pressed it into Gabriel's hand.

"Here . . . At least you'll have something to read when you're standing outside the south door of the Plant."

He strode out, leaving Gabriel to fret. Landrade trailed an air of menace in his wake, just as certain plants trail a troubling perfume.

This conversation had left Gabriel very unsettled.

Three weeks later, in the shower block, he overheard Ambresac and Chabrier talking about a "flamethrower test" that had been carried out on the air inlets for the blocs.

"Catastrophic . . ." said Ambresac.

"I know," Chabrier chimed in. "Apparently the filters got clogged with soot. The whole bloc was contaminated within seconds."

Gabriel could not help but smile. Landrade's henchmen were terrible actors, and their not-so-spontaneous exchange was clearly designed to heighten Gabriel's fear. It had precisely the opposite effect.

But that evening, while they were playing chess, the chief medical officer confirmed the tests had been carried out.

"What do you mean test?"

The doctor stared at the chessboard and, as he warily advanced his knight, mumbled, as though to himself: "The results were inconclusive. Hence the need for a training exercise. Full scale, this time. Obviously, it's going to be a fiasco, but they'll swear blindly it was a success, that the system is failsafe. Then they'll probably have the chaplain say a mass – they'll need one, and so will we."

Staring into space, Gabriel advanced his queen.

"Checkmate . . ." he said in a whisper.

The doctor packed away the pieces, satisfied with the result.

Gabriel headed back to his bunk, his feet unsteady.

*

Days passed. Caporal-chef Landrade prowled the tunnels of the fortress, busier than ever.

"You'd do well to think about what I said," he would sometimes mutter as he passed Gabriel.

Meanwhile Gabriel waited for the camp commander to order a full-scale exercise; nothing happened, and then suddenly, on April 27 at 0530 hours, the sirens shrieked.

Was this a planned manoeuvre intended to catch the troops off-guard, or had the German offensive finally begun?

Gabriel leaped from his bunk, taut as a bowstring.

Already, the corridors were echoing with the roar of shouted orders and the boots of hundreds of soldiers heading to their battle stations. Raoul Landrade and his henchmen buckled their belts as they left the bunk room, while Gabriel, buttoning his uniform, followed behind. Dazed by the wail of sirens, the din of milling soldiers forced to flatten themselves against the walls of the tunnel every time the train rattled past, and the clatter of munitions being loaded, Gabriel could not shake off the idea that the German offensive had finally begun.

His bunkmates were almost out of sight. He raced after them, writhing in a vain attempt to button his jacket, his breathing ragged, his legs trembling. Seeing Caporal-chef Landrade take a left turn fifteen metres ahead, Gabriel forced himself to run faster, but when he turned the corner, he was met by a howling mob of soldiers, led by Landrade, running towards him. Surging behind them came a thick cloud of smoke that billowed like a wave, from which panicked soldiers emerged, stumbling unsteadily.

Gabriel stood for a moment, petrified.

German gas attacks were supposed to be invisible. In some dark corner of his brain, Gabriel began to wonder whether this was something else. Some new chemical weapon? But before he could think, he was enfolded by the cloud and he felt the acrid smoke tear at his lungs. Coughing and spluttering, he whirled around, disoriented, as the blurred silhouettes of soldiers raced past, all of them shouting: This way! Head for the exit! The North corridor!

His eyes stinging from the dense fog, Gabriel stumbled on as others pushed and jostled. The smoke seemed thicker now, and this section of the corridor was barely wide enough for two men to walk abreast. At the junction of two tunnels, a sudden gust of wind dispersed the smoke, and he could see clearly once again, although his vision was still obscured by his streaming eyes.

Was he safe?

He whipped round and saw Caporal-chef Landrade pressed against the tunnel wall and pointing to one of the niches carved into the tunnel wall at thirty-metre intervals. Most were simple shelters used by soldiers when the trains passed, but some opened onto small storerooms. This was clearly one, and the steel door stood ajar. Were they near the Plant? Gabriel was convinced the generators were in the other direction . . . Landrade's eyes were streaming and he pressed his face into the crook of his elbow as he signalled for the sergent-chef to go inside. Glancing around, Gabriel saw the cloud of white smoke had reformed and was surging through the tunnel towards them. Soldiers blundered from the fog, their eyes red, gasping, screaming, frantically searching for a way out.

"This way!' roared Landrade, pointing to the half-open door. Without thinking, Gabriel slipped inside. The room was murky, a cramped tool shed lit only by a bare bulb that dangled from the ceiling. Behind him, the heavy steel door slammed shut.

Gabriel raced back and tried to open the door, but the handle spun uselessly. He hammered on the door and then stopped.

White smoke was beginning to seep under the door and through the gaps next to the hinges, as though sucked into the storeroom.

Gabriel screamed, he pounded on the heavy steel. Thick, acrid smoke poured into the room with the terrifying speed of rising floodwaters. The air began to run out.

Overcome by a coughing fit that made him double over and retch, Gabriel fell to his knees. Asphyxiated by the smoke, he felt as though his chest was about to explode, his eyes burst from their sockets. His vision was reduced to a few centimetres. Between spasms, he stared at his splayed hands. They were dark with blood.

He was coughing blood.

# 3

"Belmont, is that the name?" asked Judge Le Poittevin.

In the hospital bed, Louise looked slight and frail as an adolescent.

"And you say she's not a prostitute . . .?"

The judge spent all day polishing his spectacles with a square of chamois leather. To his colleagues, his associates, to lawyers and bailiffs, the variations on these gestures formed a language. Right now, the way his thumbs were massaging the lenses clearly indicated his scepticism.

"All I can say is, she ain't got a record," said the police officer.

"A half-time harlot . . ." muttered the judge, setting his glasses on the bridge of his nose.

He had insisted on a straight-backed chair, he was very finicky on the subject of chairs. He leaned over the sleeping girl. Pretty. Hair too short, but pretty nonetheless. The judge knew a thing or two about young women, since a goodly number trooped through his chambers at the Palais de Justice, to say nothing of those he pawed in the brothel on the rue Saint-Victoire. Behind him, a nurse was busy tidying the ward. Exasperated by the noise, he whipped around and glowered at her. The nurse merely eyed him scornfully and carried on as though he did not exist. The judge heaved a weary sigh . . . women! He turned back to Louise, hesitated, then reached out and laid a hand on her shoulder. His thumb glided over her skin. Warm. Soft. A fine filly of a girl, granted, he thought, but for the man to put a bullet in his brain for her . . . Slowly, repeatedly, his thumb followed the curve of Louise's shoulder.

"Are you finished?"

Judge Le Poittevin wrenched his hand away as though it had been scalded. The nurse loomed over the little man, her arms cradling a basin of water as though it were a baby. The judge blenched.

Yes, he was finished. He closed his case file.

In the days that followed, the doctors refused to allow him to conduct an in-depth interrogation. The hearing did not resume until the following week.

This time, Louise was awake. After a fashion. Since it was out of the question for him to begin until the police officer brought the straight-backed chair, the judge polished his spectacles and stared down at Louise, who was sitting up in bed, her arms clasped over her chest, staring into the middle distance. She had barely eaten since being admitted.

At length, the chair arrived; the judge examined it, deigned to sit, then opened the case file on his lap and – though unsettled by the presence of the nurse, who stood nearby like a sentinel – reviewed the situation. The police officer went over and leaned against the wall that faced Louise's bed.

"You are Suzanne, Adrienne, Louise Belmont. You were born . . ."

From time to time he glanced up at the girl, but she did not so much as blink, as though what was taking place did not concern her. The judge stopped suddenly and waved his hand in front of impassive Louise's face. He turned around.

"You are quite certain that she can hear what is being said?"

The nurse whispered into his ear.

"Thus far, she has said only a few barely coherent words. The doctor mentioned something about alienation, doubtless a specialist will need to be brought in to examine her."

"If she's mad as well as everything else, we're not out of the woods," sighed the judge and looked down at his file.

"Is he dead?"

Surprised, the magistrate looked at Louise, who fixed him straight in the eye. He was alarmed.

"Doc . . . Doctor Thirion died shortly after the incident . . . mademoiselle." He hesitated an instant before adding the honorific. "And just as well, too," he blustered angrily, annoyed with himself for making any concession to a girl of her sort, ". . . given the state he was in."

Louise looked at the police officer, then at the nurse, and, as though she still could not quite believe it, she said:

"He offered me money to see me naked."

"That is an admission of prostitution!" crowed the judge.

Now that he could qualify the misdeed, he was satisfied. He wrote in his file in a small, spidery hand befitting his personality, then resumed his reading of the facts. Louise then explained how she came to meet Doctor Thirion.

"I didn't know him particularly well . . ."

"Really?" The judge gave a curt laugh. "Do you just take your clothes off for the first man who comes along?"

He slapped his thigh and glanced at the police officer – Extraordinary! Have you ever heard the like?

Louise told them about the restaurant, about the shifts she worked on Saturdays and Sundays, about the doctor's habits.

"We will check your story with the proprietor." He leaned over his file and muttered ". . . and see whether his establishment has been harbouring other casual strumpets."

Since it seemed there was nothing to be gained by pursuing this line of enquiry, Judge Le Poittevin moved on to the events that interested him most particularly.

"Well then, once you were in the hotel room, what did you do?"

To Louise, the truth seemed so clear, so obvious, that she could not find the words. She had taken her clothes off, what more was there to say?

"Did you solicit money from him?"

"No. It was lying there, on the chest of drawers . . ."

"So, you counted it! A woman does not undress for a man without first making a reckoning. At least, I suppose. After all, what would I know . . .?"

He turned this way and that as though fishing for a response, but his face was flushed.

"And then what?"

The judge's fury was reaching fever pitch.

"I took my clothes off, that's all."

"Come, come, mademoiselle. A man does not part with fifteen thousand francs just to see a young girl naked, it doesn't add up."

Louise thought she remembered that they had agreed on ten thousand rather than fifteen thousand francs, but she could not be sure.

"And this is what I'm trying to understand: what precisely *were* you doing for such an extravagant sum?"

The policeman and the nurse could not really understand what the judge was hoping to establish, but the way he was fingering his spectacles betrayed a frustration that looked disquietingly like excitement.

"After all, I mean . . . One cannot help but wonder . . ."

His fingers moved more quickly over the lenses. Fleetingly, he glanced at Louise's bosom as it palpitated beneath the thin nightgown.

"Fifteen thousand francs is quite a sum!"

The conversation was deadlocked. The magistrate plunged once again into his case file and when he re-emerged, it was with a rapacious smile. Although the fingerprints, the position of the body, the angle of impact all attested to Doctor Thirion having taken his own life, there was, nonetheless, one charge that could be levelled against the girl.

"Indecent exposure!"

Louise stared at him.

"Oh yes, mademoiselle! You may think it acceptable to stroll along the boulevard du Montparnasse stark naked, much good may it do you, but law-abiding citizens cannot . . ."

"I wasn't strolling!"

Her words had come almost as a scream, her whole body trembled. The judge revelled in her reaction.

"Is that so? So what exactly were you doing without a stitch of clothing? Shopping? Ha, ha, ha!"

Once again, he turned to the policeman, then to the nurse, but they stared back impassively. What matter? Borne upon a wave of jubilation, he forged ahead in a tone so bright it sounded as though he was about to burst into song:

"It is exceedingly rare for gross indecency to be committed by a young lady eager to display her . . . (he tore off his spectacles, gripping them feverishly, almost dropping them in the process) . . . to show off her . . . (his knuckles were white) . . . to make an exhibition of . . ."

The frame of his glasses snapped.

The judge looked at the two halves tenderly, as after the

climax of coitus. Gently laying them in his spectacle case, he said abstractly:

"Your career as a schoolmistress is over, mademoiselle. Once convicted, you will be summarily dismissed."

"Thirion, yes, I remember now," said Louise.

The non-sequitur was so marked that the judge almost dropped his spectacle case.

"That's right," he stammered, "Joseph Eugène Thirion, residing at 67, boulevard Auberjon in Neuilly-sur-Seine."

Louise simply nodded. Somewhat crestfallen, the investigating magistrate closed his case file; he had so wanted her to weep. Now, had he been able to interview her in his chambers . . . Reluctantly, he took his leave.

In Louise's place, anyone else would have asked what would happen next. But she asked no questions and the judge, disappointed, left without saying goodbye.

Louise spent another three days in hospital. She barely ate a morsel.

Just as she was about to be discharged, a police officer arrived with news of the prosecutor's decision: the death had been confirmed as suicide and no charge of prostitution would be preferred.

The nurse froze. Tilting her head slightly, she looked at Louise and smiled sadly. She and the policeman both knew the young woman still faced a charge of gross indecency that would cost her her job. Neither knew what to say.

Louise took a few steps towards the door. She had arrived at the hospital utterly naked. No-one knew what had become of the clothes she had left in the room at the Hôtel d'Aragon. Except perhaps the police and the clerk of the court. Consequently, the nurse had spoken to a few of her colleagues and put together a rather motley outfit. A wool jumper that was rather too long, and a blue blouse, a dark purple jacket, a coat with a fake fur collar. Louise looked as though she had just stepped out of a second-hand clothes shop.

"You're very kind," she said, as though this were something she had suddenly discovered.

The policeman and the nurse watched as she walked away with the weary, mechanical gait of a woman who is about to throw herself into the Seine.

Instead, Louise headed straight to the impasse Pers, hesitated briefly as she reached the corner and saw La Petite Bohème, then, staring at the ground, she hurried on to her little house.

Built shortly after the Franco-Prussian war, the house at 9, impasse Pers exuded an old-fashioned bourgeois opulence; it was the sort of house that a man of private means or a retired merchant might have had built. Louise's parents had moved into the property in 1908, when they married. It was much too spacious for the Belmont family to fully occupy, but Adrien Belmont was a forward-thinking man planning on having numerous offspring. Fate had other plans: he had had only one child, Louise, before being killed in Verdun, on the eastern slope of the Ravin des Vignes in 1916.

There had been a time, before her marriage, when Louise's mother, Jeanne Belmont, had nurtured hopes. She had attended secondary school and passed her *brevet élémentaire* – a rare thing among girls at the time. Her parents and her teachers dreamed that she would go on to be a nurse or a town clerk but, at the age of seventeen, she abruptly decided to leave school. Preferring housework to factory work, she got a job as a domestic, a lady's maid who could read and dust, like something from the pages of

Octave Mirbeau. Her husband, for his part, would not hear of his wife working; it was a point of honour. After his death, Jeanne was forced to go back to housework in the hope that she and Louise might keep the house on the impasse Pers, which was the only thing they owned.

After the Great War, Jeanne Belmont had sunk into depression as one might sink into quicksand. Her health mirrored the state of the house which, with no maintenance or repairs, crumbled a little more each year. She gave up her job as a housemaid and never returned to it. The family doctor suggested it was the change of life, anaemia and finally neurasthenia – he changed his diagnoses as often as his shirts. Madame Belmont spent the greater part of her life staring out the window. She cooked (usually the same few recipes), she took an interest in Louise's schoolwork, in her diploma, in her job, and when her daughter had qualified as a teacher and no longer needed her, she took no interest in anything. Jeanne's life was so light it was almost evanescent. In the spring of 1939, her health suddenly deteriorated. Louise would often find her mother in bed when she came home from teaching. She would sit with her, still wearing her heavy coat, and take her hand. "What's the matter?" Madame Belmont would give her daughter a wan smile and say, "Nothing, I just feel a little tired." Louise would go and make her some vegetable broth.

One morning in June, she went into the bedroom and found her mother dead. Jeanne was fifty-two years old. Mother and daughter had had no chance to say goodbye.

From that moment, everything in Louise's life silently, almost imperceptibly, began to go downhill. She was a spinster, her youth had melted like an ice cream in the sun, her mother was dead, even the house was a pale shadow of what it had once been.

Louise resolved to sell the house for whatever she could get and start life again somewhere else, but the lawyer dealing with her mother's estate gave her a hundred thousand francs, a gift from the former residents of the house who had known her as a child and had wanted to provide for her future. To this was added an additional twenty-four thousand francs, being the accrued interest over a period of twenty years during which, without a word to Louise, her mother had wisely invested it. This did not make Louise a wealthy woman, but it meant that she could keep the house and pay for the renovations.

She requested a quote from a builder, haggled over every jot and tittle in the estimate. A meeting to sign the contract was arranged for one evening after she returned from work. But by mid-afternoon, the newspaper sellers along the rue Damrémont were shouting that war had been declared. The government ordered a general mobilisation. The builder did not attend the meeting. Restoring the house would have to wait for better days.

When she came home from hospital, Louise stopped in the courtyard and stared at the little lean-to her father had once used as a workshop and which her mother had once rented out for a derisory sum, since the building lacked all modern conveniences and she could not ask for more. What Louise had just experienced was so powerful, so visceral that it brought her back to the days when the little building had been occupied by the two young men who had bequeathed her inheritance. Since then, it had stood empty. Every two or three years, Louise would summon the energy to clean and air the rooms, and to throw out things that had survived her previous clear-outs. All that remained in the attic room with its low ceiling and broad windows was a coal-fired stove, a folding screen upholstered with a scene of lambs and shepherdesses and a preposterous chaise longue vaguely in the rococo style of the Directoire, with gilded garlands and festoons and a lone armrest – it was designed for a left-handed client – carved as a magisterial swan puffing out its chest. The latter was a piece that Louise loved, for reasons no-one had ever really understood, and had planned to refurbish, only to abandon it here in the attic.

She gazed at the lean-to building, the beaten-earth courtyard, the house, as though seeing them for the first time, and realised that the scene was almost a metaphor for her life, and tears welled in her eyes. She felt a lump in her throat, her legs were unsteady, she took a few steps and, with a ragged sob, sat down on the worm-eaten attic stairs that alarmed anyone called upon to use them. The ghastly sight of Doctor Thirion's head floated over the face of the young war veteran who, with his comrade-in-arms, had once found shelter in this ramshackle building. That young man, Édouard Péricourt, wore extravagant masks to hide his face, the lower part of which had been obliterated by an exploding shell. At eleven years old, Louise had been in the habit of going up to the attic room, which he shared with his friend, when she came home from school to make papier-mâché, to paint, to glue on pearls and ribbons; the walls were lined with dozens of masks, one for every conceivable mood. Even at that age, Louise spoke little; she listened to Édouard's hoarse, whistling breath, she loved the pale hands he laid upon her shoulders, he had the most beautiful eyes imaginable, Louise had never seen their like again. Because such things can happen between unlikely creatures, a sure, serene love blossomed between the mutilated twenty-five-year-old and the little girl who had lost her father.

Doctor Thirion's suicide had reopened a wound that Louise thought had healed. One day, Édouard had abandoned her.

He and his friend Albert Maillard had engineered a great

swindle, selling non-existent war memorials which had made them a fortune.

What a scandal . . .

They had had to abscond; Louise had turned to Édouard, and, as she had on the day they first met, reached out a delicate finger and traced the gaping wound on his face, the blistered, red-raw flesh like mucous membrane . . .

"Will you come back to say goodbye?" she said.

Édouard had nodded: Yes, of course. That had meant no.

The following day, his friend Albert, a former accountant whom she had always seen tremble like a leaf and wipe his clammy hands on his trousers, had managed to flee with a young housemaid in tow and a fortune in banknotes.

Édouard, for his part, had stayed behind, and thrown himself under the wheels of a car.

To him, the great swindle, the non-existent war monuments, had never been more than an entr'acte.

Only later did Louise discover just how complicated the young man's life had been.

Now, she realised that her life had not moved forward or backward so much as an inch since that day. She had simply grown older. She was thirty years old. She sobbed harder.

In the letterbox, she found a note from the school demanding to know the reason for her absence. She replied, offering no explanation, merely saying that she would resume her duties in a few days. Writing this single page was enough to exhaust her. She went to bed and slept for sixteen hours.

When she had thrown out the spoiled food in the pantry, she went out to shop for groceries and a newspaper. In order to avoid La Petite Bohème, she waited until it was hidden by a passing omnibus and ran.

For more than a week, she had not read a newspaper or listened to the radio. Seeing Parisians going about their business, she could guess that nothing much was happening on the front lines. Reading the paper today, most of what was published seemed reassuring. The Germans were struggling, their advance into Norwegian territory had stalled, and in Levanger, they had been forced to retreat 120 kilometres. They were facing a "three-pronged attack from French torpedo boats" in the North Sea. There was little to worry about. Behind his counter, Monsieur Jules was probably noisily eulogising the luminous strategy of Général Gamelin and prophesying the sound thrashing that would surely face the Germans if they dared "come round our house".

Louise found it difficult to take much interest in the news, yet she read on obdurately, in order to blot out the image that appeared whenever her mind was idle, the image of Doctor Thirion's head, half blown away.

The courts had made no attempt to understand why the doctor had chosen Louise to witness his final act when he could simply have gone to a brothel. It was a question that frequently woke her with a start. Try as she might to associate the name Thirion with the diner who came to the restaurant every Saturday, she simply could not. The judge had said he lived in Neuilly. What a curious idea, to come all the way to the eighteenth arrondissement every Saturday for lunch – surely they had restaurants in Neuilly? Monsieur Jules had said that the doctor had been "a regular for twenty years", which, in his mind, was not a compliment. While it seemed entirely reasonable to Monsieur Jules that he had spent thirty years cooking at the same establishment, the notion that a customer had come to eat there for almost as many years was beyond his comprehension. It was not so much the doctor's loyalty he found shocking as his lack of conversation. "If they were all like him, I might as well be cooking for Trappist monks!" Truth be told, Monsieur Jules had never liked the doctor.

Louise spent a sleepless night in the armchair, filling the empty hours by trying to piece together what little she knew about the doctor.

The food she had bought was disappearing fast, so the following morning, she went shopping again. A mild May day, she thought. The timorous burst of early sunshine caressed her cheek, she felt less heavy. To avoid being interrogated by neighbours and local shopkeepers, she walked some distance to buy her groceries, and found the walk invigorating.

The bright spell did not last. When she got home, there was a letter waiting. Judge Le Poittevin had summoned her to appear in his chambers at 2.00 p.m. on Thursday May 9, to discuss "a matter concerning you".

Panicked, she hunted around for the document given to her by the police when she was discharged from hospital which unambiguously stated that the matter was closed and that no charges were being preferred against her. In what was already a surreal affair, the judge's summons made no sense. Louise slumped into the armchair, all the wind knocked out of her.

# 4

Gabriel felt himself racked by another spasm, but there was nothing left in his stomach to vomit. The smoke was now so thick he could barely see a hand in front of his face. Was he going to die here, in this storeroom? His breathing was like a guttural wail, and still smoke continued to pour over him. He lifted his head: the steel door was ajar.

A breeze blew through the storeroom, creating eddies in the smoke . . .

Through his tears, Gabriel saw a layer of pure air at floor level. Without thinking, he bent down, slipped in a pool of vomit, skidded, and crawled out to the tunnel. Hurried feet raced past, some stumbled over him but did not stop.

Gabriel struggled to his feet, utterly drained. He wandered aimlessly for a long time, unable to find his way. Eventually, he saw the infirmary, knocked and, without waiting for an answer, went inside. Five of the beds were occupied. In the confusion, a number of people had suffered falls.

"Here's another one in a fine state," said the doctor looking more spectral than ever.

"I got locked in a storeroom down there in the train tunnel . . ." Gabriel's voice betrayed his terror. The doctor raised an eyebrow.

"Someone pushed me . . ."

The doctor ushered him in, had him strip to the waist, and examined him.

"What do you mean, someone pushed you . . ."

Gabriel said nothing; the doctor realised that this was the totality of the confession.

"Asthmatic!"

The diagnosis was uttered in a tone that was almost triumphant, and the insinuation was crystal clear. Gabriel had only to agree, and the doctor would put his name on the list of those unfit for service, he would be able to go home.

"No."

Somewhat sceptical, the major concentrated on his stethoscope.

"Everything's fine, Major . . . I mean, I'm feeling better."

Gabriel grabbed his shirt and pulled it back on; he was exhausted, he stank of vomit, he was pale as death, his trembling fingers struggled with the buttons.

The doctor stared at him for a moment then nodded: Very well.

The prospect of Gabriel being sent home melted away. What motivated his decision? Gabriel was not an idealist or an activist, still less was he a hero. What compelling reason could he have for not grasping an opportunity few soldiers would have passed up? He read the news. He had never believed in Hitler's protestations of peace, he thought the Munich Agreement was folly, while the rumours from Italy positively terrified him. He had not complained when the general mobilisation came, because he believed it was necessary to fight. Many had been discouraged by the phoney war, and more than once Gabriel had wondered whether he might not be of more service if he went back to teaching maths at Dole College. But life had dictated that he be here, and here he stayed. The invasion of Norway, the tension in the Balkans, the Nazi "warnings" to Sweden . . . Recent news made him think that perhaps his presence might not prove futile. At heart, Gabriel was a fearful lad, one disinclined to acts of bravery, yet he never cowered in the face of danger, and indeed took a strange satisfaction in the very situations that most terrified him.

The major kept him under observation for two days, during which Gabriel had time to mull over what had happened. For his part, the major was puzzled as to how the young sergeant had come to be locked up in a storeroom.

"You should report the incident," he suggested. But Gabriel demurred.

"These things never end well, sergent," the major insisted. "In conditions like these, we're packed in like sardines and forced to live on top of each other. We know how it starts, but . . ."

The major was clearly determined that Gabriel should file a report, because on the day the sergeant was discharged from the infirmary to resume his post, the doctor handed him an order from the commandant of the Mayenberg. A summons to appear immediately. The major, having clearly engineered the summons, seemed neither sorry nor embarrassed, instead Gabriel sensed that somewhat preposterous pomposity of men who persuade themselves that they have done their duty when in fact they have acted entirely in their own interests. He felt that he should be angry, but aside from the fact that to do so would serve no purpose, there was so much to be said that the prospect was disheartening.

Sitting in the corridor outside the commandant's office, Gabriel fretted about his situation while he waited for the commandant to deign to receive him.

When he was finally summoned, and stood to attention, steeling himself to parry any questions, he quickly realised his fears had been unfounded. The major had already filed a medical report, summarised by the commandant as "minor niggling health issues, I see, I see . . .".

"So, in civilian life, you're a maths teacher, is that right?"

Gabriel did not even have time to nod before the commandant appointed him non-commissioned officer in charge of supplies.

"Sous-Lieutenant Darasse is on furlough for three months, you will be his replacement."

A flabbergasted Gabriel felt his heart begin to race: no longer was he doomed to the subterranean murk of the Mayenberg, instead he could spend his days outside, in the sunshine and the fresh air, making trips to Thionville.

"You know the drill. You nominate three men and together you fulfil orders for the Supply Corps, you are also responsible for all out-of-pocket expenses. You are under my command. If there are any problems, you come directly to me. Any questions?"

Gabriel could have kissed the commandant. Instead, he reached out, grabbed his reassignment papers, and gave a cursory salute.

The Supply Corps was responsible for providing the Mayenberg with beef and pork, coffee, bread, rum, grains, pulses, etc., wholesale products that arrived by truck or train. All other provisions, including fresh vegetables, poultry and dairy products, fell with the authority of the "Retail Corps". Gabriel had just been appointed NCO in charge of Retail, and of all "out-of-pocket" – the cash reserves used to pay traders with whom the army did not have an account. What soldiers could not find in town, they ordered from the Retail Corps – although orders had declined considerably in the months since Caporal-chef Landrade launched a rival service.

Gabriel could breathe easily again. He dropped by the infirmary to thank the major, who stared fixedly into the middle distance and made a vague gesture that could have meant anything or nothing. That done, Gabriel raced off to pack his kit: from now on he would be billeted outdoors, near the Supply Stores. By day, he could savour the country air and by night he could go out and gaze at the stars.

"NCO in charge of Retail? Really?" Raoul Landrade whistled admiringly.

Gabriel simply gathered his belongings and, without a word of goodbye, marched down the corridor towards freedom.

Staggering under the weight of his kitbag, he stopped by the Signals Corps to hand over his order papers and sign the register. Three months from now, when the incumbent head of retail returned from furlough, he would have to come back to work here. But right now, he wanted to forget that, to treat every day as a new day. Once his papers were in order, he left the Mayenberg.

Outside, the wide esplanade was occupied by vehicles, troops loading barbed wire, small units moving along. Like a paroled convict, Gabriel greedily sucked in lungfuls of air as he headed to the Supply Corps.

By 1700 hours, he had taken up residence in his tiny, but single-bunk room, which was cold as an icebox, but had a window that overlooked the esplanade and the surrounding woodland. Hardly had he set down his kitbag than he heard footsteps and loud voices from the adjoining room, where his chosen team was to be billeted. Gabriel opened the connecting door to find Caporal-chef Landrade, with his henchmen Chabrier and Ambresac, had taken over the bunk room.

"Hey there!" roared Gabriel.

The three soldiers whipped round, as though surprised. Raoul Landrade stepped forward, smiling broadly.

"We figured you'd be wanting experienced men in this new post of yours . . ."

Gabriel stiffened.

"It's out of the question."

Raoul seemed peeved.

"Come on, you're hardly going to refuse a helping hand, are you?"

Gabriel stepped towards Landrade, his teeth clenched, his pent-up rage clearly audible as he hissed:

"You're going to fuck off out of here. All of you. Right now."

Raoul's peevishness gave way to vexation. Bowing his head, he fumbled in his pocket and extracted a blue striped handkerchief which he unfolded. Slowly and deliberately. Gabriel gasped. In the palm of his hand the signet ring, the dull gold engraved with the letters VD lay like a fat, poisonous insect. This was the ring stolen some months earlier, the ring that had been the subject of crass jokes.

"We saw you slip it into your kitbag –" Landrade turned to his henchmen – "Didn't we guys? We all saw him . . ."

Ambresac and Chabrier nodded vehemently; their sincerity seemed entirely convincing.

In a split second, Gabriel saw exactly how the threat would play out: he would be accused of theft, and, faced with the damning testimony of three witnesses, would be unable to prove his innocence. What paralysed him was not so much the thought of losing the provisional paradise to which he had just been assigned, though that would be a heavy blow, it was being wrongly accused.

Raoul quietly rolled the signet ring up in his handkerchief and stuffed it in his pocket.

# 5

Maître Désiré Migault left the Hôtel du Commerce at precisely 7.30 a.m., bought the morning papers and stationed himself, as was his wont, next to the bus stop. As he stepped onto the platform, he was unsurprised to discover that the "Valentine Boissier trial" had made the front page of all the dailies. The woman dubbed the "pretty pastry chef of Poisat", because her father owned a patisserie in the town, was charged with the murders of her former lover and his mistress. The bus dropped Désiré off some three hundred metres from Rouen Palais de Justice, a distance he traversed with a slow, measured tread that seemed at odds with a man of his age (he was certainly not yet thirty) and physique (thin, wiry and athletic).

Maître Désiré Migault ascended the front steps of the courthouse just as the crowds drawn by the trial started to arrive, and with them the local reporters. Doubtless he was pondering the terrible charge facing his client, one that could send her to the guillotine, a case based on two devastating pieces of evidence: premeditation and an attempt to conceal the bodies. To claim that young Valentine's case hung by a thread would be an understatement. "She's already lost!" commented one hack, a conclusion he arrived at when the judge declined to issue a continuance despite the accident that had befallen Valentine's court-appointed defence lawyer, who had been run over by a refrigerated truck a few days earlier. "If the judge isn't prepared to postpone the trial, it's because it's an open-and-shut case . . ."

Having deferentially greeted his colleagues, Maître Migault changed into his black robes, meticulously fastening the thirty-three buttons and donning the sash. He noticed the quizzical or incredulous looks from the members of the Rouen bar who had seen this brilliant young man arrive from Paris only a month earlier. Having moved back to Normandy for personal reasons (rumour had it that his elderly mother, who lived in Rouen, was in poor health), Maître Migault had had no qualms about stepping in at the last minute and accepting the poisoned chalice as defence counsel in this "sordid business". The gesture had made a big impression.

From the moment she stepped into the court, the defendant's considerable charm was obvious to all. Valentine Boissier was a slight young woman with a face of solemn beauty, high cheekbones and emerald eyes. Although dressed in a rather strait-laced skirt and jacket, it was difficult not to notice her shapely figure.

How her physical attributes would be weighed by the jurors was impossible to say. Pretty women were often handed down harsher sentences than others.

Maître Migault shook her hand warmly, whispered a few brief words, then quietly took his seat in front of her to begin the last stage of a trial that had begun to flag.

For his closing statement the previous day, Maître Franquetot for the prosecution – having considered the preponderance of evidence against the defendant and the inexperience of her barrister – had done little more than summarise the facts and, in a classic rhetorical flourish, demanded "the harshest possible sentence that we, as a god-fearing society . . .", etc. It was a little lacklustre. You could tell he was coasting. Those in the public gallery who had heard better speeches were wondering why they had travelled all this way to witness a conviction which owed nothing to the skilled rhetoric and firebrand tactics of the prosecutor.

The prosecuting counsel had spent his first day despatching the witnesses with a handful of questions, while Maître Migault, head bowed, frantically leafed through his case file, trying to keep a low profile – something those in the gallery could easily understand, given the overwhelming evidence. The jurors looked at him with the sort of benevolent pity they reserved for orchard thieves and cuckolded husbands.

By mid-morning, everyone in the Rouen courthouse was bored stiff.

The first day of the trial had been a damp squib, and this morning, as the trial drew to a close, promised no fireworks. The judge would give his instructions to the jurors at eleven thirty. Most expected that they would be brief. If the defence counsel truly was as hopeless as he seemed, the judge's instructions would be a formality; by noon, the jury would meet to deliberate their verdict, and everyone would be home for lunch

At 9.30, the prosecuting counsel finished questioning his last witness. Maître Migault looked up from his dossier. He stared, wild-eyed, at the man in the witness box and for the first time in the proceedings the court heard his voice:

"Tell me, Monsieur Fierbois, did you see or encounter the defendant on the morning of March 17?"

"Affirmative!" the witness shot back (he was a former soldier, now concierge). "Indeed, and I said to myself, this lass is an early bird, I said, she's got a bit of pluck about her . . ."

A murmur spread through the gallery, the judge reached for his gavel, but Maître Migault was already on his feet.

"Tell me, why did you not mention this to the police?"

"I don't rightly know. Nobody ever asked . . ."

The murmur swelled to a clamour. But what was a shock to those in the public gallery quickly became torture for the prosecutor. One by one, Maître Migault recalled each of the witnesses.

It quickly became apparent that the police investigation had been badly botched. The young defence lawyer demonstrated an exhaustive knowledge of the case, he refuted witnesses, confounded others, the court came alive, the jurors were delighted, even the judge, who was only a few weeks away from retirement, felt young again.

While this young defence lawyer pinpoints the weaknesses of the investigation, unmasks the lies and the half-truths, the unseemly haste, while he unearths long-forgotten case law precedents and probes the Penal Code, let us take a moment to become acquainted with this brilliant young lawyer who is about to win over the jury.

For Désiré Migault has not always been Maître Migault.

In fact, a year before this trial, he spent three months as "Monsieur Mignon", lowly teacher of the only class in Rivaret-en-Puisaye school, where he employed highly innovative teaching methods. The desks and the blackboard were thrown out, and the classroom was turned into a forum where the whole of the first term was devoted to drafting a "Constitution for a Perfect Society". On the day before the Inspector of Schools was due to visit, Monsieur Mignon suddenly disappeared, leaving an indelible memory in the hearts of the pupils (and – for very different reasons – in the minds of their parents).

Some months later, he was Désiré Mignard, a pilot at Evreux Flying Club. Though he had never set foot aboard an aeroplane, he presented a convincing flight log together with certificates.

With infectious enthusiasm, he succeeded in organising an incomparable tour for select well-heeled clients from Normandy and Paris aboard a Douglas DC-3, flying from Paris to Calcutta via Istanbul, Tehran and Karachi, which he was to personally pilot (in what, unbeknownst to the passengers, would be his first flight, though no-one would have guessed as much). The twenty-one passengers would long remember the moment when Désiré, in full flight uniform, revved the engines on the runway under the worried eye of his co-pilot who found Désiré's technique somewhat unorthodox, then, feigning concern, explained that he had some last checks to make, disembarked, walked into the hangar and vanished without trace, and with him the takings of the Flying Club.

Perhaps the highlight of his (still embryonic) career was a stint of more than two months as Doctor Désiré Michard, surgeon at the Saint-Louis Hospital in Yvernon-sur-Saône. He came perilously close to performing pulmonary artery banding on a patient he had diagnosed with a ventricular septal defect (from which the man did not suffer). At the last second, Désiré raised a hand to stop the anaesthetist, calmly absented himself from the operating theatre and left the hospital with the contents of the safe, having caused the patient only a minor scare and the hospital authorities some profound embarrassment. The matter was quickly hushed up.

No-one has ever discovered the true identity of Désiré Migault. All that is known for certain is that he was born and raised in Saint-Nom-la-Bretèche, where his name appears in the school rolls; after that, there is no trace of him.

The accounts from those who have met him were as disparate as his life itself.

The members of the Flying Club who met pilot Désiré Mignard described him as a fearless, dauntless aviator ("A born leader!"

one of them opined), the patients treated by Doctor Désiré Michard spoke of a courteous surgeon, serious, focused ("Not terribly talkative. It was all you could do to get a word out of him . . ."), as for the parents of the pupils taught by Monsieur Désiré Mignon, they described a shy, retiring young man ("A delicate little flower . . . A little neurotic, in my opinion.").

As we rejoin the trial of Valentine Boissier, the prosecutor, somewhat out of breath, has just come to the end of his rather confused closing argument, which, for lack of concrete evidence, he has based on principles which have convinced no-one.

Maître Désiré Migault begins his summation:

"Gentlemen of the jury, I would ask you to bear in mind that this is no ordinary case. Think of the typical defendants who appear before you. Whom have you been called on to judge in the past months? A drunken lout of a father who caved his son's skull in with a cast-iron pan, a brothel madam who stabbed a truculent client seventeen times, a former police officer turned receiver of stolen goods who bound one of his accomplices to the tracks of the Paris–Le Havre train where it was hacked into three pieces. Gentlemen of the jury, I trust that you will agree with me when I say that my client, a devout Catholic, the upstanding daughter of a respected baker, formerly a brilliant but self-effacing student at Sainte-Sophie secondary school, is a far cry from the tide of murderers and cutpurses who habitually sit in the dock of this court."

The young barrister who had initially seemed unremarkable, even bewildered, though firm and direct in his cross-examination, was now addressing the court in clear, measured tones. He was poised and elegant, his argument clear-cut and compelling, his gestures discreet and graceful. Those in the gallery had begun to warm to him.

"Gentlemen of the jury, the task of the prosecutor in this case was neither difficult nor challenging, since everyone seemed to assume that this was, if you'll forgive the idiom, an open-and-shut case."

He returned to his bench and picked up the morning papers, some of which he presented to the jury.

"The *Normandie-Express*: 'VALENTINE BOISSIER ON TRIAL FOR HER LIFE.' *Le Quotidien du Bocage*: 'PRETTY PASTRY CHEF A HAIR'S BREADTH FROM THE GUILLOTINE.' *Rouen-Matin*: 'DEATH OR LIFE IMPRISONMENT FOR VALENTINE BOISSIER?'"

He paused, gave the jurors a long, slow smile, then added:

"Rarely has public opinion colluded with the prosecution to dictate a jury's verdict. Nor pressed for a more flagrant and, let us be honest, a more egregious miscarriage of justice!"

A pregnant silence followed this denunciation.

Then began the detailed examination of the charges against the defendant, which Maître Migault placed under the critical light of what is called, somewhat curiously, "reasoned reason", an expression whose very abstruseness exponentially increased the jury's respect for him.

"Gentlemen of the jury," he concluded, "we could end this trial right now. We have here (he brandished a thick sheaf of documents) more than sufficient grounds to call for an immediate retrial, the blunders made during the investigation are legion. Just as this case was prejudged by the press, so now it is considered open and shut by the court itself. But we have chosen to fight on. Because my client is not prepared to walk free from this court on some technicality."

A ripple of astonishment spread through the court.

Behind him, Maître Migault's client almost fainted.

"She demands that you consider the facts. She demands that

your verdict be based on the truth. And as you consider that verdict, she asks that you look her in the eye. She implores you to see her action for what it was: an instinctive reflex of self-preservation. Be in no doubt, gentlemen of the jury, what we are dealing with is a crime committed in self-defence!"

There was muttering in the public gallery; the judge looked sceptical.

"Self-defence!" said Maître Migault again. "Because the supposed victim in this case is the true villain while the alleged murderer is the victim."

Maître Migault spent some considerable time detailing the beatings, the violence, the brutality and humiliation his client had suffered at the hands of the man she shot dead. The details of this horrific abuse clearly appalled the jurors and the people in the public gallery. Men bowed their heads. Women bit their lips.

Why had the defendant made no mention of these facts to the police or the investigating magistrate, and how had they come to light today?

"Gentlemen of the jury, my client held her tongue out of a sense of decency! Out of sheer altruism! Valentine Boissier was prepared to die rather than tarnish the reputation of the man she loved!"

Maître Migault went on to explain that Valentine had buried her victims, not to conceal her crime, but to ensure they had the "decent burial the Catholic Church would have denied them because of their dissolute actions".

The high point of the speech for the defence came when Maître Migault, having vividly evoked the terrible scars left by her abuser, turned to the defendant and asked her to strip to the waist so that they could be seen. There was uproar in the court-room, the judge promptly ordered the defendant to do nothing of the sort, while the crimson blush that spread over the dazed Valentine Boissier (whose shapely torso was, in fact, as unmarked as when she was a girl) made her seem demure and modest. The clamour did not subside. Maître Migault, standing stiff as the statue of the Commendatore, nodded to the judge: Very well, then, I shall not insist.

He offered a verbal portrait of "Valentine's abuser", an astute composite of fairy-tale ogre with a demonic temperament and a depraved tormentor, and concluded his speech with a blaze of oratory delivered directly to the jurors:

"Your purpose, gentlemen of the jury, is to see justice done, to sift truth from falsehood, to stand firm against the popular voice that blindly condemns. Your role is to appreciate courage, recognise selflessness, affirm innocence. I have no doubt that your compassion will ennoble you and through you, thanks to you, ennoble the system of justice of which you are the embodiment today."

While the jury deliberated and Maître Migault was surrounded by reporters, journalists and even colleagues come, reluctantly, to congratulate him, the President of the Bar slipped through the crowd, laid an arm over the young man's shoulders and took him aside.

"A minor problem, Maître, we can find no trace of your accreditation at the Paris bar."

"That is most perplexing!" the young lawyer said in astonishment.

"I cannot but agree. If you would come and see me in my chambers as soon as the deliberations are over, I would like . . ."

He trailed off, as the bell sounded to announce that the jury were coming in. Maître Migault barely had time to pay a quick visit to the lavatory.

It is impossible to know whether the closing speech swayed the jury or whether, since people in the provinces are easily bored, it was merely a sideshow that offered to the jurors the opportunity to appear virtuous, but the fact remains that Valentine Boissier, having been found guilty with extenuating circumstances, was given a sentence of three years, two of them suspended, which, given the time she had spent on remand, meant she left the court a free woman.

As for her defence lawyer, he was never seen again. Since setting aside the verdict would have entailed acknowledging that the court and indeed the entire judicial system had permitted a sham lawyer to practise with impunity, no mention was made of an appeal.

# 6

As she read and reread the summons from Judge Le Poittevin, Louise endlessly wondered and speculated about the nature of this "matter concerning you". To no avail. At night, her fears prowled the darkness, clawed at her throat. If it was related to the charge of indecent exposure, why would the judge summon her, surely it was a matter for the courts? She pictured herself before a bench of magistrates, all nervously toying with their glasses and breaking them before sending her to the guillotine, where the executioner, in the person of Judge Le Poittevin himself, bellowed: "Ah, so the young lady is eager to display her . . . her . . .", and she realised she was naked, and the judge was staring at her crotch with unsettling persistence; she would wake up bathed in sweat.

By seven o' clock on Thursday morning she was up and dressed and wearing her coat. It was much too early, since the summons was for ten o'clock. Her hands shaking, she made herself some more coffee. Finally, it was time to leave. Well, almost time, it hardly mattered if she was early. She was washing her coffee cup when the doorbell rang.

Warily, she tiptoed to the window and saw the owner of La Petite Bohème standing at the gate, tapping his foot and staring at the house. She had no desire to open the door, she did not want to talk to him. Not that Monsieur Jules had played any part in this sorry story. Louise was behaving rather like the tribunes of Ancient Rome who killed the bearers of bad news. But it was hardly surprising: she associated the restaurant with the whole grisly episode and was casting around for someone to blame, as though Monsieur Jules had somehow failed in his duty to protect her. It was strange, Monsieur Jules had only to cross the street to ring Louise's doorbell, yet here he was dressed to the nines in a tailored suit and patent leather shoes – he lacked only a bouquet of flowers. He was dressed like a man about to propose, but had the weary air of a lover about to be jilted.

Some days earlier, the bus that usually shielded Louise from La Petite Bohème had been delayed and she had been forced to venture out into the open. As she passed the restaurant, she had seen Monsieur Jules carrying the plates. It was a pitiful sight, one she heard sometimes happened on the rare occasions when she had been unable to work her shift. When it came to waiting tables, as with conversations, Monsieur Jules never listened. He would deliver the wrong order to the wrong tables, traipse through the restaurant to fetch a teaspoon, forget to bring the bread. The food – if it came – would arrive cold; diners forced to wait half an hour for their bill would grow increasingly impatient, prompting Monsieur Jules to erupt: *why don't you go eat somewhere else?* and, while the regulars sighed, the aggrieved diners would throw down their napkins, *very well, we'll do just that.* Louise's rare absences had been damaging to the restaurant's reputation and its takings. That said, Monsieur Jules had never considered replacing her: he was prepared to juggle the cooking and the service, to lose customers, but the prospect of hiring someone new – never!

Louise glanced at the clock, time was getting on, she had to open the door.

Hands behind his back, Monsieur Jules watched as she walked to the gate.

"You could have dropped in . . . We've all been so worried."

This "we", which in his mind referred to the restaurant's customers, the neighbours and, by extension, the whole world, sounded rather like a royal "we".

"What I meant was . . ."

But he could not finish the sentence. He was watching Louise. She could have opened the gate, but she had not.

They stared at each other through the wrought-iron bars, as though Monsieur Jules had presented himself at a ticket counter named Louise Belmont. She had no idea what had been said about her absence, about her return. She did not care.

"Are you alright, at least?" said Monsieur Jules.

"I'm alright."

"Were you on your way out . . .?"

"No . . . I mean, yes."

Monsieur Jules nodded knowingly, then, suddenly, he grabbed the bars with both hands, like a convict.

"Are you going to come back to work?"

Louise saw his huge face looming. His beret knocked against the railings and settled on the back of his skull, making him look faintly ridiculous. But Monsieur Jules was oblivious to that fact, because the question he had asked utterly consumed him.

Louise shrugged.

"No . . . I don't think so, no."

Something broke inside her. It was this decision, more than Doctor Thirion's suicide, more than having to appear before a judge, more than the looming charge of indecent exposure, more even than the declaration of war, that propelled her into a new life; it frightened her.

It frightened Monsieur Jules too, who reeled back, tears in his eyes. He tried to smile but gave up.

"Of course, of course."

Louise realised that she was abandoning him, and her heart felt heavy, not because she regretted leaving, but because she loved him, because he was part of a life that had just ended.

Monsieur Jules, with his ill-fitting suit, his beret askew, hopped from one foot to the other.

"Well, well . . . I'd better be going, then . . ."

Louise did not know what to say. She watched as he walked away, his fat buttocks swaying: the suit was too small, the trousers were at half mast, the seam in the back of the jacket seemed about to give up the ghost.

Rather than going out, Louise went back up the steps, fetched a handkerchief and glanced out the window as Monsieur Jules was closing the door of La Petite Bohème behind him. Only at that moment did she realise that he had asked no questions. How much did he know about what had happened? How could he know anything? Obviously, he would have noticed Doctor Thirion's absence (the first in decades), but how would he have connected her with his absence? Had there been an article in *Paris-Soir*? Did it connect the doctor's suicide to Louise?

Moments later, Louise went out and, making no attempt to hide, walked past the restaurant to the bus stop. Still shaken by her brief conversation with Monsieur Jules, she found it difficult to focus on the looming interview. From her handbag, she took the summons regarding the "matter concerning you".

"Indeed, one might say that the matter is of prodigious concern to you," said Judge Le Poittevin.

He was not wearing his glasses today; they were probably being repaired. Instead, he fiddled with a squat fountain pen just big enough for his small hands and squinted at Louise.

"You . . ."

The judge was clearly disappointed. When drained and distraught, languishing in a hospital bed, the girl had seemed alluring – he was titillated by her resemblance to Cosette at the side of the boulevard, he liked that a lot – but here, in his chambers, she seemed banal, insignificant, cramped. She looked like a married woman. The judge dropped his pen and peered down at his file.

"If this is about the charge of indecent exposure . . ." Louise said in a tone so stern she surprised herself.

"Pfft, if this were about . . ."

From the weary, disappointed tone, Louise realised that this last charge was to be dropped.

"In which case, why have I been summoned to this unjust interrogation?"

Had she used any other word, the judge might have answered. But she said "unjust" so, since he considered himself the arbiter of what was just and unjust, the judge exploded. The young clerk who took notes was clearly inured to such behaviour. He just folded his arms, looking out the window.

"How dare you suggest I am being 'Unjust'?" bellowed Le Poittevin. "You are in the presence of the very embodiment of Justice, mademoiselle. (From his tone, it was clear the words were capitalised.) And you must answer to me, to Justice!"

Louise remained calm.

"I still don't understand what I'm doing here . . ."

"*You* are not the only person concerned . . ."

Louise had no idea to whom the judge might be referring.

"Others have a vested interest . . ." he said with a certain relish.

What appeared to be bad news for Louise was good news for him.

He motioned to the junior clerk, who sighed and disappeared,

77

only to return a moment later with a woman in her sixties, dressed in mourning black, her face a picture of grief. Since there was no alternative, she took the chair next to Louise, who inhaled the woman's subtle stylish perfume, the kind of thing she had never worn herself.

"Madame Thirion, I am deeply sorry to have to impose upon your time . . ."

He gestured to Louise, who flushed scarlet.

Doctor Thirion's widow stared fixedly in front of her.

". . . while the case regarding the circumstances of your husband's . . . death . . . is closed."

He marked a long pause to underscore both the consequences of this statement and the mystery surrounding his new summons. Immediately, Louise felt anxiety rising in her throat. If the case was closed, how could she be at risk?

"There is one matter still outstanding!" the judge growled. "For although the charges of prostitution and indecent exposure have been dropped, there remains . . ."

This deliberate attempt to create suspense, so at odds with the dispensation of impartial justice, felt grotesque, obscene, and also terribly threatening. It smacked of summary justice.

". . . the charge of *blackmail*! Because, if indeed 'mademoiselle' was not selling sexual favours, what then to make of such a significant sum of money? Why, *blackmail*!"

Louise was speechless. What hold could she possibly have over Doctor Thirion? The notion was absurd.

"If you are prepared to press charges, Madame Thirion, we will launch a full investigation and prove that this was extortion!"

He turned to Louise.

"As for you, mademoiselle, it will mean three years' imprisonment and a fine of one hundred thousand francs!"

He slammed his pen down on the desk to indicate that the interview was at an end.

Louise was in a state of shock. She had only just evaded one charge and now another loomed . . . Three years in prison! She was about to burst into tears when she sensed, rather than saw, a movement next to her.

Madame Thirion was shaking her head.

"I beg you to reconsider, madame. You have suffered a serious loss. Not only the loss of a husband, but of a man of impeccable reputation, the sort of man who did not frequent women of loose morals. If he gave money to 'mademoiselle' here, there must be a reason, damn it!"

Louise felt Madame Thirion stiffen. She saw her open her handbag, take out a handkerchief and dab her eyes. Clearly, this was not the first time that Le Poittevin had urged her to press charges, and while his previous efforts had been in vain, he had not given up hope of persuading her.

"This exorbitant sum came from his own pocket! We can find out the reason and punish the guilty party!"

He gave a nervous, stilted laugh. Louise wanted to say something but was deterred by the presence of the doctor's widow, who was delicately wiping her eyes.

"We have no way of knowing that this woman did not extort other monies from your husband. This was almost certainly not the first time. How much, then, did this creature extort from your late husband? From you!"

His face lit up at the power of the argument.

"By rights, this money is yours, madame! It is your daughter Henriette's inheritance. If you do not press charges, there can be no investigation, and if there is no investigation, we cannot uncover the truth. If you will simply press charges, we can sort this out."

Louise opened her mouth to speak: she did not want anyone to think she had taken advantage of the doctor . . . In fact, she had not even taken the money, she had left the envelope on the chest of drawers . . . She was choking back words when she was curtly interrupted by the judge.

Madame Thirion was shaking her head.

"For pity's sake!" roared the judge. "Clerk!"

Impatiently he waved his little hand, things were moving too slowly for his liking, especially the junior clerk, who sighed as he crossed the chambers, took something from a shelf and went over to the judge's desk.

"What do you say to this, Madame Thirion? This is not a small matter!"

He gestured to the kitchen knife that Louise had brought to the hotel. It had obviously been found among her clothes. Seeing it in this context, tied with a handwritten label bearing an exhibit number and her name, Belmont, this mundane kitchen utensil took on a menacing appearance. It was easy to imagine it in the hands of a murderer.

"I ask you! Do you really believe that a 'young lady' who walks around with this in her pocket has innocent intentions, I ask you!"

But it was unclear to whom the judge was directing this question. The dismissal of all other charges for lack of evidence had put him into a towering rage. He was angry with Louise; he was determined to punish her.

"I implore you to press charges, madame!"

He picked up the knife as though about to stab someone, perhaps the depraved young girl he was being forced to free for want of evidence, or perhaps the widow who was denying him the means to punish the girl.

But no, Madame Thirion continued to shake her head vehemently, she did not wish to press charges, doubtless she simply wanted the whole affair to be over, once and for all. Madame Thirion got up and left the room so suddenly that the young clerk was taken aback. The judge was appalled.

As for Louise, the matter was once again closed. She got to her feet and walked to the door, fearing at every step that the judge would order her to sit back down, but nothing came. As she stepped out of the Palais de Justice, she felt a surge of relief. This time the case was truly over. Nonetheless, she had found the presence of the widow painful, and it weighed on her heart.

As she walked beneath the arcades, she was surprised to see Madame Thirion standing by a pillar, talking to a woman somewhat less elegant than she; probably her daughter, for there was a vague family resemblance. Their eyes followed her as she passed; it took all the effort Louise could marshal not to break into a run. Shamefaced, her head bowed, she walked across the esplanade.

Louise spent a day or two pacing the rooms of her house, then she sat down and wrote a note to the headmaster to say that she would be back to work on Monday.

That done, she walked down to the cemetery, as she always did when at a loose end.

She visited the family grave and filled the vase with fresh water for the bouquet she had brought. Set into the marble headstone were enamelled portraits of her father and her mother. Her parents looked as though they hailed from different generations, from different worlds. This was hardly surprising since her father had died in 1916 and her mother lived another twenty-three years.

Louise had no memory of her father, to her he was no more than an antiquated photograph, whereas everything reminded her of her mother. Jeanne Belmont had done her utmost to be a loving mother, but depression had laid her low, turned her into a spectral figure.

Louise had spent much of her childhood caring for a woman who seemed barely alive, but to whom she felt extremely close. Because they were very alike. Louise had never decided whether or not this was a good thing. Looking at the frozen image before her, she saw her own face, her own mouth and, most strikingly, the same pale eyes.

For the first time since her mother's death, Louise wished that she could talk to her, and bitterly regretted the fact that she had not known how when there was still time.

The rawness of her grief had passed now, and it was this that made her sad: grieving for the chance to be able to talk to the mother she had loved, but whom, deep down, she no longer mourned.

## 7

In appropriating Gabriel's role for himself, Raoul Landrade finally had access to a realm equal to his ambitions. On the first morning that he sat behind the steering wheel of the truck that plied the route between the shopkeepers of Thionville and the stores of the Supply Corps, he radiated the self-confidence of a man who had finally acceded to the position for which he was always destined.

In the back of the truck sat Ambresac and Chabrier, staring listlessly at the road.

"What's the wholesale grocer's name again?" said Raoul.

This question instantly set alarm bells ringing in Gabriel's head.

"Floutard. Jean-Michel Floutard."

Raoul nodded, sceptically. The struggle for power had already begun. For Gabriel, it was a losing battle. Every time he left a shop that day to supervise the loading of supplies, he saw Raoul whispering to the shopkeepers behind his back. Then Raoul would disappear for an hour, sometimes more, as though he had simply come along for the ride and was going about his business.

In the early afternoon, the three were forced to wait in the truck for almost an hour.

"Probably dipping his wick in the whorehouse," said Chabrier, ever the philosopher.

"Or playing three-card monte in some back alley," said Ambresac. "Making a little money to pay for his cigarettes. He won't be long."

At length, Raoul appeared, pushing a wheelbarrow laden with gunny sacks and wooden crates. Summoning every ounce of his authority, Gabriel gave him a dressing-down.

"I'm here now, boss, I'm here now!" Raoul sniggered.

They set off back to the Mayenberg. It was 1700 hours, this was Gabriel's first day, and the supply truck had been so late back.

The following morning, having reached the outskirts of Thionville, Raoul took a different street to a new supplier. Gabriel said nothing. This silent acquiescence, this admission that he was powerless, merely fuelled Raoul's commercial zeal. In less than a week later, Raoul Landrade had a finger in every pie in town.

Usually, the truck left the Mayenberg almost empty and returned groaning with supplies, but by the second week, it was leaving the fort laden with crates, cases, sacks. Gabriel climbed onto the bed of the truck and was about to lift the tarpaulin when he was stopped by Raoul.

"They're personal effects . . ."

Landrade's voice quavered with a latent menace that he tried to defuse with a lopsided grin, his thin lips set in a rictus somewhere between defiance and provocation.

"Just doing a few favours for our friends back in the barracks," he said, pulling the tarpaulin over the crates.

As he straightened up, he turned to face Gabriel.

"I mean, if you like, we can tell them to go fuck 'emselves, tell them we're not going to lift a finger – up to you, chief."

It was not difficult to guess the reaction of the other soldiers to such a decision. They already thought of the Retail Corps as a few lucky bastards who spent their days strutting around town while ordinary soldiers were rotting in the bowels of the Mayenberg or pouring concrete in the rain. Gabriel stepped down from the bed of the truck and climbed into the passenger seat.

Somewhere along the road, the truck hit a pothole and there came the tinkle of breaking glass; no-one said a word, but moments later the cab began to fill with the heady fumes of over-proof rum.

"We're going to make a quick stop here," said Raoul, "just a little errand for a comrade."

Before Gabriel could protest, Chabrier was in the back of the truck, handing crates to Ambresac who was standing on the pavement outside the Brasserie des Sports; Raoul, meanwhile, had disappeared inside. He was obviously filching booze and coffee from the Supply Corps and selling it to the local cafés . . .

"Here," Raoul said as he slid behind the wheel. "It's not much, but . . ."

He handed over three crumpled bills.

"This can't carry on . . ." muttered Gabriel, ashen with rage.

"Really? What are you going to do about it? Tell the brass you've been in on the whole thing for the past week? Maybe you could tell them how much you've been pocketing yourself? That should make them happy."

"I haven't pocketed a centime!"

"Oh yes you have, we've all seen you take baksheesh, haven't we boys?"

Ambresac and Chabrier nodded gravely. Raoul put an arm around Gabriel's shoulder.

"Look, just take the cash! Three months from now, your temporary posting will be over. By that stage, no-one will care . . ."

Gabriel shrugged off Landrade's arm.

"Fine, do what you like," said Landrade. "Come on boys, let's get a move on, we have work to do."

By the third week, Raoul was working a new scheme out of the military laundry facility. Sacks began to emerge stuffed with underwear, greatcoats, blankets, even shoes, all of which Raoul sold to the local farmers.

Caporal-chef Landrade was truly gifted. The personal effects and provisions were furtively smuggled out of the Mayenberg so quickly and discreetly that Gabriel sometimes wondered whether he was really seeing anything. On their return journeys, any contraband was mixed in with the official order: no-one noticed a thing.

Friday was the day when major supplies were bought. A convoy of four trucks set off in the morning, tasked with bringing back heavy and bulky foodstuffs: pulses, canned goods, casks of wine, coffee, etc. Back at the Mayenberg, everything was loaded into the trucks of the train that wound its way through the fortification's tunnel, stopping off at the Supply Corps and the kitchens. Suddenly, all the lights went out, and the tunnel was plunged into darkness. There were angry shouts from soldiers – *what the devil's going on?* In the end a call was put through to the Plant, and an electrical engineer wearing a headlamp crawled through the tunnel, cursing and blinding – I'm coming, I'm coming – and restored the power. As the lights flickered on, Gabriel just had time to see a door in the tunnel wall swing shut. Half of the supplies in the next wagon had disappeared. It was more than an hour before Landrade and his henchmen reappeared. They seemed happy with their day.

The following Tuesday, Raoul buttonholed Gabriel and took him to one side.

"Fancy a little entertainment?"

He fumbled in his pocket and brought out a slip of paper which had been rubber-stamped and bore a handwritten number and a few letters.

"If you like, we can drop you off at the door, make the usual rounds and pick you up on our way back to the fort . . ."

Landrade had just invented "whorehouse coupons". The two nearest brothels to the fort were thirty and sixty kilometres away respectively. Getting there meant taking the train. Soldiers on short-term furlough made up most of the railway's profits. Raoul grinned at him conspiratorially, holding out the coupons.

"No thanks," Gabriel cut him dead.

Raoul stuffed the paper back into his pocket. How had Landrade managed to strike a deal with the brothel madams? What rates had he negotiated, and for which personal services? Gabriel had no interest in finding out, but all too soon, he began seeing these coupons circulating: soldiers won them playing three-card monte, and before long they were being bartered for food. In less than a week, the coupons had become the illegal tender of the Mayenberg black market, run by Caporal-chef Landrade.

The whole business was getting out of hand.

Within three weeks, the "Landrade system" was operating at full throttle. Gabriel was dazed by the speed at which the operation had taken hold and the scope of its activities. Since Landrade's blackmail meant that he could take no action, Gabriel fell back on his reflexes as a schoolteacher: he took notes. Though he could not cite the precise quantities of goods circulating, or the names of Landrade's contacts, when he got back to his bunk room, he jotted down a list of all the products whose origin or destination he considered suspect, together with the dates and times they were procured. He pretended to turn a blind eye when he noticed

Landrade whispering to a butcher, a grocer, a wine merchant, but he noted every detail. When, back at the Mayenberg, cartons of cigarettes, pouches of tobacco and boxes of cigars were unloaded from the truck, Gabriel made a note.

Days passed. Gabriel's relief of being freed from the oppressive atmosphere of the Mayenberg gave way to a longing to go back, to extricate himself from a criminal enterprise that was swelling to monstrous proportions and whose organisers would, sooner or later, incur the full wrath of military justice. While he waited for this to happen, he fiddled figures, manipulated quantities and covered up embarrassing details.

But one thing followed another and, before he knew what was happening, Gabriel was pitched into the greatest maelstrom of his time, one that would forever change his life.

Just as sometimes complex operations can be solved in a split-second, so Caporal-chef Landrade's business collapsed suddenly, in the space of a single day.

It all began with an ill-timed gesture.

Gabriel discovered four jerry cans filled with diesel oil wedged between two empty boxes in the flat bed of the truck.

"It's only a couple of gallons," said Landrade. "We won't even miss it. But think what it means to the poor farmers who can barely do their work these days because of all the restrictions."

The diesel had come from the four-hundred-cubic-metre tank next to the Mayenberg that was designed to power the ventilation and filtration system that Gabriel had checked so obsessively.

To Gabriel, stealing diesel was not just another way to make a little money on the side, it meant throttling the life of the Mayenberg in the event of a chemical attack. It was an act of treason. As soon as he saw the jerrycans, he felt himself choke and gasp for air.

He wheeled round, as pale as death.

"I'll have no more of this petty trafficking, Landrade, it's over!"

He climbed down from the truck.

"Hold up!" Raoul called, running after him.

His two henchmen stepped to block Gabriel's path.

"It's over, do you hear me?"

Gabriel was bellowing now, soldiers turned and stared as he brandished his little notebook.

"I've got it all in here. Every detail of your shady deals, the dates, the times. You'll have to explain your actions to the commandant!"

Being a quick-witted man, Landrade realised the gravity of the situation in an instant, and the potential consequences. For the first time, Gabriel saw a flicker of panic in his eyes. Out of the corner of his eye, Landrade saw the soldiers moving towards them. He lashed out, a vicious gut punch that sent Gabriel sprawling, then grabbed him under the arm and dragged him out of sight, even as Gabriel hugged the notebook to his chest. Ambresac gripped his forearms as Landrade tried to rip the notebook from his hands, but Gabriel clung to it like a drowning man. Hurriedly, the three men dragged Gabriel through the tunnel and into the small storeroom lit only by a dim bulb. Gabriel felt punches rain down on his chest.

"Hand it over, you fucking bastard!" Raoul growled through clenched teeth.

Gabriel rolled onto his stomach and curled into a ball. In vain, Landrade's henchmen tried to lift him up. Ambresac, never one for half measures, kicked Gabriel in the balls with his steel-capped boot. Gabriel felt a searing pain in his gut and promptly threw up.

"Stop!" roared Landrade, grabbing Ambresac as he made to kick again.

He bent over Gabriel.

"Go on, just give me the notebook and get up, everything is going to be fine . . ."

But Gabriel curled into a ball, protecting the notebook as though his life depended on it.

Without warning, there came a wail of sirens.

Calls of "action stations!"

Opening the storeroom door, they saw soldiers racing through the tunnels.

Raoul grabbed a passing soldier who was tripping over his kitbag.

"What the fuck is going on?"

The young soldier stood, spellbound at the sight of Gabriel crawling towards the door.

Raoul shook him roughly and repeated his question.

"It's war," the dazed boy said after a moment.

Gabriel looked up.

"It's the Boche . . . They've invaded Belgium . . . !"

# 8

When Louise went to the school on Monday, the other teachers greeted her obliquely; they did not treat her as though she had been ill, no-one asked where she had been. Granted, they were all somewhat preoccupied. All male teachers who had not been mobilised in 1939 had received their call-up papers. Or had already been shipped out to the front. Either way the teaching staff had been seriously depleted, while refugee children from Belgium had arrived in droves; there was a shortage of desks, of chairs, of everything. Except, racial slurs. Parroting what they heard at home, the little French children referred to their Belgian counterparts as "Krauts"; they mocked the accents of children from Luxembourg, but also those from Picardy and Lille: by a process of capillary action, war had leached into the playground.

The newspaper headlines all led with the unexpected German offensive that had begun two days earlier. "Germany and France are engaged in a battle to the death," proclaimed Général Gamelin. It sounded martial, and therefore reassuring. Although everything was going according to plan, the sudden offensive had caught France unawares; everyone seemed bewildered. Those who had insisted that the war was nothing more than sabre-rattling kept their heads down. The newspapers insisted that the military had everything in hand. "FIERCE RESISTANCE TO THE REICH IN HOLLAND AND BELGIUM" read one headline; "GERMANS HALTED AT BELGIAN BORDER!" crowed another. Nothing to worry about. As recently as that morning, the press was insisting that Franco-British forces in Belgium had "paralysed" the enemy advance, that the brutal enemy offensive had been countered by "the powerful massed forces" of the Allies, and even that the fresh arrival of French troops had "whipped up their fighting spirit".

All this was well and good, but people could not help but wonder whether it tallied with what was actually happening. Since the previous September, everyone had been saying that the decisive weapon in any war would be information. Unsurprisingly, people feared that the newspapers were engaged in a campaign designed to bolster a conquering spirit. Hence the number of bombers that had been shot down was all the teachers talked about while the children played war games in the schoolyard.

"Ten planes a day, I'm telling you," said Madame Guénot.

"On the radio, they claimed it was thirty," said someone else.

"So, what do we make of this, then?" said Monsieur Laforgue, waving a copy of *L'Intransigeant*, which insisted fifty planes a day were being shot down.

No-one had an answer.

"*Num nos adsentiri huic qui postremus locutus est decet?*" quipped the headmaster with a knowing smile, but no-one understood.

When Louise arrived, the huddle of teachers parted, though they looked less like they were trying to make space and more like they were trying to keep their distance.

"I don't understand any of it," said Madame Guénot. "And besides, war is a man's . . ." As she trailed off, her voice took on the acid quality that presaged one of the ugly barbs that were the corner stone of her personality. "Only a certain kind of woman takes an interest in a man's affair . . ."

Two or three of the teachers turned to look at Louise. The

school bell tolled, and they all headed back to their classrooms.

When the lunchtime conversation in the canteen proved as caustic as that in the playground, Louise resolved to wait until the end of the day and have a word with the headmaster, a pedagogical relic of uncertain age whose retirement everyone had been expecting since long before Louise had joined the school. He had formerly taught Latin and belles-lettres and spoke in lofty grandiloquent circumlocutions without ever coming to the point. It was often difficult to understand what he was saying. He was a short man, with a tendency to stand on tiptoe whenever he spoke: it was like holding a conversation with a marionette.

"Mademoiselle Belcourt," he said when she had finished, "You find me profoundly discountenanced. Now, I am not one to listen to idle tittle-tattle, as you know . . ."

Instantly, Louise pricked up her ears. Rumour was the order of the day, and one of those rumours concerned her. Seeing the young woman press her hands together, the headmaster saddled his high horse.

"It is a matter of sublime indifference to me if a young woman chooses to fly in the face of public opinion, let me assure you!"

"What exactly are you talking about?" said Louise.

The simplicity of her question knocked the wind out of the headmaster's sails. His white whiskers quavered, as did his lower lip. Women terrified him. With a long, painful sigh, he opened his desk drawer and took out a piece of paper, an article clipped from *Paris-Soir* whose tattered condition suggested it had passed through many hands:

### TRAGIC SUICIDE IN FOURTEENTH ARRONDISSEMENT HOTEL

Schoolmistress, a sometime nightwalker, found naked at the scene.

The article, probably written on the very night the incident took place, was riddled with inaccuracies. The woman in question was not named, so Louise could have feigned ignorance, but she was completely distraught, her hands were trembling.

"The gutter press likes to inflame the public with matters of no consequence, Mademoiselle Belmont, as you know all too well. *Sic transit gloria mundi.*"

Louise stared into the man's eyes; she could feel him faltering. He looked like a truculent schoolboy as he dipped into his desk drawer once again and set down a second article, this one more detailed:

### HOTEL SUICIDE MYSTERY EXPLAINED
Doctor took his life while in the presence of a schoolmistress,
for whose companionship he paid handsomely.

"If I might be so bold as to offer a word of advice: *Ne istam rem flocci feceris . . .*"

The following day, Louise arrived at the school like a reluctant pupil. The music teacher tilted her head as though staring intently at something else. Madame Guénot whispered mockingly in the hallways. Louise had been ostracised; even the diminutive headmaster no longer dared look at her. When she walked down the hallways, her colleagues stared at the floor. Just as in the judge's chambers, the people here thought she was a whore.

That evening, she cut her hair much shorter than she usually did, and in the morning appeared at the school wearing make-up – something she had never done. During breaktime, she lit a cigarette.

Needless to say, the reproachful looks of her female colleagues were alternated by amorous looks from the men. Louise began to consider the idea of getting fucked by every man left in the school. She counted them as she smoked her cigarette out in the playground: a dozen, hardly an impossible task. She gazed at a prefect and imagined him taking her doggy-style on the desk in her classroom. It is impossible to know whether he read her thoughts, but he blushed scarlet and looked away.

Noting the deleterious effects of a little lipstick and mascara on his teaching staff, the diminutive headmaster sighed:

"*Quam humanum est*! *Quam tristitiam*!"

For Louise, pretending to be a whore offered only a fleeting pleasure. More than anything, she felt alone, ashamed, isolated; she threw away the pack of cigarettes.

A sudden change in military tactics provided a distraction.

A vague, nagging sense of doubt began to sweep through the school, and through the city of Paris. If the enemy invasion of Belgium highlighted the sagacity of the French générals, the Ardennes offensive confounded their expectations. The newspapers varied in their coverage of this new German incursion. While *L'Intransigeant* trumpeted the headline "GERMAN ADVANCE THWARTED", *Le Petit Parisien* was forced to admit that German troops were "advancing towards the River Meuse, between Namur and Mézières". Which to believe?

The caretaker, a sallow, suspicious man, asked querulously:

"Well, are the Krauts coming through Belgium or through the Ardennes? They need to make their mind up!"

The days that followed brought no clarification. One paper insisted "The enemy has failed to make any breach in our defensive lines", but another reported the "steady advance of invading forces".

Between the uncertainties of the war and the uncomfortable atmosphere triggered by the revelations about Louise (to which the sexual aspect added a delicious whiff of perversity, shame and taboo), life at the school was becoming increasingly intolerable.

What was she doing here, Louise wondered? No-one wanted her here and she did not want to be here. Perhaps it was time to change her life? But how? Monsieur Jules could not afford to pay a full-time waitress, and Louise's only skills were teaching children to read and serving *tête de veau sauce ravigote*. Like everyone else: she was waiting for a miracle.

When Friday evening came, she set her bag on the kitchen table, wandered over to the window and looked at the facade of La Petite Bohème. A visit from Monsieur Jules now would have been useful. As she prepared her evening meal, Louise fleetingly imagined his floundering lectures to his customers about the war with Germany; she smiled, then realised that she was eating dinner though she had not even taken off her coat. Something was clearly wrong. The inexplicable shot fired by Doctor Thirion was still wreaking havoc in her life.

## 9

"Yessss . . ."

The director was a man of about sixty. His chubby face and sullen pout made it look as though he were constantly about to burst into tears. Exhaustion, perhaps, to say nothing of his responsibilities. Running the Ministry of Information – or more accurately the Ministry of Censorship – and managing a team of five hundred agents, including graduates, teachers, professors, officers and diplomats, was no easy task. One had only to witness the hive of activity in the Hôtel Continental to realise that the dark circles under his eyes were not the result of a night on the town or a cantankerous wife.

"Monsieur Cœdes," he murmured thoughtfully, "I've met him once or twice . . . A splendid man."

The young man sitting opposite him clasped his knees and nodded respectfully. Behind his thick, round glasses, he had the curious faraway look of preoccupied people, that hesitant, febrile air the director had often noticed among intellectuals sapped by their work in highly specialised disciplines. Oriental languages. The director was holding a letter from the French School of Asian Studies signed by Georges Cœdes, warmly commending his pupil for his seriousness, his tenacity and his sense of responsibility.

"So, you speak Vietnamese, Khmer . . ."

Désiré nodded solemnly.

"Indeed, I am also proficient in Thai and Jarai . . ."

"Excellent, excellent . . ."

But in actual fact the director was disappointed. Wearily, he set the letter down on his desk. He could recognise a civil servant overwhelmed by circumstance.

"My problem, young man, is not the Orient: we already have the relevant skills. A professor of Asian languages has brought three of his protégés, so unfortunately for you, we have everything we need."

Désiré blinked rapidly; he understood.

"No, my problem is Turkey. We had only one person who spoke Turkish and the Ministry for Industry and Commerce has commandeered him."

Désiré's face brightened.

"In that case, perhaps I can be of some use . . ."

The director's eyes widened.

"My father was ambassador to the Turkish Legation," explained the young man. "I spent my childhood in Smyrna."

"So . . . so you speak Turkish?"

Désiré stifled a laugh.

"Not perhaps well enough to translate the poetry of Mehmed Pehlivan efendi, but if all that is required is to read the newspapers from Istanbul and Ankara, then, certainly . . ."

"Marvellous."

Had he searched, the director would not have found any reference to the Turkish poet that Désiré had just invented, but so happy was he that providence had sent the young man to him, that he did not think to do so.

Led by an usher, Désiré made his way through the labyrinthine corridors of the grand hotel on the rue Scribe, whose four hundred rooms were home to the teams tasked with marshalling information.

"Declared unfit for service because . . .?" said the director showing him to the door.

Désiré gestured to his thick glasses.

In this requisitioned hotel teeming with a motley crowd of besuited men, uniformed officers, harried students, overworked secretaries and society ladies, it was difficult to know who did what. Members of parliament bellowed, journalists looked for someone to blame, lawyers squabbled, ushers glided through the grand hotel in a tinkle of gold chains, professors propounded theories; in the lobby, a famous stage actor demanded an answer to a question no-one had heard only to vanish as swiftly as he had appeared. There were a spectacular number of well-connected young men and the sons of well-heeled families, since everyone wanted to be a part of this bellicose republican caravanserai. It had formerly been directed (though the term is an overstatement) by a famous playwright no-one understood who had been replaced by a history graduate from the National Library, and ruled with a rod of iron by a former opponent of censorship who suddenly found himself thrust into the spotlight as Minister for Information. The whole enterprise was a glorious shambles, but one that held a peculiar attraction to intellectuals, women, students and those in search of a cushy job. To say nothing of adventurers. Désiré immediately felt at home.

"You'll have more than enough to do with the Turkish press," said the director, laying a hand on the young man's shoulder. "You'll find that we are a little behindhand . . ."

"I shall do my best to make up the time, Monsieur le Directeur."

The usher left Désiré on the threshold of a room whose minuscule size spoke volumes about the government's lack of interest in Turkey. The desk, which took up much of the space, was strewn with newspapers and magazines whose titles Désiré could not even begin to pronounce but this fact, he felt, was of little importance.

He carefully opened them, creased them, cut out a series of random articles and made a pile, then he went to the archives, gathered up a handful of French newspapers and set about making a list of general observations about France and the Allied Forces that might have appeared in the Turkish press.

Then, safe in the knowledge that no-one would think to double-check his notes against ambassadorial messages and communiqués from a part of the world about which no-one gave a damn, he trawled through an 1896 Turkish–French Dictionary and set about writing a breathless account in which he explained that the neutrality of Turkey was the subject of an internecine struggle between the Merkez sol movement, led by Nuri Vehfik, and the pro-Western fringe group Ilımlı sağ. It was not immediately apparent what the motives were for the antagonists in the internal struggle Désiré had just cut out of whole cloth, but his report strove to be reassuring and concluded: "As the gateway to both West and East, Turkey would be an unsettling force if it decided to join the European conflict. But an in-depth review of the Turkish press clearly demonstrates a frank admiration for France and the two opposing factions are united by a respect for our country as a sincere and sturdy ally of the homeland of Muhyi Gulshani and Kemal Atatürk."

"Excellent."

The director was satisfied. He had only had time to read the conclusion, but that in itself was reassuring.

Since Turkish newspapers arrived in Paris only irregularly, Désiré spent most of his days wandering the corridors. People became accustomed to seeing him among the vast rose marble columns, in the stairways and in the courtyard, this tall, timorous young man who blinked nervously when he greeted them. He seemed so ill at ease . . . The men gently mocked him while the women smiled at him tenderly.

"Just the man!"

The director seemed more and more like a head chef overwhelmed by a sudden influx of diners. Censorship had to be applied to everything: radio, films, advertisements, plays, photographs, books, songs, doctoral theses, even the minutes of annual general meetings; there was so much to do, he did not know which way to turn.

"I need someone to man the telephones, follow me."

The telephone censorship service was based in a suite on the top floor where monitors sat at a bank of listening posts, supervising and interrupting conversations between soldiers and their families, journalists and the editors, and more generally, any conversations that might relay information of interest at home or abroad, which meant almost everything. No-one knew what to do, everything had to be monitored and censored, the task was colossal.

Désiré was given a thick folder containing a list of all the topics the service was intended to scrutinise. From the movements of Général Gamelin to the weather forecast, from the price of basic foodstuffs to pacifist ideas, from wage claims to regimental menus, whatever would be useful to the enemy or detrimental to French morale had to be rigorously expurgated.

When he plugged into the board, his first call was between an army private from Vitry-le-François and his fiancée.

"How are you doing, my darling?" the girl asked.

"Tsk, tsk," Désiré interrupted. "No questions about troop morale, please."

The young woman was clearly baffled. She hesitated, then: "How is the weather?"

"Tsk, tsk. No conversations about meteorological conditions."

A long silence ensued.

"Darling . . ." The soldier paused, waiting to be interrupted. When it did not happen, he carried on. "How is the grape harvest going?"

"Tsk, tsk. French wine is considered a strategic asset."

By now, the soldier was fuming, there was no way to carry on a conversation. He decided to end the call.

"Well, listen, my little treasure . . ."

"Tsk, tsk. We can have no mention of treasury or the Banque de France."

Silence.

At length, the young woman ventured: "Alright then, I'll let you go . . ."

"Tsk, tsk, let's have no defeatism."

Désiré was in fine form.


For two days he gave the service his all, and in fact he was disappointed when the colleague he was replacing returned from furlough but, since his work on the Turkish media took up very little of his time, he was relieved when the director temporarily posted him to the censorship of mail, where he came up with innovations that won him the admiration of all.

He opened letters from soldiers to their parents and, deciding that first and foremost he had to confront the very heart of syntax, he redacted all the verbs. As a result, addressees received letters that read: "We      muddling through, you      . We      the days chores but we      the faintest idea what      on. Some of the lads      a lot, and everyone      ."

Every morning, the service received a new batch of orders which Désiré instantly set about implementing zealously. If, for example, there was an instruction to censor any mention of the MAS 38 submachine gun, Désiré not only redacted the verbs but also every occurrence of the letters M, A and S. This produced missives like: "We _uddling through, you . We the d_y_ chore_ but we the f_inte_t idea wh_t on. _o_e of the l_d_ _ lot, and everyone ."

He was judged to be highly efficient. The director's growing confidence in Désiré meant that he was given a temporary posting to censor newspapers. Every morning, he strode into the Hôtel Continental's imposing ballroom, with its magnificent Corinthian columns and painted ceiling on which cherubs fluttered languidly, and took a seat at the long table on which were piled the proofs to be sent back to the newspapers once any proscribed information had been cut. There were some forty people working at the table, all driven by a patriotic fervour, who, armed with any new instructions (which were added to those of previous days – the list now ran to a thousand pages), were tasked with this vast undertaking.

While the waitress from Chez Daniel handed round warm beer and soggy sandwiches, there were heated discussions about the day's instructions, after which, having had their fill of contradictions and approximations, each man went about bowdlerising after his own fashion. It was not unusual for the daily instructions to produce utter nonsense. The public were accustomed to this and no-one raised an eyebrow when they read that this or that product "valued last month at . . . francs, is not worth . . . francs".

Désiré quickly earned a formidable reputation when it came to weaponry. Everyone admired the logic by which he insisted that "censorship" should be understood in its "broadest sense".

"Deduction and induction: the enemy is cunning," he would say, blinking nervously.

In the modest tone that conferred his every utterance a sheen of self-evidence, he explained that, given the linguistic connection between "arm" and "destruction" and also "damage", "victim", "innocence" and hence "childhood", all references to the family unit implicitly contained strategic elements and should therefore be censored. Thereafter, the words father, mother, uncle, aunt, brother, sister, cousin were ruthlessly expunged. A theatrical poster for a Chekhov play became "*Three* . . .", Turgenev's novel was retitled " . . . *and* . . .", there were even instances of "Our . . . which art in heaven" and ". . . r's *Odyssey*". Thanks to Désiré, censorship was elevated to the ranks of the fine arts and Ellipsis seemed about to become the tenth muse.

## 10

"Somewhere near Sedan, from what I've been told," a soldier said evasively to a question that Gabriel had not heard.

The uncertainty about their destination was not entirely surprising, given the successive waves of orders and counter-orders they had received. Initially, they were to go on foot, but having waited for an hour, they were told to go to the train station, and when they got there, on orders from the High Command, they were sent back to the Mayenberg. Hardly had they arrived than they were sent back to the station where they were finally told to climb into cattle trucks. The German offensive in Belgium had been expected, but the presence of the enemy in the Ardennes had taken everyone by surprise and the top brass were struggling to decide on their response.

Neither Chabrier nor Ambresac made the journey. Both had been posted elsewhere. Caporal-chef Landrade seemed entirely unaffected by their transfer and promptly forgot the men who had been his loyal henchmen. He was in a corner of the truck playing three-card monte with some soldiers he had not yet bilked, and a few who had gone back for more – some people never learn. He had won almost forty francs; everything he did made money. And yet he still managed to be everybody's friend. From time to time, he flashed Gabriel a smile as though everything they had been through was now in the past.

Gabriel saw things very differently; he still felt an aching pain in his groin where Ambresac had kicked him with his steel-capped boot. He felt as though his testicles had swollen to twice their normal size since the start of the journey, and he felt terribly nauseated.

As for the troops, their primary feeling was one of relief.

"We're going to bash their fucking faces in, the bastards!" roared one eager young private.

Having had their energy sapped by the interminable wait of the Phoney War, most were eager to go into battle. A group struck up the "Marseillaise", and, in the long stops that followed, there were drinking songs.

At about 2000 hours, they arrived in Sedan.

The barracks was teeming with soldiers, and they were forced to bunk down in mess halls that had been converted into barrackrooms. Noisily, they settled in, arguing over blankets with great good humour; this section of the army seemed like a body stiff from months of enforced idleness and relieved to be able to stretch its limbs.

An hour later, there were cheers and shouts of joy as Landrade tricked newcomers out of their pay.

As soon as he arrived, Gabriel ran to the latrines to survey the damage. His crotch was very tender: it was swollen and painful, but his testes had not swollen as much as he had feared. When he got back, Landrade gave him a sly wink as though, rather than being responsible for the vicious kick in the balls, he had simply played a schoolboy prank.

Gabriel assessed the throng of soldiers crammed into the mess hall. The huge gathering admirably illustrated the principle of *recombination*, a process the French army considered modern and which consisted of splitting up squads and brigades and recombining them according to some higher logic that no-one understood. Hardly anyone knew any of their comrades except for the NCO from whom they took orders. The officers were baffled; it could only be hoped that the top brass knew what they were doing.

Those who could find their mess tin were served hot soup, though it was clear as spring water. The others ate bread and passed around *saucissons* that seemed to have appeared from nowhere.

A stout lad of about twenty marched up and down between the rows.

"Anyone got a spare pair of laces?"

Raoul Landrade was first off the mark, holding out a pair of black bootlaces.

"There you go. Three francs."

The chubby lad opened and closed his mouth like a fish. Gabriel rummaged in his kitbag.

"Here, have these," he said.

From his tone, it was clear that they were free. With a shrug, Landrade put his laces back in his bag: *if that's how you want it.*

The grateful lad slumped down next to Gabriel.

"You've just saved my life . . ."

Gabriel glanced over at Landrade, his hawklike nose, his thin lips; he had already moved on and was selling packs of cigarettes to soldiers who had none. When Landrade finally turned, a half-smile was playing on his lips. Gabriel found it difficult to imagine this man sanctioning a vicious kick to the balls.

"I was one of the last to get to the quartermaster's stores," the young soldier said, unbuttoning his jacket. "The only boots they had were either too big or too small. Obviously, I took the big ones, but then I needed laces, and they didn't have any left."

The story got a laugh, and prompted another. Everyone seemed to have a similar tale to tell. One hulking lad stood up to peals of laughter when it became clear that, being unable to find the right size, he was still wearing civilian trousers. Far from proving tiresome, the vicissitudes of barracks life did little to dull the triumphal spirit of the troops. An officer was grabbed as he walked past.

"So, what's happening, capitaine, do we finally get to smash their fucking faces?"

"Oh," said the capitaine regretfully, "we'll mostly be playing walk-on parts. There won't be an attack around here for a while. That's if there are any at all! Only small squads of Krauts are likely to make it through the Ardennes."

"Well, we'll be here to welcome them!" someone shouted.

There were a few cheers, as though the energy of the soldiers was inversely proportionate to the size of their contribution.

The capitaine smiled and left the mess hall.

It was this same officer whom Gabriel went to see the following morning at 0700 hours. He had just had a message on his field radio that undermined the serene confidence he had exhibited the night before. Significant German troop movements had been detected to the north-east of Sedan.

The alert was relayed to the commandant and then to the général who loftily dismissed the news.

"An optical illusion. You have to understand, the Ardennes is a forest. Put three motorised units in there and it looks like a whole army corps."

The général stepped towards the map on the wall, where coloured pins traced a broad arc along the Belgian border. It pained him to be here, cooling his heels, playing second fiddle, when the real war was raging there. It was a terrible blow to his heroic spirit. He gave a long, wistful sigh.

"Very well then," he said, "let's send some reinforcements."

It was clear the compromise was hard won. If he could, he would have gone home.

So it was that a company of two hundred men was chosen to go and lend a hand, if need be, to the 55th Infantry Division tasked with standing guard over the River Meuse some forty kilometres away.

There was no train to take them there. Gabriel's unit, comprising some forty infantrymen, marched along the road, led by a fifty-something reserve capitaine named Gibergue, a pharmacist from Châteauroux in civilian life, and an officer who prided himself on a brilliant service record in the previous war.

By mid-morning, the blazing sun began to melt the previous night's enthusiasm. Even Landrade, on whom Gabriel was keeping a watchful eye, seemed to be struggling. With Landrade, exhaustion was usually a prelude to rage. His haggard face boded ill. The tall man who had made fun of his civilian trousers the night before was no longer smiling, and the soldier with the laces had begun to regret not taking the small shoes now that the big ones were causing blisters. In ordinary circumstance, there were eight men in their unit, but four had been posted elsewhere.

"Posted where?" asked Gabriel.

"I'm not sure, somewhere north I think . . ."

As they marched, they saw the sky in the distance streaked with orange light and plumes of rising smoke. It was impossible to say how far away – ten kilometres? Twenty? More? Even the capitaine did not know.

Gabriel found the mission unsettling. The hesitations, the uncertainties all made him nervous and on edge, the whole thing seemed about to explode. With war looming up ahead and Landrade behind, his heart was in his boots.

By now, their legs were leaden. They had already marched twenty kilometres with heavy kitbags, and there were almost twenty still to cover with their oversized packs and the canteens that hung from their belts and slapped their thighs at every step . . . Gabriel's shoulders were cut to ribbons by the leather kitbag straps he had not been able to adjust because the buckles had seized. His whole body ached. His rifle weighed a tonne. He stumbled and would have fallen, but for Landrade. They had not exchanged a word since leaving the Mayenberg.

"Give me that," Landrade said, tugging on the straps of the kitbag.

Gabriel wanted to say no, but he did not have time; he wanted to say thank you, but Landrade was already marching three paces ahead, with Gabriel's kitbag perched on top of his own.

Planes passed overhead. French? German? It was difficult to tell.

"French," said the capitaine, shielding his eyes with his hand.

This was reassuring. As were the hordes of Belgian and Luxemburgish refugees, most of them in cars, who were exhilarated to see troops marching towards the enemy. Encouragement from the local French people was more ambivalent, and invariably proffered using slogans from the previous war ("We'll beat 'em" accompanied by a clenched fist). The similarity of the gesture twenty years on was disconcerting.

The men started to grumble, they stopped to catch their breath, they had eaten nothing since breakfast, they had covered twenty-three kilometres, it was time to set down their kitbags and have something to eat.

As they passed around the bread and cheap wine, the men told jokes about life in the barracks. The funniest was one about a certain Général Bouquet who had, apparently, explained that the most effective weapon for countering a German tank was . . . a bedsheet. You needed four men, one at each corner, then, with a sweeping synchronised movement, you threw the bedsheet over the turret. Now completely blinded, the tank crew had no choice but to surrender. The soldiers laughed nervously. Gabriel had no idea what credence to give this anecdote – whether serious or not, it did not bode well. A général said that? someone roared, but no-one heard the answer because it was time to pack up and move on: Come on, boys, called the NCOs, one last push and we can swim in the Meuse, ha ha.

"Thank you," said Gabriel as he recovered his kitbag from Landrade.

Landrade smiled genially and gave a half-salute.

"At your service, sergent-chef!"

The second leg of the march was much like the first, but for the fact that the refugees they encountered were less talkative, perhaps because they were on foot, carrying their children in their arms. They were clearly fleeing the German troops, but not one of them had any useful strategic information. The only thing they worked out was the troops took shelter whenever the French approached.

For the second time that day, they passed a concrete building in the middle of the forest.

"God almighty!"

Gabriel started. Landrade was standing next to him.

"Well, well, isn't she a fine sight – the jewel in the French defence line!"

The pillboxes and blockhouses they had happened on in the forest were barely half built and exuded an air of desolation. They did not seem to be part of the same project as the Mayenberg. Abandoned, stripped of weapons and gnawed away by ivy, they looked like the ruins they were fast becoming. Landrade spat on the ground, then nodded to Gabriel's crotch.

"It'll be fine by the time we get back, don't worry."

Gabriel wanted to say something, but he lacked the strength, the energy.

Finally, they rendezvoused with the troops camped along the riverbank. Both parties were bitterly disappointed: Gabriel's unit as much as the 55th Infantry Regiment. The former because they had marched forty kilometres, were utterly exhausted and felt unwelcome; the latter because they had been expecting serious reinforcements.

"What the hell d'you expect me to do with two hundred men?" growled the lieutenant-colonel. "I need three times as many!"

By now, the aeroplanes had left, and no-one could think of a good reason to request further support. The mortar fire was distant, there had been no new intelligence beyond "the presence of large numbers of enemy troops" on the far shore of the Meuse, and that had already been explained to them: an optical illusion.

"I've got twenty kilometres of riverbank to cover," the lieutenant-colonel roared, "twelve bases to secure! This isn't a front line, this is Swiss fucking cheese, there are holes everywhere."

This was only an issue if the Germans arrived in large numbers and heavily armed, which seemed unlikely, since their primary offensive was in Belgium.

"D'you hear that, do you? What do you think that is, cats yowling?"

Everyone listened. They could hear it: the sound of artillery fire to the north-east.

"What news from the reconnaissance planes?" said the capitaine-pharmacist.

"There aren't any reconnaissance planes. There just aren't any."

Exhausted from the long day's march, the capitaine simply squeezed his eyes shut, he would have liked to rest for a moment, but it was out of the question, his superior officer had already summoned all his aides and spread out his war map.

"We'll send some men over to see what the hell the Krauts are doing on the other side of the Meuse. I'll need some troops to cover their withdrawal, so, if you post your unit here. Yours, here. Yours there . . ."

His fat forefinger traced the sinuous curve of the Meuse. He nodded to Capitaine Gibergue and indicated a tributary, the Tréguière, which followed an upside-down U.

"And I want you here. Now, get moving."

The unit picked up their rifles and loaded the munitions onto a truck mounted with a 37mm anti-tank gun, which set off, juddering down the stony forest track.

The company was now reduced to twenty men, who set off through the woods as the daylight began to fade, creating an uncertain atmosphere. To the north, the sky loured with heavy grey clouds. Although no-one said as much aloud, there were two possibilities: either the enemy made it across the river, in which case, even with artillery support, it was impossible to imagine this small, poorly armed unit could stop them, or there was nothing to worry about, and they were just spare pricks at a hoor's wedding.

Gabriel found himself standing next to Capitaine Gibergue, who was muttering "That's all we need, rain . . ." And rain it did, some minutes later, just as they reached the truck.

The bridge over the Tréguière was a small concrete construction from the previous century; it had a certain bucolic charm, was wide enough to take a heavy truck, but narrow enough that cars had to yield right of way.

The capitaine had his men cover the weapons and munitions from the downpour which was steadily intensifying: the 37mm anti-tank gun, the submachine guns (first-rate brand new FM 24/29s). They were forced to wade through mud to set up tarpaulins to shelter the camp, while six soldiers set off, belly aching, having been ordered to guard both sides of the bridge.

As so often, Landrade landed on his feet. He managed to get a posting guarding the munitions. Making the most of his rank as caporal-chef, he sat in the cab of the truck and watched the rain run off the windscreen and the other soldiers scurry around in the downpour.

Capitaine Gibergue came over to speak to Gabriel, who had set up his field radio under a tarp some distance from the main camp.

"Sergent, can you at least reassure me that you're in touch with the artillery?"

The artillerymen were posted several kilometres away. In the event of an attack, they would be called on to bombard the far bank of the river to keep the enemy at bay.

"As you know, sir, we are not allowed to make radio contact with the artillery . . ."

The capitaine stroked his chin pensively. The top brass were wary of using radio transmissions that might be intercepted. A request for artillery fire was to be made by firing a flare. But this posed something of a problem for the capitaine.

"We've been issued with new self-propelled rocket launchers, but no-one in the unit knows how to use them. And we weren't given an instruction manual."

In the distance, the treetops once again glowed crimson from the muffled shellfire.

"Probably our own artillerymen targeting the Krauts," said the capitaine.

Suddenly, without knowing why, Gabriel remembered the motto of Général Gamelin: "Courage, Energy, Confidence".

"Probably," he said. "I mean, it has to be, doesn't it . . .?"

## II

Although the vast lobby of the Hôtel Continental was already thronged, all manner of men and women continued to flood in. The moment they crossed the threshold each accepted a glass of champagne with an insouciant air honed by years of experience, then, recognising someone over by the lush plants, would call out a well-known name and push through the crowd, sheltering their glass as though from a squall.

Indeed, the blustery wind that had been blowing more than a day now, a mixture of apprehension and relief, confidence and confusion, had all of those present on tenterhooks. Finally, it had come. War. A real war. People desperately wanted fresh details. And so they rushed to the Continental, the beating heart of the Ministry of Information. Diplomats were buttonholed, journalists besieged, snippets of news trilled from one group to the next: the RAF were bombing the Rhine, the Belgians had proved to be stout fellows, one général sighed as he stubbed out his cigarette and said "The war's already over." His pronouncement made a great impression, and was promptly relayed, passing from an academic to a university professor, a demi-mondaine to a banker and thence to Désiré, whose reaction was intently scrutinised by a dozen eager pairs of eyes. For the past two days, he had been tasked with publicly announcing official communiqués to the press, and no-one, it was thought, was better informed.

"Granted," he said in measured tones, "France and her allies have matters well in hand, but from that to speak of the 'war being over' is perhaps a little premature."

The demi-mondaine let out a peal of laughter – it was her defining trait – the others merely smiled politely and waited for what Désiré would say next. They were cruelly disappointed as a man burst into the group and loudly interrupted:

"Bravo, old man! And such aplomb!"

Désiré modestly lowered his eyes. He could clearly tell that those present fell into two camps: those who admired him and those who were jealous. The preponderance of women in the former category further swelled the ranks of the envious. The unexpected support of this senior civil servant (he was something in the Colonial Ministry) was particularly opportune. Désiré's somewhat meteoric rise at the Continental had fanned the flames of comments and questions. Does anyone know where he comes from? people asked each other, but intelligence about Désiré was like military intelligence, people believed what they wanted to believe, and for the time being this modest young man, at once timid, charming and resolute, was the darling of the Continental. He reported to the assistant director of press information, a nervous, febrile man as frazzled as a live battery.

"People can say what they like about the man," he told Désiré during their first encounter, "but I tip my hat to Léon Blum for setting up the Ministry of Information. I would hardly go so far as to say he's a fine fellow, after all, the man's a Jew, but even so, a fine idea."

The assistant director spent their first meeting pacing the floor of his office, hands clasped behind his back.

"Now, let me ask you something, young man: what is our mission?"

"To inform . . ."

Désiré had been caught unawares; it was a question he had long since ceased to think about.

"Yesss . . . after a fashion . . . But why do we provide information?"

Désiré racked his brain, glanced around him, then suddenly it came to him.

"In order to reassure."

"Precisely!" thundered the assistant director. "The French army are tasked with waging war, very well. But there is little point rolling out the heavy artillery if the men responsible for operating it do not have the conqueror's spirit. And for that, they must feel that they have our support, they need our confidence. Every man, woman and child in France must believe in victory! Believe in it! Everyone!"

He stood in front of Désiré, who was at least a head taller than he.

"That is why we are here. In wartime, accurate information is less important than reassuring information. We have no truck with truth. Ours is a higher, a more noble mission. We are entrusted with the morale of France."

"I understand," said Désiré.

The assistant director studied him. He had heard much about this young man with his thick glasses and his keen intellect. People said he was unassuming (that much was self-evident), but brilliant (which remained to be seen).

"So, tell me, young man, how do you see your work here in the ministry."

"A, E, I, O, U," said Désiré.

The assistant director, who knew his alphabet, gave him a quizzical look. Désiré explained.

"Analyse, Engage, Influence, Observe, Utilise. In practice the order is different: I *Observe*, I *Engage*, I *Analyse* and I *Utilise* my findings to *Influence* morale. To keep it high."

In that instant, the assistant director knew that he had been gifted with the crème de la crème.

On May 10, when the Germans launched the offensive in Belgium and all information given to the press had to be tightly controlled, a single name was heard: Désiré Migault.

Every morning and every evening, journalists and reporters came for news from the front lines. That evening, in a solemn voice, Désiré read aloud the crucial points of the previous hours, the kind that most people long to hear: "French troops are offering staunch resistance to the invading forces" and "The enemy advances have made no significant progress". To these stock expressions, Désiré would append specifics ("around the canal Albert and on the banks of the Meuse", "in the Sarre and to the west of the Vosges") intended to enhance their verisimilitude while revealing no details that might prove useful to the enemy. Because this was the rub: to reassure, to inform, while at all times remaining vague, because the Krauts were always listening, and they had spies everywhere. Say nothing was the advice from the authorities. Everywhere there were posters reminding the citizenry that anything they said might aid the Germans, a story, whether true or false, could prove more decisive than a tank battalion, the real Ministry of War was the Ministry of Information, and Désiré was its herald.

The Ministry had invited the great and the good of Paris. This was war; this was a celebration.

All evening, Désiré found people tugging at his sleeve, asking for details, angling for classified information. A journalist from *Le Matin* took him to one side.

"Tell me, my dear Désiré, what do we know about the para-chutists?"

It was common knowledge that the Germans had parachuted people into Allied territory whose role was to blend into the crowd so that, when the time came, they could provide vital support to the invading army. These partisans, generally referred to as the fifth column, did not only include Germans, but also Belgian and Dutch sympathisers of the Third Reich; it was rumoured that some Frenchmen had been recruited from the most obvious nest of traitors: communists. Ever since the revelation that three German parachutists had been posing as nuns, people saw spies everywhere.

"Twelve of them, disguised as dwarves . . ."

"You don't say . . . !"

"Absolutely. Twelve dwarves, all of them members of the German army. Parachuted in last month. Masquerading as a group of teenagers camping in the Bois de Vincennes. Thankfully, we caught them just in time."

The journalist was shell-shocked.

"Were they . . . armed?"

"Chemical weapons. Highly dangerous. They were preparing to contaminate the Paris water reservoirs. Specifically targeting school canteens. And after that, Lord knows what . . ."

"And . . . can I?"

"A brief paragraph, no more. They're currently being inter-rogated, you understand. But as soon as we're done with them, the story is all yours."

From the far end of the lobby, the assistant director watched with paternal tenderness as his young protégé weaved his way between the groups, responding to every question in careful, measured tones. Désiré had given one reporter permission to make a note of his opinions on the German troop morale.

"Hitler finally decided to launch an attack because in Germany, people are on the brink of starvation. He had no alternative. In fact, there is a case for the French army distributing pamphlets that promise two hot meals to any German soldier who surrenders. Needless to say, the high command nixed the idea, they were worried we might end up with two or even three million German soldiers – can you imagine trying to feed them all . . .?"

The assistant director smiled: it was a glorious evening.

"An Asian languages student, I believe?" said one civil servant, nodding towards Désiré.

He had been struck by this piece of information, having himself spent eighteen months posted to Hanoi.

"Indeed," said the assistant director. "He comes to us from the French School of Asian Studies. He's fluent in a whole raft of Asian languages."

"Well then, I have someone he can talk to . . . Désiré!"

The young man turned to find himself face to face with a smiling Asian man of about fifty.

"May I introduce Monsieur Thong, secretary to the Indochinese Colonial Taskforce. He has just arrived from Phnom Penh."

"Angtuk phtaeh phoh kento siekvan," said Désiré shaking the man's hand. "Kourphenti chiahkng yuordai."

Faced with this torrent of sounds in which it was impossible to distinguish a single word of Khmer, Monsieur Thong hesitated. If this young man prided himself of his command of the language, it would be discourteous to disabuse him. Instead, he merely nodded and gave Désiré a grateful smile.

"Salanh ktei sramei," said Désiré as he moved away.

"Quite a phenomenon, is he not?" said the assistant director.

"Oh, indeed, indeed . . ."

"The Luftwaffe have attempted to make incursions into French airspace. The results have been negligible . . ."

Désiré had chosen to give his press conference in a well-lit, spacious room on the second floor which would accommodate sixty members of the press.

". . . our airforce retaliated, bombarding several high-priority military targets. Thirty-six enemy weapons were destroyed. One of our fighter squadrons destroyed eleven targets in a single day. All is quiet now between the Moselle and Switzerland."

The content of the initial communiqués revolved around two ideas: the German offensive had been expected, indeed anticipated, and the French army were in full control of the situation.

"Meanwhile, our troops are making a steady advance through central Belgium."

Since the reporters who regularly attended these press conferences sent articles (and photographs) to their editorial desks highlighting the intensity of the fighting, by the second day, Désiré opted for what he termed "controlled dramatisation".

"The German attack has been increasing fiercely, but French and Allied troops have been valiantly pushing back the desperate ploys of the enemy."

When he issued this communiqué, Désiré personally stood at the door and handed a copy of what he had said to all those who had attended.

"It's my way of taking the pulse of the nation," he told the assistant director, "I calm their fears, I instil confidence, I reinforce conviction. And I influence morale."

Three days after the start of the German offensive, a journalist naively asked:

"If the French and Allied troops are as effective as you say, how is it that the Krauts are still advancing?"

"They are not advancing," said Désiré, "they are making forward movement, that is a very different thing."

By the fourth day, it was proving more difficult to explain how the enemy he had declared could not possibly make it through the Ardennes had somehow reached the banks of the Meuse south of Namur and were now attacking Sedan.

"The Germans have attempted the cross the river at various points," said Désiré. "Each time, our forces have launched a brutal counter-offensive. Our airforce has provided effective support. The Luftwaffe is decimated."

The assistant director lamented the fact that the real war was not following the arc of these communiqués. What little anyone knew about the attack on Sedan (the high command provided barely any concrete information) suggested that the French forces were in a delicate position. Consequently, Désiré suggested they moved from "controlled dramatisation" to a policy of "strategic reticence".

"The best interests of tactical strategy make it impossible to give details of any ongoing operations at this point."

"Do you really think the newspapers will buy it?" said the assistant director, concerned by this turn of events.

"Not a bit." Désiré smiled. "But there are other ways to keep them happy."

To the reporters who expressed disappointment at the lack of details on military campaigns, Désiré offered a statement on the workings of the Allied forces.

"Everywhere, we see only courage, confidence, certainty. Our soldiers are eagerly fighting to protect this country. Meanwhile, the French high command continues calmly and resolutely to pursue a comprehensive plan drawn up in anticipation of precisely this scenario. Our armed forces are equipped with powerful weaponry, unmatched expertise and impeccable organisational skills."

## 12

A dozen men were guarding access to the bridge. It was hoped that, in itself, the submachine gun mounted on the bed of the Renault truck that barred the road would keep the enemy at bay. This seemed somewhat optimistic since the deterrent looked like little more than a police roadblock. A little further off, the 37mm anti-tank gun was aimed north. On a small truck some fifty metres away, there was a second submachine gun together with a few mortars and some crates of ammunitions.

Capitaine Gibergue spent much of the morning traipsing back and forth between the field radio ("Is there any news?") and the bridge ("Everything is fine, boys, you don't need to worry . . ."), until the arrival of the reconnaissance unit that had been sent to find out what the Germans were scheming. The unit comprised twenty lightly armed men and two motorcycles, all under the command of an officer who was visibly eager to beard the enemy in his lair. Standing with his legs parted and one hand behind his back, the officer surveyed the scene: the field radio post; Capitaine Gibergue, whom he saw simply as a reservist; the 37mm anti-tank gun; the unit guarding the bridge . . . He sighed.

"Give me your map."

"But I . . ."

"There's been a little mistake, mine covers sector 687, but we're in sector 768."

Gabriel saw the capitaine hesitate and, like him, felt as though he were being forced to hand over a crucial survival tool.

"You don't need a map to be able to secure this bridge," said Capitaine Duroc.

Gibergue handed over the map.

Minutes later, the reconnaissance unit had disappeared into the forest.

The rain had stopped during the night. The clear sky was streaked with flashes of artillery fire, and the rumble seemed to be steadily approaching. Capitaine Gibergue stared at the treetops.

"If only our planes could fly over the sector and let us know what's going on."

This was what was most frustrating: waiting, not knowing what to expect.

By late morning, the artillery fire was heavier and the explosions were getting closer every minute. There was a palpable air of unease.

Although the sky was now ablaze before them and behind, still no orders came; communications must have been cut off, there was no response from the high command. Then, finally, an air squadron flew overhead. But it was the Luftwaffe. Flying low.

"A recon mission . . ."

Gabriel whipped around. Landrade was standing next to him, his back arched, gazing at the sky. He had abandoned his comfortable seat in the truck and was looking alarmed. Gabriel was gripped by a wave of anxiety. Quickly, he made his way back to the rest of the unit, but everyone was silent. No-one said a word.

He was met by Capitaine Gibergue who insisted Gabriel send a message to military authorities. "The enemy is carrying out reconnaissance," he dictated. "They will launch an offensive within hours. We need the support of fighter planes."

Breathless and flustered, Gabriel raced back to the field radio. Was it his imagination or was the shellfire closer now? Still no answer came. Capitaine Gibergue dispatched six more men to guard the bridge.

Suddenly, the world sped up.

There came a roar of engines, intense gunfire, voices screaming. The men gripped the butt of their weapons, submachine guns trained on the bridge. But what came bursting through the forest was not enemy troops, but the two French reconnaissance motorcycles with countless soldiers clinging to them. At first, they were panting so hard that it was difficult to work out what they were saying. They paused for a second in front of Capitaine Gibergue.

"Get the hell out, boys, there's nothing we can do here!"

"Wh . . . what?" Gibergue stammered. "What do you mean, nothing to be done?"

"The Jerries are coming! The tanks are coming!" said one soldier, giving it gas. "We've got to get the fuck out of here!"

The rest of the reconnaissance unit appeared. The once-dashing Capitaine Duroc looked as though he had aged ten years.

"Clear all this shit out of here!"

He sounded as though he could clear up the situation with a wave of his hand. Gibergue demanded to know why.

"Why?" thundered Duroc. "You want to know *why*?"

He gestured to the forest on the far side of the bridge.

"Because there are a thousand tanks heading this way. Is that enough of a why?"

"A thousand tanks . . ." Gibergue's voice quavered. "We've been left swinging in the wind . . . They've . . ." he trailed off, unable to find the words.

"You've got to get the hell out of here, there's nothing you can do. We're completely outnumbered!"

At this point, the military chain of command offered a perfect microcosm of the French army as a whole. Capitaine Duroc insisted they should destroy the French weapons to prevent them falling into enemy hands, then they should head south to join up with the rest of the regiment.

For his part, Capitaine Gibergue took offence at this attitude. To abandon their position was tantamount to giving up the fight. There could be no question that he or his men would leave here without a struggle!

The two capitaines refused to look each other in the eye. Instead, without even acknowledging the other, each furiously issued contradictory orders. Duroc ordered the men to move out, which, to Gibergue, was equivalent to a retreat, so he called on the men in his unit to stay and fight. In the absence of any form of authority, everyone began to panic.

The soldiers in Gibergue's unit pressed closer and glanced nervously from the bridge to their capitaine.

"We should probably go with them, shouldn't we?" said one. To everyone's astonishment, Capitaine Gibergue drew his revolver, the one no-one really believed he knew how to use.

"We are here to guard this bridge, men, and that is what we are going to do! The first man to run will get a bullet in his back."

No-one would ever know what might have happened had the men decided to make a run for it, because at that very moment a brutal aerial bombing raid was unleashed. The first wave of German bombers cratered the ground here and there, the second ripped away the treetops in a hellish roar of bombs, explosions, conflagrations and tremors. Several soldiers were left sprawled on the ground, quivering, chests blown open, limbs ripped off. Before long, there was nothing but flames, ashes and yawning craters around the handful of French soldiers who had been tasked with defending their country's border with nothing more than two submachine guns and an antique anti-tank gun they could no longer make out through the pall of smoke and flames.

Roused from its torpor, the French artillery began to shell the woods on the far side of the bridge.

Gabriel's unit was caught between an advancing German column numbering thousands of tanks (how was it possible that reconnaissance had not seen it coming?) and French artillery trying to fend them off by shelling the far bank of the river.

Most of the able-bodied men quickly grabbed their kitbags and disappeared into the forest, howling.

Those left behind watched as their comrades weaved a path between the mangled trees set ablaze by the Luftwaffe. They glanced at each other. Then at the bridge. There were two soldiers lying there. One of the submachine guns was little more than a blackened piece of steel.

"We need to blow up the bridge before we leave, men."

Gibergue had lost his kepi, the few scant hairs on his bald pate now stood on end, his face was white as bone.

Only a dozen men remained, all stunned and deafened by the roar of shells as they whistled overhead. Among the men were Gabriel, Landrade and the fat boy with the boot laces.

"Anyone know what munitions we've got?" shouted Landrade.

"We've got some shellite rockets!" said the fat soldier, shouting so he could be heard above the commotion. "There's some detonators down there!"

Four men raced to fetch the only working submachine gun in order to bring it closer. Landrade ran to the truck, closely followed by Gabriel and the fat soldier. He scrambled into the bed of the truck, lifted the tarpaulins and rummaged around, tossing anything and everything over the side until he came upon one of the shells, which he held aloft like a trophy, grinning as though he'd just fleeced the whole unit at three-card monte.

Gabriel took the bars of explosive as Landrade passed them down and placed them under the chassis. They had ten kilos of explosives; enough to blow up the bridge.

"Shit!" said Landrade. "We've got no way of triggering the detonators . . ."

He was now sitting on the ground, leaning back against the wheel. The chubby soldier with the laces, who had taken shelter under the chassis, now crawled back. Gabriel was also sitting on the ground, one of the shells wedged between his knees.

"Alright," said Landrade, "we've got no electricity, so we'll need a slow fuse. D'you want to go get something, or are you planning to hug that shell all fucking day?"

Landrade was already climbing back into the truck while Gabriel scuttled back to the main camp and reappeared a minute later with six canvas belts which Landrade used to tie the shellite cartridges together.

Gabriel glanced over Landrade's shoulder at the pitiful little bridge, while the sky flared with the explosions that thundered all around the forest. And around Landrade himself.

Gabriel did not understand the man.

If ever there was a soldier whose first instinct would be to save his own skin, Gabriel assumed it would be Landrade, yet here he was, pulling the canvas straps tight, glaring at the bridge and muttering to himself:

"We'll put this shit under the skirts of that fucking bridge, just you wait . . ."

Together, they got to their feet, Landrade and Gabriel took most of the load while the chubby soldier whimpered and stumbled as he carried the detonators. Though, in his defence, the oversized shoes did not help. The three men weaved their way down to the river, heads bowed under the continual artillery fire. When, finally, they reached the bridge, Landrade issued the orders:

"Right, I'll set the main charge. You two, you set the others, one on the far right, one on the left. Then I'll hook the three together and . . . BOOM!"

French shells were now falling closer and closer to the river-bank, a sign that the enemy was in sight.

When they saw this motley trio show up, the soldiers clustered around the last working submachine gun by the bridge, whose mere presence seemed pitiful, heaved a sigh of relief. No bridge, no sentry duty. Although they had not been among the first to hightail it, they were more than happy to be able to run, now that a determined team was preparing to blow the bridge to Isambard Kingdom come.

Gabriel hauled his ten-kilo charge to the right-hand side of the bridge and placed it on the concrete abutment. Looking back, he saw that the chubby soldier had done likewise. The detonating charges were symmetrical. The fat kid gave a thumbs sign, and just then a shell landed in the river fifteen metres from him and he was cut in half by shrapnel and toppled into the water. Gabriel stared, in a state of shock. But Landrade was already beside him, trailing the short fuse.

"Did you see that?" said Gabriel, nodding to their dead comrade.

Landrade glanced over and saw the soldier floating, belly up.

"Fucking pity," he said, "the kid had brand-new laces." As he said this, he finished tying off the canvas rope and began tapering the short fuse.

"Go on, get out of here," he said. "I'm about to put a match to this."

Still mesmerised by the sight of the soldier's body being tossed by the current, Gabriel did not move.

"Come on, get the fuck out I said!"

Gabriel raced back to the camp, where Capitaine Gibergue was still waiting.

"Good job, boys!" he said.

By now, the rest of the unit had vanished into the forest. The two men watched as Landrade raced towards them like a man being chased by the very fuse he had just lit. Breathless, he collapsed next to them.

Instantly, he turned and squinted at the bridge.

"What the hell? I cut a short fuse, what's taking so long . . .?"

His impatience was understandable. Perhaps the charge was wet, perhaps the fuse was defective? Twenty seconds, thirty seconds, one minute. They knew they had risked their lives for nothing, since the charge would not detonate now.

As though to aggravate this disappointment and assert their own superiority, the Germans set off smoke grenades along the far bank of the Tréguière. Gabriel and Landrade had failed. Through the pale smokescreen, figures could be seen pushing dinghies into the water. The ground began to tremble, a sure sign the German armoured column was approaching the bank.

"We got to go!" roared Landrade, scrabbling to his feet.

Capitaine Gibergue laid a hand on Gabriel's shoulder: Come on, lad, we did our best . . .

It was not easy to say what was going on in Gabriel's mind. If he was not imbued with the soul of a hero, he nonetheless had his principles. He had been posted here to do a job, and he had not done it.

Without gauging the risk, he raced back to the bridge and got behind the submachine gun.

Once there, he froze. What should he do? He had seen such weapons before, but only from a distance. He laid a hand on the cartridge clip that rose above the barrel. Behind the dissipating pall of smoke, the dinghies were now clearer. Gabriel grabbed the pistol grip, swung the barrel around to face the enemy and gritted his teeth, his every muscle tensed to cushion the recoil – that much he remembered – of a submachine gun firing 450 rounds a minute.

He pulled the trigger. A shot rang out. Just one. A single pathetic bullet, like a rifle at a fairground stall.

Before his eyes, everything seemed to be happening at once. As he struggled to empty the magazine clip, he felt the ground shake beneath the wheels of the armoured trucks as they came to the bridge.

"Well, come on then, shithead, what is your next move?"

Landrade grinned and sat down next to him. So startled was Gabriel by Landrade's sudden appearance that he instinctively gripped the submachine gun, setting off a hail of bullets. Both men stared at the muzzle as though it had just spoken.

"Oh, fuck!" said Raoul, exhilarated.

Gabriel now realised that he had to squeeze the trigger twice to engage burst fire. He trained the gun on the bridge. Landrade got to his feet and, taking ammunition from a nearby crate, filled the top-fed box magazine, while Gabriel howled as he fired wildly.

Truth be told, his precision left much to be desired. Bullets were lodged in tree trunks, lost among dense ferns, a few found their way into the water, but most buried themselves in the ground tens of metres from their target.

Realising this, Gabriel tried to re-aim, but he was always either too high or too low, never where he needed to be.

"Ha ha! Go on!" screamed Raoul, laughing like a drain. "Shoot the hell out of the bastards!"

It seems as though some mischievous, impetuous gods were tickled by Gabriel's howls and Landrade's hysterical giggles, because just as the first German tank drove onto the bridge, one of Gabriel's bullets hit the charge and it exploded.

The bridge crumbled, pitching the tank into the river.

Gabriel and Raoul were blown backwards.

The collapsing bridge created chaos on the far bank. They could hear orders being barked in German, and the column of tanks ground to a halt. Gabriel, still in shock, had a vacant smile plastered over his face. Landrade nudged him.

"Maybe we shouldn't hang around much longer . . ."

In a second they were on their feet, racing into the forest, whooping for joy.

# 13

When she came home from school on Friday, Louise was over-come by the same listlessness she had previously suffered. She stoked her belly, waited for her period to start, and when nothing came, and she felt she did not even have the energy to get out of bed, she sent for Doctor Piperaud who prescribed cupping therapy and some time off work.

Saturday stole past. Then Sunday. Louise felt heavy, drained. She sat, impassive, through two air raids. Perhaps I want to die, she thought, though she did not really believe this. While sirens shrieked all over Paris, Louise lay in bed, wearing a shapeless sweater she never took off.

On Monday, she should have returned to work, but she was too exhausted. She should have gone to see Doctor Piperaud, or called him, but the very thought of getting dressed, of walking to the nearest phone was beyond her.

In the early morning, she was gazing out into the courtyard sipping tepid coffee, when the bell at the gate rang. She did not hesitate but opened the front door and was unsurprised to find Monsieur Jules standing there at the gate with his hands in his pockets.

This time, he was not dressed in his best suit – for all the good it did me last time, no thank you – but his chef's uniform and a pair of carpet slippers.

Louise stood on the threshold. There were some ten metres

between them. She leaned against the doorframe, cradling the bowl of coffee in both hands. Monsieur Jules was about to speak but was stopped in his tracks by the sight of this young woman, her hair cropped short, her sad eyes and her solemn face: she was staggeringly beautiful.

"I've come about the air raids . . .!" he said at length, in the irritable tone of someone who is tired of repeating himself. Louise nodded and sipped her coffee. The distance between them meant that Monsieur Jules had to shout, which was difficult for a man who was invariably short of breath.

"You can do what you like with your own time, Louise, but when there's an air raid, you do like everyone else, you go down to the shelter!"

On paper, the sentence seems authoritative, but Monsieur Jules began in the brusque tone he adopted when commenting on the French artillery, then ran out of steam and the command ended in a whisper, a plea, a prayer.

Were she not so exhausted, Louise would have smiled. Air raids. One of the great tragedies in Monsieur Jules' life was that he had not been appointed air-raid warden. After all, in addition to the restaurant, he owned a building four doors away whose cellar he had given to the neighbourhood to convert into a bomb shelter, in return for which he felt the role of air-raid warden was his "by right". Unfortunately, after a sorry affair marked by countless twists and turns, the prefecture offered the position to Monsieur de Froberville, "a tin soldier", as Monsieur Jules contemptuously dubbed him. Since then, the two men had been locked in a silent struggle. Louise realised that, although her absence had weakened Monsieur Jules' support, this was not the reason for his visit.

She finally tottered down the four stone steps and crossed the garden.

Monsieur Jules cleared his throat.

"The restaurant's not the same without you . . ."

He forced a smile.

"Everyone has been waiting for you to come back, you know! The customers are constantly asking me how you are . . ."

"Don't they read the newspapers?"

"They don't give a damn about the newspapers! Everyone here loves you . . ."

At this admission, he bowed his head, like a little boy caught up to no good. Louise felt tears well in her eyes.

"And when there's an air raid, you have to go down to the shelter, Louise . . . Even that old duffer Froberville is worried about you."

Louise made a gesture that Monsieur Jules interpreted as a nod.

"Well good, good, that's good . . ."

Louise had finished her bowl of coffee. Monsieur Jules thought of her as "artistic", a term he applied to young women who posed as artist's models: tousle-haired bohemians who seemed to mock the world with their wild charms, their passionate sensuality. There were one or two living in the neighbourhood who even smoked cigarettes on the street; this was how he saw Louise now, with her beautiful, impassive face, those full lips, those eyes . . .

"I meant to ask – are you alright, Louise?"

"Why, don't I look alright?"

Monsieur Jules patted his pockets.

"Right, then, I must get on . . ."

Louise went back into the house. How did she spend her time? Later, she could not remember. All that remained was a single image, one that would have seemed anodyne to anyone else, but seemed terribly cruel to her. In mid-afternoon, she realised that she had spent the past several hours leaning against the window overlooking the courtyard, in precisely the spot where her mother had stood after her father's death, a spot she never left again.

Was Louise going mad? Would she end up like Jeanne?

The thought terrified her.

The atmosphere of the house was oppressive. She boiled some water, washed and dressed, then went out, walking past La Petite Bohème without a glance. She had been shaken by her sudden resemblance to Jeanne.

Where should she go? She had nowhere in mind.

She walked along the avenue, stopped at the bus stop and waited. There was a newspaper in the dustbin. Louise reached out her hand; the woman next to her looked away: only tramps rummaged in dustbins. But as though she had forsworn all pride, Louise picked up the paper and smoothed it out. The war seemed to be going well, headlines trumpeted catastrophic enemy losses and hundreds of downed enemy planes.

On page two, there was a photograph of a huddle of people staring blankly into the camera. "BELGIAN REFUGEES AT THE GARE DU NORD TELL OF THEIR JOURNEY INTO EXILE." In the foreground was a child, a boy, or a girl, it was difficult to make out.

One paragraph caught her attention:

### PARISIAN TEACHERS WELCOME REFUGEES

The National Union of Teachers had recommended that its members make themselves available to the authorities to take in refugees arriving from Belgium and areas around the French border.

Study rooms are being organised for the refugees at 3, rue du Château-d'Eau (10th arrondissement).

Louise was not a union member. Perhaps things would have taken a different turn if the woman who had turned away moments earlier had not struck up a conversation with her neighbour:

"Are you sure the bus is still running?"

"I can't be sure . . ." her neighbour said. "I know the 65 has been cancelled . . ."

"And the number 42!" said someone else. "They're using the buses to transport the refugees."

"Now, I've got nothing against refugees, but if they're going to commandeer our buses, I can't be dealing with it. The restrictions are bad enough already, one day there's no meat, the next day there's no sugar . . . How do these refugees expect us to feed them when we don't even have enough for ourselves?"

Louise went back to her reading. The bus came and she got on, still engrossed in the newspaper: "Low-flying planes appeared above the rooftops, dropping bombs. A group of children preparing to be evacuated were blown to pieces."

She folded up the paper, glanced out at the city. She saw the Parisians who went to their work, came home again, did their shopping; she saw the military trucks, the refugees in groups of thirty being escorted by scouts, the Red Cross ambulances, a few mobile guards with rifles slung across their shoulders . . .

She had no trouble finding the place. There was a queue of people milling around outside the Trade Union Centre. She went inside.

The place was a hive of activity, people coming in lugging boxes, others going out, all shouting to each other.

Louise moved warily, as though she was a nuisance. She stood in the doorway of the great hall, beneath the huge glass ceiling. A hundred weary people were sitting or lying on wooden benches set out as in a dormitory; there were families; here and there, tables had been set out. There was a constant drone of voices. A woman in a cloak was moving between the groups, holding out a photograph. Louise only heard: "This is Mariette, she's only five . . . I've lost her . . ." Her face was haggard. How can a mother lose her five-year-old daughter? Louise wondered aloud.

"At the Gare du Nord," said a voice next to her.

A Red Cross nurse in her sixties was also surveying the great hall.

"There were so many of them that we had to tell them to go down into the basement, where trucks would come to collect them. You can't imagine the crush of people . . . You let go your child's hand for a second, you step one way, the child steps the other and when you turn around, they're gone, and however much you scream, no-one can help."

Louise gazed at the woman who was still trudging through the makeshift aisles, holding up the photograph. She felt tears well.

"And you are . . .?" said the nurse.

"A teacher, I . . ."

"You need to make a tour of the hall, find out what it is that people need. The supplies are in there . . ."

She pointed to a gaping double door. Louise was about to say something, but the nurse had already disappeared.

Suitcases were repurposed as tables, benches as beds, blankets were rolled up to make mattresses. Bread and dry biscuits were handed out to men, to haggard women cradling exhausted children while babies wailed . . .

Stranded in the middle of this crowd of lost souls, Louise did not know what to do. In one aisle, some broom handles strung together to create a washing line on which to dry clothes, mostly nappies. A little way away, a young woman was sitting on the floor, crying, her head pressed against her knees. Louise heard the gurgle of a newborn, she had a keen ear for such things.

"Can I help you?"

The young girl looked up, her face wan and tired. In her lap, a sleeping baby wrapped in a scarf.

"How old is he?" said Louise.

"Four months." The girl's voice was deep and hoarse.

"Where is his papa?"

"He put us on the train, he didn't want to just . . . You have to understand, we have a farm, cattle . . ."

"What can I . . .?"

"I forgot to bring enough nappies . . ."

She glanced at the makeshift washing line.

"And, I don't know why, but when I hang them up, they don't seem to dry."

Louise felt a wave of relief. Providing nappies was something she could do; she suddenly felt useful.

She gave the young woman's hand a firm squeeze then went into the supply room, but children's clothes and nappies were in short supply.

"We haven't had any for three days," said the nurse she had encountered earlier. "Every day they promise they'll send some . . ."

Louise glanced at the door.

"If you can find some," said the nurse, "it would be great for everyone."

Louise rushed back to the young woman.

"I'll go and get what you need, and I'll be straight back." It was absurd: she almost added "you wait here".

She left reassured, full of energy: she had a mission.

*

By the time she reached the impasse Pers, it was already 6.00 p.m. She went upstairs and opened the door to her mother's bedroom.

Louise had not set foot inside since Jeanne's death. As soon as the undertakers took away the body, she had stripped the bed of sheets and blankets, and removed everything that was on the bedside table. Next, she had emptied the wardrobe, and within minutes, there wasn't a scrap of clothing left: not a dress, not a jacket, not a single pair of stockings. Madame Belmont vanished even before she was buried. The following morning, when she headed out to La Petite Bohème, Louise had seen the four bags of clothes she had left there during the night.

Now, the room was cold and musty. She opened a window.

The wardrobe was filled with linen sheets carefully folded by her mother, just like the tablecloths and napkins that she never used. Louise's first thought had been these sheets: there was a lot of linen here, more than enough to make dozens of nappies.

She had forgotten just how thick the sheets were. She picked up five or six, weighed them in her hands, not too heavy, she could take a couple more. She happened on a fake-leather wallet in which Madame Belmont had stored keepsakes, postcards, letters. Louise had not seen the wallet in a long time. Opening it, she found a picture of her father, one of her parents' wedding, letters that probably dated back to the last war. She set everything down on the mattress, carried half of the sheets downstairs, then went back up with a burlap sack for the rest. After a moment's hesitation, she grabbed the wallet of photos and letters, hurried out and – miraculously – caught a taxi from the corner of the impasse Pers and headed back to the Trade Union Centre.

Night was drawing in. The driver was ranting about the weather and the petrol rationing. The weary Louise ignored him, and idly leafed through the contents of the wallet.

"And the number of refugees you see around," said the driver, "it's unbelievable! Don't know where the hell we're supposed to put them all."

It was true: there were many refugees, all with their suitcases and bundles. Looking down, Louise studied a handful of yellowed snapshots, postcards of seaside resorts and village squares penned in beautiful calligraphy by her uncle René – her father's brother – adorned with curlicues and arabesques. She also found letters from her parents, all dated between 1914 and 1916.

"My darling Jeanne," her father wrote, "it is bitterly cold here, even the wine has frozen solid."

Or: "My friend Victor was wounded in the foot, but the field doctor says he will be fine, he is very relieved." He signed his letters: "your Adrien".

Jeanne began her letters "Dear Adrien" and recounted details of everyday life: "Louise is studying hard at school. The prices of everything keep going up and up. Madame Leidlinger has had twins." She signed her letters: "love, Jeanne".

The vague feeling that Louise was prying into a story that did not concern her was fleeting. What she mostly felt was surprise. Again, she pictured her mother, leaning against the window frame, staring into space for days on end. But now, rather than the memory of a lost love that had plunged Jeanne into depression, Louise had only letters that were clichéd and prosaic, letters that evoked nothing except perhaps marital complacency, the hackneyed letters any soldier in war might write, and those that his wife might write in return.

Through the taxi window, Louise watched the streets of Paris flash past. It was strange. Not a word of tenderness, nothing but benign platitudes. It was difficult to see the link between the couple who wrote these inconsequential letters and the terrible heartbreak that had consumed Jeanne after her husband's death.

Louise closed the wallet, and, as she did so, a card slipped out onto the floor of the cab.

She paused.

Although it was upside down, Louise could read the name: Hôtel d'Aragon, rue Campagne-Première.

The great hall was empty.

Sometime in the late afternoon, the refugees had been taken to a relocation camp somewhere near Limoges, though no-one knew for certain.

Without a word, Louise set the linen sheets down on the floor and left the building and hailed a taxi, still clutching the card that bore the name of the hotel.

As the taxi was approaching boulevard du Montparnasse, Louise said, "You can drop me here." She made the rest of the journey on foot.

She retraced the route she had taken some weeks earlier naked, spattered with blood and totally bewildered while around her cars had honked their horns and passers-by had stared.

The hotel lobby was empty.

She walked up to the reception desk, adorned by a sign that read Hôtel d'Aragon. The lettering was not the same as on the card in her hand, the sweeping arabesques had been replaced with a more modern typeface.

How old was the card?

She was caught off guard by the sudden appearance of the old woman. She looked every bit as gaunt and unsteady; her face was stern and impassive, and beneath the lace mantilla over her shoulders Louise glimpsed a black dress with mother-of-pearl buttons. Her wig was slightly askew.

Louise swallowed hard as she heard the woman say:

"Good evening, Mademoiselle Belmont . . ."

Hers was not a friendly expression, her entire being exuded resentment.

With a curt gesture, she nodded to a small living room next to the lobby and said:

"Perhaps it might be better if we were to talk in here . . ."

## 14

No sooner had the bridge crumbled than Gabriel and Landrade broke into a run. Behind them, the machine-gun fire intensified. They caught up with others from their unit who had been running more slowly, as they passed a burnt-out truck. The trees all around them had been shorn of their topmost branches and barely came up to their shoulders, craters pierced the forest floor as far as the eye could see.

They arrived back at the place where the 55th Infantry Division had been camped, and from where they had been sent out to guard the bridge.

It was utterly deserted.

There was no sign of the lieutenant-colonel who had railed against the lack of support, or of his soldiers; of the various units that had been stationed there only hours earlier there was nothing but ripped tents, abandoned kitbags and empty tin trunks, a flutter of documents and a few spiked machine guns half buried in the mud. A truck mounted with an anti-tank gun was burning, and the smell caught in their throats. The deserted camp reeked of surrender.

Gabriel raced to the signals post. All that remained were two broken field radios, all communication had been cut off, their tiny group was alone in the world. Gabriel mopped his sweaty forehead.

They turned as one and saw, five hundred metres away, the

first Panzer tanks to make their way through the Ardennes Forest, flanked by armoured cars on caterpillar tracks.

The column emerged from the forest like the snout of a slow but savage monster, prepared to devour everything in its path.

This was the signal. They all jumped into the ditch, climbed across the rampart and disappeared in the undergrowth. A few hundred metres on, they stumbled on a path blocked by a rapidly advancing column of German armoured vehicles; the enemy seemed to be everywhere at once.

They backed away, keeping low, keeping their distance, sheltering in a dense thicket, biding their time as the seemingly endless procession of tanks passed, oblivious to the French artillery fire which, without air support, could do nothing but blindly shell the area and most of the salvos fell wide of the mark. In the space of half an hour, only two shells hit their target. The German tank column stoically sacrificed three tanks, whose smoking remains they left behind.

Initially, Gabriel had tried to count the tanks, but he soon lost track. More than two hundred tanks, to say nothing of the armoured cars and the motorcycles. An invading army passed before the eyes of the beaten, exhausted, demoralised and lonely French soldiers.

"We were betrayed," whispered someone.

Gabriel looked around. He had no idea who had betrayed whom, but he found the word oddly fitting.

Landrade, for his part, had lit a cigarette, and was fanning away the smoke. He was muttering between gritted teeth:

"We'll win because we're stronger."

The French artillery fire abruptly ceased. Whether the artillerymen had been wiped out or taken prisoner, no-one knew.

By now the German army had moved on, leaving only a

devastated forest, ruts deep enough to bury corpses, and potholes as big as the wheel of a truck.

The stragglers got to their feet and surveyed a desolate, deserted landscape. It seemed appropriate.

No-one knew what to do.

From the tracks of the vehicles, it was clear that the German army was headed west. Gabriel was the only NCO.

"I suggest we head east," he said.

Landrade got to his feet and stood to attention, his back arched, a cigarette dangling from the corner of his mouth, and executed a mock salute.

"At your service, my sergent-chef!"

They trudged for more than an hour, sharing water from the two canteens they had saved from the debacle, saying little, like men who had been left speechless by what, only a day ago, had seemed unthinkable. Like punchdrunk boxers. Landrade lagged behind, smoking, as though amused by the situation.

For some time, the light filtering through the trees made it clear they were approaching the outskirts of the forest. They pressed on, neither knowing nor caring where they were, it hardly mattered since their brains were barely functioning. They glanced around, their faces filled with fear. They felt as though they were being hunted, as though the enemy was on their tail, they had no choice but to press on. Flee. A few kilometres to the west, the war was raging, and the sky burned bright with the glow of artillery fire.

They happened on other lost soldiers. Three infantrymen, an artilleryman, a supply engineer, two men who had been on a train . . . How they had come to be in the same place at the same time was a mystery.

"Where have you come from?" asked a tall young man with a little blonde moustache who marched alongside Gabriel.

"From the bridge by the Tréguière."

The soldier looked doubtful, he had never heard of the place; if Gabriel had lost his life there, no-one would have cared.

"What about you?"

But the soldier didn't hear the question, caught up as he was by a thought that had been nagging at him for some time. He paused for a moment to stress his amazement:

"Germans in French uniforms, can you imagine?"

Gabriel shot him a quizzical look.

"It was Germans dressed as French officers who gave the order to retreat!"

He resumed his march, his voice now quavering with emotion.

Gabriel was bewildered by this assertion, something that was clear from his expression since the young man said vehemently:

"I'm telling you! Infiltrators who spoke French as well as you or I. They were the ones who gave the order to retreat, and everyone believed them. They had orders from the high command – forgeries, obviously."

What Gabriel remembered above all was a tank column emerging from the Ardennes Forest.

"Did you see the orders?" he said.

"I didn't, but our capitaine did."

Where their capitaine was now, no-one knew. They came to the edge of the forest and emerged onto a narrow road. A handful of refugees appeared as if from nowhere and hurried past, pushing handcarts. From time to time, a car or a cyclist passed, some of whom shouted: "Get out of here! Fast!"

The motley procession moved at varying speeds, the cars

disappeared quickly, the bicycles slowly, those on foot trudged solemnly, as though they formed a funeral procession.

Gabriel was about to step onto the road when he noticed a small group who had stopped by the roadside, three soldiers gathered around a map they had spread out on the wheel of an overturned sidecar that bore the ensign of the 66th Infantry Regiment. It turned out to be two officers flanking a third man who was poring over the map. Gabriel moved closer so that he could see the man's rank. A général. It was a tranquil scene, almost a still life. Three soldiers standing ramrod straight. What was most striking was the face of the général, the stunned, bewildered expression of a man dumbfounded by something utterly unfamiliar. Glancing around him, Gabriel had no problem making sense of the image: the motionless général struggling to find a solution to a problem he did not understand, and the rag-tag group of soldiers who were aimlessly following the farms, the carts and the cattle . . .

From what they could hear, the battle behind them had moved to the west. Having lingered over the sad spectacle of the général poring over his map, Gabriel was forced to quicken his step to catch up with his group, but even that group had dissolved so much that they were now dotted along the road.

He was surprised to see Landrade appear, like a jack-in-the-box, smiling in spite of the circumstances.

"Well, this is shit, isn't it? Hey, come with me . . ."

Landrade grabbed his sleeve and pulled him over to a car, a light-brown Novaquatre parked by the ditch with its bonnet open.

"I found us a mechanic!" Landrade said triumphantly, pointing to Gabriel.

The driver, a dark, broad-shouldered man, was standing next to a young woman, probably his wife. He shook Gabriel by the hand.

"Filipe."

The woman was slender, dark-skinned and quiet. Quite pretty. Was this why Landrade had offered to help them? The man was smiling broadly, grateful for this unexpected help.

"Their engine stalled," Landrade told Gabriel. 'They just need a push-start."

And, without waiting for a response, he added:

"I'll get behind the wheel. You two push. Come on, up and at it!"

He leaned close to Gabriel and whispered, "They're rich foreigners!" before opening the door and sliding behind the wheel. The car was full of boxes and suitcases.

"Put your back into it!" he roared.

Gabriel in turn grabbed the passenger door and turned. The young couple had their hands on the bonnet, straining as they pushed the car out of the ditch.

A car flashed past. In it was the général Gabriel had seen poring over the map.

A little further on, the road began to dip, the Novaquatre picked up speed, the engine spluttered, Gabriel redoubled his efforts and suddenly, with a loud belch, the car started.

"Jump in," called Landrade.

The passenger door was open. Without a second thought, Gabriel jumped onto the running board and slid in just as Landrade floored the accelerator.

"What the hell are you doing?" he shouted, looking back.

Landrade blared the car horn, forcing the carts to give way. Far behind, Gabriel could see the young couple watching as their car disappeared. The man waved his fist, Gabriel felt embarrassed, but mostly he felt furious and grabbed Landrade's elbow in an attempt to force him to pull over. In response, a fist split Gabriel's lower lip, his head was slammed against the car door. He rubbed his smarting jaw.

Dazed and half-senseless, he tried to collect his thoughts, he wanted to get out, but it was too late, the procession of those fleeing had already tapered off, the car was cruising at 50 kph.

Landrade started to whistle.

Gabriel looked around for something to stop the blood trickling over his chin and down his neck.

## 15

"We are proud to be able to tell you that, in the face of the brutal German offensive on the banks of the Meuse, the resistance of our gallant French forces has been heroic. And a triumph! Everywhere, French and Allied counter-offensives have sown confusion and doubt among the Nazi troops."

At his very first press conferences, Désiré had identified the sceptics, the doubters, those who would not be taken in. And it was to them he turned during critical passages of his communiqué, to them he addressed his most patriotic bespectacled gaze.

"The Germans' attacks are relentless, but even now the French army is building a wall that will check their advance. At no point has the enemy succeeded in breaching our defensive lines."

A murmur spread through the crowd. Désiré Migault's imperious assertions reassured everyone.

"Tell me, Monsieur Migault . . ."

Désiré glanced around, as though to work out where the voice was coming from – ah, over there on the right – yes?

"The Germans were expected to launch their attack through Belgium, but now they've launched a second offensive on the Meuse . . ."

Désiré nodded seriously.

"You are quite correct. Nazi military strategists thought they could confound our troops by creating a diversion on the Eastern

Front – a rather naive strategy for anyone familiar with our military commanders."

The phrase elicited a few chuckles here and there. The journalist was about to say something else when Désiré raised an admonishing forefinger that stopped him in his tracks.

"Curiosity is a healthy thing for a journalist. As long as, when formulating your questions, you do not foment doubt and suspicion among the populace, feelings that might be considered anti-national, indeed anti-patriotic while France is engaged in such a decisive battle."

The journalist decided not to pose the question.

Désiré invariably ended his press conferences with a brief lecture in the form of a series of talking points, each intended to bolster confidence in the French armed forces and, by extension, in the communiqués of the Ministry of Information.

"Consider our skilled, resourceful strategists, the heirs to Général Foch and Général Kellermann; our unrivalled airforce; our tanks, which are infinitely superior to their German equivalents; our fearless infantrymen . . . Each of these are factors that lead to one glorious certainty: our struggle will carry on until France emerges victorious."

Unfortunately, reality tended to run contrary to the will of the French military, thereby compelling Désiré to resort to hyperbole.

In a mirror image of the escalating fighting in the north and the east, the more unsettling the news from the front, the more imperious were Désiré's assertions.

One morning he asked the assistant director whether he genuinely felt that the ministry was the most effective voice in influencing French morale.

The assistant director pushed back his chair and wagged his index finger: continue . . .

"Despite the accuracy of our communiqués, they are treated as 'official statements' and, as such, are invariably treated with a certain suspicion by the public. Now, if I might be so bold . . ."

"Be bold, my dear fellow, be bold!"

"Well, I would say people are less likely to trust an official statement than they might trust . . . bar-room gossip."

"Are you suggesting you hold your conferences in a bar?"

Désiré gave that dry, nervous laugh the assistant director associated with higher beings.

"Certainly not, sir! I was thinking more in terms of . . . the wireless."

"A vulgar medium!" the assistant director snapped. "We are not about to lower ourselves to the standards of . . . Radio-Stuttgart! To the levels of that traitor Ferdonnet."

Paul Ferdonnet was habitually referred to as "that traitor Ferdonnet". As director of Radio-Stuttgart, in the pay of the Nazis, he had been sentenced to death in absentia by a Paris military tribunal that found him guilty of acts of treason, to wit: peddling false news intended to undermine French morale – even urging French citizens to lay down their arms. Ferdonnet was certainly perfidious, and a number of his slogans had struck home: "England supplies the guns; France supplies the bodies", "Artillery fire never reaches the générals' quarters", "While you are fighting at the front, those on detached service in the factories are sleeping with your wives". Désiré had found the approach particularly effective and believed it was something worth exploring.

"I wondered about the potential impact of a daily, prime-time slot in which a senior civil servant, on condition of anonymity, could say . . . all the things that officials cannot say."

Désiré's idea was that, since nothing is more reliable than an unofficial source, French listeners would be inclined to believe what an official told them . . . if he did so anonymously.

"The average French citizen has an intense, intimate relationship with his wireless. He believes the broadcaster is talking directly to him and talking only to him. There is no medium more appropriate than the wireless to maintain the country's morale."

The assistant director gave Désiré the incredulous look that, in him, served to mask enthusiasm.

"We need to show Radio-Stuttgart that we understand the enemy," said Désiré, "that we know him all too well."

This was the germ that produced *The Diary of Monsieur Dupont*, broadcast by Radio-Paris and relayed across the country. The programme always opened with a disclaimer stating that a high-ranking, well-informed member of the French administration had agreed to answer questions mailed in by the listeners. On condition that he could remain anonymous

"It's perfect!" said Désiré. "The listener will think that we are interested in his questions, and that we consider him someone mature enough with whom to share strategic information."

"Good evening, listeners. Monsieur S., from Toulon (Désiré insisted on this geographical preciseness which, he said, 'gave the question a topographical veracity', an expression his superior thought splendid), has written to ask 'why Germany, after more than a year of inaction, has suddenly decided to launch an offensive'? (At this point, Désiré played a brief musical phrase intended to stress the astuteness of the question and the importance of the answer.) To him, I say: Germany had no alternative. The country is bankrupt, morally and financially, there are terrible shortages of just about everything, long queues in front of empty shops. In order to avoid an uprising, Hitler had no choice but to launch an attack, to create a diversion to stem the German citizens' deep dislike of National Socialism. You need to understand that contemporary Germany is a country on its knees, one devoid of substance, or willpower. The German offensive is nothing but a desperate attempt by the Nazis to give Germany some semblance of hope. They are playing for time."

Désiré's plan was a success. From the first broadcast, Radio-Paris received hundreds of letters with questions for Monsieur Dupont. This programme was a phenomenon, one that the assistant director was only too happy to portray to his superiors as his personal initiative.

"Good evening. One of our listeners, a Madame B., from Colombes, has asked me to clarify what I called 'the terrible shortages' in Germany" – *musical phrase* – "we have seen countless examples of shortages in Germany. The lack of coal, for example, has caused serious problems. Mothers have been seen taking their children to cemeteries to warm themselves by the incinerators. Since all leather has been commandeered for use by the army, women are forced to wear fish skins to protect themselves from the cold. They no longer have potatoes to eat, since this is the staple food of the German troops, nor are they allowed butter, since this is exclusively used to oil their guns. In the past year, no home has seen a grain of rice or a drop of milk; bread is available only once a week. Needless to say, it is the weakest who most suffer from these shortages. Young, malnourished mothers give birth to sickly babies. Some sixty per cent of German children are stunted. Rationing is one of the prime reasons for the appalling spread of tuberculosis throughout the country. Millions of German children arrive at school every morning filthy for lack of soap."

In the course of his programmes, Désiré inserted nuggets of information about the French that were intended to reassure.

"It is quite inaccurate to say that there is a shortage of coffee in France," he explained one evening. "How can there be a shortage of coffee since it is still widely available. But the French love their coffee, they can never have enough. So, when they cannot get *as much* coffee as they would like, they (mistakenly) conclude that there is a shortage."

The syllogisms of Désiré Migault elicited awe and admiration from half the people at the Hôtel Continental, and fuelled rivalries and jealousies among the other half. In the corridors, people scoffed because those in high places declared themselves more than satisfied with this forceful French propaganda blitz, an area where the Germans had long been particularly effective and dangerous.

Monsieur de Varambon had appointed himself the leader of the clandestine anti-Désiré movement. He was a long man, long in the legs, long in his sentences and even his thoughts, and this was his salvation. When he got an idea into his head, he refused to budge, he would determinedly plough his furrow with mule-like obstinacy. He was the man who had slyly (but unsuccessfully) tried to unmask Désiré by introducing him to Monsieur Thong, the delegate from Indochina. He had ventured to suggest that there was something suspicious about the fact that no-one had ever heard of Désiré Migault before his arrival at the Hôtel Continental.

The assistant director had stared at him, wide-eyed.

"Are you suggesting that Monsieur Cœdes, the director of the French School of Asian Studies, is no-one?"

Monsieur de Varambon changed tack. He made the tour of

various government departments. Aside from Monsieur Cœdes, whom no-one in the ministry had ever met, no-one had ever had any dealings with Désiré Migault.

"Tell me, young man . . ."

Désiré turned around, hastily pushed his glasses up the bridge of his nose.

"Monsieur?"

"Before working here at the Continental, and before your time in Hanoi, where were you based?"

"In Turkey, sir. Mostly in Smyrna."

"So . . . you would have known Portefin?"

Désiré narrowed his eyes, racking his brain . . .

"Come on, man, Portefin!" barked de Varambon. "He's probably the most important man we have in Turkey!"

"The name doesn't ring a bell . . . Where exactly was he stationed?"

De Varambon gave an irritated shrug – let it go – turned on his heel and walked away. His trap had failed and, as he did on such occasions, he drew new strength from his failure. His investigation was far from over.

For his part, Désiré carried on his way. He was only too familiar with the light breeze that always preceded the moment of revelation, he had been dealing with them all his life, it was high time to beat a tactical retreat.

For the first time in his life, it pained him to leave his job. It felt premature. He was hugely enjoying what he was doing with this war. What a shame!

# 16

The sour-faced hotel manager folded her hands in her lap, her face was inscrutable. She glared at Louise with the grey eyes of a predatory bird. Louise was afraid of what she might hear, and unsure where to start. The two women retreated into silence, the younger kept her head bowed, staring at the patterned carpet, the elder stared defiantly at her captive prey . . .

Finally, Louise loosened her grip on the strap of her handbag and, in a quavering voice she tried to control, said:

"Madame . . . I'm sorry I don't know your name . . ."

"Trombert. Adrienne Trombert."

The response was delivered like a slap in the face. It would not have mattered how she began this conversation; the manager was merely waiting for an opening, now she launched into a rant:

"I suppose you think it's perfectly acceptable to go around killing men in other people's hotels?"

What could she possibly say to that? Instantly, Louise was back in the hotel room, she could see the old man's dead body . . . She had not thought of things in these terms; she felt guilty.

"I mean, really!" said the manager. "Did the doctor feel there was something lacking in our service when we welcomed him here? Him and his mistress? Could he not have done his business somewhere else? But apparently, he wasn't content with having the mother, he wanted the daughter too . . ."

The statement was like a punch in the stomach. Louise choked back a bout of nausea. The manager pursed her lips. She had not been able to stop herself: this was the line she had longed to say from the start, the one she had practised over and over for days and which, in the murky hotel lobby, had seemed perfect, the perfect expression of her animosity, but hearing herself say it aloud, it felt different.

It was her turn now to stare down at the carpet. She regretted what she had said. She was not a spiteful person, she was simply angry.

"It's just that . . . all this fuss . . ."

She nervously toyed with her wedding ring, she could not bring herself to look Louise in the eye.

"Can you imagine . . . The police, here in the hotel."

She looked up.

"We've never had any trouble here. This is a well-run establishment, it's not a . . ."

The word hovered in the air. This was the nub. The problem was a "brothel" problem. The problem was "whores".

"After . . . the *incident*, some of the guests, some of the *regulars* threatened to leave, mademoiselle! Guests who have lived here for years no longer wanted to stay . . ."

The incident had had a devastating impact on trade, guests, turnover.

"And obviously, none of the housemaids would go into the room to clean it. I'm the one who has had to . . ."

Louise's mind was elsewhere, still bewildered by the woman's earlier mention of "mother and daughter". She understood the reference to herself; after all, she had acted like a whore, but her mother . . .

"There was blood everywhere, even on the stairs. And the

smell . . . Do you really think this is something I should have to deal with, at my age?"

"I'm prepared to pay for the damages . . ."

Louise had savings, the idea should have occurred to her, she should have brought money with her . . . The offer of money visibly pleased the woman.

"That's very kind, but as far as that goes the family, I mean the doctor's family, were very understanding. They sent somebody, a lawyer or someone, they didn't quibble about the amount, they paid the *damages*."

Things were going more smoothly, thought the manageress, they had discussed money, talked about the problems with guests, she had said the one thing that had been preying on her mind for more than a month and, even though it had not quite had the desired effect, she was relieved. She heaved a sigh.

For the first time, she looked at Louise, not at the creature that had caused her so much trouble, but at the nervous, confused young woman sitting opposite her.

"You look just like your mother . . . How is she these days?"

"She's dead."

"Oh . . ."

Louise's mind was racing. Had Doctor Thirion been her father?

"When did you meet my mother . . .?

The manageress pursed her lips.

"It would have been . . . 1905. Yes, that's right, early in 1905."

Louise had been born in 1909.

The looming possibility of a revelation left her breathless. Imagine if she had undressed in front of . . . It was unthinkable.

"And you are sure it was my mother who . . .?"

"Oh, yes, my dear, there's no doubt. Your mother's name was Jeanne, wasn't it?"

Louise felt her throat dry. It was difficult to imagine her mother frequenting hotels. Had she been a guest here? Aged seventeen? As though she herself were being accused, Louise went on the attack:

"She was underage . . ."

The manageress clapped her hands delightedly.

"That's exactly what I said to my late husband, may he rest in peace. I said, 'René, we do not run an establishment that takes in couples in the middle of the day! I mean, what next? Renting rooms by the hour?' But you have to understand, my late husband was a friend of the doctor, they had been friends since primary school, so he insisted, he said he would make an exception, and I agreed, I mean what could I do? When you're married you have to make *conceptions* . . ."

Louise did not laugh.

"Besides," said the manageress, "it was all very correct, otherwise I would never have tolerated it. They came once or twice a week, usually twice. They would arrive just before noon, the doctor would pay for the room, and they would leave again in the early afternoon. They were very polite, I couldn't complain. Your mother would always linger a while, she was very smitten."

No point avoiding the truth, thought Louise.

"How long did they keep coming?"

"About a year, I think . . . Yes, until the end of 1906, I remember, around the time of my husband's cousin's wedding, we had a lot of guests down from the country, so we had no rooms available. I remember thinking, if they came this week, they'll have to find somewhere else, but they didn't show up. From one day to the next, we didn't see them."

Had they gone to a different hotel? The manageress clearly anticipated this question.

"They stopped seeing each other. That's what Doctor Thirion told my husband. From what he said, he was clearly hurt."

This was a relief. The relationship had ended three years before Louise was born. She could not be the doctor's daughter.

"That's why I wasn't really surprised when they came back. In 1912, it would have been."

The blood drained from Louise's face. In 1912, her mother had been married for five years.

"Would you like a cup of tea, maybe? Or perhaps you'd prefer coffee? Oh no, sorry, I think we only have tea, it's so difficult to get coff—"

Louise cut her short.

"They came back in 1912?"

"Yes. It was just like before. But they came more regularly. The doctor was always very correct, he always left a tip for the chambermaids, and your maman was clearly not a strumpet, if that puts your mind at ease. We all thought it was . . . well, romantic."

At the time, Louise would have been three years old. This was different. This was not youthful passion, it was adultery.

"I think maybe I would like some tea."

"FERNANDE!"

It sounded like the bird call, a peacock or pheasant.

A stout young woman in an apron appeared. She looked sullen.

"Madame?"

The manageress ordered tea for two, adding "my dear Fernande", as she always did in front of guests.

Louise tried to compose herself.

"So, your mother never mentioned anything?"

Louise hesitated about her answer. It was like tossing a coin, the right answer might persuade the manageress to open up, the wrong one might shut her down. She took the plunge:

"No. I'm just trying to understand . . ."

Wrong answer, she could see the manageress withdraw, she studied her fingernails.

"When she was on her deathbed, my mother said: 'I want to tell you everything, I just hope you'll understand . . .' but she died before she could tell me."

This little lie easily compensated for her blunder. The manageress gazed at her, open-mouthed. This idea of a dying woman confessing her most passionate secrets to her daughter appealed to her deepest fantasies, since she had married an impotent ex-policeman, had never had the courage to take lovers and, for want of a sympathetic ear, had never confided her secrets to anyone.

"My poor dear . . ." she said, though her pity was reserved for herself.

Louise lowered her eyes shyly, but she was still focused on the truth.

"So, you say they started coming back in 1912?"

"For two years. Then the war came, and we had other things to think about besides a little slap and tickle. What a time it was . . ."

The tea arrived, weak and tepid.

"When you first came here, the day of the air raid, I took one look at you and I said to myself, it's unbelievable how much she looks like little Jeanne, what a strange coincidence (I always called her 'little Jeanne', because of her age). Two days later, when the doctor arrived, I thought to myself: there's something fishy here. He had really aged . . . I hardly recognised him. He had been a very handsome man, let me tell you, but that's how things go, my poor husband, may he rest in peace, he was a handsome lad once too, but in the end, he had double, a double chin, a double paunch, that's life . . . Where was I? Oh yes, the doctor arrived and he requested room 311, the way he always used to do, and he put the money on the counter, I was so dumbfounded that I just handed him the key without a word. 'Someone will call to see me,' he said, just like that. And, obviously, I thought about little Jeanne. But when I saw you come in and I thought to myself, my God, it's impossible, it can't be her, it was as though time was repeating itself twenty-five years later, and that's when I thought: first the mother, now the daughter."

The manageress sipped her weak tea, pinkie finger extended, gazing at Louise over the rim of her cup. She had managed to make her jibe a second time; she was happy.

Back in the impasse Pers, Louise reread the postcards her parents had sent during the war. Every word now took on a meaning that was quite different. And infinitely sad. Madame Belmont had had a passionate affair with Doctor Thirion. Had she ever loved her husband? Perhaps Adrien had never loved her either, both their letters were so utterly banal.

Louise felt hurt, not only because she was the product of a dull, terribly clichéd story, but also because she had never imagined her mother in love, the very idea seemed incongruous. It was as if they were two different women. Now Louise could glimpse the vast continent concealed by her mother's depression. But the mystery remained. What she had just discovered did nothing to explain the doctor's decision, twenty-five years later, to take his own life in front of the daughter of his former mistress. Any more than it explained . . .

Louise froze, she took a deep breath. Was it possible that . . .?

She set down the postcards, put on her coat, went out of the house and straight to La Petite Bohème. But, rather than approaching the bar where Monsieur Jules was cleaning glasses, she turned left and sat at the doctor's usual table.

From here, she could see the front of her own house.

Jeanne Belmont's house.

Monsieur Jules sighed, wiped the bar down with a damp cloth, it was four o'clock, there was no-one in the restaurant, he took his time.

Louise sat motionless in her cumbersome coat. Monsieur Jules went to the front door, opened it and glanced outside as though suddenly interested in surveying the street, the neighbourhood, then he closed the door, turned over the little sign inscribed "Open" to "Closed", slowly made his way down to Louise's table and sat facing her.

"Good . . . We need to talk. Is that why you came?"

Louise did not answer. Monsieur Jules looked around the empty restaurant, the bar . . .

"You've come to ask me . . . Alright, what have you come to ask me?"

She could have slapped him.

"All along, you've known the whole story and you never said a word to me . . ."

"The whole story, the whole story . . . I knew a few bits and pieces, Louise, that's all."

"Well then, you can start by telling me those few bits and pieces."

Monsieur Jules walked back to the bar.

"Would you care for a drink?"

When Louise did not answer, he came back and sat opposite her, cradling a glass of wine between his fingertips as though it were a precious possession.

"When the doctor first started coming here (he nodded to the table), it would have been . . . 1921? 1922? You were thirteen. Can you imagine me saying: 'My dear little Louise, that man over there, the one who comes every Saturday, well, he's your mother's former lover!' I mean, honestly . . ."

Louise did not move, she did not blink, she gave Monsieur Jules a cold, unforgiving look. He gulped his wine.

"And then later . . . Well, time passed, you grew up, and still he's coming here every week, but it's too late."

He let out a bearish growl, as though the words "it's too late" summed up his own life.

"Your mother and the doctor, it was ancient history. It dated back to when we were – what? – sixteen, seventeen . . ."

Monsieur Jules had always lived here, his parents had lived on the rue Ordener. He and Jeanne Belmont had been at school together. Though Monsieur Jules would have been two or three years her senior.

"My God, your mother was so beautiful back then . . . The very image of you! Though she smiled a little more. Doctor Thirion's surgery was at the end of the rue Caulaincourt, everyone round here went to him. That's how they got to meet. People were really surprised. I mean, your mother had her school diploma and, rather than training to be a nurse, which is what everyone expected, lo and behold, she got a job working as a maid for the doctor's family. Obviously, I understood when I found out what was going on between them. At first, I thought the doctor was like a lot of men, he just wanted to sleep with the maid. But it wasn't like that; he was in love with her. At least that's what she told me. He was about twenty-five years her senior. And I said: 'Jeanne you can't work as a maid just because you're in love, what kind of future can you possibly have with this man?' But it was useless, she was in love too, or at least she thought she was. Your mother always was a romantic. She read too many novels, literature is not good for people, it gives them ideas."

He took another gulp of wine and shook his head – *what a mess*. Louise remembered her mother's bookshelves, the novels she had read and reread: Jane Eyre, Anna Karenina, novels by Paul Bourget, by Pierre Loti . . .

"Is that all?" she said.

"What do you mean 'Is that all?' What more do you want? They were in love, they slept together, so what!"

Monsieur Jules flushed angrily, forgetting that Louise knew him better than anyone in the world. She knew precisely what was meant by the flashes of anger he usually visited on his customers.

"I'll tell you what I want," she said quietly. "I want to know why they split up after two years. And why, five years later, they got together again. I want to understand why, for years and years, he came here every Saturday and sat at this table. I already know everything you've told me. I want to know the rest."

Monsieur Jules adjusted his beret.

"As to why he came here, he never told me and I never asked, obviously . . . But look (they both turned to the window and stared at the Belmont house), it is not difficult to guess. He probably hoped he would see her, maybe he was keeping an eye on her. But since she never went out and spent all her time staring into the courtyard on the other side . . ."

The thought made Louise's heart bleed. It saddened her to think that these two people had spent twenty-five years scarcely two hundred metres apart, each looking in opposite directions, each thinking about the same thing.

Monsieur Jules cleared his throat and pretended not to notice.

"When he started coming here regularly it was years after he moved away. I barely thought about him, in fact it was a while before I recognised him, but you know me, I'm not one to raise my voice. To me, he was a customer, so, I was diplomatic and discretion personified."

He suddenly drained the rest of his glass.

"Obviously, I wondered what the devil he was doing there, but since he always sat at the same table, the only table from which you can see your house, well, Jeanne's house . . . I assumed he was coming to see her."

"And you didn't think to tell her the doctor was coming here every Saturday, that he . . . .?"

"Of course, I did, who do you take me for?"

His anger, this time, was not feigned. But the memory of what had happened made him sad, as though he were angry with himself.

"I went to tell her that the doctor came here every Saturday. 'What has that got to do with me?' she snapped. I looked like a complete fool. And there I was, just trying to be helpful . . ."

Louise had made her first holy communion a year late, aged thirteen. That was the year when her mother began sitting by the window and barely ever moving. When Monsieur Jules told her about the doctor's visits, she had sat at that window and turned her back to La Petite Bohème.

The doctor had never called to the house, he had waited for Jeanne.

"Since she was never going to come to see him, I assumed he'd eventually give up, but it didn't seem to matter. Every Saturday he was here with his newspaper. At first, I felt sad but later I got used to him being here, I didn't think about it anymore. Until he started talking to you. I could tell there was something going on, but you didn't want to talk to me about it . . ."

A silence. Then, the question had been nagging at him from the very beginning.

"What exactly did the doctor ask you to do? I mean . . . what happened at the hotel . . .?"

He had no ulterior motive, he just wanted to know how much Louise had been hurt. So, she told him the story, the doctor's offer, her acceptance, the money, the hotel room, the gunshot.

"Jesus Christ," said Monsieur Jules. "What a tragedy. Obviously, it wasn't you he wanted to see, it was your mother, but even so . . ."

He laid his hand on Louise's.

"It was a cruel thing to do . . . If the bastard were here right now . . ."

"When they were together, what did she tell you about the doctor?"

"I don't know, she told me the things a woman tells a man when he's not the one she's sleeping with."

Louise could not help but smile.

"What about you, Monsieur Jules, did you sleep with her?"

"No, but only because she didn't want to . . ."

He patted his pockets.

"You haven't told me everything, Monsieur Jules, have you?"

"What d'you mean? Of course I've told you everything, I've told you everything I know."

Louise leaned closer. She was genuinely fond of this man, because he had a big heart, a simple heart. He couldn't lie to her, he could try, but he did not know how. She didn't want to hurt him, she took his hand and brought it to her cheek, as though to warm it.

Monsieur Jules did not know what to do. His heart felt heavy, perhaps because what he was about to reveal would hurt her even more, because he was about to reveal a secret that was not his. In the end, he snuffled loudly.

She gave him an expectant look, the same look she gave at school to timid students reluctant to take the plunge.

"Louise . . . Your mother . . . she and the doctor had a baby."

# 17

"Stop! For God's sake, stop!"

Landrade savagely pumped the brake. The car stopped in the middle of the road. Gabriel turned around. The Portuguese couple were long gone.

"There you go," said Landrade. "What do you plan to do now?"

All around, the landscape was flat and desolate.

"Haven't you marched enough? Do you really want to traipse another twenty kilometres on foot?"

Gabriel pressed a handkerchief to his cheek and stared out the window: fields as far as the eye could see. They were on a narrow road. Here and there he could see farm buildings dwarfed by the vast expanse. The few scattered thickets of trees merely added to a sense of desolation.

"Look at them . . ." said Landrade nodding to the refugees passing them by cart, by bicycle, or on foot. "It's every man for himself now. If you don't understand that, you won't survive for long, you might as well sit on a stone and wait for the Krauts."

Landrade re-started the car.

"Come on," he said with a laugh. "Everything will be fine, sergent-chef, don't make a big deal out of this."

"We stole their fucking car! We could have asked them to give us a lift."

Landrade burst out laughing and nodded to the trunks and

suitcases on the back seat. Gabriel blushed and to disguise the fact looked in the mirror to examine the bruise. His bottom lip was swollen.

There was so little traffic if felt as though they were going in the wrong direction. Gabriel found a map in the glove compartment and tried to get his bearings, they were driving east.

"Where do you want to go?" said Landrade.

"Back to the Mayenberg . . ."

"Are you joking? The Jerries will have taken the fort by now."

Gabriel thought back to the unit's frantic retreat. Their attempt to stop a heavily armed German column with the pitiful means at their disposal now seemed like an act of madness. It had served no purpose. Had they slowed the German army even by an hour? What difference had it made? He pictured the body of the chubby boy with the laces floating in the river, then he glanced surreptitiously at Landrade, who was focused on the road ahead. He might be a faker, a liar and a cheat, but he had stayed to fight . . .

How had this happened?

Were the French army really so ill-prepared?

"Time and again they told us that they couldn't make it through the Ardennes, that it was impossible . . ."

"What is it now?"

A thought popped into Gabriel's mind.

"Are we . . . deserters?"

It was a shocking word, one he could not apply to himself. Landrade didn't laugh as he usually did, but thoughtfully stroked his chin.

"The way I see it, half the army is in the same position we are."

"But lots of men are still fighting, aren't they?"

He meant, people like us, people who fought the way we did at the Tréguière bridge, but they were hardly an edifying example in

174

their stolen car, fleeing the enemy. Their duty was to fight. Gabriel was ashamed. Even Landrade did not seem too proud of himself.

"What happened?" said Gabriel.

"We were betrayed, that's what happened! The fifth column, the communists."

"What do you mean, betrayed?" Gabriel wanted to ask, but he said nothing. He remembered what the soldier with the blond moustache had said, Germans disguised as French officers had given the order to retreat . . . Could it really have taken so little to rout the whole French army? It seemed unbelievable. All Gabriel had seen was ill-equipped, ill-armed men led by ill-prepared officers desperate for orders from a high command that was nowhere to be found.

"We should head back to Paris. Turn ourselves in."

Raoul was evasive:

"The high command, yes, maybe, we'll see. But Paris . . . that suits me. Though we're heading in the wrong direction . . ."

To their left, the clamour of war had subsided. Gabriel studied the map.

"If the Jerries are heading west, we should be able to turn off a little way down the way and take the road back to Paris."

Landrade was silent for a long moment, then he lit a cigarette and looked at the louring sky, the fading light, the bleak landscape.

"God, they must be bored senseless . . ."

"Who?"

"The people who live here . . . For them, the war is probably a welcome distraction . . ."

He sounded utterly serious.

At their first stop, Landrade explored the car while Gabriel walked some distance away to take a piss. On his return, he found the suitcases disembowelled, the crates open . . . It was difficult to make out details now that night had fallen, but there were piles of clothes, trinkets of all kinds, blankets, a collection of pathetic bits and pieces of the kind you might see everywhere. Although Gabriel had witnessed things a thousand times worse over the past two days, somehow the sight of these tawdry belongings was heart-breaking.

"Nothing worth taking," Landrade growled, tossing out the empty suitcases.

Overwhelmed by exhaustion, Gabriel left him to it. He could barely stand so went back and sat in the car. Landrade climbed behind the wheel again.

"You have a little sleep, mate . . . You might be a sergent-chef, but you've got the energy of a little girl."

He chuckled. The guy was indestructible.

On the long drive, Gabriel succumbed to the purr of the engine. He felt obscurely grateful to Landrade for driving, for getting the two of them out of here.

"Shit!"

Gabriel was brutally jolted from his doze. The car had stopped. Landrade started to reverse into a narrow road lined by poplar trees.

"This looks good, doesn't it?"

Gabriel squinted into the darkness, he had no idea why Landrade thought this narrow stretch of tarmac was so promising. Yet with the keen intuition of a burglar, Landrade had sniffed out the driveway to an apparently vast country house, whose grounds were planted with tall trees. They could only guess at the size of the vast shadowy building at the end of the dark driveway glimpsed through the wrought-iron gates. The car came to a stop. The house looked deserted.

"I think we've hit the jackpot . . ."

Landrade found a toolbox, and took out pincers, pliers and a hammer. He made a deafening racket pounding and twisting the wrought iron.

"Someone's going to see us," said Gabriel, but the night was so dark they could barely see three metres.

After fifteen minutes' work, the gates finally creaked open, and Landrade whooped.

"I did it, I fucking did it! Come on, back in the car!"

Moments later, the headlights illuminated the facade of the building as gravel crunched beneath the wheels. The sweeping front steps looked like something out of a wedding photograph. All the windows were covered by heavy dark wooden shutters.

By the time Gabriel had noticed the honeysuckle and the climbing roses that festooned the walls, Landrade was already rummaging in his toolbox again and trying to break in, furiously muttering imprecations at the lock, the door, the house, its former owners and everything that stood in his way.

Finally, the lock gave way.

The entrance hall was murky. As though he already felt completely at home, Landrade raced down the hall and could be heard fumbling with something in the darkness. Suddenly, the lights flickered on: within two minutes he had found the fuse box.

The vast, sleepy family home lay waiting for the return of its owners: armchairs and sofas were covered with dustsheets which made them seem like ghostly presences, rugs lay coiled against the skirting boards like sleeping insects. Landrade stood in front of a painting, a full-length portrait of an imperious, pot-bellied man, with bushy whiskers, one hand resting on the shoulder of a supercilious seated woman.

"Get a look at the old man! You can tell the bastard crushed the life out of generations of farmers and labourers to build this little shack . . ."

Gripping the bottom of the frame, he tugged hard and it came away from the wall. He held it at arm's length, as though thinking of using it as a cloth to cover the long dining table. He slammed it against the backs of the chairs, ripping the canvas, smashing the frame, splintering the pieces on the edge of the sideboard. Gabriel was shocked.

"Why did you . . .?"

"Right," said Landrade rubbing his hands, "I'm not done here, but let's go see what they've got to eat, I'm fucking starving."

Minutes later, Gabriel watched as Landrade threw together a meal using bacon he had found in the pantry, tinned meat, onions, shallots and some white wine. It seemed clear that Landrade was better equipped for war (or at least for this war, which was unlike any other). Had Gabriel been on his own, he would simply have chewed on the smoked bacon, but Landrade set out a feast fit for a lord, with Limoges porcelain and cut-glass crystal.

"Go fetch some candles, they're probably over there . . ."

And they were. By the time Gabriel reappeared with the candles, Landrade had uncorked a vintage bottle of wine and was pouring it into a decanter ("It needs to be allowed to breathe, my friend!"). Taking a seat, he beamed up at Gabriel.

"There you go, sergent-chef, supper of the gods."

Perhaps it was the candlelight, or the stuffy atmosphere of this bourgeois mansion, perhaps it was sheer exhaustion brought on by the frantic hours they had just experienced, or perhaps it was simply the curious solidarity you feel when you have been to hell and back with someone else: it was probably all of these, but Raoul Landrade seemed like a different man. As Gabriel wolfed down the food, despite pain from his swollen lip, he gave Landrade a sideways glance. He could see nothing now of the thimblerigger, the trafficker, the brutally efficient soldier. He saw only a man spearing food with two forks and grinning like a child.

"'The order of the day is to defend our position without thought of retreat!' Landrade said, holding his glass of wine up to the light.

Gabriel did not laugh, but he allowed Landrade to pour him a glass. When he made to stand up, Landrade said "I'll get it . . ." and went in search of the coffee grinder and a filter.

"So, are you from Paris?" Landrade asked.

"I was stationed in Dole."

Raoul gave a little pout, he had never heard of the place.

"It's in Franche-Comté."

"Ah . . ."

Another name that meant nothing to him.

"What about you?"

"Me? Oh, I've knocked about a bit . . ."

He winked, and his expression was one Gabriel had seen back at the Mayenberg when Raoul would swagger back to the truck after beating up a butcher or a café owner, muttering, "Well, we showed him . . ."

It was getting late. Landrade burped loudly. Gabriel got up to clear the table.

"Don't bother," said Landrade.

He threw all the Limoges porcelain into the huge earthenware sink. The glasses and the plates crashed and tinkled. Gabriel made as if to stop him, but it was too late.

"Now we've had something to eat, let's go exploring," said Landrade. "Come on, come on."

Upstairs, a long corridor led to five or six bedrooms and a bathroom. Landrade pushed open each door.

"This is obviously the bedroom of the lord and lady," he said bitterly. He stepped inside and, though apparently calm, he looked as if at any moment he might smash everything in sight. He came back out to the corridor.

"Hey, look at this!"

Gabriel followed Landrade into what was clearly a young girl's bedroom. The walls were pink, there was a four-poster, a table, a chair, a bookcase filled with romance novels, a few soppy paintings.

Landrade opened the drawers of the painted dresser and took out various items of underwear, running them through his fingers. He held a brassiere at arm's length and studied it.

"This is the size I prefer . . ."

Gabriel, meanwhile, had wandered down the corridor, and, finding a guest room, collapsed on the bed without bothering to undress. In an instant, he was engulfed by sleep.

Though not for long.

"Get up and get in here," Landrade called to him. "We won't have much time tomorrow morning."

Gabriel shook himself awake, having completely lost all sense of time and space. Unthinkingly, he followed the caporal-chef down the corridor and into what was clearly the master bedroom. There were several large armoires.

"Here, try this on," said Landrade.

Seeing Gabriel's quizzical look, he added:

"Were you really planning to wander round in your uniform? If the Jerries catch you . . . Well, I don't know what they do with prisoners of war, but I'm guessing they're more likely to shoot them than feed them . . ."

Although Landrade was clearly right, this was a difficult step for Gabriel. Granted, they had stolen a car, but they could get rid of that. To put on civilian clothes meant no longer being an honest soldier but a deserter, someone who runs and hides, tries to slip between the cracks. For his part, Landrade did not even hesitate.

"This looks good on me, doesn't it?"

He was wearing a dark suit that was slightly too short in the sleeves, but it would pass muster.

Gabriel took out a pair of linen trousers, a checked shirt and a jumper and tried them on. When he looked in the mirror, he barely recognised himself. Landrade had already disappeared.

Gabriel found him standing in the doorway of the master bedroom pissing on the bed.

## 18

Doctor Thirion's house in Neuilly was one of those soaring square buildings set on a quiet street that are the one symbol of wealth that, since the nineteenth century, the bourgeois have been happy to flaunt. As she walked past the first time, Louise noted the stately front steps, the opulent curtains in the windows, the trees that towered over the roof – the garden was clearly behind the house. She pictured a greenhouse filled with orchids, a pond with a fountain, venerable statues, that sort of thing . . .

She walked as far as the crossroads, then retraced her steps. The neighbourhood was not busy enough that her presence would go unnoticed, a woman prowling the streets here would quickly attract attention, so she paused in front of the wrought-iron gates. A handle dangled from the long chain; Louise pulled it, setting off a shrill tinkling like the school bell announcing breaktime.

"Stillborn," Monsieur Jules had told her.

Louise had been speechless. The revelation had left her dumbstruck.

Monsieur Jules sat down and stroked his chin. Secrets are like pearls on a necklace, when the thread breaks, everything comes loose.

"I remember saying to her: 'Listen, Jeanne, you'd have to bring up this child on your own! Can you imagine the kind of life you'd have? Not to mention the child?' She agreed, but what can you do, she was only nineteen, she was confused, her mother was frantic, 'what will the neighbours say?' But Jeanne refused to get rid of it."

Overcome by painful memories, Monsieur Jules' voice dropped to a whisper.

"They packed her off to her aunt Celeste, her mother's sister."

Louise vaguely remembered the small, thin, nervous woman who only ever took off her overalls to go to mass, and the cramped little house in a working-class district of Pré-Saint-Gervais. Aunt Celeste had died shortly after the Great War, unmarried and childless, an example of those self-contained lives that leave no mark on anyone's memory.

"When was this?"

"It would have been the spring of 1907."

The parlourmaid came down the front steps and approached the gate.

Had Jeanne Belmont once worn the same black dress, the same white apron, the same black court shoes – a maid's uniform that looked like something from an operetta? Had she, too, eyed strangers with the same suspicion?

"Can I ask what this concerns?"

Did her mother have that same steely, condescending voice?

"I would like to see Madame Thirion."

"And you are . . .?"

Louise gave her name.

"I will ask the mistress . . ."

Had Jeanne also walked away with the same slow, unflappable gait, had she been the kind of servant who identifies with her masters?

Louise waited by the gates like a tradeswoman, under the blazing sun. Sweat trickled from beneath her hat.

"Madame is not available."

The servant took no pleasure in delivering this message, but nonetheless imbued it with a categorical firmness: she had orders.

"When can I return?"

"We cannot say."

This impersonal "we" accentuated a social hierarchy that began here before moving up through the great and the good, and eventually to God or to class war heaven, according to how one viewed the world.

Louise beat a retreat and set off back down the boulevard, thankful to have learned nothing more about the story. She was relieved. She would never know anything other than what she had been told by Monsieur Jules and the hotel manager; that was tragic enough.

The buses were running only erratically, but it was a long walk to the métro, so Louise waited at the bus stop.

Amid the dense traffic, Louise noticed the cars piled high with trunks and suitcases, it seemed as though half the city was fleeing. Others came and waited for the bus, grew bored and left. Louise stood, her coat over her arm, thinking about her mother's time as a housemaid. It must have been strange to wait on the family of a man who was her lover. Had the doctor suggested it? She pictured her mother, at nineteen, discovering that she was pregnant. And, having lost a child herself, how had she managed to survive the period when her daughter was crazed out of her wits because she could not have a baby? Louise tried to remember whether her mother had offered any words of consolation, but memories had begun to dim, even the image of her mother's face was fading. The woman she had known all her life seemed very different to the woman she was now discovering.

Eventually, when no bus came, it was Louise's turn to give up.

She decided she would walk, but instantly stopped when she saw Madame Thirion leaving her house.

The two women were startled to find themselves face to face.

Madame Thirion was the first to react. She tilted her head back and walked briskly past the bus stop, but it was too late, the accidental meeting had already happened. Without thinking, Louise followed some distance behind. They walked for some time, each keeping a wary eye on the other. Then, unable to bear it any longer, Madame Thirion turned around.

"Was my husband's suicide not enough for you?"

Instantly realising that this was a foolish reaction, she set off walking again, but her heart was no longer in it. She was angry with herself, it was obvious from her gait, she looked slumped and defeated.

Louise carried on following the woman, without knowing why she was doing this, or what would happen. Would Madame Thirion cause a scene? Out here, in the street, a stone's throw from her home?

"What exactly do you want?" said Madame Thirion, turning to face her again.

It was a pertinent question. Louise did not have an answer. When the young woman did not reply, Madame Thirion carried on walking only to stop once more. She could not carry on with this game any longer, such a preposterous situation was beneath her dignity. But nor was she prepared to talk here, in the street, like a fishwife . . .

"Come with me," she said commandingly.

They went into a tearoom a short distance away. Staid and stern, Madame Thirion had decided she would speak to Louise, but she wanted to make it clear that this would be a brief meeting.

"Tea, please. With just a splash of milk."

She used the same tone she did with her maid. Louise gazed at the woman's angular face, the high cheekbones, the piercing eyes, searching her memory for the sobbing woman she had encountered in Judge Le Poittevin's chambers. There was no trace of her now.

"I'll have the same, please," said Louise.

"Very well," said Madame Thirion. "Perhaps this is for the best. As it happens, I too have some questions that I would like to ask."

Without waiting to be interrogated, Louise recounted the whole story, simply and calmly, as though relating a news story that had nothing to do with her. She described the hotel, the room, but what floated to the surface was the image of Jeanne Belmont, a young girl of seventeen who, like her, had visited the same hotel, who had had an affair with this same man almost thirty years earlier.

Madame Thirion poured herself some tea without pouring a cup for Louise. The line separating their respective domains ran down the middle of the table.

"My husband was over forty when he first met Jeanne."

She, too, launched into her story without having to be asked.

"How can one even bring oneself to admit to such a thing?"

With her hands folded in her lap, her eyes fixed on the rim of her cup, this was no longer the tearful widow from the judge's chambers, nor the pompous patrician lady who had agreed to this conversation, but a woman wounded by what her husband had done.

"I did not approve of the relationship, but I understood it. Our marriage had long since disintegrated, we never truly loved each other, so, if I am honest, it was no surprise when he . . ."

She shrugged fatalistically.

"The situation was preferable to the ignominy of watching my husband sleeping with my friends. But I quickly realised that this was not simply one of the sordid affairs to which I had grown accustomed. But . . . being witness to a grand passion was more painful. More humiliating. I was always afraid I would surprise them in flagrante and I had no desire for my daughter to become aware of what was happening. I dismissed Jeanne, and they began to meet at a hotel, God knows where, I neither knew nor cared to find out."

She glanced around for the waitress, took her handbag from her lap.

"My husband had aged a lot recently – it happened almost overnight. One day, he was a retired doctor with a passion for history, literature, botany, and the next, he was an old man, his walk slowed to a shuffle, he took little care of himself, he was forgetful, he began to repeat himself. He never said anything, but I know he was aware of his decline. He wanted to end his life, he wanted to keep his dignity to the end. He was determined not to be seen as a ruin of his former self, so he chose to die. Never for a moment did I think he would do it in such a fashion . . . I can only imagine how distressing it was for you . . . . That is why I refused to file a complaint."

She was still looking towards the counter, trying to summon the waitress.

"I feel sure that he had no wish to hurt you."

It was surprising to hear this woman excuse this man she had never loved, this man who had been unfaithful to her, this man whose actions had forced upon her the ignominy of appearing in a judge's chambers.

The waitress arrived with the bill, Madame Thirion took out her purse. With three words, Louise stopped her.

"And the baby?"

Madame Thirion's hand hovered, suspended. She thought she had revealed all she needed to; but it was not enough.

"Here," she said, dismissing the waitress. She squeezed her eyes shut, marshalling her courage, then she opened them again and bowed her head.

"It came as a shock to my husband – despite the fact that he was a doctor. And Jeanne refused to . . . well, she insisted that she wanted to keep the child. For me, it was the last straw. I told my husband that he had to choose between her and me."

Louise could sense the ruthless determination that the doctor had faced in his wife.

Throughout their conversation, she had used the name "Jeanne", as though the young woman she was speaking to were not Jeanne's daughter, but merely a neighbour, an acquaintance.

"She had little choice. She was not yet twenty, she had no stable employment. She clung to the idea of this child to try and coerce my husband . . ."

Madame Thirion's eyes were steely now.

"And she moved heaven and earth to persuade him, let me tell you! But she did not succeed."

Feeling something of the fortitude and the obstinacy she had shown at that time, Madame Thirion shook her head. A silence ensued.

So many things were at stake in that fleeting moment.

What would have happened if, rather than remaining utterly calm and impassive, Louise had asked how this child had died? Madame Thirion would doubtless have invented something, and Louise would have believed her. As the wife of a city doctor, she would have known many women who had had a stillbirth she might use to add verisimilitude to her story? Madame Thirion had only to reel off a few platitudes, only too relieved for the interview to be at an end.

But Louise's stolidity won out.

She allowed the oppressive silence to drag on and, finally, Madame Thirion relented.

"The child was given up at birth. My husband took care of the matter. I insisted that he sell his surgery and we moved here, I never heard from Jeanne again and never attempted to contact her."

"Given up . . ."

"To an orphanage, yes."

"A girl, a boy?"

"A boy, I believe."

She got to her feet.

"I have no doubt that what you suffered was painful, but you did what you did for money. I never asked for anything, I simply tried to protect my family. You have compelled me to relive events that were terribly painful. I hope never to see you again."

Without waiting for the answer, she left the tearoom.

Louise lingered for a while; she had not even touched her tea. The child her mother had born to the doctor was out there, somewhere.

## 19

"French confidence is at an all-time high . . ."

It seemed only fair. After all, given Désiré Migault's success at turning even the most trifling detail into a powerful message of optimism, it was not inappropriate that he be rewarded with some genuinely good news. He could have strutted and boasted, but that was not his style. Besides, words were enough.

With a nervous forefinger, he pushed his spectacles up the bridge of his nose.

". . . now that Maréchal Pétain has been appointed to the government as Minister of State, Vice-President of the Council, it is the turn of Général Weygand to be appointed Chief of the Defence Staff and Commander-in-Chief of all theatres of war. The victor of Verdun and the protégé of Général Foch are now at the helm. France can breathe easily again: the Olympian calm and the strength of character of Maréchal Pétain has been comple-mented by the sound judgment and the innate authority of Général Weygand. Surely no-one now doubts that the very man who dictated the conditions of surrender to the Germans in 1918 will re-enact that same role within a very few weeks."

Looming at the back of the hall like the statue of the Commen-datore, Monsieur de Varambon watched Désiré's twice-daily performances, straining to unravel the mystery of this young man who had appeared out of nowhere and about whom it was almost impossible to discover any details.

After listing the details of French positions at various points on the front where the German advance had been "contained", the assembled company were afforded a second opportunity to admire the virtuosity of Désiré Migault when a journalist had the temerity to question him, not about the appointment of Général Weygand, but about the ousting of his predecessor, Général Gamelin, whose name had not been mentioned.

"The shining torch of victory is being passed from one hand to another, Monsieur, that is all. Général Gamelin forged the French forces into an impenetrable shield against the German advance, Général Weygand will now forge ahead step by step, inch by inch, until the enemy is cornered and definitively crushed. These two men, heroes both, share the same resolve, and each has the three essential qualities of a military leader: the ability to command, to strategise and to organise. 'Any troops who cannot advance must stand firm and be slaughtered, rather than surrender even a sod of the native soil entrusted to their care.' This order, first announced by Général Gamelin, will be further galvanised by his successor. France will teach Germany how miracles are made."

Like all those in attendance, Monsieur de Varambon felt a surge of admiration, but in him, admiration for others invariably curdled into bitterness. He had begun by bearding the assistant director in his office, bombarding him with questions about his young protégé, but, as the military situation deteriorated, the need for reassuring words when bad news thundered like a cloudburst made Désiré indispensable and, therefore, unassailable.

Unfortunately, the sunny spell ushered in by the appointments of Maréchal Pétain and Général Weygand was short-lived. While there could be no doubt that French soldiers were giving their all to defend every scrap of ground, it did not go unnoticed that the Nazi advance was continuing, and that their pincer movement was likely to win the day.

The Germans had launched an initial offensive in Belgium, then, when the French forces rushed to stem their advance, had seized the opportunity to launch a second offensive through the Ardennes and, in a pincer movement that would go down in the annals of military history, seemed about to drive the French and Allied Forces back to the Channel near Dunkirk.

With news like this, good luck trying to maintain French morale . . .

No matter how much they repeated that "Allied troops are valiantly holding out", it was clear to everyone who watched as the Nazis took Amiens and then Arras, that the situation was far from encouraging. It took all of Désiré Migault's considerable talents to give even a semblance of lustre to what was shaping up to be a historic rout. And to this end, he used *Monsieur Dupont's Diary* on Radio-Paris.

"Good evening, listeners. A Madame V., from Bordeaux, asks 'Why have French forces found it more difficult than anticipated to repel the attempted German invasion?' – *musical phrase* – The root cause of all our difficulties has been the fifth column, by which I mean the presence of undercover agents in this country whose mission is to sabotage the actions of the French forces. Did you know that Germany recently parachuted some fifty young women into northern France (because their presence is more likely to go unremarked upon)? These young women are tasked with sending signs to Nazi troops using mirrors, much as the American Indians used smoke signals, to reveal French military positions? They have since been arrested, but the damage has been done. We have seen evidence that traitorous farmers arrange their cows in fields to point the way to German troops. Imagine the surprise of French officers who discovered dogs had been trained by traitors to bark in Morse code! Only a week ago, French forces shot down a German plane that was about to scatter millions of locust eggs on our crops! But this fifth column also includes the communists who have infiltrated the Postal Service, disrupting the delivery of mail in an attempt to demoralise the people of France. There have been countless attempts at sabotage in our factories. The fifth column: there you have your answer, Madame V., they are the key enemy of France."

It was impossible to know whether this radio segment was effective in restoring French morale, but it was generally agreed that at least something was being done, and everyone was grateful to Désiré for his patriotic efforts.

Monsieur de Varambon spent his days scrutinising every jot and tittle of the only document he had concerning Désiré, the brief curriculum vitae that the young man had submitted to the assistant director when he had first arrived at the Hôtel Continental.

"Look! It says here: '1933, studied at the Lycée de Fleurine (Oise).' Don't you find it suspicious that this young man studied at a French high school whose archives were destroyed by fire in 1937?"

"Are you suggesting that he set the fire?"

"Of course not! But don't you see, it makes it impossible to verify his claims?"

"The fact that they cannot be verified does not mean that they are false."

"And here: 'private secretary to Monsieur d'Orsan's of the Academy of Sciences', D'Orsan died last year, his only surviving family are in the United States, we have no access to his papers . . .!"

The assistant director did not consider this evidence – consisting chiefly of missing information – very convincing.

"What exactly have you got against Désiré?"

So electrified was De Varambon by the rush of adrenaline brought by each new obstacle that, like many obsessives, he had rather lost sight of the reasons for his research.

"We'll find something . . ." he said, picking up his voluminous folder of unverifiable details and leaving, determined that he would very soon return to the fray.

Although the assistant director found Monsieur de Varambon infuriating, even he now felt a niggling doubt, one he wanted elucidated. So, he summoned Désiré Migault to his office.

"Tell me, Désiré, what was he like, this Monsieur d'Orsan for whom you worked as a private secretary?"

"A most genial man, though, sadly, very ill," said Désiré. "I was only in his service for four months."

"And . . . what exactly was your role?"

"I was responsible for organising all available documentation on a matter of quantum mechanics. The problems of precisely measuring non-commuting observables."

"So . . . so, you're also a mathematician?"

The assistant director was flabbergasted. Behind his thick glasses, Désiré blinked nervously.

"No, not really, but it was quite an entertaining task, Heisenberg's uncertainty principle states that . . ."

"Excellent, excellent, that's all very interesting, but perhaps now is not the time."

Désiré nodded – at your service – and proffered a sheet of paper on which he had written his next communiqué: "HUGE GERMAN LOSSES IN FLANDERS, STALWART ACTIONS

The young man was well aware that, however thorough his preparations, his academic and professional qualifications would not survive scrutiny indefinitely and that Monsieur de Varambon's doggedness would eventually bear fruit. But he was not worried. He was gambling on the fact that he could remain in this post until the total collapse of the French army, which was imminent.

Day by day the Nazis continued their advance, while the heroic resistance of French and Allied soldiers was limited by the strategic position of the opposing camps. Sooner or later, they would find themselves facing the Germans with their backs to the sea. There would be a massacre or a rout, perhaps both, after which there would be nothing to prevent the occupation of the whole country: Hitler might be in Paris within days. Désiré would be done with this war. In the meantime, he had work to do.

"Good evening, listeners. A Monsieur R., from Grenoble, writes to ask what we know 'about the current thinking of the leaders of the Nazi Reich' – *musical phrase* – If Radio-Stuttgart is to be believed, Hitler is overjoyed. However, our espionage and counter-espionage services have provided us with information that is rather more embarrassing to the Reich. First and foremost, Hitler is gravely ill. He is suffering from syphilis, which is hardly surprising. Though he has done all in his power to hide the fact, Hitler is homosexual, in fact he has surrounded himself with strapping young men to satisfy his fantasies, though no-one has ever heard from them. In addition, he has one testicle and has been driven insane by his chronic impotency. He spends his days climbing the walls or lying prostrate for hours. When we consider his senior staff, the situation is little better. The disgraced Ribbentrop has fled, taking with him the Nazi treasure. Goebbels will shortly be court-martialled for treason. For want of lucid, sane leaders, German troops are condemned to do the only thing that requires no thought: to blindly advance. This is something that our military leaders have long since understood, they have decided to allow the Nazis to exhaust themselves in this head-long rush and will crush them when they are at their weakest, a moment which will come all too soon."

## 20

Although the roar of battle had moved closer during the night, Gabriel slept like a log. There was only cold water, but on waking he was relieved to be able to bathe amid the opulent granite and porcelain of the owners' bathroom. Then he dressed and went downstairs to discover that Landrade had tried to loot the house.

"Hardly worth the effort, the bastards took everything worth anything when they ran off . . ."

Gabriel felt renewed discomfort when he saw them in a mirror: one in linen trousers, the other an ill-fitting suit.

"Now we really are deserters . . ."

"We're soldiers in plain clothes, sergent-chef," said Landrade, nodding to a cardboard suitcase.

"Our uniforms are in there. As soon as we find a French unit with a half-competent leader prepared to fight, we put them on, we go and kick some Jerry arse. In the meantime . . ."

He walked out of the house, climbed into the car and warmed the engine. What else was there to do?

Gabriel tried to reassure himself that at least they were heading for Paris. Landrade could do whatever the hell he liked, but Gabriel planned to report to the high command.

He studied the map. They did not know their precise position, and had no idea what was happening elsewhere; all they could see was that crimson glow of artillery fire some thirty, perhaps forty kilometres away. They could hear the shriek of the bombers, but it was impossible to tell whether they were German or Allied planes.

As they pulled out of the grounds, they were met by refugees, many more than there had been the previous day, travelling by all possible means and tracing a south-westerly line which Landrade and Gabriel joined. Was the thunderous fighting the sign of a powerful German offensive? How far had they advanced? Were they simply heading into the lion's den? It made sense to follow the refugees, but travelling blindly made Gabriel increasingly nervous.

"Let's get some gen," said Raoul, pumping the brakes.

Gabriel immediately understood why he was stopping now rather than earlier. It was because two women were cycling past.

As soon as they stopped, he saw the disappointment on Landrade's face: the women were not particularly pretty. They had come from Vouziers and were heading for Reims. Such information as they could offer was as bad as it was confusing. The Germans, having "wreaked havoc in Sedan", were heading towards Laon, or Saint-Quentin, or maybe Noyon, they didn't really know. The Nazis were destroying everything in their path, they had "slaughtered whole villages, including women and children", they had numerous planes and "thousands of tanks", paratroopers, hundreds of them, had been spotted over Rethel . . . Being local, the two women were able to pinpoint their location on the map: they were just outside Monenville.

"Right," said Landrade, "let's move it."

Half an hour later, he was fretting: he was not worried about what they had been told, he was worried about petrol.

"We're not going to get very far – it's insane the amount of fuel this monster guzzles. There's a chance we could break down on the side of the road before we find something to eat. I'm bloody ravenous, could eat a horse."

He was driving more slowly now. According to the map, the main road to Paris was about ten kilometres away. If they were going to break down, better to do so on a busy motorway than in the middle of nowhere.

The needle had just hit EMPTY when Landrade braked and rolled to a stop.

"Is it a camel?" he said, bewildered.

"I think it's a dromedary," said Gabriel.

Just ahead, the hulking animal mournfully ambled across the road, slowly ruminating, not troubling even to turn its head. They watched as it stepped over the ditch and disappeared like a mirage, then they turned and looked at each other. Tall hedgerows masked the field to their left. Landrade turned off the engine and they both got out.

Behind the hedge, on an expanse of barren land, there were three abandoned trailers, one with its gate open. This was obviously where the camel had come from. The side of the second trailer was plastered with posters of a hilarious clown with a shock of yellow hair and red lips. Landrade was as excited as a little boy.

"I love the circus, don't you?"

Without waiting for the answer, he climbed the four steps of the first trailer, turned the handle and opened the door.

"There might be something to eat."

Gabriel followed behind, anxious and wary. There was a strong smell. A musky smell he did not recognise. Inside, four cots chained to partition walls were piled high with suitcases, bags, crockery – clearly anything and everything had been hurriedly thrown together in their haste to flee. Unless this was the product of looting. The doors to the wardrobes and the cupboards stood open. There were clothes strewn everywhere. It felt less like a circus trailer than a hobo's hideout. There was nothing in the dresser drawers – everything had been ransacked. They were just about to leave when they noticed a slight movement to their left. Landrade reached out, ripped away the chequered blanket and burst out laughing.

"A dwarf! I've never seen one up close!"

A short man with a big head and narrow shoulders lay, curled into a ball, his mouth open, his eyes filled with tears, he waved his arm in a pitiful attempt to defend himself. Landrade laughed harder.

"Leave him be . . ." said Gabriel, tugging at Landrade's sleeve.

But it was futile, Landrade was spellbound.

"How old do you think he is?"

He turned to Gabriel, grinning.

"It's hard to tell with dwarves, isn't it?"

He grabbed the man under both armpits to lift him up.

"It must be hilarious seeing him run . . ."

Gabriel gripped Landrade's arm tighter. Paralysed with fear, the short man kept one arm clutched against his body, he was clearly hiding something. Landrade grabbed him roughly.

"Damn it!" he said with a laugh, "he's a strong little fucker."

Still Gabriel tried to pull him away. "Leave him, just leave him", but it was useless. Landrade had almost succeeded in dragging him from his hideout when suddenly, he let go.

"Did you see that?"

It was a tiny monkey, quivering like a leaf and clearly terrified. It was a small, warm bundle with soft fur, large ears and wide eyes that blinked at top speed. Landrade could not believe his eyes. Amazed, he cradled the creature and stared at its tiny paws.

"He seems very thin. But maybe that's normal, there are some dogs where, even if they're well fed, you can feel their ribs."

Landrade emerged from the trailer, the monkey clung to his chest to shelter from the blazing sun, gripping hard when the light blinded him. Raoul tucked the animal under his shirt, and it stopped struggling.

Gabriel stood, helpless, unsure what they should do. He turned back to the dwarf, who was still cowering, his hands shielding his face.

"I'll just . . . You need . . ." he did not finish the sentences.

Haggard and disoriented, Gabriel raced out of the trailer. Landrade had disappeared.

He heard himself anxiously shouting "Raoul!"

He walked back to the car, but there was no-one, he glanced around. He couldn't leave on his own. He had never learned to drive a car, he would be stranded here. Besides, they had run out of petrol. Fear clawed at his throat.

"Hey, sergent-chef!" Landrade called, delirious with joy.

He was riding a circus bike, a tandem with little more than handlebars and pedals. He backpedalled, suddenly causing the machine to brake hard and fall onto its side. Landrade lay there, laughing like a drain.

"Shit, try it, it's not as easy as it looks."

Gabriel shook his head, no way.

"Trust me, it's the only way. The car is going to break down within ten kilometres, what do you suggest we do then, walk?"

It was sweltering. In the car, with all the windows open, Gabriel had not realised, but out here on this patch of waste ground, he could feel the sun beating down. It was good weather for monkeys, not so much for them . . . Landrade picked up the bike, the monkey merely a lump under his shirt.

"Would you rather walk all the way in the blazing sun?"

"What about our uniforms?"

The little monkey popped a frightened head out as though it had an answer.

"He's funny, isn't he?"

"We have to give him back," said Gabriel, nodding to the trailer, but Landrade was already back on the bike.

"So, what's your plan?"

Gabriel looked around him, shrugged and climbed onto the tandem. Landrade had left him the front seat. The handlebars were small, it was difficult to pedal. Landrade giggled as though they were on a merry-go-round. The tandem wobbled, but somehow managed to pick up speed and some semblance of balance. They cycled past the car, reached the main road and, from here the ride was a little faster, a little straighter.

Landrade started whistling, he was on holiday.

"'May the thought of our native land inspire us to unwavering resolution!'" he roared.

Gabriel did not dare turn around, but he felt sure that Landrade was not doing any pedalling. Then, suddenly, for no apparent reason, the monkey took fright.

"Ow!" yelled Landrade, shaking the tandem. "The little fucker bit me!"

He grabbed the monkey by the head and threw it into the air. Gabriel saw the little creature land in the ditch. He stopped the tandem and laid it on its side. Landrade was sucking on his injured hand.

"Fucking monkey!"

Gabriel ran over to the ditch. He stepped warily, afraid he might crush the animal, but the verge was overgrown with tall grass and the brambles made going difficult. Nothing moved,

Gabriel took another step, then realised that it was pointless. He turned back, Landrade was already pushing the tandem down the road and almost out of sight. Gabriel gazed forlornly at the ditch, keenly aware that he was about to cry, an urge made all the worse because he would be crying over a little monkey that weighed less than a pack of cigarettes. He ran back to Landrade, who was standing in the middle of the road that led to the motorway.

It was as though the curtain had suddenly been raised on a very different show. They stood, rooted to the spot by the spectacle.

Hundreds of people, young and old, men, women and children all trudging in the same direction, a never-ending procession of anxious, distraught and frightened faces. Without thinking, Gabriel gripped the handlebars and they wheeled the bicycle into the fleeing torrent.

"Jesus Christ!" said Landrade, craning his neck, as though this was a crowd at a sporting event.

By chance, they had joined the throng next to a horse-drawn cart led by a whole family, including a young girl with short dark hair and a gaunt face.

"Where did you come from?" Landrade asked her with a smile.

Her disgruntled mother snapped:

"Don't talk to him, get over here!"

Landrade held up his hands – have it your way – his good humour was unaffected.

They carried on and passed a military ambulance that had broken down in the ditch and two lone infantrymen sitting on bollards catching their breath, looking hopeless.

It was a raging torrent of automobiles, horse-drawn carriages and dogcarts, here demented old men, over there a cripple on crutches who moved faster than everyone else, and there was a whole classroom, though since the children were of all ages, it might have been an entire school, and behind them, their teacher or perhaps their headmaster shouting at them to hold on to each other, not to let go, his quavering falsetto making it impossible to tell who was terrified, his pupils or he; there were cyclists with suitcases strapped to the frames of their bikes, women clutching one baby and sometimes two, and as the torrent flowed, the successive waves of people jostled, hurled insults at each other, sometimes reached out to help each other, but only briefly because it was every man for himself, and so the jostling began again. A man who had stopped to lend a hand to a farmer whose cart had tipped over, suddenly leaped to his feet screaming "Odette! Odette!", turning this way and that, his tremulous voice betraying his despair.

What struck Gabriel most was the almost palpable feeling of lassitude that radiated from the various groups that made up the crowd. The presence of a handful of haggard soldiers, their weapons missing, their uniforms dishevelled, dragging their feet, gave the scene an air of catastrophe and surrender. The flood of terrified citizens forced to flee by the German advance was gradually being swelled by their own routed army.

Suddenly, the stream encountered a four-way junction, a bottle-neck in which successive waves surged and swarmed like a drowsy mass of insects. The atmosphere of a cattle market was heightened by the lowing oxen. People moved blindly, oblivious to everyone else: there was no officer to command them, no gendarme to protect them. One short, fat corporal was wildly waving his arms, but it was futile since his orders were drowned out by the roar of engines and the mooing of cattle drawing carts piled high with mattresses, furniture and small children. In this milling crowd, Gabriel had no idea which way to turn. Suddenly, a Citroën flanked by a honking motorcyclist cut a path through the crowd, forcing people to stand aside. Behind the rolled-up window, Gabriel caught a glimpse of a senior officer's uniform and stripes.

When the procession of refugees finally made it past the junction, they opened out like an accordion that stretched over the horizon.

Landrade, as happy as a man at a funfair, chatted easily to people as they pushed the tandem through the crowds. All were fleeing the German columns now making inroads into central France, spreading panic, razing villages, and, they said, slaughtering the local populace. Landrade asked people for food, picking up a piece of fruit or a piece of bread here and there, but it was not enough. He and Gabriel were tired and thirsty, but there was little water to be found. The groups they encountered barely had enough for themselves and, in the sweltering heat, were reluctant to share. No villages dotted this bleak stretch of road.

"Let's try our luck that way," said Landrade, nodding to a signpost that read: Anancourt.

Gabriel was uncertain.

"Come on, come on," Landrade insisted.

They mounted the tandem again, zigzagged through the crowd onto open road, then reached cruising speed.

The only passing traffic was a military vehicle with seven or eight soldiers in the back.

It took twenty minutes to reach Anancourt, a village of low houses, many of them boarded up by owners who had fled. Landrade and Gabriel wandered through this apocalyptic scene like the sole survivors of some disaster.

"Oh, don't you admire the bravery of the French!" sneered Raoul.

Gabriel was shocked at the insult.

"Well, we're fleeing too . . ."

Landrade stopped dead in the middle of the empty street.

"No, we're not! And do you know why, my friend? Because civilians flee, but soldiers simply retreat, there's a big difference."

They ambled down the middle of the street. Here and there, a curtain twitched as they passed. A woman scurried past, hugging the walls like a mouse, rushed into a house and slammed the door. A man appeared on a bicycle only to vanish almost immediately. In the distance, the river of refugees continued to flow, and here, too, most of the inhabitants had fled.

The outskirts of the village loomed barely hundred metres away, as though the trunk road intersected Anancourt only by mistake and was in a hurry to leave. Letting themselves be guided by a church steeple, they turned left, then right, and found themselves in a village square almost entirely taken up by the churchyard itself. Facing it were a bakery and patisserie, which had suffered no damage, but the shutters of the café-tabac had been forced and partially rolled up.

"No, don't . . ." said Gabriel, but Landrade had already stopped and crawled through the opening.

With a sigh, Gabriel went over and sat on the church steps. His heart was heavy. The sun was pleasant, and he dozed.

He was woken by a tremor. How long had he been asleep? A heavy vehicle seemed to be approaching. On the far side of the square, the steel shutters were half-raised. The rumble of the engine drew closer. Gabriel got to his feet and ran, bent double, slipping into the dark shop. The counter was strewn with crates and cardboard boxes that had been gutted. There was a heady smell of wine.

Gabriel whipped around. The truck was clearly driving into the square. He groped his way forward, trembling like a leaf.

"Ah. So, there you are!" Landrade said hoarsely.

He was sprawling, drunk, by the open cellar door, his lips stained red, his eyes wide, his pockets bulging with packs of cigarettes and cigars.

Gabriel bent over him, *get up, we can't stay here*, but by now the truck had stopped – could it be the owner?

From their left they sensed a movement, heard a metallic crash like falling scaffolding.

With a piercing shriek, the shutters were forced up and three French soldiers rushed in, pushed past Gabriel, dragged Landrade to his feet and slammed both men against the wall, gripping them by the throat.

"Looters! So this is what you do while real men are out fighting! Fucking cowards!"

"Wait . . ." stammered Gabriel.

He felt a heavy blow to his temple and, for several minutes, he was all but blind.

"Bring the scum out here . . ." barked an officer. The soldiers did not have to be told twice: they hurled the two men through the doorway and onto the pavement where they were met by savage kicks. They were forcibly hoisted to their feet. Landrade staggered and stumbled while Gabriel tried to shield his face with his arms.

They were dragged along the pavement and beaten with rifle butts as they scrambled into the bed of the truck. The three soldiers stood with rifles cocked while the others laid into them with steel-capped boots.

"That's enough, boys," growled the officer, though he sounded unconvinced. "Come on, let's get moving."

As the truck pulled away, the soldiers clung to the slatted sides as they carried on kicking the two men, now curled into the foetal position, hands clasped at the back of their necks.

## 21

Louise was surprised by how quickly she adjusted to the notion that her mother had had a child out of wedlock. Stories of pregnant girls and clandestine abortions were commonplace. Such secrets often came to light in the best families after a death or an inheritance, and Louise did not see why the Belmonts should have been spared. What upset her, however, was that the child had been abandoned. The terrible sadness she felt was linked to her own thwarted desire to have a child. She was troubled by the idea that her mother could have done such a thing, but over time, she came to realise that it was not the face of her mother that haunted her dreams, but that of Madame Thirion. Three days after their meeting, the woman's steely, autocratic glare flickered into her mind.

"Really?" said Monsieur Jules when she told him the news. "The baby was abandoned?"

Only then did Louise realise the truth, because unlike Madame Thirion, Monsieur Jules was utterly sincere. The doctor's widow had told her the child had been abandoned, but Louise was convinced that this was not the whole story.

She visited the town hall registry office.

The whole city was in turmoil. By early afternoon, most shopkeepers were huddled behind their steel shutters as though expecting a violent demonstration. People scurried past carrying gas mask cases. A paperboy was shouting: "Devastating German attacks in northern France!" A greengrocer was loading suitcases into his van.

At this hour, the town hall should have been open, but it was closed.

Louise wandered into a café where she consulted a telephone directory, then re-emerged and headed for the nearest métro station. It was 3.00 p.m., every métro carriage was packed to capacity. Suddenly, the train jolted to a halt in the middle of a tunnel; women screamed, while men muttered things they hoped were reassuring. The electricity was restored, and fluorescent light illuminated pale, tense faces that stared at the flickering bulbs. A low murmur spread through the carriage, everyone was whispering as though they were in a church. It felt as though the oppressive heat of that Paris summer had flooded the train, and everyone struggled vainly to find a little space. "My step-sister doesn't want to leave just now because her son is sitting his bacca-laureate", one woman confided to another, who replied: "My husband promised we'd leave this weekend, but it's Thursday already . . ." When, finally, the train jolted into life, it brought no sense of calm. The train simply conveyed their fears from one station to another.

The Hospice des Enfants-Assistés, the foundling hospital that took in abandoned children, was located at 100, rue d'Enfer – "the road to Hell". The government's plans were paved with good intentions . . .

The foundling hospital was a vast, horseshoe-shaped building that framed a central courtyard. The endless rows of identical windows and the heavy doors gave the air of a gigantic boarding school. A couple of labourers were loading packing crates into a covered truck, the caretaker's office was closed, and the whole hospice exuded an eerie impression of desolation. Louise made her way through a hallway whose lofty ceiling rivalled those of a cathedral. She heard the dreary echo of footsteps in the stairwells, studied signs cluttered with arrows and peremptory instructions, passed a nurse, a clutch of nuns. One directed her to the records office, located in the south wing of the building.

"I don't know if there will be anyone there just now . . ."

Seeing Louise glance up at the large clock placed on the wall, she added:

"A lot of people asked to take annual leave" – here she gave a knowing smile – "and a lot of others just left without asking."

Louise mounted the steps of a broad, echoing staircase on which she did not meet a soul. On the third floor, under the eaves, the heat was stifling despite the fact that all the windows were open. She knocked on a door and, getting no answer, pushed it open and went in. A clerk spun round, clearly startled.

"Members of the public are not allowed."

In an instant, Louise assessed the situation and did what she most loathed: she smiled ingratiatingly. The clerk was a young man in his twenties who bore the pitted scars of protracted adolescence. The sort of lanky, awkward boy who you knew – even without knowing her – looked just like his mother. Seeing Louise's smile, his cheeks flushed crimson. In his defence, in this murky office, crumbling beneath the weight of dust, paper and tedium, her radiant smile was like a shaft of light in an ocean of sorrow.

"Could you help me?" Louise simpered. "It will only take two minutes."

Without waiting for his answer, she stepped closer, smelling his sweat, laid a hand on his desk and gazed at him, her smile now tinged with a look of supplication and gratitude that would even have pierced the armour of a stronger man. The boy glanced around, looked for some way out, but found none.

"I'd like to look at the list of children abandoned in July 1907.

"Impossible. It's not allowed."

Satisfied with his answer, and to make it clear that the conversation was over, the young man began to remove his sleeve protectors.

"What do you mean, it's not allowed?"

"That's the law. No-one is allowed to consult the register, no-one. If you like, you can make a request in writing to the ministry, but they always refuse, no exceptions."

The blood drained from Louise's face. Her distress made the young clerk feel better, it felt like retribution for the confusion she had caused him. But instead of showing her the door, the clerk carried on smoothing the folded sleeves on the wooden desk with the flat of his hand, shaking his head like a wet parrot; his silently moving lips seemed to repeat: "That's the law, that's the law." Louise stretched out her hand. The cruel contrast between his grey sleeve protectors and her delicate fingers with their deliciously domed nails shattered the boy's nerves.

"Who is going to find out?" Louise murmured. "Besides, most of your colleagues have already deserted their posts."

"It's not about that. What you're asking could cost me my job."

The reasoning seemed definitive. The boy took a breath. Surely no-one would insist that he do something that might cost him his job, his career, his future, his whole life.

"Of course, I understand," Louise said and the clerk's relief gave way to delight because this young woman understood him, and now that he felt safe, he could study her more closely. Her face, her charm, that mouth, those eyes, that radiant smile . . . She was still smiling at him. He smiled back. Oh, how he longed to kiss her. Or touch her, to simply place a finger on those lips that were a world in themselves.

"The general public are not allowed," said Louise, "but not you . . . It's not against the law for you."

The mouth of the befuddled boy dropped open and the escaping sigh sounded like a groan.

"You can look at the register and just read it out to me. I mean, it's not illegal for you to talk to me, is it?"

Louise knew precisely what was going on in this boy's mind. More or less what had gone through her mind when the doctor had made his proposition, a tangle of logical objections, feelings of helplessness and an urge to transgress.

"Just the year 1907," said Louise in a confiding tone. "July 1907."

She had always known he would give in, but as she watched him walk away, his head bowed, she felt ashamed of this dishonourable victory. How far might she have gone to know what was in the register? She shuddered as she listened to the young man shuffling between the shelves. Some moments later, he reappeared with a thick register with the legend "1907" inscribed on the cover in majestic civil-service calligraphy. With the infinite slowness of a man trapped in a diving bell, he opened the register to reveal pages neatly ruled into columns. He had not said another word. He thumbed through the pages as though unsure what to do or say.

His professional reflexes were triggered when Louise asked:

"What is this column, the one marked 'reference number'?"

"You can use the reference number to look up the case file."

He beamed; he had just had an epiphany.

"And they're not stored here."

This was a victory for him.

"The Assistance Publique will have them." He pointed to a building out the window. Victory turned to pride.

Louise peered at the register.

"There were only three registered in July," said the clerk, following her gaze.

Remembering that he had agreed to read the entries aloud, he said in a faltering voice:

"July 1, Abélard, Francine."

"The child I'm looking for is a boy."

There was only one. So it had to be him. The child Louise was looking for:

"July 8, Landrade, Raoul. Reference Number 177063."

The boy closed the register.

A new world opened up before Louise. She repeated the name over and over, she had never liked the name Raoul, but now it took on a different quality. The child would be a man of thirty-three by now. What had become of him? Perhaps he was dead . . . The very thought seemed unfair. Hers had been a lonely childhood, she had missed having sisters or brothers, cousins. This boy of about her own age, this boy with whom she shared a mother had been kept hidden from her for all these years. If he were dead, she would never get to know him.

"You said the Assistance Publique will have the file?"

"The building is closed . . ."

His heart was no longer in it, he was floundering. Louise did not even need to say a word; the boy bowed.

"But I have the key . . ." he confessed, his voice barely audible. "You have to understand, the files cannot be taken out of the building."

"I completely understand, monsieur. But there is nothing that forbids you from going into the building, and no written regulation that explicitly prevents you to be accompanied . . ."

The poor young man looked disheartened.

"I'm sorry, but no unauthorised persons are allowed to . . ."

"But I'm not an 'unauthorised person'," said Louise hurriedly, laying her hand on his. "We're almost friends, aren't we, you and I?"

They moved through the warren of deserted corridors, the young clerk walking with the heavy tread of the animal heading to the slaughterhouse.

They did not need to cross the courtyard, the clerk knew these buildings like the back of his hand; Louise followed as he weaved his way through the halls, opened doors, avoided certain corridors, mounted a staircase. The key turned twice in the lock and the door swung open to reveal walls lined with drawers. The young man gestured to Louise, who confidently stepped in, found the drawer labelled LABI – LAPE and opened it. The notion that he would read aloud for her had faded. The clerk stood on the threshold, his back against the closed door, as though to shut out some imaginary crowd. Meanwhile, Louise pulled out a slim file, laid it on a desk and opened it.

It began: "Statement concerning an abandoned child entrusted to a statutorily designated institution":

This is to state that on *July 8* at *10.00 a.m.* Nineteen Hundred and Seven a person of the *male* sex came to the offices of the Assistance Publique to give up a child.
In accordance with all applicable regulations . . .

So Doctor Thirion had personally come to give up the child. On that point, at least, his widow had not lied.

1. Child's Surname and First Name:
*Landrade, Raoul.*

2. Date of birth?
*July 8, 1907.*

3. Place of his birth?
*Paris.*

4. Remarks:
*The person who came with the child claims to be a doctor but refused to give his name. He tells me that the child's birth was not registered at the town hall and that he has not been baptised. Consequently, in accordance with the law in such cases, it was I who gave him his name and surname.*

Louise glanced at the calendar of saints on the wall. July 7 was the feast day of Saint Raoul, the following day the feast of Saint Landrade: the official had expended little effort, though Louise wondered what he did on days when two children were abandoned.

According to the file: "*The child was dressed in a white knitted jacket. He has no distinguishing features and appears to be in good health.*"

Louise turned to the end of the file:

In accordance with the law of June 27, 1904, and having regard to the ministerial decree of July 15 of the same year, and to ministerial guidelines of September 30, 1904, it follows from the aforementioned detail that the child *Landrade, Raoul* fulfils all necessary conditions to be classified as an *abandoned* child(ren).

The only remaining document was titled: "Statement regarding the placement of a ward of the state with a family".

Louise felt her every muscle tense.

Rather than being given to an orphanage, young Raoul had been placed with a family on November 17, 1907.

By order of the Préfet of the Seine and having regard to articles 32 . . .

Louise turned the page:

The child Landrade, Raoul, a ward of the state, is hereby placed with Monsieur & Madame Thirion & family domiciled at 67, boulevard Auberjon, Neuilly . . .

Louise could not believe her eyes.

She reread the last paragraph once, twice, then closed the file; she felt devastated. Having abandoned the child, for Jeanne's sake, the doctor had then adopted him. And probably raised him.

Without quite knowing why, Louise began to cry. She tried to fathom the extent of the lie. She resented her mother for abandoning a child: if you are fortunate enough to have a baby, you don't abandon it at a hospice. But she also understood the terrible injustice Jeanne had suffered. Her mother had spent the rest of her life believing her child had been abandoned, when in fact he had been adopted and raised by his father.

And his father's wife.

She closed the file and walked back to the door. It broke the young clerk's heart to see her weep.

Louise stepped out into the corridor, then turned back to thank the young man. The risks he had taken on her behalf were serious. There were no words she could say to convey her gratitude. She took her handkerchief, dabbed her eyes and, standing on tiptoe, planted a little kiss on his dry lips, smiled and then walked out of his life.

Monsieur Jules dropped the dishcloth. With a speed no-one would have thought him capable of, he darted around his counter and took Louise in his arms.

"There, there," he said. "What's the matter, my little dove?"

He had called Louise "my little dove".

She held him at arm's length and gazed at him.

Overcome at the sight of that fat face, those coarse features, she dissolved into tears.

For the first time in her life, she truly empathised with her mother.

For the first time, her heart went out to her.

## 22

To many people, Désiré had long seemed to be a paradox. It was difficult to imagine that the young man who skittered nervously through the corridors of the Hôtel Continental, hugging the walls and blinking feverishly whenever someone spoke to him, was the same man who every day, in a calm, imperturbable voice, effortlessly explained what was going on to those who did not understand, and proved himself to be remarkably well informed.

But recent military developments had shifted the focus of attention of those at the Continental and Désiré Migault, though widely considered a fount of information, was no longer of any interest to anyone, except of course Monsieur de Varambon, who continued to dig for information with the tenacity of a wire-haired terrier, something that came as no surprise to anyone, though no-one paid him any heed. Monsieur de Varambon was the Cassandra of the Continental.

All eyes were focused on the north, where French and Allied troops had been forced to retreat by the advancing German troops, who were fired up by their successes in the Ardennes and by the speed at which they had cut a swathe through the French frontline, mowing down valiant French soldiers who had been catastrophically ill-prepared for this possibility. It was becoming increasingly difficult to issue dispassionate communiqués to the press. Those reporters posted to the front lines played along, vaunting the bravery of French forces, but even they could not hide the rout at

Sedan, nor the more recent defeat in Flanders, to say nothing of the current "rear-guard action" (*dixit* Désiré) in Dunkirk, where French troops were courageously protecting retreating Allies to avoid them all being hurled into the sea. For his part, Désiré fearlessly continued to reassure the press that the Allies were "fighting valiantly", "curbing the German advance" or that French troops were "standing firm in the face of the enemy". Whereas, in fact, everyone knew that more than three hundred thousand soldiers were in imminent danger of being slaughtered by the Nazis or of finding themselves at the bottom of the Channel.

Désiré had a fresh opportunity to demonstrate his poise and keen insight when, on May 28, it was revealed that King Leopold III of Belgium had given up the fight and surrendered to the Germans.

"This is a disaster!" howled the assistant director, clutching his head in his hands.

Every fibre of his being acted as a barometer for the evolving situation. A daily photograph of the assistant director could easily have replaced the morning press conference that Désiré nevertheless continued to give in his resolute, triumphant tone.

"No, no, no, it's an opportunity!" said Désiré.

The assistant director looked up.

"Until now, we had no plausible explanation to justify our retreat. Now we have one: we were betrayed by one of our allies."

The assistant director was impressed by the obviousness of this point of view. It was simple, beautiful, elegant. Irrefutable. By late afternoon, Désiré was expounding this theory to the usual audience of journalists and correspondents.

"Fearless French forces were perfectly positioned to turn the tables, to repel the German advance and force the invaders back to our eastern borders. Sadly, the shameful surrender of the

Belgians has given the beleaguered enemy a reprieve, if only for a few hours."

The press were disinclined to accept this version of events.

"Are you saying that Belgian forces were so crucial to our strategy that their surrender turned the situation around?" asked a small-town journalist from the provincial press.

Désiré blinked and gave the weary nod favoured by teachers to indicate their disappointment at being forced to repeat themselves:

"Every military campaign is a delicately balanced mechanism, Monsieur. If a single cog is broken, everything changes."

It was at such moments that even Monsieur de Varambon could not but admire the man. Meanwhile, Désiré offered a technical elucidation to reassure even the most fretful souls.

"Though it may perhaps seem paradoxical to you, gentlemen, it could be argued that it is to our advantage to allow German troops to push us back to the Channel."

Instantly, there was uproar, but Désiré quickly calmed it with a graceful wave of his hand.

"Indeed, our allies have the means to transform this pyrrhic victory into a crushing defeat. The British navy has set up a system of underwater pipes capable of pumping oil to the surface and setting it ablaze, turning the Channel into a conflagration. Should the Kriegsmarine venture into the Channel, their ships will instantly be torched and scuppered. The French navy can then bring our troops ashore where they can finish the task they began on the sea, to wit the total destruction of the German army."

"Take a look at this!" roared Monsieur de Varambon.

He drew himself up to his full height, puffing his chest out triumphantly. He proffered a document and the emaciated, almost evanescent assistant director reached out a pale hand to take it.

It was a register of names. The assistant director thumbed through it. Having not slept for nine nights in succession, he no longer asked questions, he merely waited for answers. And such was de Varambon's impatience that the answer promptly came.

"This is the list of those who graduated from the School of Asian Languages in 1937. There is no mention of your Désiré Migault. Lest there be some mistake, I also consulted the full list of graduates spanning the years 1935 to 1939: a total of fifty-four. Not a single mention of anyone named Désiré Migault."

His delight was equalled only by his pride and his stupidity. Désiré, having been summoned to his superior's office, let out a shrill unpleasant cackle reminiscent of a bird call or a creaking door; it was fortunate that he rarely had occasion to laugh.

"Burnier."

"I beg your pardon?"

Désiré reached out and, with a forefinger as implacable as justice itself, pointed to the name Burnier, a graduate in 1937.

"My mother's name is Burnier, my father's Migault. My full name is Désiré Burnier-Migault, but I find it a bit of a mouthful, don't you?"

The assistant director could breathe once more. This was the third time that Monsieur de Varambon's deranged obsession had threatened to deprive him of Désiré; he was weary.

He dismissed his protégé.

Désiré walked down the corridor with a smile. It would take Monsieur de Varambon quite some time to find a trace of the real Burnier, who had graduated with a degree in history in 1937 and died the following year. De Varambon's efforts to unmask Désiré were constantly hindered by the mounting chaos over-whelming every area of the French public services. The postal service was unreliable. The telephone service was worse. Although de Varambon had scored a palpable hit or two, none was lethal enough to jeopardise Désiré's position at the Continental.

Though he was not unduly worried, Désiré felt a tingle at the base of his spine, something he could not put into words. Perhaps it is simply the atmosphere in the Continental, he thought.

Like a bankrupted company, the hotel had emptied considerably in the first three days of June. The hubbub of its great staircases, the tumult of its vast halls, the shouts, the cries, the questions had given way to muted whispers, hushed conversations, anxious faces and bewildered looks. People stalked the corridors as though they were the gangways of an ocean liner headed for an iceberg. Even the numbers of those attending the press conferences had declined.

On June 3, 1940, the Luftwaffe had bombed the Renault and Citroën factories. The outskirts of Paris suffered a direct hit. But even aside from the two hundred fatalities, most of them factory workers, the bombing had seriously sapped morale. This was not the first time that German bombers had targeted the capital, but, in the wake of the devastating news from the Ardennes, from Flanders, Belgium, the Somme and Dunkirk, the populace felt besieged.

The targets of German attacks were no longer other people.

Like a murmuration of starlings, hundreds of thousands of Parisians headed south.

As the assistant director's staff disappeared, Désiré became all the more indispensable.

It was at this point that a curious event occurred which, after a fashion, settled the matter.

While walking to the Hôtel Continental bright and early, Désiré stopped in his tracks a hundred metres from the entrance, spellbound by what he first thought was a dance. In the centre of the circle was a pigeon. All around it, carrion crows, those birds with their iridescent black plumage sometimes mistakenly called blackbirds. Désiré quickly realised that the pigeon was their quarry: the crows were savagely pecking at the injured bird as it limped away, desperate to find refuge. The leader of the murder of crows hopped forward, viciously pecked the pigeon then gave way to the next in line. The fight was so unequal, the slaughter so brazen, that Désiré rushed in, kicking at the crows. They warily retreated, but as soon as he took a step towards the Continental, they returned. Again, Désiré chased them off, again they came back. For the pigeon, there was no escape: stunned by the blows and limping badly, its neck taut, its feathers ruffled, it hobbled in circles as though hoping the ground would open up and swallow it.

It was then that Désiré realised that it was futile to carry on this fight. It was over. The pigeon would be slaughtered, the crows had already won.

The event, though trivial, seemed unbearably poignant to Désiré. The hounded pigeon took on an inordinate significance. Désiré had neither the strength to fight, nor the courage to watch the slaughter. He felt his chest tighten, he stared straight ahead at the revolving door, then, just as he was about to turn right and go into the Hôtel Continental, he turned left. And headed for the métro.

Never to be seen again.

The assistant director was devastated by his desertion. For him, the war had just ended in a humiliating defeat.

## 23

It was easy to track her down; sometimes luck is on your side. The doctor's daughter had not changed her name, and she was listed in the telephone directory. There was only one Henriette Thirion, with an address on the avenue de Messine.

Everything happened simply: Louise walked into the building, asked the concierge which floor Mademoiselle Thirion lived on, went upstairs, rang the bell; Henriette opened the door, recognised Louise and closed her eyes. Unlike her mother, this was not a sign of irritation or impatience, but a wave of exhaustion at the prospect of some long-feared task whose time had finally come.

"Come in . . ."

The voice was listless. Although the apartment was modest, it overlooked the Parc Monceau, albeit from a distance. The living room was entirely taken up by a baby grand piano buried beneath piles of sheet music. In one corner, a pedestal table was squeezed between two armchairs upholstered in cretonne.

"Let me take your coat . . . Sit down, I'll make some tea."

Louise remained standing. She could hear the whistle of the kettle; the clink of cups placed on a tray. An eternity seemed to pass before Henriette finally reappeared, sat down in what was clearly her usual seat. Louise sat in the other armchair facing her.

"About your father . . ." she began.

"Were you truthful in your statement to the judge, Mademoiselle Belmont?"

"Of course! I . . ."

"In that case, you have no need to explain. I have read your sworn statements. If you say they are true, that is enough for me."

Henriette gave a faint smile intended to be reassuring. She was in her fifties, and clearly unconcerned about her hair, which was now predominantly grey. She had heavy features, the eyes were dull and lifeless, hands that were large, "masculine". The word struck Louise. For some reason, it made her sad.

"I went to visit your mother."

Henriette smiled awkwardly.

"Ah, the Queen Mother . . . I won't trouble to ask if the visit went well, if it had, you would not be here."

"Your mother lied to me."

Louise had not intended to be insulting and, seeing Henriette stare at her in wide-eyed astonishment, wished she could take back her words. Then she realised that this feigned surprise was intended to be humorous. Henriette grinned.

"When it comes to my mother, lying is not lying. Some tea?"

Henriette was a measured and meticulous woman. Her gestures were poised and precise; Louise felt a little afraid of her. This was clearly a common response, since Henriette permanently smiled, as though to reassure her interlocutor that appearances were deceptive, that she had nothing to fear.

"So, tell me, Mademoiselle Belmont, what do you know of this story?"

Louise recounted what she knew. Henriette listened attentively, as though to a lurid news story. When it came to the story of the clerk at the Hospice des Enfants-Assistés, she interrupted.

"So, in essence, you seduced him."

Louise blushed.

While Louise had been talking, Mademoiselle Thirion had slowly poured herself a second cup of tea, without thinking to offer one to Louise. When it came her turn to speak, she set down her cup and folded her hands on her lap; she looked for all the world as though she were waiting for the room to be filled with music so that she might doze off.

"I remember her very well, your maman. I suspect many people have told you how much you look like her. I am not sure whether I think it is a compliment; I know how I would feel if someone said as much to me . . . There was nothing unusual about a new servant joining our household. What *was* surprising was her youth and inexperience, and – even more surprising – how long she stayed. My mother fired housemaids almost as quickly as she hired them, it was rather tiresome.

"Not long after your maman arrived, my mother simply stopped speaking to her, acting as though she did not exist. It was different for me. I would have been thirteen or fourteen at the time and Jeanne was just eighteen, so we were not so different. Except that Jeanne was my father's mistress, something that was impossible to ignore, since the whole house was suffused by their affair. It must have been quite humiliating for the Queen Mother. There was a constant blast of suppressed passion, as though a bomb had exploded in a hallway. Truth be told, my mother had scant reason to feel offended, she and my father had always had separate rooms. Once she had done her matrimonial duty by bringing me into the world, she considered herself free from her conjugal obligations. In my mother's mind, sexual relations represent the animalistic nature of men. She does not understand how sex could possibly interest a woman (there are many things my mother does not understand). She has always been more concerned about her husband's fidelity than about her husband. She could scarcely complain that papa had taken a lover, but it was a little shocking that he should invite that lover into the marital home. I do not know what reasons prompted my father to indulge in such a provocation. Perhaps my parents loathed each other even more than I believed . . . In a way, I admired your mother. It must have taken great strength of character to endure such a duplicitous atmosphere, an atmosphere that was hurtful to everyone. No-one outside the family knew anything. Neither my father (who feared for the reputation of his firm) nor my mother (who always considered virtue to be her crown jewel) had any interest in the matter being made public.

"And then, after two years, Jeanne suddenly disappeared. It was during the New Year celebrations of 1906, I remember it very well because we had guests; Jeanne had disappeared and another servant had taken over her duties. My mother's iron rule resumed, and with it the ballet of servants being hired and dismissed every month. Suddenly, my parents were talking to each other, something that had not happened in years. Hushed voices, the sort of hissing and whispering that hinted of dubious decisions, and scheming. I was fifteen at the time, I listened at keyholes, but I did not understand what was going on.

"Some months later, my father told me that he had sold his surgery and that we were moving to Neuilly. But when we got to Neuilly, there were no longer three of us, but four. There was a new baby. A boy named Raoul. Everyone in the neighbourhood thought highly of the doctor's family for taking in a little orphan. My mother cultivated a myth that proved highly successful. 'What do you expect? We are a privileged family, so we just wanted to do a little good in this world,' she would say with the humble Virgin Mary smile that made you want to slap her. She got great satisfaction from this. My father's surgery was flooded with new patients, there is little that the bourgeois love more than conspicuous virtue. The curious thing is that no-one explained anything to me. 'You're too young to understand . . .' my mother would say if I asked questions. Then one day, I am not quite sure how, I made the connection between Jeanne's disappearance and the appearance of this child. 'What nonsense you come out with sometimes,' my father said, and he blushed. 'Actually, Raoul is your half-brother . . .'"

Henriette paused for a moment and stared into the middle distance.

"At first, my father cared for the baby, but he was a very busy man. So, after a few months, he bowed to the will of his wife. He gave the baby over to her care. I quickly realised that my mother had not simply agreed to care for the child, she had insisted on it. Not out of some sense of moral obligation, but because she hated the boy. And because no-one was better placed to ensure the child was miserable. Caring for Raoul made it possible for my mother to punish everyone. My father, since the boy was a constant reminder of the love he had lost. Your mother, who had been forced to abandon her child and, though she did not know it, gave him up to the woman she had humiliated. And Raoul, of course, who suffered all the slights inflicted on bastards to punish them merely for being born."

The light was waning fast. Louise felt faintly unsettled as she peered into the depths of the apartment engulfed by evening shadows. The piano looked vaguely like a scaffold, the piles of sheet music the steps leading up to it, while above, the protruding chimney breast looked like it harboured the unseen blade of the guillotine.

"It's getting dark," said Henriette. "I'll turn on the lights."

She took away the tea tray.

One by one a series of lamps cast pools of light around the living room, dispelling the threatening shadows of Louise's imagination. Henriette reappeared with a bottle and two small glasses.

"It's fruit brandy," she said, handing a glass to Louise. "Tell me what you think."

At the first sip, Louise had a brief coughing fit, set down the glass and brought her hand to her chest. Meanwhile Henriette had already refilled her own glass and was idly sipping, staring into the void.

"I was sixteen years old. We had a baby in the house. Can you imagine!"

Louise could easily imagine. Her fingers had begun to tingle, she picked up the glass and made an effort not to drain it in one gulp.

No sooner did she put it down than Henriette poured her another and made the most of the opportunity to refill her own glass.

"He was a lovely little boy. Always smiling. The wet nurse, who was exceptionally lazy, was only too happy for me to take care of him, she spent half of her time out in the garden, reading newspapers and smoking cigarettes. She rarely changed him, since it was too much work, so Raoul learned to walk wearing a heavy nappy. At night, I would soothe his rash with talcum powder and stroke him for a long time to get him to fall asleep. In a sense I was just playing with dolls, of course, but I was also the only person in the house who really loved him, and babies sense these things.

"As soon as Raoul could walk, everything changed. The Queen Mother descended from Olympus to 'care for the child'. She fired the wet nurse and did as she did with the other servants, hiring and firing nannies every other month. There is nothing more damaging for a small child than constant changes: they have no routine, no stability. The nannies were to care for him. My mother would deal with his education. It was a task she took to with relish. Finally, she had found a role that suited her, one that allowed her to publicly play the selfless mother raising her child while taking secret delight in ensuring that he failed. She never gave him a moment's peace. In anything. She forced him to eat the food he hated in the name of healthy nutrition; she forbade him his favourite games in the name of a healthy education. For my mother, everything was about health: her own. What she inflicted on Raoul was what was good for her, what relieved her pain. Having to watch that harpy relentlessly grind the child down was the greatest torment of my life. Raoul was a sweet boy, you know. But all the privations and the prohibitions, the lack of affection, the constant displays of authority, the pleasures denied, the punishments meted out, the hours he was forced to spend locked in a dark room screaming in terror, the never-ending home-work to be endlessly repeated, the humiliations, the years spend at brutal boarding schools, to say nothing of the sneering contempt, all these things crushed and broke him. Deep down, he was not a bad boy. I did what I could in secret, I dressed his wounds behind the scenes, it was nerve-wracking. And my father? It is no insult to say that he was a weak man. As cowards always are . . . He had definitively cut all ties with Jeanne. He should have had the courage to tell her he had used his contacts to get their boy back, to raise him unbeknownst to her, to weather her under-standable outrage, the lawsuit that she could have brought against him, but he was weak. My mother had prevailed. In the early years, Raoul was difficult, later he became frankly impossible. He lied, he cheated, he stole, he absconded from every boarding school, clashed with every teacher. My mother would say: 'See what he's like! The badness is in his blood!' Everyone in the neighbourhood felt sorry for her."

Henriette fell silent for a moment.

"I didn't notice it right away . . . Then, one day, I realised that my father had simply snuffed out. He was a man crushed by the weight of his own past. Gradually, he shut himself away in his little world, he became unreachable . . ."

Louise felt a pang of anguish.

"And you never told Raoul the truth . . .?"

"Courage is not our strong suit in the Thirion family."

"So, what became of him?"

"As soon as he was of age, he enlisted in the army. By the time he was demobbed, he had qualified as an electrical engineer. He is an intelligent young man, quick with his hands. He was called up again last year, he's fighting at the front."

Night had drawn in. Henriette had refilled their little glasses, and both of them sipped. Being unaccustomed to alcohol, Louise was worried about having to get up to leave – would she reel and stagger like a drunk?

"Do you have a picture of him?"

The thought came out of the blue: she wanted to see Raoul – what did he look like? Later, she would wonder whether she had hoped to see a resemblance, however slight, between them, discover that she had a . . . twin. In the end, we always think about ourselves.

"Yes, I'm sure I have one."

Louise could feel her heart pounding.

"Here . . ."

Henriette handed her a yellowing photograph with scalloped edges. Louise stared at it. Henriette smiled, she felt moved. The photo was of a ten- or twelve-month-old baby who looked like any other baby. To Henriette, it was the picture of the child that she had loved; to Louise, it was just a baby.

"Thank you," said Louise.

"You can keep it."

Henriette sat down again, engrossed in her impenetrable thoughts.

In giving away the photograph, did she feel as though a great weight had been lifted from her, or was she already regretting the gesture?

The apartment looked different in the half-light. No longer the hideaway of a woman who lived for her piano, but the refuge of a lonely, solitary creature.

Louise thanked Henriette as the woman walked her to the door:

"Raoul only ever writes when he needs something," she said. "I don't take offence, he always was like that, a mountebank . . . Even the army hasn't changed him, he is still a ne'er-do-well. Obviously, I love him, but . . . In his last letter, he asked for money, he told me he is in Cherche-Midi military prison in the 6th. He swears it's a miscarriage of justice, but then, he would. He probably pilfered some général's medals and sold them for scrap gold. I don't let it worry me these days. Tomorrow it will be something else."

The two women shook hands.

"Oh," said Henriette. "Just a moment . . ."

She disappeared and returned carrying a sheaf of envelopes tied together with string.

"These are the letters your mother wrote to my father, I found them in his study."

She handed over the packet.

As she made her way downstairs, Louise felt drained.

Discovering that Jeanne Belmont's son was a petty con artist was a disappointment, but there was something crueller still: her mother had never known the truth about the existence of her son, or about the hell he had suffered as a boy.

Raoul Landrade had never known the truth about his mother, or about the love affair of which he had been the tragic consequence. What lies had he been told?

Did he even know that the man who took him in was his real father?

She shoved the sheaf of envelopes into her bag.

And went back to cry on Monsieur Jules' shoulder.

June 6, 1940

## 24

The street had witnessed countless celebrations, Bastille Days, weddings, people heading off on holidays, but today there was no celebration, no joy. Harried fathers loaded suitcases into cars, mothers raced around clutching babies to their breast, the pavement was littered with mattresses, trunks, chairs, as though the whole street had simultaneously decided to do a moonlight flit.

Standing smoking a cigarette at the dining-room window, Fernand watched the milling crowd and thought about this leave-taking.

He had been seriously considering the subject ever since the astonishing scenes at the mass in Notre-Dame three weeks earlier.

He was head of the mobile guard unit dispatched to maintain order on the square outside the cathedral. The solemn, tightly packed crowd that spilled onto the bridges over the Seine looked as though they were waiting for the Messiah. Instead, they watched as the vicar capitular of Paris, wearing the bishop's golden cope, a mitre on his head, his staff in one hand, greeted the Président du Conseil, the ambassadors, the Ministers of State and Monsieur Daladier. To Fernand, it seemed astonishing that all these politicians – radicals, socialists, freemasons – arrived as a delegation to pray to a god in whom they did not believe, but what was most worrying was the presence of thousands of servicemen in full dress uniform. Seeing the army's top brass, Maréchal Pétain, Général de Castelnau, Général Gouraud, et al., Fernand could not help but wonder why, when the country was being invaded by an age-old enemy, they had nothing better to do than attend mass.

When the loudspeakers set up on the square assailed the disconsolate crowd with the strains of "*Veni Creator Spiritus*" ("Come, Holy Ghost, Creator, come from thy bright heav'nly throne; come, take possession of our souls . . ."), followed by a sermon from Monsignor Beaussart ("Come, Saint Michael, who hath defeated Satan . . .") and finally the voice of the Vicar Forane, Monsieur Brot, ("Our Lady of Paris, pray for us!"), it was clear that the government and the military had reached a point where they no longer knew which way to turn.

The mass was interminable, and Fernand could not help but wonder how many kilometres Generaloberst Guderian's Panzer Division had covered during that time.

The bells of Nôtre-Dame pealed out above the crowd. Seeing the clergy and members of government slowly emerge from the cathedral with heavy tread, it was clear to everyone that God had just been appointed Commander of the Armed Forces.

Fernand reckoned that within two or three weeks, all of these good people would have fled. Rumours of a mass exodus were everywhere. Even within his own brigade, a lot of men had already vanished, including officers, on pretexts that no-one had the heart to question.

By the time he had set off home, Fernand had come to the decision that – in spite of the state of her health, or indeed because of the state of her health – he would send Alice away. She clutched his hand and, in that husky voice that always made him shudder, said:

"I couldn't think of leaving without you, my love."

But she instantly suffered fierce heart palpitations that made a case for doing just that.

These convulsions invariably plunged Fernand into despair:

he felt utterly powerless; there was nothing to do but wait. He laid a hand on his wife's heart, shocked by the pounding heartrate that could lead only to catastrophe.

"Not without you," she said again. There was a tremor in her voice.

"Alright," said Fernand, "alright."

He cursed himself for his cowardice, he should have insisted, decided for her. Was the war somehow to blame for the fact that Alice's health had markedly deteriorated in recent months? The palpitations had become more frequent and more intense; doctors insisted that she needed rest.

So, if she would not leave without him, should he go with her? Should he, like so many of those in the brigade, take a train to the countryside? His sister lived in Villeneuve-sur-Loire, she had a small grocery shop there. She had written to say "Why don't you come and stay with us for a while, surely the war effort can spare you. Or do you think you're indispensable?"

Not indispensable, no, but the closer the enemy came, the greater the sense of duty to stand firm. He was a mobile guard of twenty-two years standing, and if Paris had to be defended, what right had he to run off and hide at his sister's? He had given himself until June 10, the date of his birthday. It was absurd: absconding on his forty-third birthday was no better or worse than doing so the day before or the day after, but these were absurd times.

It was the dustcart that made him change his mind.

Not the one that rolled down his street every morning at five o'clock to the clang of galvanised dustbins rolling over the pavement, but the dustcart that, shortly before 8.00 a.m. on June 5, pulled into the yard of an incineration plant in Issy-les-Moulineaux that he had been sent to guard. But what, exactly, was he guarding? It was highly unusual to send a mobile guard unit to provide security for a lorry full of household rubbish.

Usually, the only visits to this modern plant were official: the local member of parliament would come to give the glad hand, a senator would pay a visit to "his" factory as though it were somehow his by virtue of his office, but four inspectors in suits and ties eyeing everyone suspiciously was something Fernand had never seen.

No-one knew which department they represented; they had not said a word. Although they swaggered into the plant as though they owned the place, they seemed slightly taken aback when they saw the gargantuan structure, the four gaping incinerators, the fast-moving conveyor belts, the tangled fretwork of steel walkways and steps.

Each worker had to report to an official tasked with checking their identity and getting them to sign an attendance sheet. "Government orders!" snapped one inspector, loosening his necktie which, paradoxically, gave greater credence to the statement. They all signed.

Fernand was told to have his men guard the doors, the ovens and the conveyor belts; only then did the huge steel gates swing open to allow the truck through. The labourers were ordered to unload the truck and burn the contents.

There was nothing but paper. Official forms, spent counterfoils, receipts, communiqués of various sorts, payslips, out-of-date certificates and carbon copies – a huge mountain of bureaucratic paperwork that hardly seemed to warrant immediate incineration, and yet the tension was so electric it felt as though the inspectors' careers were at stake.

The dustmen spent all morning pushing barrows that groaned under the weight of sacks marked Banque de France, each weighing as much as a dead donkey.

Those in charge, wielding clipboards and wristwatches, spent the morning quantifying, regulating, jotting notes, passing comment, observing the backbreaking work with that self-important bumbledom that incites a powerful loathing of pencil-pushers. They constantly tinkered with the workflow; clearly, no-one had the first idea how to burn so much paper in such a short time.

Fernand was standing guard by the conveyor belt on which the sacks rolled towards the incinerators. He nodded to one of the labourers, a man of about forty who, despite his stubby legs and a paunch that spilled over his waistband, seemed to have inexhaustible reserves of energy and had spent the morning opening sacks and tipping the contents into the chutes without breaking a sweat.

The sacks were counted as they were unloaded from the truck, the numbers checked at each stage and ticked off on a form when they reached the furnace. Late in the morning, the inspectors left the plant without a word of goodbye to anyone, still arguing over the number of labourers required, changes to the workflow, the time at their disposal.

By the time Fernand arrived home, he had made his decision. Alice would leave Paris as soon as possible, but on her own, since he had work to do at Issy-les-Moulineaux.

"What work?"

"Work, Alice! Work!"

He said the word with such solemnity that what Alice heard was not "work" but "duty". And she could not understand how, in this unsettled period, any duty could prevent Fernand from leaving Paris with her.

"Will you be here long?" she said, worriedly.

Fernand did not know. A day or two, perhaps a little longer, it was impossible to say. Sensing his intransigence, she did not press him further.

Then Fernand went to see Monsieur Kieffer.

Earlier in the week, he had heard the man say he was planning to go to stay with a cousin in Nevers, so he would have to drive through Villeneuve-sur-Loire. Fernand buttonholed Monsieur Kieffer as he stood on the doorstep, holding a cardboard box. The man tilted his head and re-lit his Gitane Maïs. From the expression on his face, Fernand could tell he was hesitating.

"It's just you and your wife, isn't it?" Fernand said. "Surely you'll have space in the car?"

Monsieur Kieffer was a postal inspector, a lucrative position, he had a son serving at the front and a Peugeot 402 – second-hand, admittedly – cars that were so roomy that, when sitting in the back you could almost stretch your legs out.

"Space, pfft . . . Not really," said Monsieur Kieffer. "They're not as spacious as you'd think."

It was not a categorical no, it sounded more like a qualified yes.

For his part, Monsieur Kieffer was thinking about Alice. Although everyone said she was sickly, she had a lovely pair of titties and an arse like nobody's business.

"As to the conditions," said Fernand, "I mean food and petrol and suchlike, you tell me . . ."

He suggested this as a possibility, one he did not really believe applied. The friendship between the two men was unequal, since Kieffer, who considered himself a success, looked down on the mobile guard, whose only distinguishing characteristic was that he had the most buxom wife in the building. Monsieur Kieffer stared into the middle distance. Fernand's request was tempting, to be able to spend time with such a woman . . . And have his petrol paid into the bargain.

"It's just that . . . it's a serious responsibility."

"I was thinking four hundred francs," ventured Fernand.

It was immediately clear that this did not meet expectations. Kieffer shook his head slowly, sucked pensively on his cigarette as a shimmering silence settled over them.

"The thing is . . ." he said at length, "they cost a lot, these trips, you can't imagine."

"Why don't we say six hundred francs," said Fernand anxiously, since this was almost all the money he possessed.

"Well, since we're neighbours, I'll do it. We'll be setting off tomorrow, mid-morning, does that suit you?"

The two men shook hands, though without looking each other in the eye: each had his reasons.

When Fernand told Alice he had come to an arrangement with Monsieur Kieffer, she said nothing. Kieffer gave her lecherous looks whenever they met on the stairs, tried to rub against her "accidentally" when he stood aside to let her pass, but Alice had ignored him. If she took offence at every man who leered at her or allowed his hand to slip, there would be no end to it. And Fernand was too quick-tempered for her to broach the subject with him; besides, she was perfectly capable of dealing with the situation.

Fernand took out a map of France, and together they traced the route the car would take to Villeneuve-sur-Loire. Even given the current situation, it was a two-day trip. There was no mention of Alice's health, but two days on the road was a long time.

"Why don't you come with me?"

Alice did not give up easily.

Fernand knew that he was making the right decision, but there was no way to explain it. What would Alice think if he started talking about Persia and the *Thousand and One Nights*? It would sound ridiculous. And yet . . .

They had been married for twenty years. Alice's failing health had meant she was forced to stay at home, and could not have children, but she did not care, she had never had the makings of a mother. Or a housewife. Grudgingly, she did the housework, but spent the better part of her time reading novels. Alice's dream was not to raise a family with a police officer, but to travel.

Egypt, the Nile, this was what she longed to see.

Or, better yet, Persia. Yes, these days people said Iran, but it was not the same, the *Thousand and One Nights* was Persia. These were the tales that fired her imagination. In fact, when he gazed at her as she reclined on the sofa, Fernand often thought that his wife looked a little like an Eastern princess. He would laugh when she talked about the ottomans, the gilded furniture inlaid with ivory, the rugs, the heady perfumes, the baths of ass's milk, but it was a forced laugh since his salary barely allowed them to holiday in Villeneuve-sur-Loire. Alice always said that she did not really mind, and perhaps this was true. But as time passed, the journey began to seem crucial to Fernand. The idea of a trip to Persia was his penance, it embodied all the guilt he had felt having to watch, helplessly, as the woman he loved faded month by month.

The following morning, Fernand kissed Alice and helped her into the back seat of Monsieur Kieffer's car, next to two crates and a suitcase.

"It won't take long, my love, you'll be there the day after tomorrow, and you'll be able to get some rest."

Alice smiled and squeezed his hand. She was deathly pale. Fernand did not know what to do, I'll be there as soon as I can, he whispered, I'll meet you at Francine's, but already the engine was roaring into life, smothering his last words; Fernand walked around the car and said to Monsieur Kieffer, I'm trusting her to your care, and Kieffer gave him a smug smile.

As the car pulled away, Fernand stood on the pavement and waved. The last thing he saw was Alice's delicate hand emerge from the window waving goodbye, see you soon.

He headed back upstairs, exhausted and worried, beleaguered by doubts and qualms: had he done the right thing? Had he just abandoned Alice? The apartment looked empty, like the stage set for a play that has long since closed. He barely slept a wink that night.

The next morning, he stood at the window and watched as other cars set off.

It was 5.00 a.m. Soon, the sun would rise into the sky over Paris, the street seemed wider, several cars had vanished during the night.

He shook himself, put on his uniform and went downstairs to the rear courtyard and fetched the heavy burlap sacks, still caked in soil from the potatoes they had once held.

Then he got on his bicycle.

His salvation now depended on a dustman.

## 25

The military guardhouse at Cherche-Midi was something halfway between a prison and a barracks. It had the dingy cells and
cramped exercise yards of a jail, with food as stodgy as it was
dismal. But it was staffed by the obtuse, pig-headed personnel of
a military barracks, who insisted on iron discipline and meticulous organisation. This was a lot to deal with even under normal
circumstances, and the circumstances were far from normal.
The looming prospect of a crushing, irrevocable military defeat
weighed heavily on the prisoners who, in the eyes of the
warders, represented all the misdeeds that had led to this imminent defeat.

Those incarcerated at Cherche-Midi included a broad swathe
of political prisoners and deserters. The former chiefly came from
among the anarchists and communists and included saboteurs,
alleged spies and supposed traitors. The latter included deserters,
draft evaders and conscientious objectors. Between the two were
the soldiers convicted of common law crimes, a disparate bunch
including looters, thieves and murderers. Having previously had
a couple of spells in prison, Raoul Landrade adapted more easily
than Gabriel, although conditions here were worse than he had
experienced anywhere else. He spent sleepless nights tossing and
turning on a straw mattress even a bear would have rejected.

The atmosphere in the guardhouse was nerve-racking. As the
enemy advanced, so the antipathy the wardens had initially felt

for the prisoners at Cherche-Midi veered towards abject loathing. The pulse of war could be felt in every hallway in the prison. It was an echo chamber for all the grievances of the French army. When French troops were defeated at Sedan, when Calais was captured by the Nazis, blows and punishments rained down on the imprisoned; when the French managed to protect the Allied retreat at Dunkirk, there was a return to normal hours in the exercise yard.

Twice, Landrade and Gabriel had been separated only to be reunited. Each time, Gabriel pestered him to testify to his innocence.

"Don't worry, things will settle down," Raoul said. "We'll be out within a month."

Nothing seemed less certain. The French army had no qualms about sending whole contingents of soldiers to be slaughtered, but it refused to tolerate that any among them might be criminals. The army felt sullied by the association.

Raoul's optimism stemmed from the fact that he always managed to wriggle his way out of difficult situations. Always. Sometimes it was with difficulty and he had to make minor sacrifices, but his logic was that, had they suffered what he had since childhood, most people would be long dead, whereas he was still standing.

Within days, he had canteen privileges. People are fascinated by thimblerigging because it is rooted in the evidence of their senses, which they trust implicitly. Though he would have denied it, Gabriel could not help but admire his friend's ingenuity. Almost as soon as he arrived, Raoul duped a warder into posting a letter without submitting it to censorship. "It's just a note to my sister," he said. The warder felt that fair was fair, he had lost at the shell game, so he agreed.

Landrade had also tried to reason with Gabriel when he shouted "I demand to see a lawyer!" to the admitting officer.

"You demand . . ."

"What I mean is . . ."

He did not have time to say another word before the rifle butt in his belly left him gasping for breath.

"Calm down," Raoul said.

"I wouldn't want to be in your shoes," said a soldier who had been arrested for stabbing a fellow soldier during a drinking binge. "They go pretty hard on looters in here. I don't know why, maybe they think it's bad for troop morale."

A terrified Gabriel immediately sat down next to Raoul.

"When they question you, you have to tell them the truth," Gabriel pleaded over and over.

Raoul amused himself by offering different rationales each time, Gabriel had no idea what he really thought.

"What do you mean, the truth?" Raoul would say. "I can hardly claim you weren't there since you were caught in the act."

"In the act?" roared Gabriel. "What act?"

At which point Raoul would grin and slap him on the back.

"Just joking, sergent-chef, just joking."

Raoul was fond of Gabriel. He had proved his mettle at the Tréguière bridge. Landrade was choleric by nature, blowing up bridges was in his nature, he had spent his whole life dealing with violence, so warfare came naturally to him. But in a timorous little maths teacher, it was more surprising. Raoul felt that Gabriel had acquitted himself handsomely.

As is often the case with prisons, the Cherche-Midi was one of the best-informed places in Paris. Visitors to the guardhouse came from all walks of life, so it was easy to corroborate any rumours. In the early days of June, the news was worse than ever.

Events at Dunkirk had shaken even the most deeply held convictions. The terrible period during which French and Allied troops were said to be heroically resisting the German advance had serious consequences for the prisoners. It was at this point that the powers that be (meaning the government) began to consider what to do about military prisons, of which Cherche-Midi was the jewel in the crown.

From the first signs of tension with the Germans, all departments had been ordered to ensure that anything of value was safe in the event of defeat. Crates, boxes and sacks containing anything and everything that could not be allowed to fall into the hands of the invading army were shipped off. There were numerous stories of government departments burning documents or shipping them out under cover of darkness. The government itself was considering relocating from Paris to avoid the risk of being taken hostage, adding insult to injury.

And so the case of the prisoners at Cherche-Midi had to be considered.

It was common knowledge within government that the place was teeming with terrorists, most of them communists, who – in the opinion of anyone who was not a communist – had connived with the Nazis. The time had come to decide what should be done with them if worst should come to worst, which was precisely what was happening. Many of those in high places assumed that these prisoners, chiefly members of the fifth column, would be liberated by those communists still at large in Paris, and would place themselves at the service of the German troops, supporting them in their plans to occupy the capital and control the citizenry.

The threat haunted prisoners and warders alike. The closer the

Germans came, the more ominous the atmosphere and the more hostile the guards, who did not want to be arrested by the Germans for guarding the enemies of France.

On June 7, a copy of *Le Petit Journal* brought in by a warder made the rounds. "Our troops are standing firm against the German invasion." An official statement from General Headquarters confirmed: "Troop morale is excellent." The following day, newspapers were forced to concede that the French air force was outnumbered "by ten to one". On June 9, headlines read: "German attacks have sharply intensified between Aumale and Noyon".

Then, suddenly, on June 10, shortly after 11.00 a.m., an eerie silence settled over the Cherche-Midi guardhouse. No-one knew what was happening, but rumours were spreading like wildfire. "The Krauts are marching into Paris," some said confidently. "The whole government has done a bunk," insisted others. The warders were uncharacteristically tight-lipped, which was not a good sign.

After more than two hours of glacial silence it was clear to everyone that something was amiss.

Then, someone finally said aloud what everyone was thinking. "They are going to shoot the lot of us."

Gabriel almost passed out. His breathing was ragged, he was gasping for air.

"Oh, for Christ's sake," said Raoul, "you can't be coughing and spluttering when they shoot you, where's your dignity!"

He was lying on his bunk, idly toying with the knucklebones he had got from another inmate. In a way, the jacks served as his worry beads. He was as panicked as Gabriel, but he was used to hiding his feelings.

When there was no denial, the rumour spread from cell to cell. A voice shouted, "They can't just gun down hundreds of prisoners out it the yard, what would they do with the corpses?" Another called: "If they start loading us onto trucks, it'll be because they've decided to shoot us somewhere else."

Out of the blue came the order:

"Gather up all your belongings and step outside your cells!"

There was a deafening racket, the guards banged on the bars with their truncheons as they threw open the cell doors and roughly pushed the prisoners out.

"If they're letting us take our belongings, they must be transferring us to another prison," said Gabriel, assuming the prospect of a firing squad was fading.

"Or they don't plan to leave anything behind," said Raoul, quickly packing up a comb, some soap, a brush, some dry biscuits and his underwear.

Already, a guard was prodding them to get them out of the cell.

Within minutes, all the prisoners were in the exercise yard. The prisoners muttered amongst themselves, no-one knew anything. Out in the street, dozens of Moroccan snipers and armed mobile guards flanked a fleet of military trucks.

"If any of you try to make a run for it, it's the death penalty!" barked an officer. "We'll fire without warning."

The prisoners were brutally herded into the trucks.

Raoul found himself next to Gabriel who was white as a shroud, a feeble smile playing on his lips.

"Sorry, sergent-chef, but this time, I think we're done for."

## 26

Although it was the middle of the day, there were very few people in the métro. Paris was half empty. Sitting on a wooden seat with a backpack wedged between his feet, Fernand was keenly aware that he must be a curious sight: a uniformed mobile guard with a haversack, clearly heading somewhere . . . But no-one seemed surprised. The orders telling him to report for duty to Cherche-Midi prison had given no further details of his assignment, and Fernand wondered how easy it would be to keep an eye on the bag, about which he was beginning to feel a little embarrassed.

Alice had been gone for four days now, and so much had happened in the interim that he no longer felt a flicker of the hope and the enthusiasm that had prompted him to persuade Alice to travel with that moron Kieffer. By the morning after her departure, he was regretting his decision. What he had been expecting had not happened. He and his unit had been dispatched to the Gare d'Austerlitz, where thousands of people attempting to flee the city were vying for seats aboard the few trains that might or might not ever leave. A train crammed with people eventually ended up going nowhere, while another, on the opposite platform, suddenly juddered into life, though no-one could say where it was bound. Dijon according to one man, only to be corrected by another who said, no, it's going to Rennes. Fernand gathered his unit together. He sent a guard to the station office to find out what was happening, but no-one there knew who was in charge, so the guard trudged back, none the wiser, and then had trouble finding the unit, which was now on the other side of the station dealing with a scuffle that had broken out between Belgian refugees and people hoping to travel to Orléans.

Fernand surveyed the chaos. Thousands were spreading stories they had heard on the radio: "I heard on *Monsieur Dupont's Diary* that the Krauts plan to chop off the hands of every child they find on the way to Paris." The story grew and twisted. Fernand heard one man say that the Krauts weren't going to chop off children's hands, they were going to decapitate their mothers. It's all shit, he thought.

What he had anticipated, the project that had prompted him to send Alice on ahead and postpone his own departure had not materialised, it had been nothing but a mirage, a blind hope, he was a fool.

On Friday, he put a call in to Villeneuve-sur-Loire. His sister's grocery shop had the only telephone in the neighbourhood and, these days, the only thing less reliable than the telephone service was the railway.

Miraculously, he managed to get through. Fernand's principal worry was allayed only to be replaced by another. Alice had arrived safely, in fact it had taken her little more than a day to get there from Paris, but she had immediately left again.

"Left again . . . To go where?"

"I'm sorry," said the operator, "I'm afraid I have to cut short this call."

"Well, when I say she left . . . She hasn't really left, she's at the ch . . ."

The call was cut off before his sister could finish her sentence. But then again, his sister rarely finished her sentences.

Orders for him to report to Issy-les-Moulineaux finally arrived on Sunday. Perhaps his faith in God had not been misplaced after all. He could have danced for joy.

By the time Fernand arrived in Issy, it was 8.00 a.m. and the inspectors were already there, though there were fewer of them this time. No doubt many of the pencil-pushers responsible for the operation had discovered some urgent reason to go and see what the weather was like in Orléans – they say the Loire is lovely this time of the year. Those who had survived the sudden epidemic of wanderlust stood around, looking pale, glancing at each other nervously as they assigned tasks. The labourers (as they referred to the dustmen) lined up next to the foreman and calmly waited to see what would happen next. A strange atmosphere pervaded the incineration plant, no-one could work out why they had been summoned here on a Sunday.

Once again, the labourers were asked to sign an attendance sheet, and the identity cards of the mobile guards were checked. Everything was going smoothly until the rubbish truck arrived and the dustmen realised it was going to be a gruelling day, since, at a glance, they could tell there had to be eight or ten tonnes in there . . . But that was not the pièce de résistance. About an hour later, once guards had been posted at every gate and inspectors strategically stationed to monitor the truck, the conveyor belt, the chutes, the gangways and the incinerator funnels, the first sacks were finally unloaded.

The sacks were not stuffed with crumpled old documents, but with crisp, freshly-printed legal tender – fifty-franc notes, hundred-franc notes, five-hundred-franc notes, thousand-franc notes. Everyone's head started to spin.

Fernand spotted the short man with the pot belly he had seen tirelessly lugging sacks two days earlier and the two exchanged a look. Like him, the man seemed dumbfounded. A single thousand-franc note was almost as much as he earned every month, and the first sack he dumped onto the conveyor belt weighed at least forty kilos. You did not have to be a genius to work out that, in the course of a day, they would end up burning three or four billion francs. The Nazis were at the gates and the government's pathetic response was to burn the loot before they arrived.

Inspectors posted at ten-metre intervals counted the bags.

Meanwhile, dustmen, who had spent their working lives sorting through tin cans, bicycle pumps, and orange crates, hauled sacks stuffed with enough cash to buy the plant and pay the staff for the next five generations. But people can get used to anything. At first, the dustmen were overcome by the sight of the untold riches each sack represented, but by midday, they were blithely tossing shovelfuls of banknotes as though they were trowelling cement. They resigned themselves to watching money that had never been theirs go up in smoke.

Fernand was the only one who felt a twinge of satisfaction, his hunch had been right: the previous load had simply been a dry-run.

They were coming to the end of their mammoth task.

One of the inspectors yelled that the numbers did not tally: one burlap sack was missing.

One empty sack out of nearly two hundred, thought the dustmen, who gives a damn? The inspectors, it turned out, gave a damn. To them, a sack was not simply a sack, it was a symbol. And it was not missing, they insisted, it had been stolen.

Two inspectors, together with Fernand and two mobile guards scoured the plant in search of the sack, and eventually they found it. It had fallen under the walkway that led to the furnace. Finding the empty sack here meant that its contents had been incinerated, it was easy to understand how such a thing might have happened – the working day was almost done. Almost, but not quite. The dustmen, exhausted by their backbreaking work, were about to leave when they were recalled – hey, you lot, back here – the beckoning forefinger and the stern, headmasterly glare . . . Fernand rounded up his men and listened to the inspectors' deliberations. When they had finished, the order came, swift and specific: right, you lot, strip!

It was worded rather more officiously, but the message was the same.

One of the dustmen protested, a second chimed in, then a third: We're not going to take our kit off here, we're just plant workers . . . When the inspectors insisted Fernand summon reinforcements, the men were flabbergasted. Things were getting serious.

Fernand frowned at this disturbing turn of events.

He positioned himself in front of one of the labourers and calmly told him to take off his overalls. To submit. The worker stared at him, his eye wide and expressionless, he looked like a heron. Then he unbuckled his belt and began to unbutton his flies. One by one, the others followed suit, all except for one stupid moron who started yelling, no bloody way I'm stripping, that's not what I'm paid for. By the time he had thundered his outrage, he was the only one still dressed.

At as sign from one of the inspectors, the men turned around and raised their arms. They had all done military service, so being naked around other men did not embarrass them, but to have to strip here, at their place of work, in front of a bunch of besuited bureaucrats was a different matter . . .

As they pulled on their clothes again, the big lummox was still hopping from one foot to the other, but he had stopped bellowing. He had little choice now, so began to unbutton his jacket. All eyes were on him, except those of his colleagues who were busy getting dressed. The guy was sweating like a pig. With a pained sigh, he shoved down his work trousers. Peeking from the seams of his underpants was a large wad of fifty-franc notes.

"Take him away!" barked the senior official.

If he expected howls of protest, none came. The order fell like a stone into the silence.

Fernand stepped forward and quietly told the man to remove the money from his unmentionables and get dressed. An inspector gingerly counted the bills, holding them with his fingertips: eleven fifty-franc notes.

The other dustmen shot him a pitying look as he was hauled away by Fernand's unit. Although the governmental practice of not allowing the poor to get away with even a fraction of what was permitted the rich was well established, it was sad nonetheless.

At this point, something curious happened that would be remembered by all present for some time. A small number of Banque de France officials came and shook hands with the dustmen. Once this little ceremony had begun, it seemed unstoppable, such that all the officials shook hands with everyone. While the gesture was prompted by the best of intentions, the gloomy cortege looked more like a funeral. A grateful nation thanking the dustmen and simultaneously offering its condolences.

The pot-bellied labourer gave Fernand a friendly nod and disappeared. The foreman stayed behind to lock up the plant.

While two officers from Fernand's unit carted the duplicitous dustman off to the police station, Fernand left the plant, bid his colleagues goodnight, mounted his bike and, making a sweeping detour that took him back to the incineration plant, along the perimeter wall to a little equipment. Opening the door, he saw the little bicycle trailer he had left there a day earlier and, inside, the huge pile of hundred-franc notes – the hastily dumped contents of the missing sack.

Fernand divided the loot into two bags, left the larger one for the pot-bellied labourer to collect during the night, loaded the other into his bicycle trailer and set off back to Paris.

When he got home, he found a message telling him to report to Cherche-Midi prison the following day at 2.00 p.m. The attached orders read "mission: undetermined" and specified only that all officers should bring "such personal effects as might be necessary for a brief trip".

As he wondered what the mission could be, Fernand brought the sack upstairs. He did not trouble to count the contents. It contained several million francs – more than enough to take his wife to Persia.

At the thought of Alice, his resolve weakened. He decided to call her again the following day.

The order to report to Cherche-Midi lay on the table like a reproach. Could he simply ignore the orders and leave? Now that he had all this money, surely it made sense for him to flee, as others had, and to rejoin Alice?

Had there been no mission, Fernand would have had no qualms about leaving Paris and going to Villeneuve, but he could not imagine himself flouting a direct order. He knew that he would go where he had been posted; it was in his nature.

He decided to stuff as much of the money as he could into a haversack and piled the rest into a suitcase, which he stashed between two crates in the cellar.

Now here he was, on the métro, a bag stuffed with cash wedged between his feet.

He took out the dispatch again and reread the address to which he had been summoned. He did not like the look of it one bit.

## 27

When Louise arrived at Cherche-Midi military prison she was met by barriers preventing people from approaching the main gates. The women standing behind the barriers looked fretful and anxious.

"They've cancelled all visits," said one woman. "I've been waiting here since gone noon . . ."

You could hear the panic in her voice.

In the distance, uniformed officers came and went. Now and then the women would heckle the soldiers. "What time are they going to let us in?" "Are we expected to just stand around all day and all night?" "We've come all the way from the provinces!" And one brave woman who roared: "We've got rights!", a remark that fell like a stone into a bottomless well.

Although their pleas had been loftily ignored, the little crowd gathered at the corner of the rue du Cherche-Midi were determined to make themselves heard. Louise could sense a palpable unease among the gendarmes (unless they were mobile guards, Louise didn't know much about uniforms . . .) as they glanced towards the end of the street. Would the women try to knock down the barriers? Would they have to force the crowd to disperse? Beneath their kepis their eyes betrayed their embarrassment at the thought that they might have to use brute force against a gaggle of women.

*

Singly and in small groups, mobile guards emerged from the nearby métro station, carrying a bundle of clothes, a towel, almost nothing. As they came to the barrier, they were harangued by the women: "Do any of you know what's going on?", "Why have prison visits been cancelled?", but they trooped past, some bowing their heads as though fending off a hail of stones, others ramrod-straight and dignified, staring straight ahead to make it clear they were unbowed. Some of the younger men made to say something, but the older men silenced them with a glare. They trooped through the barriers and joined their colleagues outside the prison. Some went inside while others lingered for a last cigarette, deliberately turning their backs on the women to stress their lack of interest.

"Adjudant-chef!" shouted a woman who recognised an officer's rank. "Surely you must know what's going on, nobody's told us anything."

This particular officer had a haversack strapped to his back, he was clearly expecting to travel, in which case he must know something.

The woman blocked his path; Fernand stopped.

"Are you taking them away?" she said.

Who was the woman talking about?

"We've got a right to know!" said another woman.

The prisoners, probably. Fernand glanced at his colleagues who were chatting animatedly and staring at him.

"I'm sorry, I don't know any more than you do." He seemed genuinely sorry. Louise watched as he elbowed his way through the women then walked away.

"If they don't know what the hell is going on, then . . ." a voice piped up.

But she had no time to finish before it appeared, a convoy of buses, moving slowly, keeping bumper to bumper. The engines' rumble boomed against the stone walls and made the pavements quake, there was something impressive about their unhurried advance. As though witnessing the arrival of a distinguished guest, the crowd of waiting women parted to allow the buses to pass.

The fleet of some ten buses rolled slowly to the prison gates and stopped, bumper to bumper. They were standard-issue TCRP buses, but the windows were obscured by dark-blue paint, giving them a strange and spectral appearance. The remaining officers who had been standing outside the gates, raced into the prison. All that remained were the buses, motionless as birds of prey.

And the handful of women staring at them.

# 28

It was the wait that was killing people: not just the fearful but the feared. The three hundred prisoners having been ripped from their cells now stood, shivering anxiously, in the exercise yard. Rifles at the ready, some sixty mobile guards and two platoons of Moroccan infantrymen paced up and down, all anxious about orders that did not arrive or were incomplete.

Capitaine Howsler – a tall man with the haggard countenance of a knight-errant but none of the innocence, whose inexpressive features were his most prized military asset – refused to respond, even to his own men.

Fernand had summoned his unit. Ordinarily, they should be six, today they were only five. The day before, Durozier had told him that he was leaving Paris, his wife was eight months pregnant, he had to get her to safety. If he had to be a man down, Fernand would have preferred it were the cretinous Caporal-chef Bornier. Some alcoholics are bloated by their vice, some are shrivelled by theirs. Bornier was among the latter, angular, all skin and bone, driven by a frenetic reserve of energy which was probably why he never seemed drunk; he was constantly burning calories, racing this way and that, incapable of standing still. He was the kind of alcoholic you see at a party, dancing and twirling with his beer in front of the band. His nose was as sharp as his wits were dull and he was constantly spoiling for a fight. In this prison yard, he looked more frenzied than usual.

Capitaine Howsler did a roll call and then parked six prisoners in a corner of the yard, guarded by twice as many soldiers.

"The condemned men," Raoul whispered to Gabriel.

Fernand's unit was assigned the task of guarding the common-law criminals, some fifty men. Rather than standing calmly in front of the prisoners, who were lined up in rows of three, Bornier prowled around them restlessly, toying with his rifle, darting suspicious glances that only served to heighten the fears of the prisoners, who were muttering amongst themselves.

"Silence!" snapped Bornier.

As soon as he wandered off the whispers started up again. Some said Prime Minister Daladier had ordered that all military prisoners be "removed", but what exactly did that mean? "It means 'evacuated'," muttered someone. They clung to this inter-pretation, it being the more reassuring. The other possibility was "executed". No-one could believe it, but the guards seemed nervous and on edge . . . "D'you think it's because they haven't got their orders? Or because they know they're going to have to shoot us?" Someone mentioned mass graves in Vincennes. Gabriel felt as though he might faint. He had been loudly proclaiming his innocence ever since he arrived at Cherche-Midi prison, but, then again, who hadn't? The prison was full of innocent men, except for the communists, since everyone agreed that they were guilty.

The communists were the heart of the problem, Capitaine Howsler confided to the officers gathered around him:

"We have clear evidence that the communists are planning to loot arsenals and munitions stores, seize weapons and use them to carry out attacks. We know the order was given last night, and the plan is already in motion. There's a serious risk that the communists here will try to revolt and encourage the anarchists and saboteurs to join them . . . Communists are the mortal enemies of France."

Fernand surveyed the exercise yard. Right now, the mortal enemies of France stood, shoulders stooped, hands shaking, staring in terror at the soldiers. None of this boded well.

"So . . . what are we supposed to do with them?" said Fernand.

Capitaine Howsler stiffened.

"You will be given your orders in due course."

He insisted on a second roll call. Fernand set his bag down next to the wall where he could keep an eye on it and called out: "Albert, Gérard; Audugain, Marc . . ." Each prisoner had to shout "Here", and a mobile guard would then point to where he should stand and Fernand would tick the box next to his name.

Gabriel, pale as death, found himself standing two rows behind Raoul Landrade, who was also clearly distraught.

Everyone stiffened abruptly when they heard the rumble of engines from the street outside.

The purring of the diesel engines put an end to the guesswork, rumours froze in mid-air, one prisoner pissed his pants and fell to his knees, the Moroccan infantrymen grabbed him by the armpits and dragged him to the group of condemned men only to let go before they reached them, leaving him sprawled on the ground, moaning.

"Line up in pairs!" roared the capitaine.

Caporal-chef Bornier, tense as an archer's bow, echoed the order more loudly. Fernand went over to tell him to stay silent and wait for his orders, but did not have time. The lines of prisoners shivered as the gates swung open to reveal the convoy of vehicles. Blue-painted buses that looked like hearses.

"All attempts to escape are punishable by death!" said the capitaine. "We will fire without warning."

Bornier opened his mouth, but the situation left even him speechless.

The small group of condemned men would not be going anywhere. They were left kneeling in a circle in the prison yard, their hands on their heads, surrounded by as many rifles as there were necks to aim at.

Fernand slipped his arms through the straps of his haversack, slipped it onto his back and then cocked his rifle with his fellow officers. The prisoners shuffled forward between the lines of Moroccan infantrymen and were pushed onto the buses.

"There will be no stops until we reach our destination. We have strict orders to keep driving, whatever happens."

A blow from a rifle butt sent Gabriel sprawling onto the floor of the bus, he scrabbled to his feet and raced to sit down. He saw Raoul sitting at the other end of the bus. No-one said a word. The prisoners' knuckles were white, their necks tensed, the throats dry.

When they saw the shambling cortege of prisoners emerge, the women still gathered around the barriers were stunned.

They strained their necks, scanning the faces as they fleetingly appeared before disappearing into the buses with their blacked-out windows. They could hear the shouts of the soldiers as they savagely jabbed their rifles into the prisoners' backs.

"They're taking them away!" one woman shouted.

Louise had found a space among the other women. She alone did not know who she was supposed to be looking at. Any of these men might be the one that she was looking for, the brother she had never known. It was all too fast, too far away. Hardly had she scanned the line of prisoners than they disappeared. She had seen nothing.

The first bus pulled out and was slowly heading towards the women, preceded by two officers marching at a brisk pace.

As they came closer, the women huddled together to block the street, but the barriers were brutally pushed back against the pavement, the bus accelerated, and they were forced to give way. It was impossible to see what was happening inside the vehicle. Then came the next bus and the next. The women could only stand helplessly and watch as the convoy passed. They were no longer shouting; their voices would have been drowned out by the roar of the engines.

Before they knew it, the street was deserted.

The women stared at each other. They clutched their handbags to their chests, they talked over each other, they were all haunted by the same question: "Where are they taking them?"

A few theories flashed but quickly fizzled out; in each woman's mind, the answer was the same.

"You . . . you don't think they're going to shoot them, do you?" a woman in her fifties said, her eyes brimming with tears.

"They looked very strange, those buses . . ."

Louise assumed the buses had been painted so that the operation could proceed incognito, but she said nothing. The street was empty, the prison gates were closed, there was nothing to be done. Without another word, the women slowly walked away, their hearts heavy. A sudden shout made them all turn back.

One of the women had seen the small door set in the prison gate open and a man dressed in a suit appear.

"He's one of the warders," said the woman, "I know him."

They all surged forward. Louise raced back to join them. Seeing this flock of determined women swoop on him, the man was rooted to the spot. He quickly crumbled under the hail of insults and questions and blurted out:

"They've been transferred . . ."

Silence.

"Transferred where?"

He had no idea, he said, and the women knew he was sincere. The threatening horde that had besieged him was once again a little group of terrified wives, mothers, sisters and fiancées. The warder, who had five daughters of his own, felt sorry for them.

"Someone said they're heading south," he added, "but where, exactly, who knows?"

The fear of their loved ones being shot gave way to the fear of losing them. Everyone's first thought was Orléans. The thousands of Parisians fleeing the city daily were all heading to the Loire. Everyone assumed that, long before it reached Beaugency, the German army would be defeated. Or exhausted. Or demoralised. Or, better yet, the French army would have mounted a defensive front or even a counter-offensive. Nightmare had begun to give way to fantasy. The idea was clearly preposterous, but because it served a purpose, it spread far and wide: Orléans was the new Jerusalem.

Louise was one of the first to head for the métro station. Since hearing the name Raoul Landrade, in her mind he had begun to take on, if not a life of his own (she did not know what he looked like as an adult), then a substance, a solidity. Should she stop trying to find him? Wait until the situation improved?

"Until the situation improves?"

Monsieur Jules gave Louise the little pout he used with his clientele to express incredulity.

"But, let's start at the beginning: who is this Raoul Landrade?"

"My mother's son."

From his reaction, anyone would have sworn the thought had never crossed Monsieur Jules' mind. He rolled his eyes to heaven.

"If you say so . . . But why exactly do you want to track him down? Who is he to you, huh? No-one! Not to mention he's banged up in a military prison, so it's pretty clear the boy is a bad lot. How did he end up in Cherche-Midi? Did he kill a général? Did he do a deal with the Krauts?"

When Monsieur Jules got the bit between his teeth, there was no stopping him. His regular customers simply battened down the hatches and waited for the storm to pass. But not Louise.

"I've got things I need to tell him!"

"Oh, really? What things? You know nothing, nothing except what you've been told by the widow Thirion. He probably knows more than you do."

"Then he has things to tell me."

"I'm sorry, my little Louise, but I think you're raving mad!"

He counted off on his fingers. He liked to hammer home his arguments. It was, according to him, the most effective strategy to browbeat his adversary. First, he brandished not his thumb, but his forefinger, which he considered more categorical:

"First, how do you know that this man is not a danger to the public? He's been in jail, so we have a duty to ask the question. If he's heading for the guillotine, are you going to claim his head to have it stuffed? Secondly (his index was joined by the middle finger to create a V signalling inevitable dialectical victory), you don't know where they were taken! Orléans is just a guess, it could just as easily be Bordeaux, or Lyons, or Grenoble. Who knows? Thirdly (three fingers now jabbed at his adversary like Lucifer's trident), how are you planning to get there? Are you going to buy a bicycle and ride through the night with a military column? Fourthly . . ."

This was always where Monsieur Jules juddered to a halt; "fourthly" was always the most difficult to find. So he would fold his fingers into a fist and let it fall to his side like a man who preferred to give up rather than to enumerate the long series of arguments at his disposal.

"Alright, alright," said Louise. "Thank you, Monsieur Jules."

He gripped her shoulder.

"I won't let you do something so stupid, Louise! You have no idea what you're getting into! The roads are crawling with thousands of refugees and deserters."

"What do you suggest I do? Wait here in Paris for the Nazis to arrive? Hitler has said he'll be here on the 15th!"

"I don't care, I'm not interested in Hitler. But you are not leaving, and that's that."

Louise nodded wearily. Monsieur Jules could be exhausting. Slowly, she shrugged off his hand, walked through the restaurant and left.

What should she take with her?

As she randomly stuffed clothes into a suitcase, she mentally reviewed Monsieur Jules' objections. She took down the Post Office calendar and studied the map of France, tracing the course of the Loire. She had no idea how to get there. A train was out of the question, everyone said that the train stations were under siege. For a long time, she stared at the serpentine road that led to Orléans. She could not be the only person looking for a ride, most Parisians did not own a car but still somehow managed to flee the city. I'll work something out, she thought, but already Monsieur Jules' arguments had worn down her resolve.

She carried on stuffing clothes into the suitcase, although she already knew that she would stay.

Even if she did manage to find Raoul Landrade, what would she say when they suddenly came face to face? "Hello, I'm your mother's daughter"? It seemed faintly ridiculous.

An image flashed into her mind, a man with a sinister scowl dressed in a convict's uniform, like a character in a cheap novel.

Her courage deserted her, and she sat down next to the suitcase. She sat there for a long time, overwhelmed, lost, helpless.

She turned on the light, then went downstairs to see what time it was. As she passed the window she was stopped in her tracks.

She raced upstairs, picked up the suitcase and crammed everything on the bedspread into it, raced down again, grabbed her coat and threw open the door.

Standing by the gate, Monsieur Jules, in a black suit and patent-leather shoes, was polishing the bonnet of his beloved Peugeot 90S, which had not left the garage for almost a decade.

"Looks like we might need to find somewhere to inflate the tyres . . ."

He had a point, the car looked as though it was already riding on its rims. The once-blue bodywork was as dull as a mourning mirror.

As they passed La Petite Bohème, Louise saw the rolled-down metal shutters and a sign that read: "Closed for genealogical research."

## 29

The thin young man sitting next to Landrade was shivering from head to toe and seemed to be in poor health. Raoul did not rate his chances of survival. The sort to suddenly make a run for it and get shot in the back.

Armed mobile guards were posted at three-metre intervals along the central aisle, while Fernand kept an eye on everything from the open platform at the rear of the bus.

The first minutes were harrowing. The prisoners studied the guards, wondering whether, half an hour from now, they might not be summarily executed.

The minutes crawled past.

Although the windows had been thickly daubed with paint, Raoul found a tiny gap through which he could peer without having to visibly contort himself. He could see the Place Denfert, the bus stopped for a second and he heard a newsboy shout: "*Paris-Soir*! GERMANS OCCUPY NOYON! *Paris-Soir*!"

Raoul could not remember precisely where Noyon was, it was somewhere in Picardy, a hundred, maybe a hundred and fifty kilometres from Paris. The Nazis would soon reach the gates of the capital. Clearly there was some connection with their hurried evacuation from Cherche-Midi.

The traffic was so heavy that the buses were moving at a snail's pace. The guards quickly tired of standing and Fernand gave them permission to sit on the jump seats.

Raoul was keeping a weather eye on the caporal-chef guarding the central aisle. He was concerned by his air of palpable hostility. He knew the type: cut and dried, shoot first, ask questions later. Raoul had known men like him in the army: excitable, impulsive to the point of being foolhardy, incapable to keeping a cool head, vicious bastards who considered their uniform a form of entitlement. "Bornier", he had heard. He planned to avoid him like the plague.

His superior officer, the adjudant-chef, was a man of about fifty, heavy but solidly built, with a receding hairline, a walrus moustache and the sort of sideburns no-one had had in decades. He was the calmest of the officers. Raoul filed away these details in his memory, the stance of the guards, the way they signalled to each other, everything that might one day prove useful. Vital.

The idea that they were leaving Paris was becoming a reality. As fears of mass graves in Vincennes faded, the prisoners, though still tense, felt less frantic as the minutes passed. The atmosphere was a little less grim. Raoul even dared to turn around and shoot Gabriel a quick glance, only to be reprimanded by a mobile guard with a vicious blow to the back of his seat. More bark than bite. The bus was clearly governed by the same rules that had applied in the prison. Raoul waited patiently until the guard's back was turned, then glanced at the adjudant.

Fernand strove to appear calm. Ever since the capitaine had given him his list of prisoners, he had been wondering what would he do if he were ordered to shoot these "enemies of France"? He had not worked his way up through the ranks to end up in charge of a firing squad. But if he refused, what then? Would he be accused of treason? Would he be shot?

Fernand was also worried because of the contents of his haversack. He had felt compelled to bring it with him, since he had no way of knowing if he would make it back to Paris, or when, or whether any of his things would still be there. He had had no choice, he told himself, you had no choice.

He had heard the headlines about the German advance. If the Nazis occupied the city, every available apartment would be commandeered, and his little nest egg would disappear. He smiled at the thought of some Kraut finding a suitcase stuffed full of banknotes in his cellar. Would it be an upstanding Nazi who would report the find to his superior officers, or some crafty bastard who would keep his mouth shut? In the meantime, he had put his haversack on the luggage rack above the prisoners. Covering it with his coat would have been tantamount to putting a sign on it saying "This bag contains valuables, hands off!" His only options were bad and worse. In a sense, he had brought less with him than anyone else; since the money took up all the space where his clothes should have been, he did not even have the "personal effects necessary for a brief trip" recommended in the orders issued to him.

All those aboard vaguely saw this bus as a metaphor for the times. While the country was foundering, this bus with its vehicle was heading to an unknown destination, from which no-one could be sure they would return, by forcing a path through crowds of panic-stricken Parisians all fleeing in the same direction . . .

Somehow, the bus managed to pick up speed. Prisoners and guards alike felt relieved that they had managed to get away, to escape the slaughter, the carnage. They gradually retreated into their own worlds.

Fernand was thinking about Alice. If she were to have a heart attack, would his sister Francine know what to do? Were there doctors in Villeneuve who had not yet fled?

Fernand and Alice had met twenty years earlier. Perhaps

because they were both only children or because they had never found love, they had clung to each other like ivy, clinging tighter when they had no children – something neither of them regretted. Alice was everything to Fernand. Fernand was the love of Alice's life.

Then, one morning – back in 1928 – Alice had a funny turn, a dark, clawing sensation in her chest that moved through her, draining the colour from her face and the warmth from her hands; she gazed sightlessly at Fernand. He was staring at her when she suddenly collapsed at his feet. In that moment, their lives were cracked from top to bottom, like a delicate vase that was somehow still in one piece but would need to be jealously guarded in order to survive. From then on, their lives were circumscribed by danger, illness, death and – greater still – the fear they might be separated.

Fernand was a Catholic but had never been particularly devout. He started to attend church again, though he made no mention of this to Alice. In Fernand's mind, to do so would be demeaning, it would show weakness. And so, when he took her to mass, he would stand outside and smoke cigarettes in the courtyard, only to go to a different mass in secret on his way to the barracks. In his relationship with God he was cheating on his wife.

Suddenly feeling the need to reassure himself, he glanced up at the bag on the luggage rack, then down the central aisle to make sure his men were alert as the bus rattled over potholes, then, lastly, he surveyed the prisoners. He scanned the list he had been given: names, dates of incarceration, judicial status and reasons for their arrest. Of the fifty men, there were only six communists, the rest of his contingent was made up of thieves, rapists, looters, and petty criminals. Thugs and punks, to his mind.

*

Through the chink in the paintwork, Raoul saw a signpost for Bourg-la-Reine. The road was increasingly crowded, the bus driver constantly had to honk his horn to get through. Outside their suburban houses, people were lashing bundles to the roofs of their cars, while traffic wardens stood at junctions vainly attempting to direct traffic that was all going in the same direction. Fernand gave the order to open windows so officers and prisoners could breathe more easily. The commotion was louder now: the shouts and cries, the revving engines, the drivers leaning on their horns.

It was beginning to get dark, and the prisoners were thirsty and starving. No-one was keen to stick their head above the parapet, but when it came to pissing, someone had to do something. It was the young man sitting next to Raoul. He was no longer trembling, but his face was still ashen and contorted by fear. He raised his hand like a schoolboy. In an instant, the squat alcoholic guard, who had been lulled into a doze to the purr of the engine, was on his feet, his rifle cocked.

"What d'you want?"

The adjutant-chef also stood up, he held out his hands in a sign of appeasement.

"I need to take a piss," stammered the prisoner.

No-one had considered this eventuality. It was always possible to tell the prisoners that they had to wait, but no-one knew when they would be able to relieve themselves. They had been issued strict orders: no stops.

Fernand turned around. They had left Paris and the suburbs behind; the road was clearer now. He whispered orders to his men and so began a slow procession as the prisoners were escorted to the rear platform where they pissed onto the road while a guard jabbed a pistol into their kidneys.

This interlude provided something of a diversion.

The prisoners had begun to whisper amongst themselves. Fernand signalled to his men not to intervene. When the young man came back to his seat, he said to Raoul:

"What were you banged up for?"

"Nothing!"

The word just came out, like an elemental truth.

"What about you?"

"Distribution of subversive literature and membership of a proscribed organisation."

This was the standard charge used to arrest communists. There was a tinge of pride in the young man's voice as he rattled it off.

"You're a fucking moron . . ." said Raoul with a laugh.

As it grew darker, the bus drove on, but the driver was careful to keep the headlights off. Things had sped up since they passed Étampes and they had begun to overtake the refugees.

At about seven o'clock, Fernand started to worry about food supplies. The capitaine had not mentioned anything. The rushed evacuation, the vague orders, the ad hoc organisation all signalled a challenging mission. Then again, thought Fernand, the whole country is falling apart, why would *this* mission be properly planned and prepared?

Finally, they came to the outskirts of Orléans. It was eight o'clock.

The buses pulled into the car park of the central prison. The mobile guards were left to supervise the prisoners, while Capitaine Howsler took the officers aside.

"Right, we're here," he said in a tone that betrayed his sense of relief. "Now, it may take a little time to process the prisoners and get them into the jail. Security issues. While I sort out the orders, I need you lot to keep an eye on things here. Right, hop to it!"

He rang the bell on the great prison doors as though he were merely a visitor. A hatch opened and he launched into a long conversation with the sentry posted on the other side. It sounded as though no-one here was expecting them. Sensing that his junior officers were watching, he angrily whipped around.

"Go on, hop to it! What did I tell you?"

Fernand climbed aboard his bus again. He instantly sensed that the atmosphere had become more volatile in his brief absence. As one, the prisoners and the guards turned to stare at him. They had all been taken by surprise by this stop.

Caporal-chef Bornier shot him a frantic glare.

"We're sorting out the details of the transfer!" Fernand said, before moving around to have a quiet word with each of his men:

"This is probably going to take a bit of time, so we can't afford to drop our guard."

Having assuaged their fears somewhat, he stepped off the bus and leaned against the side while he lit a cigarette. Some of his fellow officers on the other buses had had the same idea and soon there were five of them, smoking in silence and staring at the prison gates which remained obstinately closed. After a moment they were joined by Bornier. He was not a smoker since all of his activities were motivated by booze. No-one knew how he managed to drink on duty without ever getting caught. Fernand wondered whether Bornier had smuggled a few bottles on board the bus. It was hardly impossible, after all, he himself had managed to smuggle almost a million francs in large bills.

"What the bloody hell is going on?" snarled Bornier.

Fernand could not remember the man ever saying anything

in a calm, considered tone. Every utterance, every sentence, was offensive and querulous, studded with expletives, as though Bornier was constantly demanding redress for some injustice against him.

"These things always take a bit of time," said someone.

"You'll see, they're going to leave us here with our shipment of fucking thugs!"

The officers turned and stared at the huge, hulking shadow of the prison.

"If it was up to me, I'd shoot the bloody lot of them . . ."

What was most surprising was that no-one disagreed. Not that any of them actually wanted to shoot anyone, but this eerie darkness, the hasty departure from Paris, the buses with their painted windows, these prison gates that remained stubbornly shut, the uncertainty about what might happen next, all these things left them too weary and too exhausted to argue.

"What's that?"

One of the other guards nodded to the book sticking out of Fernand's pocket.

"It's nothing, it's . . ."

"You're not telling me you've got time to bloody read?" said Bornier.

Everything he said had an undercurrent of reproach.

"So, what is it?"

Fernand reluctantly took out the little paperback. The *Thousand and One Nights*. None of the men had ever heard of it.

"It says *volume three*, so does that mean you've read the first two?"

Fernand, embarrassed, stubbed out his cigarette.

"I just took the first book I could find, it's only to help me get to sleep . . ."

Bornier was about to say something when they heard a disturbance coming from their bus. The caporal-chef rushed forward, but Fernand barked:

"Stay there!"

He grabbed Bornier's shoulder, as he felt compelled to do from time to time, and said what he always did:

"You wait for my orders!"

Like a spring that gradually accumulates tension each twist and turn, the prisoners' growing fears had suddenly been unleashed when they saw one of the exhausted guards reach into his knapsack and take out a *saucisson* and a loaf of bread. Never had charcuterie so nearly triggered a spontaneous mutiny.

In a bound, Fernand was on him.

"Put that away now!" he growled between gritted teeth.

"What about us, when do *we* get to eat?"

Fernand whipped around, but it was impossible to say which prisoner had made this plaintive cry, only that it was clearly shared by the others. A tremor ran through the bus, one that might herald a full-blown riot. The guards trained their rifles on the prisoners and their colleague, blushing furiously, stuffed his sandwich into his bag.

No-one had had anything to eat or drink for more than six hours. Worse still, all the men were stiff and tired. To Fernand, the situation didn't smell good.

"It won't be much longer," he said. "In the meantime, we'll get you something to drink."

The click of rifles being cocked was followed by silence. Fernand climbed down from the bus.

"Is there anywhere we can get water?"

Nobody knew.

"The river Loire's just down there," said Bornier. "But if you want to drown 'em, the easiest way would be to drive the bus off the bridge."

"Yeah, we should probably get them something to drink," said another guard. "My lot are starting to grumble, we don't want the situation to deteriorate . . ."

Fernand walked over to the great prison door, rang the bell and waited. The hatch was opened, and a face appeared in the half-light.

"Do you know if it's going to take much longer?"

"I don't think so, no, we should get them moving soon."

"Oh. That's good, because . . ." Fernand gave a little laugh intended to lighten the mood. "Because . . . there's a lot of thirsty men on those buses!"

"Well, they'll be thirsty a little longer, then . . ."

As if to prove the point, the door swung open, and Capitaine Howsler emerged. The six senior officers looked at him anxiously.

"So, um . . . things aren't going exactly to plan . . ."

He hesitated.

"What was the plan?" said Fernand.

Under normal circumstances, Howsler was a confident officer, he had trained at the military academy and was not much given to self-doubt. But the circumstances were far from normal, and he seemed shaken. Over the past weeks, he had begun to notice that what was happening on the ground did not quite tally with the views of the Chiefs of Staff. The fact that a miserable provincial prison was now refusing to provide accommodation for a group of prisoners sent by the prison authorities undermined his habitual calm certainty.

"Well, it looks as though there wasn't one," Howsler confessed. "My orders were to transfer the prisoners here, but they're telling me they don't have room."

"What about provisions?"

"That comes under the responsibilities of the regional military," said the capitaine, relieved that he had an answer. "They're supposed to deliver fresh supplies tonight . . ."

Everyone instantly realised that the supplies, like the transfer, would not go to plan.

The capitaine checked his watch. 2100 hours. Behind them, the hatch in the prison door banged open.

"Cable for Capitaine Howsler!" roared a voice from inside.

The capitaine hurried back while his officers stood and stared at each other.

"Personally, I don't know what we're waiting for . . ." said Bornier, nodding to the buses, " . . . we'll end up shooting them sooner or later. If it were up to me . . ."

Fernand was about to say something when the capitaine reappeared, clutching the cable, looking triumphant.

"We've been ordered to fall back to Gravières camp."

No-one knew where or what this was.

"It is far?"

Before the capitaine answered, another officer said, "And what about the provisions . . .?"

"Everything has been arranged. Now, get moving!" said the capitaine.

"Why don't we get them something to drink first," ventured Fernand.

"Don't you bloody start!" snapped the capitaine. "Gravières is fifteen kilometres from here, they can wait another fifteen minutes."

This time Fernand offered no explanations, not even to his own men; he was looking pale and uneasy. The men watched as he got onto the bus and, after a curt nod, signalled the driver to start the engine. They set off again; this shilly-shallying was beginning to get on Fernand's nerves.

"Where do you think they're taking us?" whispered the young communist.

Raoul had no idea.

After fifteen minutes, the bus began to slow and Landrade peered through the chink in the paint. It was a clear night, and he could just about make out the landscape, the farmhouses, the country lanes. The bus made a sweeping U-turn then came to a halt in front of a line of barriers and barbed wire . . .

Fernand was the first to get out. Before issuing any orders, he first wedged his haversack under the chassis of the bus.

One by one, the prisoners stepped down and gave their name and number, a guard ticked the list.

When Landrade got out, he found himself next to Gabriel.

They both stared at the Indochinese soldiers who were lined up in what looked like a guard of honour, but whose rifles were trained on the prisoners. Further away, near the entrance to the camp, was another row of armed soldiers, this time French.

The prisoners were lined up in threes and ordered to march. The first man to stumble got a bayonet blow to the groin and the two who tried to hold him up were pistol-whipped to cries of "Fucking bastards, fucking Krauts!"

Raoul, who had planned to ask if he could have a drink, suddenly changed his mind.

"Our glorious past has lighted our way . . ." he whispered to Gabriel. But he didn't laugh the way he usually did when mocking military slogans.

They could see rows of huts in the camp, reminiscent of the graves in a military cemetery.

# 30

From the moment they set off, Louise had been wondering whether they would get there faster on foot. The car started to splutter before they even reached the avenue de Saint-Ouen.

"It's the spark plugs," said Monsieur Jules, "give them a minute, they'll sort themselves out."

The Peugeot was a 1929 two-door model that Monsieur Jules had driven on precisely four occasions: on the first, when he collected the car from the garage, he had managed to hit a milk truck at the first junction; the drive back to the garage was the second. The third out, the following year, was to attend the wedding of a distant cousin in Gennevilliers. This, then, was his fourth excursion. Although, over time, the paint had dulled, Monsieur Jules polished the car every fortnight. And, for reasons known only to himself, he always kept the petrol tank and radiator topped up, and the spare tyre properly inflated.

It was obvious from the way he drove that Monsieur Jules had had very little practice. Before they set off, he swapped his patent-leather shoes for carpet slippers, a sartorial choice that probably did not make his task any easier.

Louise suggested they give up, but Monsieur Jules gripped the steering wheel harder and carried on, as though driving a tractor. They would simply have to wait until the car broke down or they were involved in an accident, which was bound to happen soon.

After an interminable wait, they found a garage and inflated the tyres, then headed south. Traffic was bumper to bumper, so they were moving at a snail's pace.

"Good job we remembered to take a spare can of petrol, don't you think?"

The car reeked of it.

When they reached the avenue d'Orléans, all the traffic was heading in the same direction: south. An unending line of cars, into which were crammed people, crates and suitcases, and most of which had mattresses lashed to the roofs.

"So, 'south' – that's all they told you about where they were sending the prisoners?" asked Monsieur Jules for the tenth time and, when Louise said yes, he said, for the tenth time "We'll have a hell of a job finding them."

This time, he added:

"Here we are, moving at a crawl, but they'll be belting along! You won't see a convoy like that stuck in traffic."

Louise was increasingly aware that Monsieur Jules was right, their attempt was doomed to fail. Not simply because the traffic seemed to be moving more and more slowly, but because they had no idea where they were going.

"South means Orléans, what else could it mean?" said Louise.

Curiously for a self-professed military strategist, Monsieur Jules had only the most approximate notions. He simply nodded and gave Louise a sceptical look intended to signal that he had other ideas. As he lit a cigarette, he swerved and scraped the left bumper against a lamp post.

There had been nothing sensible about the plan to try to follow the Cherche-Midi convoy, but one look at the three-lane stream of cars ahead was enough to know that it was now impossible to turn back.

The traffic inched forward, mostly in second gear, sometimes in first. At about 8.00 p.m., the endless tailback took a detour, then ground to a halt. Louise got out to stretch her legs. Every female passenger seemed to be looking around for a patch of undergrowth that afforded shelter from prying eyes, every thicket was suddenly a public convenience with a queue of women patiently waiting, keeping one eye on their cars lest they should move off – which never happened.

Louise took advantage of this break to talk to the women around her. Had any of them seen a convoy of TCRP buses with windows painted blue? It sounded ridiculous. What would a fleet of Paris commuter buses be doing on a national motorway? And what was this nonsense about blue windows . . .? The question elicited only shrugs and surprised looks; no-one had seen anything of the kind. Undeterred, Louise did not go back to her car, but walked up and down the line of cars, talking to drivers and passengers, always getting the same answer.

She retraced her steps and reached the car just as it was about to pull away again.

"You almost had me worried!" said Monsieur Jules.

She climbed in, put her arm in the door.

"Did you say you were looking for a fleet of TCRP buses?" said a woman in the car next to theirs. "They drove past us earlier this afternoon. Just outside Paris, near Le Kremlin-Bicêtre at about three of clock. They were heading south, towards Orléans."

It was 9.00 p.m. The order was passed from car to car that they should drive with no lights for fear of enemy bombers. One by one, headlights flickered out like a string of votive candles. Being unaccustomed to driving at night, Monsieur Jules simply hooked his bumper to the towbar of a large trailer transporting four families and all their worldly goods.

The prison convoy had a six-hour head start on them and, at the rate things were moving, they were not likely to reach Orléans for two days . . .

After a while Monsieur Jules unhooked the car, pulled onto the verge, got out and went to open the boot of the car. Louise saw him reappear with a hamper full of food, a saucisson, a bottle of wine, some bread. They climbed the embankment and Monsieur Jules spread a white linen tablecloth on grass already wet with dew. Louise smiled.

For the space of an hour, their escape from Paris was transformed into a bucolic night-time picnic.

There were the mobile guard, soldiers and infantrymen from Indochina and from Morocco – all of whom seemed to have landed up at the camp for different reasons. The one thing they had in common was their uneasiness. Fernand sensed the tension the moment he stepped off the bus. The line of armed soldiers outside the camp entrance gave the distinct impression that the convoy – both prisoners and guards – was unwelcome.

In the late afternoon, Luftwaffe squadrons had been spotted high in the sky. Those guarding Gravières were alarmed at the thought of the defenceless camp being strafed by enemy fighters; they were not prepared to die for prisoners they considered the dregs of society.

Capitaine Howsler, still stiff as a ramrod, held a confab with his counterpart, an officer responsible for a group of inmates from La Santé prison. It was clear that, being last to arrive at the camp, they would have to take what accommodation remained: six buildings without latrines, ringed by barbed wire. From a distance, the buildings with their narrow windows looked like blockhouses. Howsler asked how many prisoners were being held in the camp.

"Including your lot, a little more than a thousand."

When Fernand heard this, he was unnerved.

A thousand prisoners they would have to guard for how long?

The capitaine ordered a fresh roll call, and this time – on orders from the high command – the prisoners were frisked. One by one, they were searched by the Indochinese soldiers and only then were they allowed to enter the building. The first twenty-five commandeered the bunks, while the others had to fashion a billet from the few bales of straw. Raoul and Gabriel resigned themselves to creating a makeshift berth. The militant communist appeared, shivering, and lay down a metre away. His teeth were chattering. Gabriel lent him his greatcoat.

"What's the matter, Red?" said Raoul. "Did Uncle Joe not send you any blankets?"

Whether it was hunger, fatigue or disease, the boy was clearly in a bad way.

Fernand sent one of his men to fetch water. When Bornier only brought back four buckets, it sparked heated arguments. Long experience had taught Fernand that it was better not to get involved, and he was right. A tall, heavy-set prisoner managed to persuade the others, if not to compromise, then at least to cooperate. Fernand wasn't sure that rationing would work as well when it came to food.

"So, the local military are responsible for delivering supplies and provisions?" Fernand asked the capitaine.

Howsler slapped his forehead – ah, yes, another thing to deal with! He went and consulted his counterpart but came back none the wiser. No-one seemed to know. The most recent supplies, delivered the previous day, had proved woefully inadequate to feeding seven hundred prisoners, and a full-scale riot had been averted only when the guards fired warning shots into the air. Now they were at almost a thousand.

As he invariably did, Raoul Landrade used this period to move around and chat to everyone or, as he put it, "have a meet and greet". In a clear sign that things had taken a turn for the worse, no-one seemed interested in playing his shell game. Worn down by hunger and exhaustion, the prisoners had no time for people like Raoul.

This was something that had not escaped Fernand's notice. He was concerned by the way the prisoners were grouped together. The communists hated the anarchists who despised the informants who in turn loathed the deserters, the situation was further complicated by the respective loyalties of the saboteurs, the draft dodgers, the defeatists and the alleged traitors, all of whom scorned the common-law criminals who, for their part, made clear distinctions between the thieves, the conmen, the looters and the murderers; none of whom wanted anything to do with the rapists. Ah, yes – and then there were those far-right Frenchmen, the crypto-fascists whom everyone else here referred to as "cagoules". There were only four of them, including a journalist, a certain Auguste Dorgeville, who advocated Franco-German reconciliation and was the de facto leader by virtue of the fact that he was twenty years older than the other three.

Fernand and his men had been allocated an adjoining room that was barely more comfortable than the prisoners' dormitory excepting that the guards each had a straw mattress. Fernand wedged his haversack under his camp-bed. It was almost 2300 hours, no-one had eaten, and there was no prospect that food would arrive that evening. He drew up a rota for guarding the prisoners and took the first watch so that his men could get a little rest.

Hunger had begun to gnaw at his belly. They would all have to hold out until morning when fresh supplies were bound to be delivered. In the meantime, there was one problem that transcended all socio-political categories and clan affiliations: the latrines. Heading back after a last cigarette, Fernand spotted a prisoner tossing a clump of straw through the half-open window.

From the smell, it was clear what it was. Fernand realised he had to do something urgently, before the air became completely unbreathable.

"We need to organise trips to the latrines," he informed his men.

"I don't need to go," muttered Bornier.

"It's not for you, it's for the prisoners."

"Then I *really* don't need to go."

"Too bad, you're going anyway."

The prisoners, in groups of three, were escorted to the latrines by a mobile guard who had to stand and supervise. It was a harrowing experience for all concerned. The murky building had not been hosed down for four days and stank like a cesspit. The first prisoners to use it emerged a sickly green. The others decided against. Tomorrow morning, Fernand would have to set up a latrine duty. He made a mental note to add cleaning supplies to his growing list. He gave permission for the prisoners to piss against the fences. "Anything else, you do it in the latrine, or you don't do it at all!"

Gabriel made do with a quick piss against the fence. Raoul headed into the latrines and came back looking cadaverous. Once the prisoners were done, the guards secured all doors and windows. Inside, the prisoners watched as the shutters closed and they heard padlocks being snapped onto the bolts.

Gabriel started to gasp for breath.

"Hey, sergent-chef, don't go having an attack," said Raoul, "we're not in the Mayenberg now!"

His laugh was rolling around the room when Fernand came in to stand guard and immediately imposed silence.

"No moving around without my permission, and no talking."

Most of the men dozed off. Sitting in a chair with his rifle on his lap, Fernand turned a deaf ear to the occasional whispers here and there.

"Are you sleeping?" said Gabriel.

"I'm thinking," said Raoul.

"About what?"

Built on slightly higher ground, the latrines offered a panoramic view of the whole camp. Raoul's sole reason for going there – holding his breath – had been to survey the site, the soldier's sentry rounds, the routes they took, the surrounding countryside bathed in moonlight. The camp was vast and complex. Raoul counted all the possible exits and entrances and came back bewildered. The camp was considerably less secure than Cherche-Midi prison, but the increased number of armed guards gave him pause for thought.

The word "escape" quivered like electricity through Gabriel's brain.

"You're insane."

Raoul shifted closer. His voice was barely audible, but the anger was palpable.

"No, you're the one who's out of his fucking mind! Don't you get it? There is no organisation in the camp, no food, no orders, the guards don't know what to do with us. What do you think they'll do next time the Krauts show up?"

This was something that preoccupied Gabriel as much as the other prisoners.

"You think they'll give us to the Nazis as a welcome gift?"

This did not seem likely.

"And even if they did," said Raoul, "what would the Nazis do with us? Offer us prime position in the Glorious Army of the Reich?"

This seemed even less likely. But Gabriel remained sceptical.

"How can we possibly escape? We've got no papers, no money."

"If you don't get the hell out of here soon, my friend, your choices will be a bullet in the chest or a bullet in the back . . ."

As if in answer to his fears, Gabriel heard the chattering teeth of the young communist lying next to him.

"One less commie, I suppose," said Raoul, turning to face the wall.

The whispered conversations gradually subsided. Fernand checked his watch, there was an hour left on his watch. He had left his haversack under his bed so as not to attract attention, and though it was highly unlikely that anyone would go through his belongings, he felt uneasy. A guilty conscience, he thought. Whenever he felt racked by guilt, he thought about Alice. He had not been able to put a telephone call through to Villeneuve. He longed to hear her voice, if only for a second – that was all he needed to know whether she was feeling good or bad, worried and anxious or happy and well-rested. The tone of her voice told him everything he needed to know. It was infuriating that he was trapped here.

He thought about the bag of money, about the suitcase he had left in the cellar, how would he explain these things to Alice, who was so honest, so . . .

He had yielded to temptation, but the thought of the trip to Persia that had seemed so alluring now seemed like a waste. He had stooped to theft to fulfil a fantasy that Alice would never share, because deep down he knew it would not come true . . . By stealing the money, hiding part of his loot and taking the rest with him, Fernand had become the kind of man Alice would never have wanted to marry.

"Silence! Don't make me come over there!"

Shouting at the prisoners made him feel a little better. Half an hour and he would be able to get some to sleep. He would lie on his side, the way he did when he hugged Alice to him and they slept like nestling spoons.

The following morning, at 0600 hours, Capitaine Howsler summoned all the officers, NCOs and infantrymen responsible for guarding the inmates from Cherche-Midi prison.

"For the avoidance of doubt, all supervisors are under the command of the mobile guard unit. There must be no fraternising with the prisoners, unless you want to find yourself on the other side of the fence."

As he listened to this stirring speech, Fernand inspected the "supervisors" – ageing, visibly disheartened infantrymen who had been sent back from the front knowing that this would be their last mission before they joined the ranks of the defeated in one of the shortest wars in military history.

Within an hour, it was clear that the supervisors were ill-equipped to deal with the anger of prisoners who had not eaten for almost two days.

Bornier strode into the prisoners' dormitory like an avenging fury.

"If you're not happy, we can break out the machine guns . . . !" he bellowed.

Bornier's distinct advantage was that he was brutally honest. If his words did little to assuage the prisoners' hunger, they at least calmed their anger. When Raoul saw him, red-faced, howling, his finger on the trigger, he realised that his assessment had been right: this man was dangerous.

Fernand arranged exercise details, ensuring the various tribes stayed together to avoid any brawls between these men who were already on edge.

During morning, some prisoners managed to make games of

checkers or dominoes using scraps of torn paper. Raoul managed to win himself a straw mattress playing the shell game.

Capitaine Howsler was keyed up, constantly running back and forth to the field radio to request orders and demand supplies, but his calls went unanswered or he got through to an officer who had no information and promised to make enquiries, but never radioed back.

When their turn came to go out and stretch their legs, Gabriel did limbering-up exercises while Raoul casually wandered away and managed to spend some minutes chatting to a veteran soldier who did not give a damn about the capitaine's orders.

"The Nazis are just to the west of Paris," the soldier told Raoul. "They've already crossed the Seine . . ."

If the Germans took Paris, the war was over. That was certain. What would the military authorities decide to do with its thousands of prisoners?

As though in answer to his question, there came the howl of air-raid sirens. Prisoners and guards threw themselves on the ground. Minutes passed. Raoul was lying near the door. German bombers passed overhead but the expected shelling did not come and silence returned. A short time later, there came the roar of French planes.

"They always show up late, the fuckers . . ." said Bornier.

Raoul sidled up to Gabriel.

"That's when we need to make our escape. During a bombing raid. Everyone will be lying on the ground, no-one will by paying any attention to us."

"And how exactly do you plan to get out of the camp?"

Raoul said nothing. He was thinking his idea through, surveying the camp from a new perspective.

"When the next raid comes, I'll know whether it's feasible."

Raoul continued to nose about. Every time they were allowed out of the dormitory, he spent his time discreetly counting the number of steps from one place to another, assessing the best routes, working out alternatives.

Shortly before 1400 hours, when the supplies truck finally rolled into the camp, Fernand panicked. There was a single loaf of bread that weighed no more than a kilo and a half, a tin of pâté intended to serve twenty-five. And a round of Camembert that might feed fifty.

In order to distribute the rations, Fernand was forced to have guards train their rifles on the queue of prisoners who quickly became mutinous and aggressive.

"We're going to die from starvation," said one.

"Would you rather die from a bullet in the belly?"

Bornier was clearly in a black mood. Had he already polished off his reserve of cheap wine?

"Well?" he said, stepping closer. "Is this what you want?"

He jabbed the barrel into the prisoner's paunch, the man dropped his ration and hurried to pick it up.

"Easy now," said Fernand. "Calm down."

He clapped Bornier on the back in a friendly fashion, but it was futile. Bornier was determined to press his advantage:

"You should be grateful we feed you fucking scum!"

As he watched this scene, Gabriel frowned: Raoul had been right.

"I swear, the first bastard who kicks up a fuss, I'll . . ."

Bornier did not get a chance to finish the threat before Fernand steered him back towards the barracks and signalled to another guard to take over.

By the time they had finished, it was clear that they were also running low on tobacco and cigarettes.

At some point during the afternoon, one of the prisoners wandered over to the little rubbish tip where the soldiers threw their coffee grounds. He brewed up a pale beige concoction which he handed around.

As night drew in, Fernand gave the order for the prisoners to return to their dormitories and stationed soldiers and mobile guards at every entrance.

## 32

"Don't worry, Louise, I can sleep under here."

Monsieur Jules' attempt to play the benevolent gentleman depended on his ability to slide under the chassis of the car, as he might to change the oil. Given his corpulent build, this had perhaps been somewhat optimistic. Louise could feel the car rocking as he made his attempt. Out of pity, she did get out to see what was happening, but a little later she heard snoring from the roadside where he had finally found refuge on a scrap of blanket.

Leaning out of the car window, she stared at Monsieur Jules, who was sleeping on his back, his paunch proudly on display, his arms folded over his chest. For a moment, she thought he might be dead. Three seconds later she realised her mistake when a sonorous snore made his cheeks quiver. But that fleeting moment was enough to remind her of the immense part he played in her life.

For her part, Louise lay curled up on the back seat, which was so narrow she spent the whole night clinging to it tightly so as not to fall off, while she dreamed of scaling sheer cliffs. Meanwhile, there was the continuous rumble of traffic from the cars that dared not pull off the road for fear their place would be taken by someone else, or that, in their absence, the whole caravanserai might have moved on.

After their brief picnic, while Monsieur Jules had been attempting to shimmy under the chassis, Louise had opened the bundle of letters given to her by Henriette Thirion. She had intended to take the photograph of baby Raoul with her but now suddenly remembered that, in her hurry to leave, she had left it on the kitchen table . . .

In the dim, waning light, she began to read her mother's letters, some thirty in all.

The first was dated April 5, 1905:

> *My dearest love,*
>
> *I had vowed not to write to you, not to impose, yet here I am doing both. You will probably hate me, and with good reason.*
>
> *If I am writing now, it is because I did not answer when you asked me about my silence, my "mutism", as you called it. The truth is, I am still overawed by you. Not that I am afraid of you – I could never love a man of whom I was afraid – but everything you say fascinates me, is all so new to me that I can think of nothing better to do than drink it in. I am silent only so that I can revel in the moment, in your presence, and every time I emerge more alive than before.*
>
> *Yesterday, when we parted, my whole body was quivering . . . Such things are best not spoken, much less written, so I shall say no more.*
>
> *Know only that, when I am silent, in means "I love you".*
>
> *Jeanne*

Jeanne would have been seventeen when she wrote this. As besotted as any young girl who has fallen for an older man. It would not have been difficult for the doctor to win her affection. Jeanne was far from stupid, she knew how to write, she had passed her high-school diploma and, as Monsieur Jules said, "she read novels" – as was clear from the style of her letters. What effect had her declaration of love had on this man in his forties? Had he smiled at her naive romanticism?

Louise was surprised by her mother's youthful passion, something she had never experienced herself. To Louise, the vicissitudes of love were as alien as an undiscovered country. Not that she was envious, on the contrary she admired this young woman who could so immerse herself in an affair from which she could not reasonably hope for much. Louise had never had the opportunity, or if so, she had not seized it; she had been in love, but never passionately so, she had made love, but had never known this heady intoxication. Jeanne had written love letters, not so Louise. Oh, the love letters themselves were commonplace, almost banal. And yet there were moments when Louise was struck by the sincerity and the sheer abandon of her mother's words.

In June 1905, Jeanne wrote to Doctor Thirion:

*My dearest love,*
*Be selfish.*
*Take, take all, take everything.*
*In my every sigh, hear the words "I love you".*
*Jeanne*

The light had faded. Louise put the letters back into the bundles and tied them with string.

Jeanne addressed the doctor by the formal "*vous*". He, doubtless, spoke to her as "*tu*". To Louise, this seemed neither odd nor affected; this was how their relationship had begun and so it carried on: some things are innate.

As she drifted off, Louise wondered how much the doctor had loved Jeanne.

Louise and Monsieur Jules were not alone in feeling at the end of their tether. The previous day the crowd had grown weary of the slow-moving tailback that was as discouraging as it was terrifying. Their nerves frayed, they scanned the skies for Luftwaffe bombers.

In the morning, Louise had set off with a number of other women in search of water. Everyone felt grubby. They found a welcome at a nearby farm, where they were allowed to draw water from the well. The other women in the group were all gossips and rumourmongers.

"Italy's just declared war on France," said one.

"Bloody bastards . . ." muttered another.

No-one knew to whom she was referring. The silence that followed was heavy with menace. They could hear a distant roar of aeroplanes but, looking up, saw nothing in the sky.

"Italy will be the last straw," said one woman, "as if things weren't bad enough."

The conversation quickly moved on, partly because of their eagerness to have a quick wash and bring water back to the families they had left on the motorway. Stoic resignation did the rest. Did anyone know whether the road was any clearer up ahead? Where might it be possible to buy petrol, eggs, bread? One woman needed shoes. "The ones I'm wearing weren't made for walking," she said. "Shoes! I'm not sure I have anything in Madame's size!" quipped another, and the women – including the butt of the joke – burst out laughing.

As Louise headed back to Monsieur Jules, she saw that the torrent of fleeing Parisians had steadily grown. Since they first set out, they had barely covered forty kilometres and had more than twice that distance still to travel. If the exodus continued, how long would it take to reach Orléans, two days, three?

"I know," said Louise.

"What do you know?"

"You're just dying to tell me that you were right, that it was a stupid idea to leave Paris."

"Did I say anything?"

"No, but that's what you're thinking, so I'll say it for you . . ."

Monsieur Jules threw up his hands, then slapped them against his thighs, but he said nothing. He knew that Louise was not angry with him, but with herself, angry at the situation, at life itself.

"We need to find petrol . . ."

All the drivers were probably thinking the very same thing, but no-one knew how to do it.

The caravanserai set off again. Lorries, vans, dustcarts, delivery tricycles, ox-drawn carts, coaches, delivery vans, tandems, hearses, ambulances. The motley assortment of vehicles on the motorway was like a showcase of French engineering prowess. The assortment of luggage was equally varied: suitcases, hat boxes, eiderdowns, commodes and lamps, bird cages, cookware and coat racks, dolls, wooden crates, steel trunks, even dog kennels. It looked as though the country was holding the largest flea market in history.

"You have to admit it's strange," said Monsieur Jules, "all those mattresses strapped to the roofs of cars . . ."

It was true that there were countless mattresses. Were they intended to protect the owners from aerial machinegun fire, or to allow them to sleep al fresco?

Those on foot and on bicycles moved faster than the cars, which lurched in fits and starts, damaging gearboxes, radiators and clutches. From time to time, gendarmes, soldiers, herds of volunteers tried to direct the traffic into lanes, but were powerless in the face of the dogged determination of thousands of vehicles intent on inching forward at any cost.

As the car juddered another twenty metres, Louise once again untied the string that held Jeanne's letters.

"That's your mother's handwriting . . ." said Monsieur Jules.

Louise was surprised.

"There weren't many girls as pretty as she was. Or as intelligent."

He looked heartbroken; Louise waited for him to carry on.

"Reduced to being a maid-of-all-work, I ask you . . ."

He turned off the engine. He could crank-start it when the time came, but it was important to allow the engine to rest as much as possible.

In July 1905, Jeanne wrote to Doctor Thirion:

> *My dearest love,*
> *I must be a truly wicked person . . . Any decent, respectable young woman would feel ashamed at the thought of going to a hotel with a married man. But I feel nothing but joy, as though sin were the most delightful thing in the world. It is so deliciously immoral.*

"So," said Monsieur Jules, unable to contain his curiosity, "was she proud to have a job as a skivvy?"

Louise shot him a glance. The word was not in his vocabulary, especially when it came to Jeanne.

"I haven't got to that part yet," she replied.

"Where are you?"

Louise could have handed him the letter and allowed him to read it for himself, but something stopped her – modesty, perhaps, or shame, she was not sure. Instead, she went back to her reading.

> *There is no part of me that is not yours by now and yet, each time, I feel I am surrendering a little more of myself to you. How can that be possible?*
>
> *I truly wish that I could die, you know. I was not joking when I said it, though I can understand why it upset you; it is a simple fact. But it is not a wish born of sadness, quite the reverse, it is a longing to leave this world with the best that life can ever offer me.*
>
> *You clapped your hand over my mouth when I said it. I still feel your hand pressed against my lips, just as I can feel you inside me, wherever I am, whatever the hour.*
>
> *Jeanne*

Louise was taken aback by the sheer intensity of her mother's passion.

"Is it sad?" said Monsieur Jules.

"It's . . . love."

She did not know what else to say.

"Ah, love . . ."

She found his sceptical, mocking tone infuriating; it was insulting. She bit her tongue.

In the afternoon, a series of military convoys passed, imperiously cleaving a path through the melee and trailing behind it a vacuum that accelerated the progress of the caravanserai. Although the traffic was no less dense, for a few hours it flowed more easily. Here and there, at a crossroads, or by the roadside, people would encounter others with whom they had spent an hour the previous day. There was time to say hello or exchange a few words before the convulsive contractions of the caravanserai swept them up and deposited them a little further on, among other neighbours, behind other cars.

Some thirty kilometres outside Orléans, traffic suddenly ground to a halt, as though the metal snake had decided to stop for a doze. Monsieur Jules, who was worried about running out of petrol, turned off onto a by-road where they came upon a farm.

Something had changed.

The days when farmers were happy to allow people access to their wells without charge were long gone (though barely twenty-four hours had passed). The farmer demanded twenty-five francs for the use of his barn. Because of the risks, he said, though he did not specify which ones.

# 33

The first supplies, which arrived at the camp shortly before 0700 hours, were reserved for the staff and the guards.

The prisoners watched from the windows as Indochinese soldiers unloaded the military van. Fearing a riot, Fernand ordered his men to keep out of sight while they ate. Meanwhile, to create a diversion, he ordered a sanitation detail so that the prisoners could wash. But the huge basins of hot water quickly ran out for lack of firewood and, after the first few prisoners, the others, faced with tepid, dirty water, declined.

"We'd rather eat," growled one.

Fernand pretended not to hear.

Two hours later, another supply truck arrived. The inventory was quickly done: a loaf of bread sufficient to feed twenty-five, and one spoonful per prisoner of cold sticky rice that had clearly been cooked the day before.

"Nothing I can do about it, adjudant-chef," said the capitaine irritably. "There's a war on."

Fernand had no time to respond when, from behind him, Bornier roared:

"You've already had your share, scumbag!"

The panicked freeloader, a journalist named Dorgeville, was betrayed by his quivering jowls. Instantly, other prisoners fell on him, knocked him to the ground and started to beat him.

Others came to his aid, and then the anarchists piled in.

Fernand ran forward, but the brawl was already too big to be contained, he had no choice but to draw his gun and fire a warning shot.

Even this was not enough. Soldiers had to separate the struggling prisoners, jabbing rifle barrels into their ribs, or rifle butts against their necks as blood flowed through the dust. A group of particularly frenzied prisoners faced down the soldiers. Such was their hunger that they were prepared to do battle, even if it meant fighting with their bare hands.

"Fix bayonets!" roared Fernand.

Although almost as panicked as the prisoners, the soldiers instinctively formed a line, bayonets fixed and ready to charge.

For a moment, it seemed as though the prisoners would rush the soldiers. Fernand bellowed.

"Prisoners, line up in twos! Quick march!"

One by one the mutinous prisoners gave up and fell into line. Dorgeville tried to struggle to his feet, clutching his ribs with both hands, and had to be helped up by three comrades. The prisoners reluctantly trudged back to the barracks.

Fernand grabbed Bornier's collar.

"You pull a stunt like that again," he said through gritted teeth, "and I swear, I'll have your stripes! You'll end up in a sentry box!"

The threat was purely hypothetical. It was impossible to imagine how Fernand could implement such a sanction. But it had taken Bornier twenty-three years of service and superhuman efforts to rise to the rank of caporal-chef. This was the most he could ever hope to achieve, and nothing terrified him more than the prospect of being stripped of his rank, forced to climb down the few rungs of the ladder he had managed to scale, and ending up an orderly in a sentry box outside some ministry.

Fernand stalked off and lit a cigarette – the one Alice always never allowed him to smoke. "Never before noon" was her phrase. He watched as the prisoners slowly trudged back to their dormitories. Then, having come to a decision, he went and reported it to the capitaine.

"I don't want to hear another word about it, adjudant-chef."

This was a tacit approval.

Fernand summoned his team and delegated a quick-witted young man in his early thirties named Frécourt to lead a group comprising two other mobile guards and four soldiers.

From the window of their dormitory, Raoul and Gabriel watched as the small group left the camp.

"Are they going for supplies?" asked Gabriel.

Raoul was not listening; he was busy studying the north fence of the camp. He pointed to it.

"That's our way out."

Gabriel screwed up his eyes.

"We'll have to move fast, but there's a chance that the air-raid siren will give us just enough time to duck out of sight behind that old storehouse."

It was a derelict building with shattered windows and gaping doorways whose only advantage was that it masked part of the barbed-wire fence surrounding the camp.

"And what do we do when we get there?" said Gabriel.

Raoul pulled a face.

"We probably curl up and die, but I can't see any other solution . . ."

Gabriel had initially been resistant to Raoul's idea of escaping but now, although hunger was making it difficult for him to think straight, he was forced to admit that things at the camp were quickly turning sour. They had just witnessed a near riot, the guards were increasingly volatile, brawls had already broken out between the prisoners, the pervasive hunger was driving everyone insane, to say nothing of the news that the Nazis were now just west of Paris . . . An hour earlier, Gabriel had approached a guard to ask whether a doctor could check the young communist whose teeth had been chattering ever since he arrived. Before the guard could answer, Caporal-chef Bornier strode over.

"A doctor? Anything else you need, you little faggot? I wouldn't send a fucking vet to care for you lot!"

He waved his bayonet. "Now, if you need a little injection . . ."

Gabriel held his tongue.

Although he had not formally agreed to Raoul's escape plan, his rational mind was already weighing their chances of success. They would have to be in the right place at the right time. They would have to trust to luck. And to help each other to get across the barbed wire. It would be impossible to escape this camp alone.

Moments after Fernand had sent his little group out on their mission, two veteran soldiers came to find him.

"The Germans are approaching, sir," said one.

This was hardly news.

"If things go badly, we're going to end up being prisoners too. And if the Jerries throw us in with that lot, I don't fancy our chances . . ."

"We're not there yet," said Fernand, but he sounded less than convincing.

"There's no artillery, no airforce cover, sir. Who's supposed to defend us if the Nazis show up?"

Fernand stared at the two men, stony-faced.

"We're waiting for orders."

He did not believe this any more than they did, but what else could he say? Capitaine Howsler was permanently glued to the field radio, and any soldier who tried to ask a question was shooed away like a fly.

To keep the prisoners calm, Fernand organised an exercise detail. When Raoul and Gabriel's turn came, they casually strolled towards the north fence, only to be stopped by a soldier.

"What the fuck are you doing?" he shouted, aiming his rifle.

He was a stocky, red-faced man, clearly overcome by the heat. From his rising, querulous tone, it was obvious that he was fretful; he was clearly ill-equipped for this ordeal. Raoul had gauged the situation in an instant. He took out a cigarette, offered it to the soldier.

"We're just trying to steer clear," he said simply. "We don't want to get caught up in a fight. Some of the prisoners are pretty volatile . . . "

Gabriel was taken aback. Not just by Raoul's presence of mind and consummate ability to lie, but by the fact that Landrade somehow still had cigarettes when no-one else had.

The soldier nodded slowly, as though embarrassed to accept, but the guards clearly had no cigarettes left either because, after a furtive glance, he stepped forward and grabbed the cigarette.

"I won't smoke it now . . ."

He slipped it into the breast pocket of his uniform.

"I'll save it for tonight . . ."

Raoul nodded and lit his own cigarette.

"Does anyone know what's happening?" he asked.

"If you ask me, we're well and truly screwed here. The Jerries are moving fast, and we haven't had orders for ages . . ."

As if to confirm his worst fears, a reconnaissance plane passed high overhead and the three men looked up and followed its path.

"Yeah," Raoul said, "it's not looking good, that's for sure."

The guard's silence was tantamount to a confirmation.

"Right, now I need you to head back to the barracks, boys. Don't make me . . ."

Raoul and Gabriel raised their hands, palms out – no problem.

In the early afternoon, the little group dispatched by Fernand returned. Frécourt leaned close to the superior officer and gave his report in a low voice.

The adjudant-chef nodded. Then he quickly strode over to the barracks, opened the door to the officers' room, grabbed his haversack and came out again. He assembled a small group, including Bornier (whom he was reluctant to leave unsupervised) and young Frécourt, commandeered the only flatbed truck in the camp and headed for the nearest farm, which was located near La Croix-Saint-Jacques. They would start there.

As they drove, Fernand racked his brains, trying to work out how he should go about it.

By the time the truck pulled into the farmyard, he still had not come up with an answer.

## 34

Monsieur Jules was not by nature a patient man, as regulars of La Petite Bohème could attest. Two nights without a bed, including one sleeping in straw, did not help matters. It was something the farmer who had provided accommodation came to realise when he demanded two francs from Louise for the bucket of water she planned to use to wash her face. Monsieur Jules lumbered into action, his battered carpet slippers raising dust, advancing like a pachyderm, shoving over anything in his path: the people in the farmyard, the farmer's son, the dogs, the cowherd who waved a pitchfork and was rewarded with a blow that would have felled an ox. Monsieur Jules grabbed the farmer by the collar, clamped his Adam's apple between thumb and forefinger with surprising precision and squeezed so hard that the man fell to his knees, his eyes bulging, his face crimson, panting for breath.

"How much did you say, buddy? I didn't quite hear."

The farmer flailed his arms wildly.

"Speak up . . ." said Monsieur Jules, with a scowl. "How much did you say?"

Louise rushed over and calmly laid her hand over Monsieur Jules'. He instantly let go, and the farmer fell to the ground.

Monsieur Jules glowered at the assembled company – what do you want, a photograph? Those present decided it was wisest to look away.

"Take the bucket of water, Louise. I think we can afford it."

While she doused herself in icy water in a corner of the stable and Monsieur Jules stood guard outside, Louise wondered about his curious behaviour. For the first time, Monsieur Jules did not seem like Monsieur Jules.

She emerged from the outhouse to find he was no longer standing outside. She spotted him in a barn, next to a tractor, and walked over.

"I can't give you any more," the farmer was saying apologetically as he filled the jerrycan with petrol. "We'd have none left to run the farm."

Monsieur Jules said nothing but stared at the jerry can, keep pouring, a little more, that's it . . . Good! He screwed on the cap, took his booty and, without a word of thanks, he strode over to Louise.

"I think we have enough to get us to Orléans, there might even be a little left over."

There was a little left over.

The Peugeot 90S guzzled petrol, but for the first hour or two, the traffic seemed strangely fluid. The endless procession of cars moved in fits and starts, sometimes flowing, sometimes stalling.

As they drove, Louise picked up the bundle of letters.

"More letters from Jeanne?" said Monsieur Jules.

As he turned to look at Louise, he drove straight into the wheel of a cart, and the front wing of the car started flapping like a mortally wounded insect. Monsieur Jules did not stop, he did not apologise. "All's fair in love and, especially, in war," he muttered.

Since they first set off from Paris, the Peugeot had lost a little of its finery: the rear bumper on the outskirts of Paris, a headlight just outside Étampes, the right indicator light some twenty kilometres further on, to say nothing of the countless dents and scratches acquired along the way. Anyone seeing it drive past could tell the car had been in the wars.

*December 18, 1905*

*My dearest love,*

*Why did you wait until the last minute to tell me? Were you trying to punish me? For what? Suddenly, I find myself bereft, knowing I will not see or hear from you for two long weeks, you come and tell me this, and then you turn and leave. I would rather you had stabbed me. Oh, you kissed me, and you held me, but it was not the same, it did not feel as though you were leaving your mark on my body, it felt . . . as though you were apologising. But for what? I have never asked anything of you, my love, you are free to leave just as you are free to do anything. But to say it as you did makes me feel as though you have abandoned me twice over. It was needlessly cruel. What did I ever do to you? How have I failed you? And to pretend that your decision to move away was made only yesterday . . . As if you would close down your surgery without telling any- one . . . Why do you feel you have to lie to me? I am not your wife.*

*In fact, you simply put off telling me because you knew how much it would hurt me, isn't that the truth? Tell me it is, swear to me that it is only out of love that you have caused me this pain.*

"Well," Monsieur Jules interrupted, "I don't know whether she loved the doctor, but she obviously loved writing to him."

Louise looked up. Monsieur Jules stared stubbornly at the road. "Yes, she did love him."

Monsieur Jules looked dubious. Louise was surprised.

"No, no, it's nothing," he said. "Call it love if you like. What do I know . . .?"

*Whenever you are away, I count the days, the hours, it bears me up, but two weeks without you near . . . What do you expect me to do with so many hours and days?*

*Your absence stretches out before me like a desert, I go around in circles, I do not know what to do with myself, I feel empty.*

*I wish I could scrape away the snow in the yard, dig a hole and slip inside to hibernate until you return, wake only at the precise moment when you are here again, when you lie on top of me. I have to hide away and weep.*

*All my tears are yours.*

*Jeanne*

The church of Saint-Paterne was striking ten o'clock as they arrived.

Orléans was bedlam. Everywhere they looked there were weary families, nuns scurrying around like mice, the town council was overwhelmed. A feverish, desperate atmosphere pervaded the city, people desperately scrabbling to find out where they could eat, where they could sleep, where they should go.

"Okay," said Monsieur Jules. "Shall we meet up back here?"

Before Louise could answer, he had already disappeared into the nearest bar.

Although she felt ridiculous asking people if they had seen "TCRP buses with windows painted blue", no-one seemed particularly surprised. In the flood of people looking to find a gas cylinder, a wheel for a pram, somewhere to bury their dog, a woman with a bird cage, postage stamps, spare parts for a Renault, a bicycle tyre, a working telephone, a train to Bordeaux, asking whether anyone had seen Paris commuter buses a hundred kilometres from the capital did not seem incongruous. But Louise got no answer, not from the prison where she could find no-one to ask, not on the public squares or along the river, not on the roads leading into the city, nowhere. No-one had seen the bloody buses.

By mid-afternoon, she went back to find Monsieur Jules who was sitting in the car, stitching up his tattered slippers with a needle and thread.

"Luckily, I brought a sewing kit with me," he growled as he pricked his thumb. "Shit!"

"Give it here," said Louise, taking the slippers from him.

Exhaustion had begun to carve lines and wrinkles into her beautiful face which only served to highlight her velvet lips, her shimmering eyes, and made you want to hug her. As she sewed, she gave Monsieur Jules a broad account of her peregrinations through the town.

"People have too much to think about to be paying attention to the scenery," she said at length, "they only notice the things that matter to them."

Monsieur Jules heaved a stoic sigh. Louise paused for a moment.

"I don't know what everyone is waiting for. Now that we've made it as far as the Loire, shouldn't it be . . .?"

She did not know how to finish her question. What had the hundreds of thousands of refugees been hoping when they fled Paris? That the Loire would be a new Maginot Line? Their most fervent hope had been that they would encounter reinvigorated French forces, an army prepared to resist, perhaps even to gain some ground, but they found only scattered, haggard soldiers and abandoned military trucks, the French army had melted away. In the past two air raids, not a single French plane had been spotted. The Loire, it seemed, would be just one more rest stop on the journey taken by a panicked populace.

The prospect of finding the TCRP buses and Raoul Landrade amid the surging tide of refugees seemed impossible. And going back to Paris was unthinkable.

"From what I've heard, the Nazi advance and the sudden influx of refugees has scared the shit out of everyone in the city," said Monsieur Jules, watching as Louise sewed his carpet slippers. "As the refugees flood in from the north, the people of Orléans are heading south . . ."

Louise finished her task.

"How far do you think you'll get in these slippers?"

"As far as the camp at Gravières."

Louise stared at him in astonishment.

"Don't look at me like that, I didn't spend all day hanging out in bars because I'm a lush, I did it out of a sense of duty! I did the rounds of five bars. If we don't find this guy you're looking for soon, I'll die of liver failure!"

"Les Gravières?"

"It's about fifteen kilometres from here. That's where they took the prisoners. They showed up the day before yesterday. Sometime around midnight."

"And you didn't think to tell me this before?"

"So? I needed my slippers to be able to drive, otherwise how are we supposed to get there?"

*

317

Gravières camp was not marked on any map. Monsieur Jules had to stop off at three bars to get directions and he was quite tipsy by the time they reached the broad, unpaved road where he was forced to brake sharply by a chain barrier blocking the route and a sign that read "MILITARY CAMP".

"Sorry," he said to Louise, who had almost been thrown through the windscreen.

"Thank God we're finally here," she said solemnly.

"It was all the investigating I had to do, I'm completely bushed . . ."

"So, what are we hanging around here for?" said Louise, nodding at the road ahead.

"We're hanging around here until we know what we're doing. If we remove that chain, we'll be trespassing on military land, have you any idea what that means?"

He was right. If they forced their way past the barrier, they would come to the military camp. Louise pictured watchtowers, barbed wire, armed guards. What good would it do?

"I thought maybe I could chat to one of the soldiers, or to a guard," she said.

"If you want to get yourself arrested for soliciting outside a military camp, that's certainly a good plan."

"Or talk to one of the soldiers as they're coming out."

"From what I've heard, there's more than a thousand prisoners banged up in there, so if you're going to talk to a soldier, he'd have to know every single one of them . . . "

Louise thought for a moment and then made a decision.

"We'll wait a while. If we don't try to enter the camp, no-one can stop us hanging around. We'll just wait here; someone is bound to walk past."

Monsieur Jules muttered something that might have been an agreement.

Louise took out Jeanne's letters. Every time she picked up the bundle, she untied the string, and when she had finished, she tied it up again.

May 1906. Jeanne was eighteen years old and had just been employed to work as a maid in the doctor's house.

As she began to read, Monsieur Jules got out of the car and used a chamois to polish the Peugeot. It was a preposterous exercise, like painting a dustbin about to go to a rubbish tip. Perhaps he missed polishing the zinc counter at La Petite Bohème. He worked with broad, sweeping gestures.

*My dearest love,*

*I'm sorry, I'm sorry, I'm sorry, I know that you will never forgive me, and I know that it is all my fault. You have every right to hate me for doing something so vile, so contemptible, so shameful, but you cannot blame me more than I blame myself . . .*

*I only realised what I had done when I found myself standing in front of your wife. I have often pictured her (I hated her without ever having met her because you belong to her and there is nothing left for me), and in spite of my hatred, I prayed that she would throw me out onto the street. But God has clearly abandoned me to my shame and infamy, because, rather than throwing me out, your wife offered me a position.*

*Oh, the look on your face when you walked into the living room to find me serving tea . . . I was so miserable I wished I could beg forgiveness from you, from both of you, yes, even from your wife.*

Suddenly, she became aware that Monsieur Jules was at the car door. He was cleaning the windows, like a petrol station attendant.

How long had he been standing next to her door? Had he been reading over her shoulder?

To hide his embarrassment, he breathed out, creating a halo of mist on the glass and then buffing it briskly, striving to look busy, scratching a spot on the glass with his fingernail. It was surprisingly assiduous for a man who could not drive ten kilometres without smashing into a streetlamp or running over a cow. Engrossed in her reading, Louise made no attempt to stop him. If he wanted to read over her shoulder, let him.

*You'll tear up this letter, and sooner or later you will proclaim the truth and have me kicked out of the house, which is no more than I deserve for my monstrous selfishness: I wormed my way into your home in order to hurt you, to shame you, but it is I who have been shamed.*

*But what you do not understand is that you are my whole life. Foolishly, I believed that by intruding on your life, you would be forced to choose and to protect my life. It was malicious, I know it. But you have to understand that you are all I have.*

*Now, I live in fear of bumping into you in the very home where I thought I could seek shelter from you . . .*

*Throw me out, do it quickly, I will carry on loving you more than my life.*

*Jeanne*

Monsieur Jules had moved away now. Louise could only see his back, his head was bowed as though he were studying an insect at his feet or searching for a key that he had dropped. There was something about his stance, something slumped and heavy, his shoulders sagged.

Puzzled, she got out of the car and walked over to him.

"Is something wrong, Monsieur Jules?"

"It's just the dust," he said, turning to face her.

He wiped his eyes with his sleeve.

"It's a bloody nuisance, all this dust."

He fumbled in his pocket then turned away as if to blow his nose. Louise did not know what to do. There was no more dust in this godforsaken corner of the forest than there was in La Petite Bohème. What was going on?

"Oh, fuck!" he said suddenly.

A military truck had just appeared and was heading towards them.

"Sorry," he said to Louise, then clambered behind the wheel.

It took him a moment to find the clutch pedal, then he fumbled with the gearstick and put the car into reverse. Up ahead, the truck driver braked hard and honked his horn, clearly infuriated, while a soldier jumped down to move the chain and shouted.

"Get out of here, this is a military camp, you've no business being here!"

As Monsieur Jules reversed, the Peugeot hit a tree, and though it was a loud crash, at least it left the road clear.

The soldier hooked the chain back onto the barrier.

"Go on, beat it! This is a military camp!"

The truck's tyres shrieked as it passed close to the Peugeot.

"Follow them."

Monsieur Jules looked puzzled. In that moment, Louise desperately wished that she knew how to drive a car.

"Don't get too close, but follow the truck."

Only when the Peugeot was back on the road and they could clearly see the rear of the military truck as it rounded each corner, did Louise explain.

"The guy in the front seat, the officer, he's an adjudant-chef. I saw him at Cherche-Midi prison when they were taking the prisoners away. I'm going to try and talk to him."

# 35

The farmer was a man who was proud of his belly, of his sprawling farm, of his submissive wife and of the convictions that had not changed one iota since they were passed down to him sixty years earlier, the legacy of four generations.

When Fernand saw him, he knew what he had to do.

"The rest of you, wait here . . ." he said, grabbing his blue haversack as he jumped down from the truck and bellowed: "I am authorised to requisition . . ."

He briskly covered the thirty metres that separated them, but this left more than enough time for him to see the farmer's face fall. From the way the man stiffened, stuffed his fists into his pockets and hunched his shoulders, Fernand knew that he had adopted the right strategy. He stopped in front of the farmer and roared:

"I am hereby authorised to requisition . . ."

His back was to the truck, so none of the members of his unit saw the broad smile he gave the farmer as he lowered his voice and said:

"Obviously, all produce requisitioned is paid for . . ."

For the farmer, this was good news, but it was not enough. What was being requisitioned, and how much would be paid for what was taken?

"I need a hundred eggs, twenty-five chickens, a hundred kilos of potatoes, lettuces, tomatoes, fruit, whatever you have . . ."

"Well, first off, I ain't got all that stuff . . ."

"Well, then, I'll take what you do have."

"Thing is . . . we'll have to see."

"Look, I can't stand around here all day. I'm requisitioning your produce, and I'm paying for it, full stop. Is that clear?"

"Hang on, hang on, hang on."

"How much are the eggs?"

"About five francs each."

Five times more expensive than usual.

"Right, I'll take a hundred."

The farmer did some mental arithmetic. Good God, that was five hundred francs.

"I got twenty, maybe thirty, but that's all . . ."

The regret in his voice was profound and sincere.

"I'll take them. How many chickens?"

Despite feeling sad that he did not have the quantities required, the farmer was having the time of his life. He was selling chickens for eight times more than he could get at market, lettuces for ten times more, tomatoes for twenty times more and potatoes for thirty times more. For each foodstuff, he marshalled an argument to justify the price: the shortages, the rain, the sun, but this officer was the kind of moron you meet once in a lifetime, a meathead prepared to believe whatever he was told.

Suddenly, a doubt floated into his mind.

"Hold your horses a minute, how is this going to be paid for. Because let me tell you right now I don't do credit."

Fernand, who was watching the last of the food being loaded into the truck, did not even bother to turn around.

"Now. In cash."

The farmer was thinking to himself: the French army is a fine institution, but I wouldn't trust it with my wallet.

"Come with me . . ."

They walked off and rounded the corner of a barn. From the haversack, Fernand took a wad of hundred-franc notes as thick as a capon's thigh. The farmer stared, dumbstruck.

"There you go."

Fernand made to walk away. But, just as the farmer was stuffing the money into his trouser pockets, he turned around.

"Oh, yeah – I meant to say. The Jerries are about thirty kilometres from here. If you stick around, you're in for a rough time."

The farmer's face was ashen. Thirty kilometres . . . How was it possible? Only last night, they were still outside Paris, he had heard it on the wireless.

"So, what about you lot, the infantry or whatever it is you are, where are you based?"

"We've just taken over the camp at Gravières to defend the local villages. And the farms."

"Oh, good," said the farmer, reassured.

"But not you. You'll have to defend yourself."

"Wha . . .? Wh . . . why wouldn't you defend us?"

"Because you're selling produce to us, which means that as far as we're concerned, you're not a farm, you're a supplier, it's not the same thing. Oh, and one more thing: the Krauts don't requisition, they just take over the place and help themselves, and when they leave, they torch the place. Thugs, the lot of them, but you'll find out for yourself . . . Anyway, keep your chin up."

Fernand should have felt ashamed for telling such lies, but the thought of the farmer waiting in fear of an enemy that would arrive eventually consoled him.

The team called at two cooperatives, three bakeries and four farms where they requisitioned potatoes, cabbages, turnips, apples, pears, a few hams and some cheeses. Everywhere they went,

Fernand would roar "Requisition!" for his men to hear, then take the owner aside, open his blue haversack and take out a bundle of hundred-franc notes.

He made the most of the time when the team spent loading up the truck to buy things he could give to his men as a bonus, little things he could hide from the other guards.

The war began to seem like a godsend to the local farmers selling their produce at a profit, often a large profit, sometimes an indecent profit. Fernand did not count the cost, he bought anything and everything that could be eaten without requiring much preparation.

As they were driving through Messicourt, he suddenly shouted "Stop!" The supplies slid across the bed of the truck, the soldiers fell over each other, but Fernand had already jumped down from the cab – wait for me here – and run into a post office which, by some miracle, was still open.

In a second miracle, there was a postmistress.

"Does this telephone work?"

"When it feels like it. I haven't been able to raise the operator for two days now . . ."

She was a lean woman with the look of a truculent governess about her.

"Let's give it a try anyway," said Fernand, giving the woman his sister's number in Villeneuve-sur-Loire.

Through the window, he could see his men smoking as they gazed around them at the empty pavements and the deserted streets, amazed that a humble adjudant-chef serving with a mobile guard unit could manage to requisition so much food when the military authorities could barely deliver enough Camembert to feed thirty.

"There's no answer from the exchange."

"Can you keep trying?"

While the postmistress was trying to put the call through, Fernand walked over to the counter.

"You decided not to leave?"

"Of course not – who would run the post office?"

Fernand smiled. Suddenly the woman looked away.

"Ginette? Hello, it's Monique! So, you came back?"

Whoever Ginette was, she launched into a long and detailed explanation which the Messicourt postmistress punctuated with little guttural sounds; that done, they put the call through to Ville-neuve. The postmistress pointed to one of the telephone cabins.

"Well, well, so it's you, honey!"

It was not so much that he was in a hurry, or that it had not occurred to him to ask his sister how she was, he simply could not contain himself.

"How is Alice? Tell me, how is she?"

"I don't know if I can rightly say . . ."

Fernand felt a cold wave run through him, as though his body had suddenly been drained of blood.

"She spends all her time at Bérault chapel . . ."

His sister's voice was grave, almost traumatised. At first, Fernand could not understand what was so . . . Then it dawned on him. He knew the little chapel at Bérault, it was out in the middle of nowhere, an ancient, derelict building half-buried by ivy, ringed by a cemetery of crumbling gravestones. From what he remembered, part of the roof had fallen in.

"The thing is, my love, it's very far away . . ."

Distance is a relative notion; his sister had never been further than Montargis. Fernand seemed to remember that the chapel was a few kilometres from Villeneuve.

". . . so, she's taken to sleeping there."

This was a little difficult to understand. It was not surprising that Alice should become more devout during this period, she firmly believed that she owed the fact that she was still alive to her religious faith. But from that to sleeping in a remote chapel, miles from his sister's grocery shop? Fernand quickly realised that the chapel was being used to house refugees.

"She says there's hundreds of them, that she can't just abandon them, and I understand, I do, but if it costs her health . . ."

"Have you told her she's being unreasonable?"

"As if she'd listen to me! And, besides, she hasn't been back to Villeneuve since she started sleeping out there, so I haven't had a chance to talk to her."

It was frightening to think that Alice, whose heart could give out at the slightest effort, was spending day and night in a make-shift refugee centre in a disused church. Where did she sleep? Was she expected to do manual work? Fernand was convinced that Alice would have told no-one about the state of her health . . .

He stared out the window as he listened to his sister. He could take the truck, drive straight to that bloody chapel, find Alice and make sure she was safe . . . It was that or feed the prisoners. For an instant, he found himself in Bornier's shoes, resenting and despising the prisoners. It was perhaps this unsettling resemblance to the caporal-chef that persuaded him to be sensible.

"I'll be there very soon . . ."

His sister, feeling she had failed to care for Alice, was now sobbing uncontrollably. How could Fernand be expected to go back to work in such circumstances?

As he emerged from the post office, Fernand saw his men standing, staring wide-eyed. Following their gaze, he saw a young woman, pretty, with blue eyes and a wan expression, coming to speak to him.

"Adjudant-chef, sir?"

Louise did not know how to address military officers and could not remember how the prisoner's wife – or daughter – had addressed him when he first appeared at the end of the street, carrying his blue haversack, walking towards Cherche-Midi prison.

Fernand stood, frozen. He was still shaken by the conversation with his sister and panicked by what she had told him about Alice, torn between his duty as an officer in the mobile guards and his need to be with her. The sight of this young woman, standing, holding out a letter, all but broke his heart.

"This is for a prisoner named Raoul Landrade . . ."

She had the hoarse voice of a harried woman.

Landrade, Landrade, Fernand racked his brain.

The young woman's hand was trembling. She was standing next to an old Peugeot that was obviously on its last legs. The chubby-faced man wearing a beret sitting behind the steering wheel, was probably her father.

Landrade. The name rang a faint bell.

"Raoul?"

Louise's face lit up, her beautiful lips curved into a smile, a smile like Alice's, the smile for which Fernand had done, and would do, anything in the world.

"Yes, Raoul Landrade," said Louise. "If you could . . ."

Fernand took the envelope. It was strictly against regulations, of course, but the times were propitious for transgression. His tour of the farms and the cooperatives, the lies he had already told and those he would tell, were they within "regulations"?

"What has he been charged with?"

No, thought Fernand, he could not go so far as to divulge the charges proffered against someone.

Except that, in that moment, as he came out of the post office, his head spinning from the alarming news about Alice, it was himself that he saw in this young woman's anxious face. Both were lost lovers, possessed by a categorical need for reassurance.

"Looting . . ."

Instantly, he regretted the word; Louise understood, and lowered her eyes as though he had not answered.

He stuffed the letter into his pocket and, out of principle, said:

"I cannot promise you anything . . ."

But that, in itself, was a promise.

Capitaine Howsler was in panic.

"If there's only food enough for your group, we'll have nine hundred rioting men on our hands, it's impossible."

"There is food enough for everyone, sir. Not much, but probably enough to see us through the next two days. Enough to restore calm. After that . . ."

What should have been good news seemed utterly mysterious to the capitaine.

"How did you get all this?"

"Requisitioned it, sir."

Was it really as simple as that?

"The army now has an account with these suppliers. If we win the war . . ."

"Are you taking the piss?"

"In that case, the Germans will inherit the debt."

Howsler could not help but smile.

The potatoes were cooked in large metal basins, the hams cut into small pieces, the chickens used to make *soupe grasse*; there was almost enough fruit for every man, the others could have cheese. Prisoners were delegated to cook the food under the watchful eye of soldiers who were just as hungry.

Fernand took his unit aside and handed out what he called a "bonus", something small they did not have to share. Some got *saucissons*, others tins of meat, Bornier was given a bottle of brandy. As he grabbed the bottle his lips trembled and his eyes misted over. Fernand wondered how long this "bonus" would keep his brutish tendencies in check and was not optimistic.

In principle, the arrival of supplies should have done much to boost morale, but this was interrupted by an air raid.

Everyone threw themselves on the ground. This time the Nazi bombers were not high in the sky, but somewhat lower. It was a reconnaissance flight. Everyone realised that this was a prelude to a bombing raid.

Two squadrons passed overhead, flying out and back, each time lower than before. From above, the hundreds of men sprawled on the ground must have looked like people close to death who had only to be rounded up and machine-gunned.

If the Germans were well informed (as everyone knew they were), it was unlikely that they would bomb a site known for harbouring men who favoured their cause. No-one could work out what was going on.

When the air-raid siren sounded, Raoul made the most of the confusion to pinch three apples, then he and Gabriel raced off, their bodies bent double, and sought shelter in a spot from where they could see the former supply stores.

"Excellent . . ."

Raoul was happy; his instincts had not failed him. One obstacle had been overcome, but there remained a second. Even if they could reach the derelict warehouse, they still had to find a way to get through the barbed-wire fence.

"That ladder . . ."

It was Gabriel who spoke.

As the Luftwaffe flew past again and the men on the ground covered their heads with their arms, Raoul and Gabriel took the opportunity to crawl a few metres.

Raoul brutally gripped Gabriel's wrist in congratulations. *Jesus, what a brilliant idea!* Lying next to each other as the ground quaked beneath the bombers, the two men glanced at each other. Next to the disused warehouse lay long wooden ladders of the kind used by decorators or roofers. It was an obvious solution. They would lay a section of ladder over the barbed wire, crawl across it, and then lay another section . . . Until they had crossed the barrier.

When the Nazi bombers had finished their tour of inspection, the men got to their feet. They were disconcerted by the threat of imminent bombing, but by now the soup was ready. And there was bread.

A roll call was carried out. There were four every day, not counting the ad hoc checks of individual barracks. Escape attempts vied with German bombers as the chief concern among the guards. Finally, everyone was allowed to eat.

To avoid fights, prisoners were served in small groups. Those at the back of the line grumbled, afraid that there would be nothing left when it came to their turn. Bornier, who never set down his rifle, would rush at them.

"You want to wait, or would you like a bellyful of bayonet right now?"

His enthusiasm for his bayonet was obsessive; everyone sensed that he would not think twice before using it. Two weary fellow officers led him away. This fatalistic gesture further worried Fernand. If things carried on like this, everyone would be worn out and there would be no-one prepared to try and calm Caporal-chef Bornier.

Fernand spoke to one of the officers in charge of the other barracks and suggested they give the prisoners half an hour's exercise before confining them to their dormitories. The men had eaten, the air raid was over, they could be allowed to walk around the yard.

"Prisoner Landrade!"

Raoul stopped in his tracks. Had he been indiscreet? Had their escape plan been guessed? Slowly, he turned around. The adjudant-chef was striding towards him.

"Body search," he snapped.

The apples. The three stolen apples.

"You lot, stay where you are," the officer shouted to three of his men who were coming to lend a hand.

Compliant but worried, Raoul stood with his legs apart and his hands clasped behind his head as he felt the adjudant-chef frisk the various places which, according to regulations and experience, might serve to hide a weapon. He quivered as the officer's hand felt an apple, then a second apple . . . He closed his eyes and prepared himself for a beating. From a few metres away, Gabriel watched as the scene played out . . . but saw nothing, the officer's hands continued their slow, systematic search.

"All good. Right, move on!"

Astonished and still uneasy, Raoul walked over to the corner of the warehouse where Gabriel shot him a quizzical look. Raoul was about to say something when he felt a piece of paper in his back pocket that had not been there before.

"Routine search," he said.

But Gabriel was no longer listening. One of the other prisoners had just announced the news: "Paris has been declared an open city."

The news spread like wildfire. Making the most of the uproar,

Raoul wandered off to the corner guarded by two soldiers where prisoners were allowed to urinate. Like everyone else in the camp, the soldiers were discussing the shocking news and paid little attention to Raoul, who took the piece of paper from his back pocket. It was an envelope. From it, he took out a letter which he read quickly.

*Dear Monsieur Raoul*

*You do not know me; my name is Louise Belmont. Since I fear that you may decide to throw this letter away, let me immediately set down a few details that will, I hope, persuade you that I am not mad.*

*You were abandoned as a child on July 8, 1907 and taken in by a family on November 17 of that same year. The civil registry officer named you Raoul Landrade, taking the names of the saints for July 7 and 8. You were raised at 67, boulevard Auberjon in Neuilly, by the family of Doctor Thirion.*

*I am your half-sister. We share the same mother.*

*I have important information I wish to communicate to you about your birth and childhood.*

*I have overcome many difficulties in order to find you, and the present circumstances are hardly propitious to a family reunion. Consequently, in case I cannot meet up with you, I wish you to know that I live on the impasse Pers in the eighteenth arrondissement. Should you not find me there, you can ask for information from Monsieur Jules, the proprietor of La Petite Bohème, located on the corner of the street.*

*If I may, I would like to sign off: Yours affectionately,*

*Louise*

Meanwhile:

"Open city?" the young communist said to Gabriel. "What does that mean?"

In all the time he had been at the camp, he had not taken off his hood, and his bouts of shivering had abated only briefly, after he had had food, but his pallid face and the dark circles under his eyes did not bode well.

"The Nazis have made it to Paris," said Gabriel. "We could try to defend the city, but if we do, they'll carpet-bomb and reduce it to a pile of rubble within days. By declaring it an 'open city', the government is saying they don't have to destroy Paris. They are handing it to them on a silver platter."

The consequences were dire. The government that had gifted its capital to the enemy would have to flee to avoid being taken prisoner. Meanwhile, the fate of all the prisoners here in the camp at Gravières depended on decisions made by the military authorities of a devastated country.

"So, we're going to end up being picked off by the Jerries, is that it?" said Bornier.

Fernand did not know what to say.

He felt a dull ache in his lower back, his chest was tight, as though covered by a scarab shell.

He went over to sit on a rock. As he bent down, his pocket gaped to reveal the spine of his book. He took it out. On the cover of the *Thousand and One Nights*, the sultry, shameless Scheherazade whose crimson veils covered only her breasts and her groin, had twin locks of jet-black hair – just like Alice – that formed an inverted heart on her forehead.

Fernand felt his eyes well with tears.

What the blazes was she doing at Bérault chapel?

He felt at sea, floundering to find some hidden meaning in the incomprehensible situation in which he found himself. He was surprised to find himself praying. Though he had recently attended mass without his wife, he had never prayed like this, alone. He stopped and glanced around: this was no way for an officer to be seen, given the circumstances . . . To give himself an air of composure he closed the book and looked around for the prisoner who had sought privacy to read his letter.

Instantly, he felt mortified. Why had he stooped to doing such a thing? Had he been mollified by the telephone call to his sister? Was it a fitting action for a man of his rank and standing? What would he think if another officer had done such a thing? He was ashamed that he had gone against regulations.

Then the thought occurred to him: what if the young woman was a spy?

What if the letter was a signal? Could there be a connection between the looming occupation of Paris and the arrival of this message?

Convinced that he had allowed himself to be duped by this young woman, who had used her charms to take advantage of him in a moment of distress, Fernand decided to demand an explanation from the prisoner.

He strode over to Landrade, his rage further fuelled by his wounded pride.

The whole camp turned to watch as the heavyset, yet remarkably swift adjudant-chef rushed, head down, at the prisoner who was staring into the clouds, squinting as though unable to believe what he saw.

Fernand never arrived at his destination.

He was halfway there when a dull roar shook the air above the camp, swiftly growing louder and louder until all eyes were staring into the sky.

Fernand was stopped in his tracks.

With a deafening shriek, the squadron of German bombers moved, casting a dark, shifting shadow on the ground below. The adjudant-chef completely forgot what he had been doing as he saw the planes drop bombs on the station barely five hundred metres away. The ground shook for miles around, guards and prisoners looked on, dazed, but their stupefaction quickly gave way to terror. The prisoners threw themselves on the ground, shielding their heads with their arms.

Raoul shot Gabriel a look: this was the moment they had been waiting for.

June 13, 1940

June 17, 1940

# 36

Fernand had been mistaken, the roof of Bérault chapel had not collapsed, though it was pockmarked here and there by holes. But sheltering from the rain was a secondary concern compared to the pressing issues of food and hygiene.

Alice had counted fifty-seven refugees, with more arriving every day. "Don't worry," the priest would say with his usual smile, "if they come, it is because God has guided them here." Nothing, it seemed, could shake him. When Alice first arrived at the chapel, he had welcomed her with a laugh.

"An unpaid volunteer? There is no such thing, my child, God always finds a way to repay us!"

It had been this, the priest's unfailing good humour, that had melted her heart. To say nothing of his determination, his resourcefulness, his fighting spirit . . . He seemed to be everywhere at once, and did not hesitate, as he himself put it, to "get his hands dirty".

"Jesus does not look to see whether the hands stretched out to him are clean or dirty."

That Thursday morning, Alice found him down by the little stretch of river next to which the chapel had been built. The small river made up for the lack of running water, which was in danger of posing a health risk.

Alice crept down the steep bank.

Around the soutane that whirled with the priest's every sweeping gesture, there were seven or eight refugees hard at work. The priest never asked anything of anyone; people were drawn to him. He had only to pick up a hammer or a spade for men and women to flock around.

"Can we help you, Father?"

"Well . . ."

The exclamation invariably made him burst out laughing, but then, most things made him laugh, which was doubtless why children adored him – they were constantly under his feet, tugging at his soutane, and he would often organise a football match or a game of hide-and-seek only to break off in the middle, saying: "That's not all, my children, but the Good Lord cannot do everything Himself!" and head back to repair the church, to treat the wounded and the sick, make cakes of soap from fat and wood ash or peel vegetables to make soup.

He started his day after Lauds at about five in the morning, and stopped only for Sext at noon, and for Vespers at about 7.00 p.m.

"Yes, yes, I know," he would say. "It's not the full set of offices, but I think God will excuse us off Terce and Compline."

In fact, he devoted much more time to God than the canonical hours. Whenever the needs of the refugee centre meant that Alice had to seek him out in the cell of monastic austerity that he had fashioned for himself, she invariably found him kneeling on his prie-dieu, rosary in hand, praying.

Between the three daily canonical offices he referred to as "Jesus breaks", he could be seen racing around solving one problem after another, whether begging or borrowing supplies, utensils, tools or materials, or laying siege to officials in what remained of the departmental administration, always with a smile on his face, as though life were one big joke created by a fun-loving and protective God.

His project this morning was to build a flush toilet using a hand pump he had found in an abandoned farm. It would pump water up from the stream and, once flushed, would rinse the toilet bowl, so that the lavatory was always clean.

When Alice happened upon him, he had his soutane hitched up and was squatting in the mud, urging on his team as they pulled the pipe up to the outhouse. On the count of three, everyone heaved.

"Jesus, Mary, JOSEPH!" he roared. "Jesus, Mary, JOSEPH!"

At each "Joseph!" the pipe rose another metre.

Alice saw him in profile and, as so often, what most struck her was the hole in his chest. Everyone noticed the neat, round hole in his soutane. A bullet. From strafing fire during an air raid somewhere in Paris.

"My bible," he would say to anyone prepared to listen, "I always keep it close to my heart."

He would take out the book, its cover scorched, its pages pierced by a bullet that had lodged midway through, a bullet he now wore on a chain around his neck. Whenever he moved it jangled against his crucifix. "It's like a sheep bell," he would say, "I am one of the Lord's flock." He still used the bible, he refused to get another. Reading from pages half-devoured by a bullet posed him no problem whatever.

"Ah, Sister Alice!" he said, without stopping his efforts.

This was what he had called her from the day she first arrived, and she had come to terms with it.

She walked down the bank to where he stood, looking pre-occupied. The pipe had now reached the outhouse and two men were attaching it to the pump.

"Let's give it a go," he said.

There was a dull gurgle as one of the men pumped the handle. The priest stared dubiously at the pipe. Nothing came out.

There was a moment of uncertainty during which the priest cupped his hands at the outlet of the pipe. And, as though God had simply been waiting for this gesture to work in His mysterious ways, the pipe disgorged a prodigious quantity of excrement.

"Ha! ha! ha!" he roared joyously, holding aloft his shit-filled hands. "Thank you, Lord, for this Thy offering. Ha! ha! ha!"

He was still laughing as he washed his hands in the river and as he walked up the bank to Alice, who was trying not to allow herself to be affected by this trivial situation.

"There are four new arrivals," she said, striving to sound as reproachful as she could.

"Well then, why the long face?"

This was a ritual between them. Alice kept saying that, at the rate refugees were arriving, within a few days the chapel would be filled to capacity and overcrowding would be their chief concern. To which the priest always replied that to turn people away was not in the "spirit of the house of God".

They walked up the hill towards the chapel. The priest kept his soutane hiked up, revealing a pair of muddy clodhoppers.

"Rejoice, sister! If God has sent new souls, it is because he has faith in us. Should we not be grateful for all that we have?"

Alice was more pragmatic in her accounting. It was difficult enough to feed those they already had. True, most of the refugees, buoyed up by the priest's enthusiasm, were not defeatist, and actively worked to find fresh supplies, but even so, the chapel had its limits. The nave and the transept were completely full – some people would have to sleep outside – and there were not enough able-bodied people, nor was there enough medicine or bandages. Simply drying the laundry took up a vast swathe of the cemetery where thirty generations of the faithful lay at rest. The priest had turned the remaining part of the cemetery into a refectory, where the flat gravestones had been propped up to serve as tables.

"Isn't this all a little . . ." ventured Alice.

"A little what?"

"Sacrilegious?"

"Sacrilegious? But, Alice, the good monks buried here have shuffled off their mortal coil, have fed the good earth with their bodies, what makes you think they would refuse a table to those who are hungry? Is it not written 'With thine eyes, thou shalt create light; with thy heart, thou shalt create hope, and with thy body, thou shalt create the garden of the Lord'!"

This was not a verse that Alice remembered.

"Where does it say that . . .?"

"The book of Ezekiel."

When it came to the cemetery, she had given in, but this time Alice was determined to make the priest see reason. Since they had no nurse, she had taken responsibility for all medical care. Thankfully, there were no seriously ill babies, or old people on their deathbeds, but no-one here was healthy, they had been worn down by exhaustion and poor nutrition.

She was about to try again but had to stop, her heart was hammering fit to burst, she felt dizzy.

Feeling she might faint, she bowed her head, pretending she was merely out of breath. She felt mortified at the thought of complaining, here among these uprooted families faced with the horrors of war, and in the face of the herculean efforts this priest had made for everyone, yes, she would have felt mortified if she had to reveal that she was ill, as though it was somehow unseemly to draw attention to herself.

During these giddy spells, when the threat of illness loomed, her thoughts immediately went to Fernand; she missed him terribly, the thought of dying without seeing him again was slowly killing her more surely than her faulty, failing heart.

She waited a few seconds and, as soon as the spell had passed, she walked slowly towards the priest.

"It's unreasonable, father. Taking in more people is putting the very existence of the refugee centre at risk and . . ."

"And, and, and . . . Firstly, there are no refugees here, only people in danger. Secondly, this chapel is not a 'refugee centre', it is 'the house of God', which is a very different thing. Here, we do not make choices. We leave those choices to the Lord. Our task is simply wait with open arms."

"Father Désiré! Most of these 'children of God' are sick, exhausted and malnourished. They have not seen a piece of meat for weeks. You cannot be certain that you can save them, and by taking in more, you are risking the lives of those already here. Is that really the Lord's will?"

Father Désiré stopped and stared down at his shoes, lost in thought. He looked nothing like the enthusiastic young priest she knew and loved. In his tense, pale features she could see only help-lessness and confusion.

"I know, Alice. You are right . . ."

His voice quavered, Alice was afraid he might cry, she did not know what to do.

"I have given the matter much thought," he said. "Why would God in His mercy uproot millions of people? What sin have we committed to deserve such hardships? Never have the ways of the Lord seemed more mysterious to me . . . But, by dint of prayer, I have seen the light. Look around you, Sister Alice, what do you see? In many people, this catastrophe has brought out base instincts, rank selfishness, blind self-interest. In others, it has kindled the desire to help, to love, it has awakened a sense of solidarity. This is what the Lord is saying: choose your camp. Will you be among those who turn in on themselves, who close their doors and their hearts to the poor and the destitute, or will you be one of those who opens their arms not *despite* the difficulty, but *because* of the difficulty. When faced with selfishness, with the threat of loss, with the instinct to think only of ourselves, our only strength, our true dignity, is to come together, do you understand? To come together in the house of God."

In Alice, emotion often prevailed over conviction. She nodded: I understand.

"And remember: 'Reckon not the travails or the hardships, for the house of God is a haven where the heart knows only how to give.'"

When he made up these biblical verses – by far the aspect of the work he most enjoyed – Désiré was not always successful, but in this case, he was not unhappy with how the scene had played out. Every day, his persona became grander and more refined. If the war carried on, within six months he would be a candidate for canonisation.

He took Alice's hand in his and the two slowly walked up the hill. Alice would have liked to say something, but nothing came.

They stopped when they saw the chapel, the cemetery, the garden, the adjoining meadow, the tarpaulins stretched between posts, the two roasting pits turning slowly, the brick oven built by a farmer with a talent for masonry and used by another refugee, a baker from Brussels, to make biscuits and vegetable tarts and pies. From the far right-hand corner, next to the canvas shelter Father Désiré used as his "office", some fifteen metres of wire suspended from electricity poles served as an antenna for the crystal radio set Désiré used to keep abreast of the war.

Father Désiré was right, thought Alice. When she surveyed

what this twenty-five-year-old priest had managed to achieve in the space of ten days, moved by a radiant faith that nothing and no-one could resist, she felt certain that he could triumph over any misfortune.

"Well," said Father Désiré, whose colour and whose smile had returned, "don't you think we are managing?"

Alice nodded. It was futile to argue; he always managed to convince you eventually.

They crossed the yard and went into the chapel.

To make up for the lack of bedding, Désiré had persuaded the manager of a factory in Lorris to part with hundreds of metres of hessian which he used to make huge sacks which were stuffed with straw to create bales that, after a night or two, took the shape of perfectly acceptable mattresses.

As soon as Désiré appeared, everyone flocked to him, the mothers grasped for his hand to kiss it (Easy now, he would say with a laugh, save your kisses for the Pope's ring!), men respectfully blessed themselves. To all the refugees drawn by rumours that there was "a saint at Bérault chapel", he was a saviour. "It is not I who have saved you, but the Lord. It is to Him you should give thanks." Most of the refugees had turned up shattered and hopeless; he had fed them all, calmed their fears, given them hope: they all now believed in heaven.

As the reader can see, Désiré was in his element. His inventiveness was constantly challenged, his imagination was working at full throttle. This man who had never believed in God revelled in the role of saviour. Peacetime would have made him a convincing guru. Wartime offered him a cassock which he had seen, if not as a sign, at least as an opportunity.

The cassock had belonged to a priest cut down by a bullet on a little road outside Arneville.

348

When he came upon the body of the priest, Désiré had felt moved. The black soutane reminded him of the incident with the crows outside the Hôtel Continental. Had his flight from Paris been prompted by remorse at playing such an active part in that vast enterprise of lies and misinformation? Had he felt, for the first time in his life, that this incarnation had not benefited those around him? Had his innate generosity fallen victim to his passion for reinvention? We will probably never know. Without a second thought, Désiré had pulled the body of the priest out of the ditch and swapped his clothes and his suitcase for those of the dead man.

He set off walking. With every step he entered into his character and was pervaded by his new vocation. By the time he had walked a kilometre, he was a priest.

He was particularly proud of his story about the bible. The idea had come to him while when he came upon a demoralised soldier sitting glumly on a milestone. Désiré entered into conversation with him and, in a dress rehearsal for his new role, tried to boost his morale. He also took the opportunity to filch the soldier's revolver, which he later used to perfect the bible pierced by a bullet.

Désiré had stumbled on Bérault chapel quite by chance while looking for something to drink. There, he found two families from Luxembourg who were shattered after the long trek from the village; as they had fled the German advance, they'd lost almost everything they possessed, including their illusions. Everywhere they stopped, they were treated as outsiders. As the Nazi troops continued to advance, solidarity among the French faded, encounters were more unfriendly, self-interest was more acute than ever, selfishness and short-term decisions became the order of the day, and no-one suffered more painfully than foreigners. "Go ask your king to give you some water," someone snarled at a Belgian asking for a glass of water.

When Désiré appeared, the two families mistakenly assumed that he was the parish priest of Bérault. Sensing the misunderstanding, Désiré smiled broadly.

"You are welcome in this house of God," he said, opening his arms wide. "You are at home here."

He had gone from being a simple man of the cloth to being a parish priest.

Hour after hour, day after day, more families arrived seeking refuge, most of them foreign, since French families avoided the chapel, considering it a kind of ghetto. The larger the group became, the greater their need, and the more Désiré warmed to his new role. For a pretender, what better role than that of priest?

He had hardly been at work a week when Alice appeared in the doorway of the chapel, eyes brimming with tears to see the miracle she had heard of when she first arrived in Villeneuve.

When Désiré had approached, she had been unable to resist falling to her knees and bowing her head. He had laid a hand on her head, a light, warm, caressing hand.

"Thank you for coming, my child."

He had held out his hands and helped her to her feet.

"God has guided you here because we have need of you, of your presence, your affection and your passion."

As they walked on towards the chapel and the new arrivals, to whom Father Désiré now offered his most welcoming smile, he paused for a moment, leaned close to Alice and whispered:

"Your heart is filled with the love of God, my child, that is good; but do not ask too much of that same heart . . ."

## 37

As shells rained down on the derelict train station, the ground beneath the Gravières quaked.

Raoul and Gabriel were waiting for the moment when everyone was lying face-down on the ground so they could run to the old supply store when, from the middle of the yard, the adjudant-chef roared:

"Everyone, back to barracks!"

The bombing of the area was intensifying. The soldiers and the mobile guards grouped together, rifles trained on the prisoners, and marched towards them, forcing them to retreat to their dormitories.

The prisoners were panicked at the thought of a bomb hitting the building and causing it to cave in on top of them. They felt as though they were being cast into a dark pit from which they would not emerge alive. That these foul-smelling dormitories would be their coffin.

As bullets screamed across the sky above their heads and the planes began dropping bombs closer and closer to the camp, the prisoners faced down the soldiers. Fernand instantly realised that he was about to lose control of the situation; something Raoul also quickly spotted.

Had the adjudant-chef sensed that Landrade was about to make his escape?

Did Landrade see, in this moment of panic that overwhelmed guards and prisoners, a last chance to put his plan into action?

For a fleeting moment, the two men stared at each other over the heads of the milling crowd.

A wave of terror rippled through both groups.

Bornier took out his pistol and fired into the air.

The air was thick with the shriek of aeroplanes. And yet this bullet, although less piercing and less deadly than the bombs exploding a hundred metres away, resonated with astonishing clarity because every prisoner assumed it was intended for him. The Nazi raid faded into the background. Their real enemies were the soldiers intent on killing them. They huddled together and stood firm. This was the second time that a riot loomed, this time almost beneath the enemy bombs. This would be a fight for survival; everyone was ready. Realising that their best ally in their plan to escape was this collective fear, Raoul and Gabriel moved to the front of the group.

Bornier aimed his pistol and strode forward.

Fernand rushed at him, desperate to avoid disaster, but it was too late.

Bornier lowered his weapon and fired two shots; two men crumpled to the ground.

The first was Auguste Dorgeville, the crypto-fascist "cagoule".

The second was Gabriel.

Stupefied, the prisoners froze. It was enough. In an instant, the soldiers were upon them, weapons aimed at point-blank range; the prisoners shuffled back, then, as bombs exploded on the edge of the camp, they raced into the dormitories for shelter. It was over. Three of the journalist's comrades grabbed his feet and dragged away his body. Raoul, meanwhile, took Gabriel under the arms and hauled him off.

"That's enough," he screamed, seeing the French bayonets trained on him.

The doors were padlocked, the shutters bolted.

Furious, and terrified at being caught in a trap, the prisoners pounded on the window. Gabriel's head rolled from side to side. Raoul quickly ripped the trousers next to the bullet hole from which blood was trickling, creating a pool that slowly seeped into the grooves between the poorly fitted floorboards.

The bullet had gone straight through Gabriel's thigh but had missed the femoral artery.

"He needs a tourniquet," said the young communist, visibly upset.

"Does he, now?" said Raoul, hurriedly rummaging through his belongings. "With doctors like you, the Supreme Soviet won't get very far . . ."

He ripped up a shirt, rolled it into a ball, and used it to put pressure on the wound.

"Instead of talking horseshit," he said, "why don't you go find him something to drink?"

The young man walked off. He was so stick thin that, seeing him walk, it looked as though he was dancing.

Gabriel recovered consciousness.

"You're hurting me."

"I have to put pressure on the wound, my friend, I need to stop the bleeding."

Gabriel's head fell back; he was deathly pale.

"It's alright, sergent-chef, you're alright, don't you worry."

As though to indicate that history had turned a page on this incident, the German bombing raid ended almost as soon as the bolts and padlocks were shot home.

Nothing remained of the train station. Blue and orange flames rose high above the treetops – a fuel dump had obviously been hit – and black acrid smoke plumed into the heavens.

Outside the barracks, Fernand stood, stunned, reflecting on the damage caused by a bloodstain in the dust. The clamour of the prisoners had died away. They too seemed to be waking from a nightmare after the sudden departure of the German bombers.

Caporal-chef Bornier had holstered his pistol. His hands were shaking. He did not know whether he had salvaged the situation or whether it was he who had set it off . . . No-one knew.

As for Fernand, he was not thinking of where to point the finger of blame. He was simply in a state of shock at the realisation that they had stooped to firing on their prisoners.

Behind that door, two men lay wounded, perhaps gravely wounded: this could lead to a massacre.

The other dormitories had also been locked and shuttered. The mobile guards, the soldiers, the Indochinese and Moroccan infantrymen stood around in small groups, shaken by what had just happened.

Hands clasped behind his back, Capitaine Howsler was pacing up and down the yard. Everything about him seemed to exude smug self-satisfaction: the camp had not been hit, his men had successfully quelled the panic, everything was for the best. But a keen observer – in this case, Fernand, who was walking towards him – would have seen in his deeply furrowed brow and the twitch of his lips the same dull dread that had affected every other soldier.

Where was the French artillery?

Where was the air force? Did the enemy now rule supreme and unchallenged over French skies?

Were they facing a total rout?

A swift glance at the padlocked buildings around the camp was enough for the soldiers to gauge the enormity of the task that lay ahead, and the uncertainty of their mission.

They were about to leap into the void; no-one could say how all this would end.

## 38

Louise was not at all convinced that the adjudant-chef would give her letter to Raoul Landrade.

"He probably just took it so I would go away . . ."

"I'd be surprised," said Monsieur Jules. "From what I saw, he looks like the sort of man who's well capable of saying no."

Now that the letter was gone, and the army truck had left, what should they do? The German army was on the march; trying to go back to Paris would be walking into the lion's den. Stay here? They might as well just wait for the lion to open its maw and devour them. There was only one solution, one that millions of refugees had already accepted: keep heading south. To where? No-one knew. They simply fled.

"We could have dinner here," said Monsieur Jules, "but we can't stay overnight, the place is deserted, it's dangerous."

"Dinner . . .?" Louise said sceptically.

There was nothing to eat. Monsieur Jules reached onto the back seat of the car an exhumed a paper bag from which he produced four sandwiches. And a bottle of wine.

"Since I was doing the rounds of the bars to try and find your friend, I thought I might as well stock up on provisions."

How Monsieur Jules had managed to procure four sandwiches at a time when buying a glass of water would have been a heroic feat was a mystery. Louise said nothing, but threw her arms around his neck.

"Alright, alright, that's enough, that's enough . . . Especially when you see this . . ."

He nodded to the open sandwich. The slice of ham was paper-thin. He got out his corkscrew, opened the bottle, then they set about chewing their way through the stale bread.

Louise took out the bundle of letters.

Monsieur Jules stared out the windscreen, brooding and knocking back glasses of wine at a worrying rate.

"I wouldn't mind a little glass," said Louise.

Monsieur Jules shook himself from his reverie.

"Oh, I'm sorry, my darling, excuse me . . ."

His hand shook as he poured, Louise had to steady the neck of the bottle to stop wine spilling everywhere. For a man who owned a bar . . .

"Are you alright, Monsieur Jules?"

"Why, don't I look alright?"

His tone was aggressive. Louise sighed: this was how he was, surly and sullen, and a world war was not about to change that. She went back to her reading.

The letter was dated June 1906, from the period when Jeanne Belmont was working as a maid in Doctor Thirion's house.

> *My dearest love,*
> *I have created a situation without weighing the possible consequences.*

Louise sensed Monsieur Jules leaning towards her, reading over her shoulder.

Had she wanted her reading to be strictly private, she would not have done it here, in the car, in his presence. And so, she pretended not to notice and carried on reading. It was a long letter.

Jeanne explained how guilty she felt at taking a position in the doctor's household, but she had very mixed feelings because, she wrote, "*of the joy of feeling your presence everywhere, all the time. For the moment, I am revelling in my role as a usurper, because it makes my life complete.*"

As she set down the letter, she noticed that Monsieur Jules had tears in his eyes. The fat tears of a fat man with a big heart.

A disconcerted Louise simply laid a hand on his arm; he did not shrug it off. His nose was running. Louise fumbled for a handkerchief and wiped his face, as one might do a child.

"Come on," she said, "come on now."

"It's her handwriting, you understand?"

Louise did not understand, but she waited, handkerchief at the ready. Monsieur Jules stared straight ahead.

"Look, I wasn't a doctor, so maybe that's why . . ."

From the lips of anyone else, it would have sounded non-sensical, but not coming from Monsieur Jules. Suddenly, Louise realised how blind she had been, how cruelly she had treated this man.

"I never loved anyone in this life the way I did your mother, you understand?"

There, he had said it.

"No-one."

He took the proffered handkerchief.

Now the floodgates were open, the torrent came.

"I watched as she got herself mixed up in that affair . . . What could I do, huh? She wouldn't listen to anyone."

He stared at his empty glass and toyed with the handkerchief. Out of the blue, as though he had had an epiphany, he turned to Louise.

"I was a fat guy, you know? It's a peculiar thing, being a fat guy. People like to confide in you, but it's never you they fall in love with."

Monsieur Jules sensed that he was beginning to seem ridiculous. He cleared his throat.

"So, I married . . . Oh my God, I can't even remember her name. Germaine! That's it, Germaine . . . She ran off with one of your neighbours, and she was right to do so. If she'd stayed with me, she would have been miserable, because there was only ever one woman in my life, and that was your mother."

The sunset, which can all too often seem mawkish, lent this moment a tender solemnity.

"I never loved anyone but her . . ." he said again.

This bald statement, which he had doubtless said to himself a million times, was too much. The tears returned and, one by one, Louise wiped them away thinking to herself that, in a sense, she was in the same boat as Monsieur Jules. Both of them had longed to be loved by this woman whose passion was focused elsewhere. At this though, she felt a lump in her throat. For two people to hug in the cramped Peugeot amounted to an acrobatic feat; they managed it effortlessly.

"I'll carry on reading, if you like . . ."

"If you like . . ."

"This is from the end of 1906."

"Ah, so Jeanne is pregnant?"

"I think so."

The first words, "my dearest love", were hard to bear. They were painful, simple, necessary.

> *My dearest love,*
> *You will not abandon me, will you? I have given my*

*whole life to you, surely you cannot leave me in the state*
*I am in.*

*I shall wait for your reply; I live only for you now.*
*What shall I do if I do not have you.*

*Write soon.*

*Jeanne*

"What did he reply?"

"I don't have his letters, only the ones Maman wrote."

How long had it been since she last thought of her mother as "Maman"?

"Oh, who cares . . . What does the next letter say?"

*December 4, 1906*

*My dearest love,*

*In a little while, I shall leave. I have accepted your*
*reasons. I have accepted your promise.*

*I say this only now, because there is nothing more to be*
*done. I am terribly scared. To know that it is your baby I am*
*carrying, your baby that I will give up breaks my heart.*

*I beg you, please do not abandon me again.*

*Jeanne*

Monsieur Jules said nothing. He clutched the damp handkerchief and furrowed his brow. His head rocked on his shoulders
as though moved by the breeze.

Louise carried on reading.

*July 10, 1907*

*My dearest love,*

*This letter will be brief, I cry so much that I can do*
*nothing else.*

*Never did I imagine that this moment would come: I do not want to see you anymore. Not that I no longer love you, that would be impossible. But something inside me is broken. I am no longer myself. Perhaps later, if I still mean something to you. Oh, if you had only seen the baby's little face . . . I saw it only for an instant. Everyone bustled about so that I would not see him, it was terribly cruel, and so, in spite of the pain, I got up and crossed the room quickly enough that no-one had time to stop me. I ran over to the nurse who was cradling him in her arms, and I pulled away the coverlet hiding him.*

*Oh, that little face!*

*It is burned into my mind for the rest of my days.*

*I fainted. When I came to myself, it was too late, that is what they said to me, it's too late, there is nothing you can do now.*

*I spend my days weeping.*

*Despite the suffering that this has caused me, I still love you, but to see you, now, is more than I could endure.*

*I love you, and I leave you.*

*Jeanne*

Monsieur Jules had regained his composure.

"She told me the baby was stillborn. Can you make sense of that? Why did she not tell me the truth? If she couldn't have told me, who could she have told? Who?"

Jeanne had given birth, had seen her baby in the moment he was ripped from her. That single image justified all the effort that Louise was putting into trying to find Raoul.

Now, she was no longer doing this for him, she was doing it for Jeanne, for the mother who had suffered so much.

"September 8, 1912," read Louise.

She and Monsieur Jules glanced at each other. The love affair unfurling in this small bundle of letters was taking a new turn now.

Jeanne had married Adrien Belmont in 1908.

Louise had been born the following year.

Five years after walking away, Jeanne had once again taken up with the doctor, while she was still married.

Who had initiated this reunion? It was Jeanne: *"I am so happy just to know that you have not forgotten me, that you have agreed to see me again . . ."*

She was simple in her reasoning: *"I could bear it no longer. I distanced myself from you, but you were always there inside me, so I made my decision. If I was to be damned, better to be so in your arms . . ."*

Louise shuddered.

"You're not cold, are you?" said Monsieur Jules.

Louise said nothing; for a long moment she stared out the windscreen at the waning golden light that seemed to fall from the trees.

"Sorry? No, I'm not cold . . ."

Had Louise known her father better, these letters from Jeanne would have been painful, but to her, he had merely been a photograph, and a poor one at that, scant reason to feel pain.

"Do you want to hear the rest?"

"If you don't mind . . ."

*November 1914*

*My dearest love,*

*Why would you do such a thing? Does this war so badly need more men to die that you should decide to enlist when there is nothing to compel you?*

*Are you so intent on leaving me?*

*Every day, I pray that little Louise will not lose her papa. Must I weep every night so that this war will spare my only love?*

*You tell me that you love me, but what sort of love can it be if you choose war?*

*You will come back, won't you?*

*Come back for me. And keep me for yourself.*

*Your Jeanne*

The fact that Doctor Thirion had enlisted came as a surprise. At the time, he would have been over fifty (not that the army turned anyone away, especially not a doctor, there was work enough for everyone) and he had decided to risk his life at the front.

The question Jeanne had asked was the one now on Louise's lips: why? Out of conviction? It was possible.

Unexpectedly, Louise remembered the two war veterans who had rented a room from her mother after the war. Jeanne had never been prepared to rent out the lean-to before. Had she seen in them something of the two men she had loved who had also enlisted?

"It never occurred to me that a man like him would have served in the war," said Monsieur Jules.

Louise, too, found the doctor's patriotism a little suspect. This was the moment when she genuinely regretted not having the letters that the doctor had written. It was difficult to understand this love affair, more difficult still when one knew only one side . . . What was certain was that the doctor had sacrificed himself. He had signed up to defend his country. Or to defend his love.

*My husband was killed on July 11.*

*J.*

The note was written on a page torn from an exercise book.

This time, her father's death brought a lump to Louise's throat.

What a waste their marriage had been. Even she, as a child, had served no purpose. Louise blew her nose.

"Come on now," said Monsieur Jules, hugging her to him.

There was only one letter left.

It was Monsieur Jules who read it. His voice was deep and tremulous, at each word it sounded as though he might cough.

*October 1919*

*My dearest love,*

*To write this last letter to you is as poignant as the memory of our first meeting. My heart beats now as it did then.*

*The only difference is hope, since you have deprived me of that. Since you refuse to be with me, to live with me, now that it is possible.*

*You know that it is killing me, but you do so just the same.*

*I console myself by living with the love I bore you. I owe a duty to my little Louise whom I will not abandon as you have abandoned me. But for her, I would die at this moment. With no regrets.*

*I have loved only you.*

*Jeanne*

They were the same words Monsieur Jules had said barely an hour earlier. All loves are alike.

So, now that she had been widowed and could start a new life with him, it was the doctor who refused.

"The bastard," muttered Monsieur Jules.

Louise shook her head.

"He had decided to raise Jeanne's son Raoul. Without ever telling her. By this point, it was too late. He was a prisoner of his own secret. Had he left to be with Jeanne, Madame Thirion would have told her everything . . . Whatever the case, their affair was over. The doctor was bound hand and foot, there was nothing he could do."

The two sat for a moment and contemplated the damage wrought by this relationship.

Monsieur Jules had drunk almost a whole bottle of wine by himself. Louise's glass was still half full. By tacit agreement, they both shook off the memory. Louise emptied her glass out the window while Monsieur Jules got out and crank-started the car.

Without a word, they drove out of the woods.

Gone now was the golden light of sunset, and they found themselves on the dark road heading out from Orléans, surrounded by carts filled with furniture, passing meadows where thirsty horses jumped fences. The rich had long since fled, this was an exodus of those who could scarcely walk: a motley mix of soldiers and farmers, civilians and cripples, a whole nation on the move, the girls from a brothel on a public omnibus, a shepherd with three sheep.

The Peugeot lurched along amid a stream of refugees that mirrored this country that had been sundered, abandoned. Everywhere were faces and more faces. A never-ending funeral cortege, thought Louise, as she gazed into this mirror of our sorrows and of our defeats.

Having covered some twenty kilometres at a snail's pace, the Peugeot came to a standstill in a huge tailback on the road to Saint-Rémy-sur-Loire.

Next to them, a woman pushing a cart filled with bundles of clothes.

"Have you any water left?"

Monsieur Jules said that there was a bottle somewhere in the boot. He said it grudgingly, his tone clearly half-hearted. Louise got out to fetch it and offered it to the woman.

"I won't say no . . ."

The contents of her cart were not bundles of clothes, but children. All three of them asleep.

"The two eldest are eighteen months," said the woman, "the little one is not even nine months yet . . ."

She ran a children's nursery in a town whose name Louise did not recognise. When the mayor ordered an immediate evacuation, parents had rushed to collect their children.

"All but three, I've no idea why . . ."

She had clearly been brooding on this *why* ever since she set out.

"They're good people, the parents of the elder two, something must have happened to stop them . . . As for the baby girl, we didn't really know her mother, she'd only just arrived . . ."

The woman was shaking with fear and exhaustion.

"She's got it hard, the baby, she's not weaned yet . . . What can you do? She can't eat solids yet, she'll only drink . . ."

The woman handed back the bottle of water.

"Keep it," said Louise.

Monsieur Jules was honking the horn. When the caravanserai set off again, there was no way of knowing whether it would advance a metre or a thousand metres; this was how people got lost in the maelstrom. Louise picked up Jeanne's letter, not because she had any desire to reread it, but as an instinctive reflex that betrayed her anxiety.

Hardly had she snatched it up when, unannounced as always, tragedy struck. This time in the form of a pteranodon several hundred metres ahead, its vast wings unfurled. With a thunderous howl, it flew so low that it looked as though it might devour everything: tarmac, trees, cars and refugees. Instead it strafed the hundred-metre stretch of road with machine-gun fire, then banked and soared with a deafening roar. Thrown to the ground, the refugees found themselves flattened, petrified, devastated by this sudden, violent apparition and they wished the earth would open up and swallow them.

Monsieur Jules had lain down next to the open car door. Louise had stayed in the car, so terrified was she that she did not have time to get out. A dull crash projected her forward and her head hit the windscreen, her body shook from the ear-splitting shriek of the sirens while the short, flat impact of the bullets seemed to bore through her. It was impossible for anyone to tell if they had been hit, since their minds had ceased to function.

Then, the pteranodon's siblings appeared, two, three, four of them, all eager to join the fray, to sow terror, each fuelled by the same scrupulous, efficient, murderous fury, engines blaring like the trumpets of Jericho, shattering willpower, cutting bodies to the marrow, bursting eardrums, plunging into ribcages, engulfing minds. The wild machine-gun bullets shredded everything in their path. Numbed and petrified, her hands clapped over her ears, Louise no longer knew whether she was alive or dead. Sprawled on the front seat of the car as it juddered and jolted, terrified by the staccato burst of bombs and gunfire, she no longer felt anything. Her mind, like her body, was utterly drained.

Then, as abruptly as they had arrived, the pteranodons flew off, leaving a heartrending silence.

Louise takes her hands from her ears.

Where is Monsieur Jules?

She shoulders open the door. The bonnet of the car is crumpled and smoking. Unsteady on her feet, Louise walks around the car and sees Monsieur Jules lying on his belly in the road, his bulbous behind seems to take up all the space. She bends down and touches his arm, he slowly turns to look at her.

"You alright, Louise?" he asks in his cavernous voice.

He gingerly gets to his feet, pats his knees, looks at the car: their journey is over, there is no car. In fact there is nothing. For as far as the eye can see, there are lines of ruined vehicles, bodies lying on the tarmac; from everywhere come groans and whimpers, and there is no-one to help.

Louise stumbles forward.

A few metres away, she spots the blue dress of the woman from the nursery, she is lying on her back, her eyes wide. A bullet has ripped through her throat.

In the cart, the three babies are wailing.

"I'll stay here," says Monsieur Jules, who is now standing next to her.

She looks at him, failing to understand. He looks down at his carpet slippers.

"I'm not going to get very far on foot . . ."

He nods at the three distraught children.

"You'll have to take them with you, Louise, they can't stay here."

Monsieur Jules is the first to hear the rumbling in the sky. He looks up.

"They're coming back, Louise. You've got to get out of here!"

He pushes her, lifts the handles of the cart and hands them to her – *go on, get going.*

"But what about you . . .?"

Monsieur Jules does not have time to answer before the first fighter plane starts to strafe the road. Louise grabs the handcart and pushes; it is surprisingly heavy, it takes all her strength, but finally she gets it to move, she takes a step.

"Go on!" roars Monsieur Jules. "Go on, get out of here!"

Louise turns back.

Her last glimpse of him is of a fat man wearing carpet slippers standing next to the wreckage of a Peugeot who, without a thought for the planes hurtling towards him, machine-guns blazing, stands waving for her to go, to save herself.

Electrified by fear, Louise steps over the body of the woman in the blue dress whose throat is spurting blood. She crosses the hard shoulder.

The babies are bawling; the planes are closer now.

Already, Louise is running through the field, pushing the cart . . .

## 39

"*Credo um disea pater desirum, pater factorum, terra sinenare coelis et terrae dominum batesteri peccatum morto ventua maria et filii* . . ."

Oh, how they loved that!

Désiré launched into his oration, despite not having even rudimentary Latin. And since he had rarely attended mass, he had no idea what precisely he was supposed to do. So he improvised masses after his own fashion, delivered in a language reminiscent of Latin (albeit vaguely), peppered here and there by the only phrase he did know: *In nomine patri et filii et spiritus sancti,* at which points the faithful, pleased to have found their bearings, chorused Amen!

Alice had been the first to doubt.

"The mass you said, Father, it was very . . . disconcerting."

Delicately, Father Désiré removed the chasuble he had found in the suitcase belonging to the priest, who had doubtless now been buried wearing the clothes of Désiré Migault, then he said:

"Yes, the Ignatian liturgy . . ."

Alice meekly admitted that she had not heard of it.

"Even the Latin . . ." she ventured.

Father Désiré gave her a broad smile and explained that it was drawn from the order of Saint Ignatius, who performed a form of religious service "that pre-dated the Second Council of Constantinople".

"Our Latin, one might say, is the original. Closer to the source, closer to God!"

And, when Alice explained her confusion ("We don't know what to do, Father, when to stand, when to sit, when to sing . . .") he had reassured her:

"It is a simple, plain liturgy. When I raise my hands like this, the congregation stands. When I do this, they sit. In the Ignatian rite, the faithful do not sing, the priest does so on their behalf."

Alice spread the word; no-one seemed surprised by anything any longer.

". . . *Quid separam homines decidum salute medicare sacrum foram sanctus et proper nostram salutem virgine . . .*"

Many more refugees had arrived over the past days. As a result, even the choir was now overrun, such that mass had to be said in the apse and the side chapel, both of which were full to bursting for every service. Désiré was so popular that there was not room for everyone who wished to attend. Out in the cemetery, the faithful heard mass through the broken stained-glass windows.

During the day, when weather permitted, Désiré would say mass in the open air. Boys fought amongst each other to serve as the altar boy because, during pauses in the service, he would turn and wink at them, as though he were one of them and was only playing at being a priest.

"*Confiteor baptismum in prosopatis vitam seculi nostrum et remissionem peccare in expecto silentium. Amen.*"

"Amen!"

Désiré's greatest frustration was the fact that, busy as he was doing a hundred and one different things for his flock, he did not have as much time as he would have liked to indulge in his favourite pastime: hearing confession. He was fascinated to discover how many sins they found to confess, these people who were merely victims. Désiré was liberal and generous in his absolution; everyone was happy to confess to him.

"Father . . ."

It was Philippe, a Belgian as round as a beer barrel with a girlish voice. He was suspected of bigamy, since he was travelling with twin sisters whom no-one could tell apart. It was thanks to Philippe, who had been an engineer in civilian life, that the priest's crystal radio set was so acute that the congregation had as much information as the highest-ranking military authorities.

"It's gone seven o'clock . . ."

Father Désiré looked up from his sewing (he was making sleeping bags for the new arrivals while listening to the radio news, which confirmed that Châlons-sur-Marne and Saint-Valery-en-Caux had been taken by German troops).

"Let's go!"

Two or three times a week, Father Désiré drove to the government offices in nearby Montargis in a military truck he had found abandoned a few kilometres from the church, having run out of fuel. Désiré had found petrol and driven the truck back, removed the tarpaulin cover and, on the bed of the truck, leaning against the cab, he mounted a large cross that had been ripped from the walls of the church during a thunderstorm. Almost two metres tall, the crucifix was turned to face the open road.

"Now Jesus can light the way," he explained.

Since "God's Chariot" constantly belched exhaust fumes, the crucified Christ would appear, wreathed in whorls of opalescent smoke that looked like angels. As they drove through Montargis, passers-by would make the sign of the cross.

From the clatter of the engine, Georges Loiseau, the sous-préfet, would know that he was about to receive a visit from

Father Désiré, who would appear some moments later, bursting into his office without bothering to have himself announced, since there were almost no staff left other than Georges Loiseau, a calm, determined man who had resolved to remain in his post until the invading forces ousted him.

"I know, Father, I know!"

"Well, then, my son, if you know, what have you been doing about it?"

Father Désiré had been demanding to speak to a civil servant, a rare creature in these troubled times. He wanted a list made of all the refugees at Bérault chapel, stipulated that they be granted rights and demanded that the administration provide subsidies that he might use to house, feed and tend to the group; in addition, he had requested that he be allocated a doctor or a nurse.

"There's no-one here, Father . . ."

"You're here! Why don't you come in person. Jesus will thank you."

"Are you saying that Jesus Himself is there?"

The sous-préfet liked to joke with Father Désiré, it was the only way he found to distract himself from his gruelling workload, since he spent most of his time issuing orders to the few staff he had left, trying to find the means to aid the numerous refugees flooding into the département, mobilising the gendarmeries, the social services and the hospitals – it was exhausting.

Désiré smiled.

"I have an idea."

"Good God!"

"You're telling me!"

"I'm listening."

"Since you are devoting all your energies to desperate cases, and never come to visit the chapel because we somehow manage to get by, what would you do if, say, I allowed a dozen refugees to die of starvation?"

"A dozen? It's not many . . ."

"How many deaths will it take for you to intercede?"

"To be honest, Father, I can't see myself making the trip for less than twenty."

"Should I ensure they're all women and children?"

"That would be very thoughtful."

The two men smiled at each other. Both were faced with the same task; filling the yawning gaps left by war. This exchange was a sort of ritual, after which they discussed more serious issues. Désiré had never left the office empty-handed. Once, he had come away with the two jerrycans of petrol he used to fuel God's Chariot (so he could come back and beard the sous-préfet in his den), on another occasion, he had been given permission to take equipment from the local school canteen.

"What I really need is some sort of presence, you understand? A medical officer."

Loiseau had never told the priest that he still had a number of nurses at his disposal, but the situation at Bérault chapel was becoming increasingly worrying. He had not yet had the chance to visit, but the alarming increase in the number of people being housed at the makeshift refugee centre had forced him to rethink.

"I'll send you a nurse."

"No."

"What do you mean, no?"

"You won't send her, I'll take her there right now."

"Very well. But, since I know you'll never give her back, I will come and pick her up again in person. Shall we say Tuesday? Ten o'clock?"

"Will you conduct a census?"

"We'll see . . ."

"Will you conduct a census?"

The sous-préfet was tired. He gave in.

"Alright."

"Hallelujah! For that good deed, Monsieur Loiseau, you deserve a mass. What do you say to a little mass?"

"Fine, I'll come to the mass . . ."

He truly was worn down.

She was a nun with the Daughters of Charity. Young. With a wan face and stern features.

She offered Philippe a long, pale hand.

"Sister Cécile."

A little nonplussed, the Belgian reverently took her hand, then went back to loading the nurse's boxes and suitcases onto the bed of the van.

The drive back from Montargis followed a complex, sinuous route, one that allowed Father Désiré to visit the neighbouring farms and take whatever he could to feed those living in the chapel. He rummaged through kitchen gardens ("Are those tomatoes I can see over there?"), explored cellars ("You have enough potatoes here to withstand a siege, surely you can give me half to do the Lord's work?")

"It's extortion," said Alice, the first time she made the journey with him.

"Not at all. Can't you see how happy they are to donate?"

As they passed through Val-les-Loges, Father Désiré waved to Cyprien Poiré, who was tilling a field in which there was a calf tied up.

"Turn right," shouted Father Désiré.

Philippe the Belgian braked hard, not to satisfy the demands of Father Désiré, but because the road ahead was blocked by an interminable line of military vehicles.

"If that's the French army, I can't help but wonder whether they're heading in the right direction," said Father Désiré, ". . . because the Germans are that way, if I'm not mistaken," he added, nodding in the opposite direction.

The young nun smiled. At the prefecture, they had talked about nothing else all morning: the Seventh Army had begun a retreat to the Loire, and the vehicles they could see were probably the advance guard.

"Where in heaven are they going?" Désiré wondered aloud.

"I believe they are headed for Montcienne," said the nun, "though I cannot be certain."

Once the column had passed, God's Chariot was able to turn onto the dirt road that led towards the Poiré farmstead, an extravagant term for a place with only two buildings. Cyprien, a turbulent farmer, lived there with his mother, Léontine, with whom he had quarrelled. An age-old dispute divided mother and son, they did not speak, but lived in two houses that faced each other. This allowed them to peer out their windows, glower and curse at one another without having to stir abroad.

God's Chariot pulled into the farmyard. Father Désiré stepped out and surveyed the two buildings with a satisfied air. The nun came out to join him just as old mother Poiré appeared.

"Good day, my child," said the priest.

Léontine simply nodded. The sudden appearance of this priest in his black soutane, flanked by a nun wearing a white habit left her overawed, as though God had personally sent a delegation.

"I've come for the loading ramp for the trailer, could you tell me where it is?"

"The loading ramp . . . what would you be wanting that for, Father?"

"So I can load the calf into the back of the truck."

The blood drained from Léontine's face. Désiré explained that Cyprien had just donated the calf to Bérault chapel.

"That there is my calf," Léontine protested.

"Cyprien says it's his . . ."

"I've no doubt he did, but that calf is mine!"

"Very well," said Father Désiré in a conciliatory tone. "Cyprien wished to offer it to the Lord, you wish to take it from Him . . . It is your decision."

He turned on his heel and headed back to the truck.

"Wait, Father!"

Léontine stretched out a finger and pointed to a pen surrounded by railings.

"If he's giving you the calf, then I'll give you the hens."

On his return, when Cyprien saw his chickens getting loaded into the back of the truck, he saw red and instantly offered the priest the calf that belonged to his mother. He had no need of the loading ramp; he hoisted it into the truck himself.

## 40

Five or six other prisoners were gathered around Gabriel, peering through a chink in the shutters, trying to see what was happening in the yard. Most were exhausted having spent a sleepless night. Dorgeville, the cagoulard, had spent the whole night whimpering; just as the other prisoners were about to drift off again, he would howl with pain. "Die, you fascist fucker!" roared the anarchists, with the communists sporadically chiming in.

It was not yet o600 hours, but from what was going on in the yard, it was clear that the soldiers and the mobile guards were already in marching order. Strapped up tight in their uniforms, they were passing around cigarettes while keeping a watchful eye on the tense officers gathered in a circle around the capitaine.

"What's going on?" said the young communist, who had managed to struggle to his feet.

"The bombing raid yesterday has them scared shitless," said another prisoner, his eye pressed to the crack. "They're making decisions . . . and it doesn't look like it's going well."

As always whenever the group felt threatened, this news spread like wildfire and a dozen other prisoners rushed over to the window – what's happened, let me see . . .

"I don't know what they're plotting but . . . it looks like the adjudant-chef doesn't agree with the capitaine."

Gabriel laid a hand on the communist's shoulder; the young man was still very weak and often racked by fits of trembling.

"You should go and get some rest."

Then he went back to watch what was happening. The adjudant-chef was talking now. The capitaine's stiff, military bearing made it clear that there was conflict in the air.

Gabriel's sense of the adjudant-chef was constantly shifting. The previous evening, while Caporal-chef Bornier – doubtless riled up by lack of alcohol, to say nothing of his temperament and his hatred of the prisoners – had shown his true colours, the adjudant-chef had remained calm and unruffled. He seemed determined not to allow himself to be engulfed by the wave of panic about to overwhelm guards and prisoners alike. Gabriel knew that it was only through the adjudant's good graces that the prisoners had had anything to eat the previous night. No-one troubled to wonder how he had managed to get fresh supplies, however meagre, to feed a camp of almost a thousand starving souls . . . The men were too hungry to ask questions.

Late in the afternoon, when the adjudant-chef came to check on the wounded, Raoul had asked for fresh water and clean dressings, and the officer had personally come back to share what he had managed to find between Gabriel, who was still suffering from the wound to his thigh and needed pain relief, and Dorgeville whose foot had swollen to double its size. The bullet was still lodged in the wound, and he urgently needed a surgeon. The adjudant-chef was clearly concerned.

Gabriel's injury was less serious than had been feared. The bullet had cleanly cut through the thigh muscle, and while the gash was painful and gory, it was not particularly worrying.

"It's just the muscle, sergent-chef," Raoul had reassured him. "In a couple of days you'll be running like a hare again."

Then night had fallen, and with it had come the plaintive wails of Dorgeville.

Raoul was more worried than he had ever been. For a long time, he lay on his back, clutching the letter from Louise, whose words were already engraved on his memory. The name Belmant or Belmont meant nothing to him, but whoever this woman was, she knew what she was talking about. His date of birth was accurate, as was the address of the house in Neuilly. At the mere mention of the boulevard Auberjon, he felt a dull ache. Never had he been as miserable as in that vast mansion, being tormented by that mad bitch, Germaine Thirion, who was hypocrisy personified.

"I am your half-sister," the letter said. "We share the same mother." How old was this woman? She could be older or younger than he was, anything was possible, women have been known to have babies twenty years apart. But one sentence kept coming back to him: "I have important information I wish to communicate to you about your birth and childhood."

She knew more than he did. Raoul did not even know the date on which he had been placed with the Thirion family.

"Can't sleep?" said Gabriel.

"I've slept a little . . . What about you, sergent-chef, are you in any pain?"

"It's throbbing a lot. I'm worried it will get infected . . ."

"You don't need to worry, I cleaned out the wound, it'll heal in its own good time, it's bound to hurt for a little while, but you'll be fine."

They were whispering, their faces only inches apart.

"Can I ask you something?"

"What?"

"That letter . . . how did you get it?"

Raoul was not naturally given to confidences, and to talk about the letter would entail revealing its contents. He did not like this idea. There are some children who are rendered fearful and ultimately cowardly by blows, sufferings and misfortune. For Raoul, they served only to strengthen his character, moulding him into a man who was tough to the point of provocation, one steeled against spontaneity and effusiveness. But this letter, like a message from the heavens, had stirred something in him that had shaken his very soul; the mystery at the heart of the letter left him restless, revelations about his mother, his real mother, awaited him, and he felt ill-prepared. It is possible to make your peace with not having a mother, especially if you have a substitute that you can cordially loathe. But Raoul had never allowed himself to think about his other mother, his real mother, the one who he said – at various times, at various ages – had "abandoned" or "lost" him, "protected" or "sold" him: there were many variations.

"You don't have to talk about it . . ."

"I got it from the adjudant-chef," Raoul muttered. "He slipped it into my pocket when he was frisking me."

Gabriel found this baffling. Had Raoul known the adjudant-chef before? Why would an officer play postman for one of his own prisoners?

"It's a letter from my sister . . . well, sort of . . ."

The situation was confusing. Raoul had always thought of Henriette as a sister, though he knew she was not. Should he now acknowledge some woman he had never met, might never meet, as his real sister? The escape plan had failed and, now that Gabriel was injured, it was impossible to try again. The prospect of breaking free and finding this woman seemed remote.

He was haunted by a host of details. Among them, the date November 17, 1907, when he had been taken in by the Thirion family.

"How old is a baby when he's weaned?" he asked.

The question was so surprising that Gabriel was convinced he had misheard.

"I don't know. I'm an only child, so I've never had another baby around," he said, "but I'd say between nine and twelve months, something like that."

Raoul had been four months old when placed with the Thirion family.

He felt suffocated by these doubts, he needed air. Abruptly, he sat up.

"Are you alright?" said Gabriel.

"I'm fine, I'm fine," Raoul lied, tugging at his collar so he could breathe.

Landrade had always been volatile. In his dealings with Gabriel, he had been by turns aggressive, violent, scheming, even cruel. His new attitude was something Gabriel dated to the incident at the Tréguière bridge. A triumph that would not go down in the annals of military history, but one they had accomplished together. Gabriel had never liked the idea of "comrades in arms", it was something that showed up only in novels, a cliché he had no desire to fulfil. And yet he had to admit that a bond had been forged between them.

Gabriel watched Raoul tug at his collar and stretch out his neck, gulping air. Perhaps this had something to do with his talk of babies, perhaps he was thinking about his childhood. Out of the blue, two images resurfaced. The first was of the vast mansion they had looted, when he had stumbled on Raoul Landrade pissing on the master bed. The second was one that he had un-consciously filed away: Raoul, in Cherche-Midi prison, bribing a warder to post a letter to his sister.

"What's your sister's name?"

Raoul did not move. What should he say? Henriette? Louise?

It would seem idiotic to say "I don't know", although this would have been the best answer. He simply handed the letter to Gabriel.

The dormitory was too dark to be able to read. On the far side of the room, a beam of light was coming from beneath the door leading to the officers' quarters. Gabriel silently hobbled to the far side of the dormitory, lay down on the floor and, holding the letter in the faint glow, he deciphered rather than read Louise's letter.

"They look like they're going to lay into each other," said a prisoner with his eye pressed to the crack in the window.

Outside, in the middle of the yard, the adjudant-chef was going toe to toe with the capitaine. It was a symptom of the times: superior rank was no longer enough to wield authority over one's subordinates.

"Our orders are to advance to Saint-Rémy-sur-Loire," the capitaine said, waving a map he had procured from somewhere or other. "At Saint-Rémy, we will be issued with fresh supplies. Provisions should be there before nightfall."

This information was not greeted with the expected enthusiasm. The fresh supplies promised two days earlier had never arrived, and but for the miracle performed by a resourceful adjudant-chef, everyone in the camp would have starved. As a result, soldiers and prisoners alike had grown wary of good news and promises made by the military authorities.

"From Saint-Rémy, the prisoners will be taken in trucks to the Bonnerin camp in Le Cher," said the capitaine, shooting a glance at Fernand before continuing. "The mobile guard units will be relieved when we reach Saint-Rémy, which marks the end of their mission. All other units will carry on to the Bonnerin camp where they, in turn, will be relieved."

Fernand heaved a sigh of relief. As far as he was concerned, the news could scarcely be better. Travelling by truck, they would reach their destination in a couple of hours, at which point he would be officially relieved of his duties. He had only to travel another ten kilometres to reach Villeneuve-sur-Loire – less, in fact, since Bérault chapel was midway between the two. He could be at the chapel by noon and find Alice. After that, the two of them could spend time with his sister, or go back to Paris, whichever events dictated.

"At least, that's the theory," said the capitaine.

Everyone froze.

"In practice, we have no trucks to drive to Saint-Rémy, so we will have to get there on foot."

This news took a moment to percolate into the minds of those present. Taking almost a thousand prisoners on a forced march along the open road, during which they would have to be watched and guarded, but also treated, since some were wounded . . . The whole idea was insane.

From the capitaine's silence, it was clear that more bad news was to come.

"In addition, a number of units are being redeployed to shore up the defence of the country. Consequently, our workforce will be somewhat reduced."

Everyone turned to look at the workforce that remained. It was mostly comprised of Moroccan and Indochinese infantrymen, since many of the ordinary soldiers had been shipped out at first light.

"We have thirty-four kilometres to cover. We shall set off at 0800 hours, and should arrive at Saint-Rémy at 1800, which is perfect."

With the naivety of the overconfident, he was amazed by the

coincidence that, according to military calculations, Saint-Rémy was precisely a day's march from Gravières camp.

"I have decided that the prisoners will be divided into eight groups of 120, each commanded by an NCO from the mobile guards with fifteen men under his command."

Fifteen men to guard a group of more than a hundred . . . Fernand groped for something to say.

"It's impossible."

The words had come out as a roar. The capitaine turned and glared at him.

"Excuse me?"

The other NCOs looked at Fernand, relieved that someone else had dared to criticise this plan which beggared belief.

"It would be impossible for us to guard a thousand prisoners on the open road . . ."

"Nevertheless, that is the mission entrusted to us by the high command."

"And there are no trucks, no trains?"

The capitaine said nothing as he carefully rolled up his map.

"Get on with it!"

"One moment, sir . . . I have two wounded prisoners, one of them can barely walk, the other cannot even stand. And . . ."

"I've got wounded men in my barracks too," muttered another NCO, so quietly that no-one ever knew who it was.

"That's too bad for them."

The capitaine called for silence and then, articulating each word, he said:

"Our orders are to leave no-one behind."

The threat was self-explanatory.

"Meaning . . .?" Fernand pressed him nonetheless, unable to believe his ears.

Capitaine Howsler had not expected to have to explain himself at this precise moment, but, having little choice, he said decisively:

"On May 16, Général Héring, Military Governor of Paris, requested permission from the highest echelons of state to fire without warning on escapees and runaways; this permission was granted him. I consider that it is equally applicable to us. Runaways and laggards amount to the same thing."

The ensuing silence was filled with images as each man imagined such a situation.

"What about the code?" said Fernand, his voice firm and unwavering.

For a moment, Capitaine Howsler was dumbstruck.

"What do you mean, the code?"

"Article 251 stipulates that 'no prisoner should be forced to travel unless he has been assessed and deemed fit to withstand the rigours of the journey'."

"And where did you come up with that, pray tell?"

"The Code of the Gendarmerie."

"Really? Well, when the day comes that the French army is subject to the rules of the gendarmerie, come back and we can talk about it. But right now, you are under my command, and you can stick your code where it might do some good."

The discussion was closed.

"Get moving, God damn it! Sort out food for the mess this evening, feed the leftovers to the prisoners. I want us up and out at 0800 hours sharp!"

Fernand gathered his unit together.

"We are being asked to transport a hundred prisoners over a distance of more than thirty kilometres. But we have no vehicles."

"So we're supposed to . . . what? Hoof it?" said a shocked Caporal-chef Bornier.

"Can you think of an alternative solution?"

"So we're expected to run the risk of being machine-gunned for that scum?"

From the crowd came several murmurs of approval; Fernand was determined to brook no argument:

"Yes. And that is precisely what we are going to do."

He marked several seconds of silence before adding, in a tone he hoped was encouraging:

"Once we've done that, our mission is over. By tonight, it will all be over and tomorrow we can all go home."

Fernand bit his lip. Home . . . It was increasingly difficult to believe in such a place.

The reaction from the prisoners was no more enthusiastic.

"Saint-Rémy," said one, "that's thirty kilometres at the very least."

Gabriel struggled to his feet and gestured to his wounded thigh.

"It's pretty painful . . ."

"Let me have a look."

Raoul removed the bandage. During his time in the army he had seen wounds of all kinds.

"It doesn't look too bad . . . Try to walk on it."

Gabriel took a few steps, he was limping, but he could walk.

Dorgeville's wound was another matter. Unless a surgeon could be found, and quickly, septicaemia would set in.

Getting a thousand prisoners ready for a ten-hour march was not simply a matter of clicking one's fingers. The preparations dragged on. What little food was left was distributed so there would be no provisions to carry. On several occasions, NCOs had to intervene to ensure that food was shared out fairly and to avoid clashes between the prisoners. Capitaine Howsler moved between the groups, cracking his rolled-up map like a whip. As he issued his final orders to the men under his command, he seemed more than satisfied with this turn of events. The few soldiers who had not been redeployed donned their caps and watched the pitiful spectacle.

Having gathered up the few belongings they had brought from Cherche-Midi, the prisoners lined up in pairs and waited beneath the blazing sun. The guards who were to flank the march seemed few and far between.

It was almost 1000 hours.

The capitaine insisted that "to comply with regulations governing the transport of prisoners in time of war", the guards load their rifles in full view of the prisoners. The resounding clack of rifle breeches was grave and ominous.

"Any attempt at escape will be immediately quashed!" roared the capitaine.

He moved to the head of the procession and ordered the first unit to move out. Then, with a blast of his military whistle, he set off with a long, determined stride.

The first hundred prisoners marched away in crocodile formation, raising clouds of dust on the dirt road.

"The groups will move out one by one," Fernand said to his unit. "We'll be bringing up the rear. We need to avoid the column becoming spaced out, allowing those in front to get too far ahead of the other. The important thing is that we stay tightly grouped. Those leading shouldn't march too fast, and those bringing up the rear have to be careful not to lag behind."

While in theory this sounded feasible, many of the men had their doubts. Although they had been issued many orders since the German offensive began, this was by far the most fatuous.

They waited for a long time, watched as the various groups set off in turn.

Since Fernand had spent some of his money procuring supplies for the camp, he now had more space in his haversack. Turning away from prying eyes, he quickly kissed the cover of his battered copy of the *Thousand and One Nights* and stuffed it into the bag.

Then came the moment for him to blow his whistle.

High above them, a German fighter squadron was flying past. It was almost 1100 hours.

## 41

Louise raced through the meadow, pushing the little cart in front of her. The babies wailed and, behind her, the German fighters were once again strafing the road with machine-gun fire. Out here in the open we're easy targets, thought Louise, quickening her pace. One of the wheels caught on an exposed root, the cart almost tipped over, but she caught it just in time; the children howled even louder as she raced on. Obviously, it was unlikely that one of the German fighter pilots would have the urge or the inclination to break formation in order to pick off a lone woman dashing through a field pushing what looked like a wheelbarrow, but her throat and her chest tightened at the thought of being mown down. She forced herself to focus on the line of trees in the distance, which she had almost given up hope of reaching; her breath was ragged and wheezing, she could feel her lungs burning.

She had run away without a thought, without a thing, and for an instant she was once again that young woman, stark naked, running blindly down a boulevard . . .

At length, out of breath, she stopped and turned back. By now the road was far behind her, too far for her to be able to make out what was happening there, but the roar of the fighter planes and the shriek of sirens was so loud it was if they were directly over-head. She set off again and, reaching the trees, she found that they lined a narrow path, on which she turned right. Her whole body felt ablaze with fear and exertion. Gradually, she slowed her pace, panting to catch her breath. All around were undulating hills, here and there a copse or thicket, and on one side a single farmhouse. What should she do? Go to the farm? Remembering the welcome she and Monsieur Jules had received from local farmers, she thought it best to press on. A kilometre or two ahead she could just make out some woodland.

Abruptly she became aware that the three babies had not stopped wailing since their escape, and she felt a surge of panic rise in her throat.

She stopped, bent over the makeshift cradle and, for the first time, she looked at the three children. The two boys were dressed in blue, hand-knitted baby clothes. Louise took a corner of the coverlet and wiped their runny noses. The gesture seemed to calm them. That, and perhaps the sight of a human face . . .

"Come on, now," she said, lifting one out of the cart. "So, can you stand up by yourself or not?"

The little boy stood on the ground, one hand gripping the wheel of the cart. She set down the second boy. She spoke to them softly, all the while glancing to the left, towards the road where all sign of the German attack had now disappeared; the sky was once again as calm and peaceful as a shroud.

She picked up the baby girl, cradling her in her arms as she stared at the plumes of smoke from the burning cars in the distance. She crooned a lullaby and the baby settled.

She twisted her body and inspected the handcart, lifted the blankets where the children had been lying and found the bundle of Jeanne's letters she had tossed there; the only thing to survive, purely and simply because she had been holding it when catastrophe struck. She slipped the bundle under the blankets and continued her search of the cart. She came upon some tin plates, a knife and fork, a jumble of clothes, a hunk of bread, a canteen of water, two jars of preserved fruits, some tins of biscuits, a bar of melted chocolate, three tins of vegetables, a bag of rice and one of baby milk powder. Sitting on the grassy verge with the youngest child between her legs, she broke off pieces of bread which she gave to the twin boys, who, in unison, sat back on their behinds and began to chew hungrily. The baby girl smelled foul. Louise searched, found an unused nappy and set about changing the baby. She had no idea how the three points fit together and, finding no safety pin, simply swaddled the baby and tied the nappy into a knot that was unlikely to hold for very long. She decided to throw away the soiled nappy rather than taking it with her – how could she wash it?

Night was drawing in. Feeling apprehensive, Louise once again glanced towards the lone farmhouse; something about its isolation and the horseshoe curve of the roof made it feel remote and forbidding. She put the twins back into the cart, settled the baby next to them and continued on her way.

*Marlbrook the Prince of Commanders*
*Is gone to war in Flanders*

This was the song that popped into her head. For a while, it lulled the children.

As she walked, alone, down the long, straight path that led to the distant woodland, Louise tried to make a list of all the things she needed to do: feed and change the children, find a place for them to sleep, and, most of all, find a home for them – where could she leave her foundlings?

*"The news I bring, fair lady,"*
*With sorrowful accent said he,*
*"Is one you are not ready*
*So soon, alas! to hear."*

In her mind, she saw Monsieur Jules standing alone in the road, "Go on, Louise, get out of here!" Had Monsieur Jules been mown down in his carpet slippers on a country road by a German fighter plane?

*They watched as his soul drifted off,*
*'mid the sprays of laurel wreaths*
*They watched as his soul fluttered away,*
*Across the barren heath.*

Temporarily sated by the bread, the twins had drifted off again, but the little girl still wailed. Louise was at the end of her tether, overwhelmed by her sudden flight and the onerous responsibilities imposed on her by fate . . . Sometime later, she could be seen pushing the cart with one hand, and using the other to hold the little girl, whose face was pressed into the hollow of her neck.

By the time she reached the trees, the whole countryside was shrouded with tendrils of fog. It was not a wood, as she had thought, but a line of trees flanking the same road she had fled two hours earlier. A stream of refugees walked on with heavy tread, carrying heavy cases. There were a few bicycles, but not a single car . . .

Louise struggled to get her bearings. Was the place where she had left Monsieur Jules and his charred Peugeot to her left or her right? All three babies were awake now. She urgently needed to get organised, to find the children something substantial to eat, something to drink, to change their nappies . . . "She is not even weaned . . ." the phrase drifted up from her memory. How should she feed a baby who had not yet learned to chew? Did she have what it would take? Beset by these and other doubts, Louise once again joined the onward surge of refugees, determined not to stop until she had resolved these questions, singing loudly in an attempt to soothe the sobs that shook the handcart:

*Some embraced their wives,*
*With many a sigh and moan.*
*Some embraced their wives,*
*But others were quite alone.*

The long road was lined with ditches filled with cars and trucks like corpses in a cemetery. Engines steamed and smoked, doors gaped wide amid the mangled wreckage revealing yawning suitcases and crates that had been swiftly emptied by feverish hands. Louise walked quite quickly, in part because the stream of evacuees seemed to be thinning, but also because some had chosen to stop for the night, pitching makeshift tents made of blankets, sheets and scraps of tarpaulin, all of them praying that the rains would not come to heap misery upon catastrophe.

It was the campfire that urged Louise on. A fire of matchwood built next to an embankment, and around it, a family, eating hungrily, with their backs to the road.

Louise stopped as she drew alongside. Heads turned when they heard the wails of the three babies. In a flash, Louise saw the indifference on the faces of the two adolescents, the father's scowl, the mother's sadness.

Louise lifted the twins down and sat them on the verge and,

cradling the baby in one arm, set out what little she had, disparate foodstuffs ill-suited to preparing a meal. Again, she broke off bread to feed to the twin boys. Seated near the fire, the wife watched out of the corner of her eye. From the fields came the insistent lowing of cattle. Louise opened the bag of dried baby food that smelled faintly of vanilla, and added some to water in the tinplate bowl. Instantly, large lumps appeared. The boys chewed on their bread and watched her curiously, the little girl was growing impatient; Louise used the back of a spoon to crush the lumps, but still the formula refused to blend.

"It won't work unless you heat the water."

The wife had got to her feet and was now standing beside Louise. About fifty, heavy set, wearing a floral print dress that resembled a bedspread.

"Leave her be, Thérèse," said the man still sitting by the fire.

But the woman was clearly accustomed to this injunction and paid no heed. She took the bowl and poured the contents into a small saucepan: the family was much better equipped than Louise. While she heated the mixture on the fire, her husband whispered to her, disjointed phrases of which Louise could make out only the man's querulous overbearing tone.

Louise, meanwhile, set down the baby and gave her a rattle – a wooden whistle with a little handle that the girl waved – and dug out the jars of fruit, but the lids were screwed tight and Louise did not have the strength to open them. She walked over to the fire; the man watched her approach as though spoiling for a fight. She addressed the taller of the two adolescent boys.

"I'm not strong enough, could you . . .?"

The boy took the jar, twisted the lid with a satisfying *pop* and triumphantly proffered the jar in one hand and the lid in the other as though they were the spoils of war.

"Thank you," said Louise, "you're very kind . . . ."

He could not have been happier if she had offered to spend the night at a hotel with him.

The mother was stirring the baby food.

"Careful, now. It's hot."

Feeding the baby proved a difficult task. The little girl whimpered constantly, anxiously waiting for a breast or a bottle, and opened her mouth to spit out what little Louise managed to feed her. After half an hour, Louise and the baby were both exhausted. The twins were sitting on the grass, playing with the blanket. At this point, Louise had the idea of diluting the baby food until it was almost a liquid and managed to trickle a few spoonfuls into the little girl, who promptly fell asleep with almost nothing in her belly, as though sapped by these futile efforts.

For the first time, Louise was able to study the child. Her features were delicate, her eyelashes beautifully curled, her lips pink: Louise found her beauty intensely moving. Fleetingly, she remembered a line from one of Jeanne's letters: "Oh, if you had only seen the baby's little face!" She was struck by the curious parallels in their fates, hers and Jeanne's; both had lost a baby. Now here Louise was with three babies to look after.

The twin boys were smiling and playful. When Louise played at making the spoon, the rattle, the cup disappear, they giggled happily. The two adolescents had turned away from the fire now and were watching this pretty young woman with her pale hands, her wan, exhausted face lit up by a painful smile.

Two hours later, all is quiet.

The children have been changed, the baby girl had woken up again and Louise managed to get her to swallow a few more spoonfuls of the now-cold formula.

To sleep, the best she can do is to curl up in the cart like a dog, with the baby against her belly and one twin on either side.

High above, the deep-blue sky is speckled with stars; the children's breathing is deep and calm. Louise strokes the little girl's soft, warm head.

## 42

Fernand tooted his whistle as he set off with his unit, though any music lover would have heard in it an undercurrent of worry that clashed with the self-assured, soldierly blast given by Capitaine Howsler. It had taken more than an hour for the seven groups, each numbering just over a hundred prisoners, to set off. Fernand, concerned about how some of the prisoners would withstand the gruelling march, had allowed his group to remain seated while they waited their turn.

He had made the most of that time by honing his strategy. Fearing that the swiftest would quickly leave the slower men behind, he would march at the head of the column and post Caporal-chef Bornier somewhere near the middle, where his aggressive impulses were less likely to manifest themselves.

As it happened, Bornier was posted right next to Raoul and Gabriel who, despite being told to line up in alphabetical order, had managed to stay together. While the guards were prepared to overlook such minor details, it was clear from the loaded weapons and tense faces of the mobile guards, and the nervousness of the Indochinese infantrymen, that no other contraventions would be tolerated.

During the long wait before they set off, discipline had been lax, and the prisoners had been able to talk in low voices. Who knows where the news had come from – such is the mystery of prison life – but there were rumours circulating about the state of the war. Some said Général Weygand intended to sue for peace. Whether this was true or false was irrelevant, what mattered was that this was the first unambiguous suggestion of defeat, and attributing the statement to the Commander in Chief of the French Forces spoke volumes about the mistrust that now greeted official military communiqués announcing that France had the enemy in check.

"What?" said Raoul.

He had not quite been himself since receiving the mysterious letter from Louise Belmont. And earlier that morning, perhaps weary of thinking about it constantly, and fuelled by a sudden rage, he had torn up the letter and scattered the shreds, but this changed nothing, since he was still consumed by what it had said.

"We'll get through this, you'll see," said Gabriel. "You'll be able to find this woman and clear things up."

They were prisoners, facing charges of looting and probably desertion, but right now they were more likely to be gunned down on this road than they were to face a court martial . . . Gabriel's optimism was ridiculous, and he knew it.

"What I mean is . . ."

Raoul Landrade was staring at his boots. Without looking up, he said:

"She would have been – what? – thirty, thirty-five . . . No older . . . You can still have a kid at that age . . ."

Gabriel wondered who Raoul was talking about, but could not bring himself to ask.

"The problem is," Raoul said, turning to look at Gabriel, "what if that old hag Mother Thirion *is* my real mother . . . I mean, she'd have been about the right age, wouldn't she?"

"But why would she give you up and then take you back three months later?"

"That's the bit that worries me. I think she was forced to. It would explain why she always hated me . . ."

There: he had said the word.

"It's not finding out who my real mother is that scares me, it's the fact that it might turn out to be that bitch . . ."

Raoul had grabbed Gabriel's arm and was gripping it tightly.

"I mean . . . I can't see the old man being my real father. Maybe that's why she had to give me up. Because she got knocked up by some other guy. And the old man was furious that she'd cheated on him and forced her to take me back. In which case . . ."

Anything was possible, of course, but Gabriel did not have much faith in this explanation, which sounded more like the result of bitter brooding than logical reasoning.

"Shut your bloody cakeholes, you fucking homos!"

Bornier was pacing up and down the lines of seated prisoners waving his rifle and ordering them to be silent. No-one seriously thought he would shoot while they were sitting in wait to leave, but a rifle blow to the head or the ribs was perfectly possible.

They heard the adjudant-chef blow his whistle.

It was finally time to leave.

Gabriel was limping a little, but his wound had not reopened. Dorgeville's health was altogether more worrying. Supported by two of his comrades, the journalist hobbled slowly and painfully; it was difficult to imagine him marching the thirty kilometres to Saint-Rémy. The young communist, also helped along by his comrades, was to the rear of the column. Although Gabriel could not see him, he knew the lad was also in bad shape.

The column quickly began to stretch out, to a hundred and fifty, then two hundred metres. At regular intervals, Fernand would wait at the side of the road and urge the laggards to quicken their pace, only to have to rush back to the head of the column to order the leaders to slow down. After two hours of playing the border collie, he was exhausted.

The afternoon sun blazed in the anxious atmosphere. Refugees also heading towards Saint-Rémy initially stopped to allow the prisoners to pass, but seeing the length of the column, ended up walking alongside them, making the guards' duty more difficult. The shouted orders for them to clear the way merely led to insults. There were calls of "traitors", "spies" and "fifth columnists". The less the refugees understood of what was happening, the more they saw the prisoners as enemies. Fernand was not worried that a column flanked by armed guards should be verbally abused by the refugees, but their naked aggression made an already absurd situation more excruciating. How, he wondered, could the military have been so stupid as to order the forced march of more than a thousand prisoners escorted by a handful of soldiers and guards?

In the middle of the afternoon (by which time they had been marching for four hours), Fernand gave the prisoners permission to stop and drink from a nearby stream, though they remained under armed guard. If they were to make progress, he could hardly stop them quenching their thirst, but each time he bent the rules further unsettled the men, and the adjudant-chef was beginning to feel out of his depth.

Looking back down the road, he could no longer see the rear of the column. The prisoners were walking in groups of two, three and four while guards and soldiers marched alone. It seemed clear that some men had made their escape. Already, some faces seemed to be missing from the group. But, short of gathering all the prisoners together and conducting a formal roll call – which would simply add to the delay – there was nothing to be done.

At about 1600 hours, they were still six kilometres from their destination. From time to time, he heard a distant gunshot up ahead, and then another, as though he and Alice were walking in the countryside during hunting season.

Like Fernand, Capitaine Howsler was worried about how the column had begun to stretch out and so, at 1800 hours, he stopped by the roadside to ensure that all of the groups were making steady progress. The pace, he realised, was continuing to slow. His scowl reflected the deep disappointment of a man who has been bitterly reminded that events refuse to bow to his will. He glared vindictively at the prisoners, but also at the soldiers and the mobile guards, who were in no better shape than their charges and were pathetically panting while the first groups, already far ahead, were within a kilometre or two of their goal.

Shortly afterwards, Fernand's group was divided in two with the arrival of a convoy of military trucks that blocked the road. No-one knew where they were headed but, since the prisoners could do nothing but wait, they sat down and recovered their strength.

By this point, Gabriel was struggling. His wounded leg had suddenly given way beneath him, and he had fallen hard. Raoul had been unable to break his fall. A few hundred metres on, Landrade briefly swerved to grab a broken wooden slat from an abandoned cart and tied a rolled-up shirt to one end to fashion a makeshift crutch. Gabriel would not be able to walk any faster, but he would be in less pain.

They began to overtake breathless, lame or exhausted prisoners from groups that had set out earlier. Gradually, the rear of the column became comprised of prisoners who were unlikely to reach their destination. Dorgeville, the journalist, who was being carried by a group of comrades now so exhausted that they had to stop and rest more frequently, had long since been left behind. The little group was barely visible in the distance.

Fernand had passed Capitaine Howsler some time back when it dawned on him that the capitaine was not posted by the roadside simply to check the progress of the march. He was lying in wait for the stragglers.

Panicked, Fernand turned back and broke into a run.

Raoul had his arm around his friend's shoulder.

"You go on ahead," said Gabriel, panting for breath.

"Yeah, like you can manage without me, knucklehead!"

Making the most of the lax surveillance, they stopped for a moment and sat down, and it was then that they realised that it had been some time since they last saw the young communist, looking like a ghost, being dragged along by two comrades almost as weak as himself.

Suddenly they saw Capitaine Howsler striding towards them, flanked by Caporal-chef Bornier and a small group of stiff, stolid Indochinese infantrymen.

"You, stay here and guard this lot," he said to Bornier.

The caporal-chef proudly threw back his shoulders and, gripping his rifle, he shifted his furious glare from Gabriel and Raoul to the straggling communists.

Meanwhile the capitaine and the infantrymen marched towards the rear of the column, to a tiny group of laggards. From a distance, the tall, rigid figure of Capitaine Howsler was visible, standing in the middle of the road while the Indochinese infantrymen lined the stragglers up along the ditch.

There was a shouted order.

A gunshot rang out.

Then another

And a third.

Raoul whipped around. Two or three hundred metres up ahead, the adjudant-chef was racing down the road waving his arms and shouting something that no-one could make out. Caporal-chef Bornier was deathly pale.

"On your feet!" roared the capitaine.

They had not seen him arrive. He was shouting at Gabriel and the young communist. But as the two men struggled to stand up, he bellowed:

"Out of the way!"

He was furious. He gestured to the able-bodied prisoners.

"You lot, stand aside!"

Raoul realised that all the pieces were now in place for the denouement of the tragedy.

Three prisoners had just been slaughtered and dumped in a ditch.

Now, two wounded prisoners were about to get a bullet in the head.

As Fernand, running and gasping for breath, drew closer shouting "Stop! Stop!", the capitaine turned to Bornier.

"Soldier! Execute these men. That's an order!"

Raoul reached out, gripped Gabriel's makeshift crutch and pulled him to his feet. Meanwhile, the Indochinese infantrymen had reappeared and were staring at Bornier, whose lower lip was trembling.

Fernand's voice rang out:

"Stop!"

But he was still some way off, his face contorted from a stitch in his side.

"Take aim!" thundered the capitaine, drawing his revolver.

Bornier raised his rifle, but his hands were shaking, his eyes vacant . . . He trained the gun on Gabriel, who seemed about to say something. He, too, was shaking, his legs had turned to jelly, and he stared down the barrel of Bornier's rifle as though waking from a nightmare.

Raoul, meanwhile, still gripping the improvised wooden crutch, gauged the distance separating him from the capitaine, the caporal-chef and the Indochinese infantrymen.

Finally, Fernand arrived, gasping and spluttering.

"Stop!" he shouted again.

"Fire!" roared the capitaine.

But Caporal-chef Bornier had already dropped his rifle which now pointed at the ground, he was shaking his head, tears in his eyes, it was almost as though he was the one about to die.

Then the capitaine raised his arm, aimed his revolver and fired at the young communist, who was brutally thrown backwards. His arm still raised he turned to Gabriel.

Abruptly, the scene paused and all eyes turned to scan the skies. The capitaine froze, his pistol still cocked.

Less than a kilometre away, a German fighter squadron was strafing the road.

The infantry men ran and dived into the ditch. Bornier threw himself on the ground.

Raoul bounded forward, swinging the makeshift crutch against the legs of the capitaine, who crumpled to the ground. He raced past Fernand, who was lying on the road. In an instant, he was kneeling next to Gabriel, grabbing him around the waist, throwing him over his shoulder, then he set off at a run.

The capitaine lay, stunned; Bornier seemed to have been turned to stone, meanwhile the infantrymen in the ditch had their arms over their heads.

Just as the fighter squadron passed overhead, Fernand drew his revolver and aimed at Raoul, who was barely ten metres away.

He fired, twice.

## 43

The cow turned its head and let out a thunderous moo.

"Slowly, now."

Louise half whispered, half shouted, waving her hand. The adolescent nodded that he understood. Louise turned to the other boy and gestured for him to veer to the right.

She turned around. Standing by the ditch, arms folded, the father watched the scene in the fervent hope that the attempt would be a fiasco. The older of the two boys was holding a rope which, Louise knew, would be useless unless the cow was biddable.

At another nod from Louise, all three of them stepped forward.

"Easy now, girl," said Louise. "Easy now."

The cow nodded but did not move. She had spent all night lowing in the field on the far side of the road, and this had given Louise the idea.

"She's lost her calf," she explained to the two boys. "She's got so much milk her udder is hurting, and, well, all that milk . . ."

She was cradling the little girl who had woken in the early hours and had not stopped crying since. The two boys preened like toreadors, their chests puffed out, prepared to take on the whole world. This proved unnecessary. The cow made no attempt to move as they crept towards her.

"Come on, girl," Louise said. "Come on."

She winked at the two boys as they reached the animal, impressed by its sheer size. They patted its flank gently.

Standing by the roadside, the father kept his arms folded. For a fleeting instant Louise was reminded of Monsieur Jules, who often adopted that stance with customers.

She set down the saucepan, knelt down next to the huge udder and grasped one of the warm, swollen teats. All three started as the cow nervously flexed her hind leg. Louise squeezed the teat. Nothing came. She tugged harder, but to no avail. She had no idea what to do. The milk was there, but she did not know how to extract it.

"Why won't it come?" said the older of the two boys.

He tried his luck. The cow swung her tail, whipping their faces but, sensing that they might relieve the painful pressure, made no attempt to move. Louise tried again, tugging and squeezing, but it was futile. The three looked at each other, disappointed and hopeless. Louise was reluctant to admit defeat; there had to be a solution.

"Out of the way, you lot . . ."

It was the father. Imperiously, he strode forward, a brusque wave of his hand simultaneously indicated exasperation at the incompetence of others, his impatience for the work to be done and his disgust at being forced to perform a menial task that reminded him that he had once been a farmhand.

Kneeling down in front of the udder, he propped the saucepan between two clods of earth, gripped a teat in each hand and, with a single squeeze, sent a powerful jet of milk into the grass. This was followed by the metallic lapping of the liquid as it filled the pan. The cow gently shook her head.

"You!" The father turned to one of his sons, "Go fetch me something bigger, go on, shift your arse!"

He had not so much as glanced at Louise.

"Thank you," she muttered.

He made no response. Milk frothed in the saucepan; the son reappeared carrying a bucket. Louise could see that it was dirty, but she said nothing; there was milk enough to feed the three toddlers for a whole day, perhaps longer, if the milk did not turn . . .

The jars of fruit were emptied out to make room for the milk. The baby girl had been fed and winded and was now asleep, smiling wanly. The twins had milk moustaches which Louise wiped away with a cloth of dubious cleanliness.

"Good luck," said the mother.

"Thank you," said Louise as she set off again. "You too."

The two boys watched as Louise faded away like a mirage.

Everyone seemed determined to carry on as far as Saint-Rémy-sur-Loire. Rumours were rife about what awaited them there, some claimed there were shelters, food, a semblance of government while others said it was full of Nazis raping wives in front of horrified husbands before lopping their heads off – worse than communists, they were. But the rumours had changed little since they first set out from Paris four, five or even six days earlier. In fact, the rumour had become such a cliché that it no longer terrified anyone.

Louise stopped several times, lifted the twins down and allowed them to walk a little way. It was good exercise, but it would also tire them out and help them sleep, allowing her to press on.

Her few provisions were dwindling, she was almost out of water and by late morning the milk had soured. She needed to find clean nappies for the children. Her legs felt so heavy that she would gladly have given ten years of her life for this nightmare to end. Finding a home for the children had become an obsession. She had to entrust them to someone who would know how to look after them.

It was as they passed the signpost indicating they were coming into Saint-Rémy-sur-Loire that the baby got a bout of diarrhoea.

The town was overwhelmed by the flood of refugees, the mayor's office was under siege, the vast wedding hall now housed whole families, as did the fire station yard, the three primary schools, the town hall, the square Joseph-Merlin; the forecourt of the church of Saint Hippolytus looked like a Gypsy encampment; the Red Cross had pitched their tent in front of the secondary school where soup was served from dawn to dusk – until yesterday: now there was nothing left to serve, and no sign of fresh supplies. It was to the Red Cross tent that Louise headed, the central meeting point, the social hub, a forum awash with news and gossip.

Entering the town was like stepping into a different epoch, a savage world where leaving your cart meant never finding it again and setting a child down meant losing it forever. "My baby is sick . . ." she said as she tried to make her way to the Red Cross tent. "So what? We all have sick children, that's no excuse!" snapped one woman as Louise tried to manoeuvre the unwieldy cart. "Don't you go running that thing over my feet!" shrieked another, and Louise apologised. Crowds pressed around the tables manned by beleaguered volunteers asking when supplies of food would arrive, only to be told that no-one knew. It was a battle royale for people to reach this tent only to go away disappointed: come back later, there were shortages of everything: medicines, clean nappies, vegetables to make soup, everything.

Louise, like everyone else, came away empty-handed; the baby was screaming, the twin boys were howling, it was enough to make anyone give up hope – not to mention the baby's chronic diarrhoea, probably brought on because the cow's milk was too rich.

Where was she supposed to give up foundling children?

Someone suggested the mayor's office, but there was no-one there to confirm or deny this. The Red Cross, suggested another woman, but Louise had just come from there and they had said that it was impossible, that they might perhaps take in babies in two or three days' time, but right now there was nowhere to house them, no volunteers to care for them. Meanwhile, the baby girl reeked to high heaven, and Louise's arms were caked to the elbows.

She looked for a drinking fountain and found there was a queue, but the others allowed her to go first, mostly to get out of the way since the baby sounded as though she were dying. Louise gritted her teeth, she needed three pairs of hands – they're not mine, she explained, I don't suppose you know if there's somewhere that takes in foundlings . . .?

The baby needed urgent medical care. Louise's despair gave way to blind fury.

Abruptly, she turned and wheeled her cart to the front of a café on the square and, leaving the twins outside despite the risk, she scooped up the baby and marched inside and up to the counter where she set down the bag of rice, three carrots and the potato that she had managed to procure.

"I need to make soup for the little one, she's very ill," she told the owner.

The café was crowded, but it was impossible to say whether they were customers or simply lurking, some were drinking, others were eating, but everyone was ardently discussing the snippets of news that had reached the town.

"The Norwegians have surrendered . . ."

"Général Weygand said the situation is hopeless . . ."

"For the Norwegians?"

"No, for us . . ."

"I'm sorry, dear, we don't make soup here. We don't have anything to make it with. You need to go and talk to the Red Cross . . ."

He was a ruddy-faced man with thinning hair and yellow teeth. Louise lifted the squalling baby and set her on the bar.

"This child will be dead within a few hours if she's not fed."

"That's too bad, but I don't see why you're telling me."

"I'm telling you because you can save her life. I just need a gas stove and some water, is that really asking too much?"

"But, but, but . . ."

He was dumbstruck by her effrontery.

"I'll leave here her on your bar until she dies. That way, you can all watch her die . . . Come on, then!"

Every voice in the café fell silent.

"Come on, then, come and look. This baby is going to die . . ."

The silence uncoiled, snakelike, and pricked at their collective conscience while the infant writhed in pain and reeked of diarrhoea.

"Right, well . . . just this one, mind . . ."

A woman appeared. An ageless woman who might have between thirty or fifty, it was impossible to tell.

"You go ahead, I'll mind him."

"It's a girl," said Louise.

"What's her name?"

There was an awkward pause.

"Madeleine."

The woman smiled.

"Madeleine. That's a pretty name . . ."

As she used the rice and vegetables to make soup for the twins, carefully saving the cooking liquid to give to the baby, Louise tried in vain to remember where she had come up with the name she had just blurted out.

# 44

From the eight slatted wooden crates came the cackling, cheeping, gobbling and quacking of a dozen hens, a dozen chickens, three turkeys, five ducks and two geese. They stuck their heads out between the slats as though impatient to have them cut off. The problem was the calf. Tied to the side of the truck by a piece of string, it tottered and lurched. God's Chariot manoeuvred slowly. At every bend, the calf looked as though it might topple over the side.

"Tell me, Father," said Sister Cécile, "what are you planning to do with that animal."

"I'm planning to eat it, Sister, what else?"

"But I thought we abstained from meat on Fridays," said Sister Cécile.

"The refugees at the church are abstaining four days out of five, Sister," Father Désiré said imploringly. "I think the Good Lord knows that . . ."

Philippe the Belgian kept turning around to ensure the animal was steady on its feet.

"And are you planning to slaughter it yourself, Father?"

Father Désiré made the sign of the cross – Jesus Mary and Joseph.

"Certainly not. God spare me such a hideous ordeal."

They both turned to look at the magnificent calf with its wide-set ears, its soft brown eyes, its wet muzzle.

"It's a quandary, Sister, I grant you."

"What you need is a butcher," said Philippe the Belgian in a tone so shrill that made them all start.

"Do you have such a man among your flock, Father?" said Cécile. "Surely God attends to your every need?"

Désiré merely spread his hands as if to say: the Lord will provide.

The calf on the bed of God's Chariot was greeted with great enthusiasm by the refugees at Bérault chapel. The courtyard was cleared, and while the animal was tethered to a stake in a field next to the cemetery, water was set to boil so the chickens could be plucked.

"Isn't he glorious?" said Alice to Sister Cécile.

They both gazed as Father Désiré herded the geese to the delighted laughter of the children.

"Glorious is indeed the word," said Cécile.

The two women went into the side aisle where Alice had hung sheets to serve as partitions between the refugees who were most gravely ill. Exhausted, ill-nourished, ailing, with wounds that refused to heal . . .

As Alice applied new compresses to dress a varicose ulcer ("A little meat would be welcome, the protein will help them to heal . . ."), the nun noticed Alice's wedding band.

"Married?"

"Twenty years now . . ."

"Is he in the army?"

"More than thirty years . . . he's a mobile guard."

Alice lowered her head, racked by sudden emotion. There was an embarrassed silence.

"It's just that I've had no word from him. He stayed behind in Paris, I don't know why, he was supposed to join me here, but . . ."

She fumbled in her pocket, took out a handkerchief and dabbed her eyes as if in apology.

"I don't know what's happened to him."

She attempted a smile.

"Every day, I pray with Father Désiré for Fernand's safe return." Sister Cécile patted her hand.

Having tended to the sick, the nun asked Alice to come with her to speak to Father Désiré.

"You have three patients here who urgently require hospitalisation." She turned to Alice. "That varicose ulcer could become gangrenous. The adolescent boy has symptoms that I think may point to diabetes, but I have no way to verify that here. As for the other man, you tell me there has been blood in his stool for several days now, which would suggest a serious intestinal problem."

Alice was so overcome she was shaking, she felt horribly guilty. Father Désiré put his arm around her.

"None of this is your fault, my child, you have done everything you could with little or no means. Indeed, it is astounding that all these people are still alive. No-one has died, and that miracle is entirely down to you."

Sister Cécile tried to be pragmatic.

"There are no free beds at Montargis hospital. And there is no other hospital nearby."

"Then we shall need God to intervene," said Désiré. "But, while we wait for His succour, perhaps we might do our best – what do you say?"

He asked Philippe the Belgian to ready the truck; as he always did before setting out he called for God's Chariot as though there were horses to be harnessed. The nun made the most of these few moments to take Alice to one side.

"You have done excellent work here, Alice. Bravo. It cannot have been easy . . ."

There seemed to be an implication in her words that Alice could not quite make out, so she did not immediately respond.

"But, the fact remains that we can give only what we have . . ."

Did this mean they should give up? Abandon all these people to their fate? Alice nodded vaguely, considering the subject closed, and made to leave, but Sister Cécile stopped her. She had grasped Alice by the arm and now slid her hand down to clasp her wrist, while she brought her other hand up to Alice's face, her thumb tracing a curve beneath the eye.

"The fact is, there are not three, but four cases that I think need urgent care. You've not been well, have you, Alice?"

As she spoke, she took Alice's pulse and palpated her neck; what had been a conversation was now a clinical examination.

"Please, don't move," said Sister Cécile in a stern voice.

Without asking permission, she laid a hand on Alice's breast, next to her heart.

"You did not answer my question. Have you been unwell?"

"I've had some concerns, but . . ."

"Your heart?"

Alice silently nodded. The nun smiled at her.

"It would be good for you to get a little rest now. As I said, there are no beds free at the hospital, and I worry that Father Désiré may not be able to find a solution, but . . ."

"Oh, he'll find one," Alice interrupted. "Never fear, he will find one."

Her voice held such conviction that the nun was a little shaken.

"Sister Cécile!" Father Désiré smiled from the running board of the truck, now idling and ready to set off. "We go in search

417

of Providence. On the way, we will pray for the Lord to send help. Two of us stand a better chance in entreating his intercession . . ."

Less than an hour later, God's Chariot rolled into Montcienne barracks, where the 29th Infantry Division were now quartered, the same soldiers they had seen drive past Cyprien Poiré's farm.

The sudden appearance of God's Chariot caused something of a stir. The soldiers, devastated by the order to retreat, and awash with rumours like a plague of rats of an imminent armistice, were stunned as they saw the huge cross, the agonising Christ wreathed in white smoke and, at His feet, a priest dressed in a black soutane, his arms raised, imploring heaven to come to his aid.

There was a hushed silence. Many of the men quickly blessed themselves. Colonel Beauserfeuil stepped out into the yard.

The sign of the young nun climbing down from the cab brought a lump to the throat of every man present; to some, because she was wearing a cornette, to others because this apparition, garbed all in white, might well have been an angel.

Father Désiré stepped down and stood next to her. Together, they made a formidable pair.

"Father . . .?" said the colonel, a square-headed man with pale eyes and bushy sideburns that merged with a thick white beard and a reddish, almost orange moustache.

"My son . . ."

From the colonel's reverent, almost deferential greeting, Désiré knew he was a religious man.

"I truly believe that God has sent me to you . . ."

They retired to the colonel's makeshift office to converse.

Out on the parade ground, the soldiers were smoking, staring at the nun waiting patiently next to the truck, and at Philippe the

Belgian, sitting behind the wheel as though fearful that someone might steal it. One soldier broke ranks and stepped forward. A moment later, Sister Cécile was the centre of attention, they offered her coffee, she smiled; perhaps a glass of water? She declined.

"But if you could spare us a few sacks of coffee, some sugar and some biscuits, I would gladly accept . . ."

Meanwhile, Father Désiré and Colonel Beauserfeuil were standing at the window of the office, looking at the subject of their conversation: a heavy vehicle emblazoned with a red cross, a crucial component of a military field hospital.

"I'm afraid it's impossible, father, as I'm sure you can understand . . ."

"May I ask you a question, my child?"

The colonel merely waited silently.

"Some hours ago, it was announced on the radio that Paris had been taken by Nazi troops. They say the flag of Nazi Germany is flying atop the Eiffel Tower. How long, in your opinion, before the government surrenders to the enemy?"

It was a hurtful formulation. To ask for an armistice was to sue for peace; to surrender to the enemy was to accept defeat.

"I don't see what . . ."

"I shall explain, my son. How many wounded have you here in the barracks?"

"Eh . . . at this precise moment . . ."

"None. You have none. In my chapel, a dozen people will be dead by tomorrow, a dozen more by the day after tomorrow. I do not care what you will tell your superior officers, all I care about is what you will tell the Good Lord when you finally appear before Him. Will you be able to tell Him without compunction that you chose to heed your superiors rather than heeding your conscience? Remember . . . The children of Israel said unto the

Almighty: 'Give us the path and we will follow it. Show us the way and we will make it ours' . . ."

Before his glittering career at Saint-Cyr Military Academy, the colonel had attended a Catholic secondary school. But try as he might, he could not remember this bible verse.

Swiftly, Désiré continued:

"Should the need arise, the truck can be returned to you within two hours. In the meantime, who here will need it? Whereas to us, my son . . . 'Know ye that the hand of God doth stir when the heart of Man has faith'."

Decidedly, the colonel's memory was not what it had once been, because this verse was also unfamiliar to him.

Désiré was rather pleased with these flashes of inspiration. Oh, how he loved this job! Improvising verses was tantamount to rewriting the Bible.

The field ambulance turned around and followed God's Chariot. The colonel saluted as it passed. In it were medicines, bandages and instruments together with a medical officer who had been tasked with bringing the truck back within forty-eight hours.

In the cab of the truck, Sister Cécile turned to Désiré.

"You are extremely convincing, father . . . Remind me again, what order do you belong to . . ."

"Saint Ignatius."

"Saint Ignatius . . . How curious."

Father Désiré gave her a quizzical look.

"I simply meant that yours is a rare breed."

Désiré heard a note of steely determination in the young woman's voice, and gave her his broadest, most seductive smile.

Lest there be any misunderstanding, Désiré was not a ladies' man. Though not for want of opportunity, since he had won the favours of countless women in his many incarnations. Whether a lawyer or a surgeon, a pilot or a teacher, women found him attractive. But he had one self-imposed rule that he never broke: no women while on duty. Before, yes; afterwards, by all means; but never while on duty. Désiré was a professional.

No, the dazzling smile he bestowed on Sister Cécile was merely his way of playing for time. Not the brief interlude that separates question from answer, but the much longer reprieve we tend to grant to those we find attractive. Their charm suspends our disbelief for a time, we put off the careful consideration of our doubts in favour of the pleasures of the moment.

Because what he had intuited in Sister Cecile's tone had not been mockery. It was a tone that invariably triggered an internal warning. Someone had misgivings about his persona.

It was an all-too-familiar tone, one he knew would inexorably force him to flee; one to which he was inured. Nonetheless, something in the back of his mind nagged at him. Why had it happened so soon? They had known each other for less than a day . . .

## 45

Raoul carried Gabriel on his back through a hundred metres of woodland, then, panting, set him down.

"Fucking hell, we got those bastards, didn't we?"

He gasped for breath, unable to believe that he was there, then he threw Gabriel over his shoulder once more.

"We can't hang around, we've got to get moving."

Gabriel was in a state of shock, in his mind the capitaine's pistol was still trained on him, over and over the same bullet pierced the young communist's head, the sound of the gunshot filled his mind, he felt sick to his stomach, his wounded leg refused to bear his weight, and if Raoul had not carried him, he would have remained stock still, waiting to be found and slaughtered.

In fact, the German fighter squadron had not been strafing the road. Perhaps it was a reconnaissance flight. But in that case, why nose-dive towards the road? To scare the fleeing populace? It was possible. It was difficult for anyone to know what was happening in this war.

They had made it some three hundred metres into the dense forest. Gabriel could just make out a road through the undergrowth. Suddenly, he realised it was the same road they had left.

They had come full circle.

Up ahead, the body of Dorgeville was rotting in a ditch, a little further, the young communist lay stiff and cold, and there were doubtless others.

"Come on, this way, sergent-chef, let's get you in here."

Parked on the verge was a removals van with an Italian name emblazoned on the tarpaulin. They had passed it shortly before the appearance of the capitaine with his pistol and his Indochinese infantrymen, and the breathless adjudant-chef shouting for him to stop.

"Coming back this way is completely illogical," Raoul explained as he hauled Gabriel into the bed of the truck. "It'll never cross their mind. They'll look for us further down the road, heading towards the Loire, not behind them."

Gabriel curled into a ball; he felt an overwhelming desire to sleep, meanwhile, Raoul kept an eye on the road through a hole in the tarpaulin.

"You get some shut-eye, my friend," he said without turning round, "it'll do you good."

Overcome by exhaustion, Gabriel instantly fell asleep.

He remembered waking in the morning but, still in shock, he had dozed off again.

Now, he was alone.

He managed to roll onto his side and crawl as far as the tarpaulin. The van was parked by the side of the road, which he could see lazily meandering into the distance beneath the morning sun. The flood of refugees had dwindled somewhat, and adhered to the laws of chance, which arranges things and people in clusters. A hundred or so would pass, followed by hours when there was scarcely a soul to be seen, and then the stream would begin again. Most of those Gabriel saw were cyclists with backpacks. Given the shortage of fuel, there were hardly any motor vehicles.

Suddenly, Gabriel threw himself flat on the truck bed as a column of military vehicles passed. French troops. They had no problem getting hold of petrol. They, like the refugees, seemed to be following the course of the Loire. Where were they headed? Then he remembered that Raoul had said "You wait here, I'm going to go for a little stroll." My God . . . They had narrowly escaped being slaughtered by the side of the road. Given their assault on the capitaine and their subsequent escape, if they were arrested now, they would face a firing squad, but Raoul had gone out "for a little stroll" as though they had just checked in to a hotel in a foreign city and he was eager to see the sights. The road quaked as the convoy rumbled past. If Raoul were captured, what would become of me? thought Gabriel, and instantly felt like slapping himself for even thinking such a thing: Raoul Landrade had saved his life, and here he was thinking only about himself.

This qualm lasted only as long as it took the convoy to pass, a blind, blundering caterpillar that left in its wake a terrible void, a feeling of abandonment. Gabriel glanced around. The removals van he was in was not particularly large. A Henri II dresser lashed to the slatted side took up most of the space; people had made off with other things – the floor was strewn with torn hessian sacks and broken crates: looters had been and gone.

Gabriel's leg felt numb, but the bandages showed no signs of fresh blood. Gingerly, he removed them to look at the wound. It was oozing pus. This alarmed him. Hearing a voice, he huddled behind the dresser. It was Raoul.

"A whole rabbit, now that's a stroke of luck, isn't it?"

He popped his head under the tarpaulin.

"What's up, sergent-chef? Are we under attack?"

But before Gabriel had a chance to react, he had turned back to the road and was muttering:

"A whole fucking rabbit. I tell you, we're blessed."

At the thought of the rabbit, Gabriel heard his stomach growl.

When had he last eaten? That was one reason why he felt so weak. But a rabbit . . .

"How are we going to cook it?" he asked.

Raoul's face reappeared, he was chuckling.

"Don't worry, there's no rabbit left, my friend. He gobbled it whole."

Gabriel leaned out of the truck.

"Allow me to introduce Michel," said Landrade.

Michel was a huge dog, its fur streaked grey with a white patch on its belly, a wet black nose and a lolling pink tongue that was at least a foot long . . . It must have weighed at least seventy kilos.

"That's how you make friends with Michel here. I found a rabbit and I gave it to him. Now we're friends for life, aren't we, Michel?"

"But the rabbit," Gabriel timidly protested, "we could have tried to cook it and . . ."

"Yeah, yeah, I know, but no good deed goes unrewarded. If you need proof, just look at what we've brought you."

Gabriel stuck his head out of the truck again and saw a large wooden crate mounted on wheels, still emblazoned in blue letters with the advertising slogan "My Favourite Soap is Monsavon". As Gabriel watched Raoul tie a piece of rope around Michel's chest, everything became clear.

"If Monsieur le Baron could favour us with his presence . . ."

And so, with Gabriel seated in the soapbox drawn by Michel, they followed Raoul Landrade who was singing at the top of his lungs:

"We will beat them! We will triumph because we are the stronger!"

By virtue of some curious cross-breeding that doubtless included a generous genetic helping of Italian Mastiff, the

425

supremely placid, surprisingly powerful dog easily pulled the little cart. Once Landrade had stopped singing, their onward progress was marked only by the cast-iron wheels on the road, a shrill squeal that bored into the soul.

Raoul had made the most of his morning stroll and now had his bearings.

"Saint-Rémy-sur-Loire is about twelve kilometres in that direction," he explained. "Trouble is, we're likely to be recognised there. The best thing would be to bypass Saint-Rémy and go straight to Villeneuve. We should be safe there. And we can get everything we need to treat your leg."

Raoul's plan was to keep heading south. They were deserters, looters, prisoners on the run, so unsurprisingly they would be wanted men. The wisest route would be one that avoided bridges and major thoroughfares. Further down the road, they could turn east, find some way to cross the Loire and reach Villeneuve, after that, they would see.

At their first stop, both men realised that this cunning plan had its drawbacks. Michel constantly had to stop to drink and they could only guess how much food they would need to feed him . . . Raoul had found the dog chained to a post in the courtyard of a house outside the village. His owners had probably been afraid that he would follow them. As soon as they stopped, Michel ambled over and laid his snout on Raoul's knee.

"He's a great mutt, isn't he?"

Gabriel remembered the little circus monkey Landrade had previously been enamoured of, an episode that had not ended well. Michel's sheer size meant that Raoul could not toss him into a ditch, but it was difficult to tell how this new adventure would end.

Their status as wanted prisoners forced them to take endless detours along secondary roads to avoid the flood of refugees taking the more direct route. It would be a long journey, and food would be more difficult to find. More importantly, Gabriel would need medication.

"It's nothing," Raoul would say, "I just need to drain the wound . . ."

Needless to say, they did not have the necessary instruments to do so.

427

## 46

Once Louise had fetched the twins from the cart parked outside, the woman who had helped her with the baby watched over them while Louise prepared the rice and soup. When it was ready, the woman sat them in the rear of the café so that Louise could feed the two boys and the baby.

"Hey!" roared the owner from behind the bar. "Not on the billiard table, you'll ruin the baize!"

"Oh, shut your hole, Raymond," said the woman without turning around.

Louise never found out who she was: his wife, his mother, his lover, a neighbour or just a regular?

The chink of glasses behind the counter, the hiss of the coffee percolator, the clatter of crockery on the zinc-topped bar . . . The sounds reminded her of La Petite Bohème. What had become of Monsieur Jules? Louise could not picture him dead. She did her best to convince herself that he was alive and, most of the time, she succeeded.

The past hour had left her utterly drained. Like the children, she had not eaten in some time. She felt grubby and dirty.

The woman led her into a back room where there was a sink and a tap. From a cupboard, she produced two rough dishcloths, nodded to a sliver of soap and said:

"I'll lock the door behind me. Just knock when you're ready."

It was the sort of perfunctory catlick that prostitutes do in hotel rooms, thought Louise. She washed herself and then her underwear, which she wrung out and put back on still wet.

Before knocking on the door, she stood on tiptoe, opened the cupboard, grabbed a handful of cloths and stuffed them into her blouse, took a deep breath, then put them back.

During her absence, the woman had changed the children's nappies. Louise realised it was time for her to leave. The woman had done everything she possibly could.

"Thank you," she said. "I don't suppose you know where I can leave the children? They're not mine."

Yes, she had been to the town hall. No, the Red Cross said they could not take them in. Well, maybe she could try the police station. The woman spoke haltingly, as though afraid that Louise would leave the three toddlers on the billiard table and make a run for it.

Once again, Louise found herself on the street.

The woman had given her three bottles of water, the cooking liquid from the rice in a jar, and a bundle of cloths. She had wrapped a cake of soap in a piece of newspaper. Louise felt cleaner, the children had been changed and fed. But in a few hours, she would have to start all over again. She felt a terrible weariness. She noticed that she had not set the baby girl with the twins, but was cradling her with one arm and pushing the cart with her free hand, which made the process more difficult.

Louise made a mental list of the things she needed.

She passed a woman pushing a pram.

"Excuse me, I don't suppose you have a nappy you could spare?"

The woman didn't. By the fountain, she asked another woman: "Do you have some washing powder you could give me?"

And since she did not have a sou:

"You wouldn't have two francs, would you? There's a man selling apples over there."

Imperceptibly, without even realising, Louise became a beggar-woman.

She had left Paris to find a man named Raoul Landrade, she could have been one of those women she had seen in the Gare du Nord, walking past rows of benches clutching photographs in their outstretched hands. And now she was stretching out her hand begging for a crust of bread, a cup of milk, a piece of sugar.

Indigence is an unerring teacher. Within a few short hours, Louise learned the apposite words to use depending on whether she was begging from a man, a woman, from the young, from the old, learned to present the expression of flushed humiliation, or the pallid face of despair.

"This little one is Madeleine, what's yours called?"

After which, she would casually say:

"I don't suppose you have some baby clothes you could give me, even clothes for a two-year-old would do . . ."

By late afternoon, she had amassed nappies to change the three children (having rejoined the queue for the water fountain on the main square), and food enough for the twins. She had a kilo of apples, three nappies, some safety pins, and a length of string. A young father gave her a romper suit while his wife was not looking, but when she tried it on one of the twins, it was too big. She had also found a length of tarpaulin which she kept rolled up in the cart in case it rained. By the end of the day, pulling the cart was backbreaking work. From beggarwoman to thief is a small step. Louise enviously eyed each pram she passed. She stood for a long moment, as though waiting for someone, watching a mother who had to leave her pram unattended for an instant, but when it came to it, she changed her mind and quickly walked away, ashamed not because she had considered stealing, but because she had been too cowardly. I'd make a terrible mother, she thought, yet still she pushed the cart with her left hand while cradling the baby in her other arm, constantly babbling to the little girl and singing lullabies, walking along the street in rags and tatters, she looked like a madwoman.

By the end of the day, she was deadbeat.

Being now reduced to the status of a vagrant (that was one of Monsieur Jules' pet words), Louise found a sudden dislike to town life. Since there was nowhere that would take in the children, she decided to leave; perhaps she would have better luck in the countryside. Should she go to the police station, as someone had suggested? Leave the children at a farm, perhaps? She thought about the Thénardier clan and shuddered. She hurried on.

Leaving the town, she took the main road heading towards Villeneuve.

The little girl had come down with diarrhoea again, Louise had to change her twice in quick succession; she could not carry on like this, she had already used up all the cloths and rags. The baby's belly was swollen, and she sobbed continually. She was clearly in pain.

It was then that the rains came. Fat raindrops promised a downpour, the sky above was black, the few cars splashed water onto the verge, and before long Louise's feet were frozen. Quickly, she pulled out the length of tarpaulin but as she tried to pin it over the cart to shelter the children, the wind whipped it away and she watched as it soared, fluttering its wings, twirling in the air like a kite on a string.

She gathered up all the fabric she had and used it to cover the children, who had begun to howl at the first flash of lightning.

She considered abandoning the twins. She could retrace her

steps and leave them at a church, someone would surely take them in. She sobbed bitterly, but the rain engulfed everything, her tears, the road, the trees, she could barely see a hand in front of her face. She continued to pile up the clothes; don't be scared, she shouted to drown out the rumble of thunder, all the while thinking, yes, surely someone will know how to take care of them, not someone like me. A thunderbolt struck in a field just to her right, and the three children wailed louder.

Louise looked up at the sky, she spread her arms wide; it was over.

The wild rain whipped and stabbed at her, she became delirious, she saw hideous faces in the dark roiling clouds, daggers and spears in the jagged flashes. She thought she had been struck by lightning when, framed against the clouds that boomed like an angry giant, she saw the huge cross appear in the distance, heading straight for her. But the cross, it seemed, was real; it was mounted on a truck.

A man jumped down, hair plastered to his head by the rain, smiling like an angel, a young man in a black soutane.

"Bless you, my child," he roared above the rolling thunder, "the Lord has taken pity on you . . ."

# 47

The long penal march had come to an end on the airfield to the north of Saint-Rémy.

Now, the prisoners were jumbled together, sitting around haphazardly on the concrete runway with no distinction between the various groups.

"Are they all here?" said Capitaine Howsler.

"I'm afraid not . . ." said Fernand.

The officer blenched. There could be no doubt that there were considerably fewer prisoners than had set out.

"Call the roll!" barked the capitaine.

The non-commissioned officers took out their crumpled lists and began a long litany of names which were met by countless silences, after which they gravely intoned "missing". The capitaine, pacing up and down, was limping slightly, the after-effects of the blow Raoul Landrade had dealt to his calf. Fernand collated the various lists, ticking off the names on his own and announced the result.

"Four hundred and thirty-six men are missing, sir."

More than a third of the prisoners had made their escape. Scattered somewhere along the road, almost five hundred looters, thieves, anarchists, communists, draft dodgers and other miscreants were running free. In the eyes of the authorities, the army had considerably boosted the numbers of the fifth column with traitors and spies . . .

"Many of those missing are, in fact, dead, sir."

This news seemed to cheer the senior officer. In war, those missing in action represented defeat; the dead represented victory. The NCOs were consulted and a list made of the dead. In each case cause of death was noted.

"Thirteen dead, sir," said Fernand. "Six prisoners were shot while attempting to escape. Seven other prisoners were . . ."

How could he put it?

"Yes?" prompted the capitaine.

Fernand did not know what to say.

"They were . . ."

"Laggards, adjudant-chef, they were laggards."

"Exactly, sir, laggards, who were also shot."

"In accordance with orders."

"In accordance with orders, absolutely, sir."

Although no-one expected it, fresh supplies were delivered. Enough to feed a thousand men. At the camp in Gravières, they had starved, now there was almost too much food to go round.

"Tell me something, adjudant-chef . . ."

Fernand turned around. The capitaine took him to one side.

"You'll write up a report of what took place at kilometre 24, will you not?"

Kilometre 24: this, henceforth, was how they would refer to the incident in which he had played a direct role.

"As soon as possible, sir."

"Give me a verbal report now, so I have a sense of what you plan to write."

"Well, sir . . ."

"Come on, come on!"

"Very well. Having executed three stragglers at kilometre 23, you dispatched a sick man with a bullet to the head. You were about to do the same to a prisoner suffering from a wound in his leg . . ."

"A prisoner who was dragging his feet!"

"Quite so, sir. Then, taking advantage of a momentary diversion caused by an approaching German fighter squadron, one of the prisoners knocked you down and, together with his accomplice, made good his escape."

The capitaine stared open-mouthed at Fernand, as though seeing him for the first time.

"Excellent, adjudant, excellent! And you, what did you do during their escape."

"I fired two shots, sir. Unfortunately, my shots went awry . . ."

"Because . . ."

"Because I was focused on going to the aid of a senior officer who had been wounded, sir."

"Impeccable! And did you pursue the runaways . . .?"

"Indeed I did, sir, I pursued the escaped prisoners."

"And . . ."

"And I turned left, sir, whereas it would seem that the fugitives turned right."

"And . . .?"

"My primary duty was not to chase down two fugitives, sir, but to safely escort one hundred and twenty prisoners to Saint-Rémy-sur-Loire."

"Precisely . . ."

The capitaine was visibly satisfied. Every man had done his duty. No-one was to blame.

"Needless to say, I shall want the written report before you leave."

Fernand's ears pricked up at this.

"Absolutely, sir, in fact my men have been asking when they will be relieved."

"As soon as the prisoners leave for Bonnerin army base . . ."

"And that will be . . .?"

"We don't yet know, adjudant-chef. A day, perhaps two, I am waiting for orders.

It was never-ending.

The airfield was even less suited to housing six hundred men than the camp at Gravières had been. There were a number of army tents, but no cot beds. Although more than enough food had been delivered, there was no field kitchen, so they ate their soup cold – though it would have been no better hot.

Fernand rounded up the prisoners for whom he was responsible. Of the hundred who had started out, there were now sixty-seven. Twenty-three per cent missing, he thought, significantly better than the average.

He decided that discipline could be relaxed a little.

"We don't know how long we will have to wait here," he told his men.

"You mean we're going to be here for ages?"

Bornier regularly needed things to be repeated; it was something Fernand was accustomed to.

"No-one knows. But if things drag on, this rogues' gallery will soon start to get worked up. So, right now, let's let them get a bit of fresh air."

In this, as in everything, Caporal-chef Bornier was incapable of thinking ahead, but, unusually on this occasion, he did not rant and rave. He, too, had been shaken by the incident at kilometre 24, and was still carrying the weight.

And so, the prisoners were allowed to talk amongst themselves.

Groups and clans re-formed – such things survive all else – and they differed widely as to their opinion on their situation. Some thought they had missed the bus and should have tried to escape earlier. Others were convinced that they were alive only because they had not made the attempt. The communists had lost three of their own, the fascists two and the anarchists two. They were keenly aware that the guards' threats were not empty rhetoric.

Night fell silently over the airfield. The only sound was the whine of German planes high in the sky. But soldiers and prisoners alike had grown used to it.

Fernand's mind was filled with dark thoughts. Having nothing else to hand, he had made a pillow of his blue haversack. His head was resting on more than half a million francs. This money was the reason he had not left Paris with Alice, and it disgusted him. What a waste. He had become a thief to gratify a soaring fantasy that the war had deftly exploded in mid-air. He would have been better advised to carry out his mission . . . To the list of slurs he heaped upon himself (thief, liar, coward, etc.), he could now add traitor. He had had the two runaways in his crosshairs and had deliberately fired two shots into the air. Without a second thought. It was an instinctive reaction he now understood: he had just watched his capitaine kill a sick prisoner with a bullet to the head; he could not imagine himself shooting an unarmed man in the back, especially when, some hours earlier, he had given that same prisoner a letter from his fiancée: it had not forged a bond between them, yet it was something similar.

Furiously, he turned over. He slipped a hand into his haversack, felt the sheaf of banknotes, fumbled for his book and gripped it tight. He missed Alice terribly.

## 48

"So, the storm did not visit us?" said Father Désiré, somewhat surprised, as he climbed down from God's Chariot.

"No, God be praised!" said Alice, who had been thinking about the urgent measures needed to protect the camp if the storm had decided to visit Bérault chapel.

"God be praised, indeed!" said Father Désiré.

"What has happened to you, Father?"

He was soaked from head to foot. His soutane was dripping.

"A gift from Heaven, my child. Or, rather, four."

As he said this, he opened the door of the truck and helped down a wild-eyed young woman cradling a baby in her arms. Alice felt deeply moved. The Blessed Virgin is never portrayed as a short dumpy woman, and if Alice were to describe how she imagined the Holy Mother she would have said: this is she. The young woman with the austere, almost stern features had clearly suffered, she was drawn and haggard, but, perhaps because she was holding a baby to her breast, she radiated something simple yet fierce, an animal sensuality. Like the priest, she was soaked to the skin. Alice rushed to fetch a blanket and draped it over the woman's shoulders.

In order to make room for the woman and her three children, Father Désiré had travelled home on the flatbed of the truck, whipped by the wind. Whenever Louise turned to look at him through the narrow rear windscreen, he was upright, despite the rocking of the truck, his arms flung wide, his face turned towards the heavens, shouting at the cross and the crucified Jesus: "Thank you, Lord, for all Your mercy!"

Désiré was in fine form.

Louise took a step or two, attempted a smile, handed the baby to Alice then turned back to the cab and lifted down the twins, two panicked toddlers who stared at everything with a mixture of eagerness and fear.

"My God . . ." said Alice.

"Those were my words, too," said Father Désiré.

What Louise could see was beyond her comprehension.

She had just fled a city made brutish by war, where keeping three small children alive was a herculean task. Now here she was, surveying a sort of makeshift encampment of tarpaulins strung from wires, straw mattresses, piles of wooden crates, and everywhere a bustle of activity – some distance away, chickens were roasting on a spit, behind this was a vegetable garden equipped with a network of grey pipes that irrigated the crops, while further away, in a small paddock, a calf with wide, gentle eyes stood next to a patch of waste ground where four pigs were snuffling; and at the centre of everything was a hulking Red Cross van with a makeshift awning. All around there were men toiling, women going about their business, laundry flapping in the wind, tables fashioned from gravestones, children running between the tents; freshly caught fish spilled onto the grass and were being scaled and gutted by women with sharp knives. To the right was an area furnished with rickety chairs and broken sofas where old people sat, chatting, while to the left there was a large shed that looked like a chicken coop, but was filled with children laughing and splashing water in each other's faces, running, falling and scrabbling to their feet again. A woman in a black smock who looked like a farmer's wife stepped over the low fence and said in a firm but gentle voice: "That's enough now, children, let's have a little calm."

"Welcome, sister, welcome to the house of the Lord."

Louise turned and stared at the young priest who seemed to have appeared from nowhere. He was about thirty, with dazzling eyes, delicate eyebrows, a determined chin and a smile that was simple, forthright and joyous.

"So, what is the matter with this baby?"

A worried Sister Cécile was already feeling the little girl's stomach.

"I haven't been able to feed her properly . . . I had no . . ."

"We just need to get someone to make up a bottle for her. Don't worry, everything will be fine." Sister Cécile turned and went back to her other duties.

"Well now," said Father Désiré, "Alice will look after you and the baby, and as soon as this little angel has had her bottle, we'll find a space for you. I'll take care of these two little ones, twins, aren't they?"

"They're not mine . . ." Louise began, but the priest had already disappeared.

On the other side of the chapel there was an improvised nursery where nappies had been hung up to dry next to a table piled high with a motley array of soaps, talcum powders, lotions, bottles and dummies of various brands from various places.

Louise changed the baby while Alice prepared a bottle of formula, dabbed a little on the back of her hand to check the temperature and decided it would be fine. Louise looked enviously at Alice, at the ample bosom that was surely every woman's dream. As she did so, she struggled to fasten the nappy.

"It's easier if you fold it this way . . ."

"I know, I know," Louise stammered. "I'm just tired . . ."

"Then fold this under, that's right, and tuck it in here . . ."

Finally, the baby was changed and dressed.

"What's her name?" said Alice.

"Madeleine."

"And yours?"

"Louise."

Next came the bottle, which the little girl sucked eagerly.

"Come over here," said Alice. "We'll be a little more comfortable."

Hammer in hand, Father Désiré was putting the finishing touches to a sty to house the pigs. Night was drawing in. The two women sat on a stone bench next to the main door of the chapel. From here, they could see the whole of the camp.

"Extraordinary . . ." Louise said, sincerely.

"Yes," said Alice.

"I was talking about Father Désiré."

"So was I."

They smiled at each other.

"Where is he from?"

"I'm not quite sure," said Alice, knitting her brow. "He did tell me . . . But it doesn't really matter, what matters is that he is here, now. What about you, where are you from?"

"Paris. We left last Monday."

Having been fed and winded, the baby girl was beginning to doze.

"Because of the Germans?"

"No . . ."

The word had slipped out. How could Louise explain that she had left Paris to look for a half-brother whose existence she had only discovered a few days earlier? That she had been reckless enough to set out on the road to ruin with a restaurant owner in a pair of carpet slippers who . . .

"I mean, yes. Because of the Germans."

Alice told Louise everything she knew about the camp, how Father Désiré had created it with his own bare hands. As she described his indefatigable energy, there was a note of admiration in her voice, but also a tinge of amusement, almost of mockery.

"You find Father Désiré amusing?"

"I have to admit, I do. It all depends on how you look at him. On the one hand, he is a priest, on the other, he's a child. You can never tell which will win out, it can be very surprising."

There was a brief silence as Alice struggled to find the right words.

"Your children . . . Is the father around?"

Louise blushed, opened her mouth to say something, but could think of nothing. Alice averted her eyes.

"Your twins are in there (she nodded to the chapel). That's where we put the toddlers during the day, there are three women who take turns looking after them."

"I can help out, too . . ."

Alice smiled sweetly.

"Take your time. You only just got here."

## 49

They spent the first night sleeping in a barn, after a meal of salad leaves and fruit scrumped from an orchard. Michel had sniffed at the vegetables and fruit, and then sloped off.

The hay smelled good, the countryside was serene, and had Gabriel not been so worried about his leg, he would have happily drifted off to sleep.

"Do you think he'll come back?" Raoul said worriedly.

The barn was pitch dark.

"He's hungry," said Gabriel, deciding that honesty was best. "He'll probably have to roam far to find something to eat. I don't know whether he'll come back . . ."

Now and then, the two men felt a mouse scurrying between their feet.

"Why did you tear up the letter?" said Gabriel after a moment's silence.

"I was sick and tired of thinking about it . . . but it's still got me all riled up."

"Because . . ."

"Because of that bitch . . ."

"Was she really cruel?"

"You can't begin to imagine. You won't find another kid who spent as many hours locked in a dark cellar as me. I never said anything, never complained, and that really made her mad. What she wanted was for me to bawl, that's what she wanted, to hear me sob. To hear me beg. But the more she punished me and the more she locked me up, the more I defied her. At ten years old, I was probably strong enough to kill her. But I saved that for my dreams; I never fought back, never raised a hand to her, never complained, I would just stand there and stare at her, it drove her out of her mind."

"Did you ever wonder why she . . .?"

"The way I figure, she wanted another child, she'd had a daughter and she wanted a son. But she couldn't have another kid. I can't think of any other reason. So, they took me from the orphanage and . . ."

The explanation seemed unsatisfactory, but it hurt nonetheless. And he could think of no other.

"I suppose I was a disappointment."

A terrible admission.

"They couldn't give me back, it's not done, that's the law, if you take a kid and you end up with a moron, you're stuck with him."

"But, adopting an infant, only four months old . . .?"

"What better way to give the impression it's your own?"

It was clear that Raoul had carefully considered the matter; he had an answer for everything.

"And there was no-one in the family to defend you?"

"There was Henriette, but she was still very young. And the old man was never around, he was always out visiting patients. Or in his surgery. There would be people in his waiting room at all hours. We barely saw him. He thought I was a problem child. He felt sorry for his wife . . ."

Late that night, Michel padded back into the barn. Though he stank of rotting carrion, Raoul let the dog lie next to him.

*

The night did little to improve Gabriel's health. By morning, the wound was septic and weeping pus.

"Right," Raoul said authoritatively, "what you need now is a doctor with instruments who can drain the wound and give you fresh dressings."

It was difficult to imagine this was possible. The nearest town was precisely the one they had hoped to avoid, but now they found themselves forced to head for Saint-Rémy-sur-Loire. The river was somewhere to their left, but they would have to walk some distance in order to find a bridge.

They hitched Michel to a leash and set off for the Loire.

If they managed to find a way to cross the river, they planned to leave the dog on this bank. It had been Raoul's decision. Feeding him would be a Sisyphean task. Besides, the three of them together were bound to attract attention. Michel could not tag along.

Gabriel knew things were off to a bad start because Raoul seemed to have lost his drive and determination, his face was tense and anxious. Quick-witted as he was, he could work out how they could cross the river, or how they would get to Saint-Rémy without being arrested by a random gendarme or a soldier; worse still, they had no idea of the position of the German army. And perhaps the idea of having to abandon Michel, as his owners had done, led him to think dark thoughts.

They reached the banks of the Loire shortly before midday. Although the river was not particularly wide at this point, it was daunting nonetheless; it was at least a hundred metres to the far bank, and then there was the current to consider.

"Sit!" Raoul ordered Michel. "Stand guard! If anyone comes, eat them, that should keep your belly full . . ."

Then he disappeared.

An hour passed, and then another. Not for an instant did it occur to Gabriel that Raoul might have run off. It was a curious certainty. Perhaps he had no choice: the pain in his leg was excruciating, he could not even touch it, he was haunted by the word gangrene, so even imagining that Raoul had abandoned him was beyond his capabilities.

It was almost 4 p.m. when he saw Michel get to his feet, sniff the air and disappear. Twenty minutes later, his return was heralded by the gravelly voice of Raoul, swearing like a trooper. But the voice did not seem to be coming from the field, nor the road to Gabriel's left; it was coming from the river to his right. Somewhere downstream, Landrade had found an abandoned skiff and somehow managed to tow it upstream, against the raging current, a task that would have defeated many men.

"Are we supposed to row across?" said a panicked Gabriel.

"Um, no . . ." said Raoul, ". . . I couldn't find the oars."

His trousers were caked in mud up to the knees and he was sweating profusely; he was exhausted from the effort. With no oars, it was difficult to see the point of the boat.

"It looks like Michel will be coming with us after all . . ."

Some minutes later, the dog was harnessed, but this time he was not pulling the Monsavon cart, he was swimming. With his snout just above water, he was frantically doggy-paddling, towing the boat containing the two fugitives across the Loire.

When they reached the far shore, the exhausted dog lay on the bank, panting hard, his tongue lolling, his eyes staring. Meanwhile, Gabriel was hopping on one leg, doing his best to haul the Monsavon cart out of the boat while Raoul was hunkered down, patting Michel's flank.

"Getting us across the river was no mean feat, I tell you. There's many a dog would have died in the attempt."

Michel was clearly ailing. The constant lack of food coupled with the sheer effort of dragging a boat against the raging current had sapped his strength; his paws were limp, and he was gasping for breath.

And so it was that two men, one leaning on a crutch fashioned from a fence post found lying in a field, and the other drawing a cart in which lay an ailing dog the size of a calf, trudged into a little hamlet called La Serpentière, a clutch of four or five houses, and rang the doorbell of the only house whose shutters were not closed.

An elderly woman appeared, warily opening the door only a crack: What is it?

"We're looking for a doctor, Madame."

From the old woman's expression, it seemed as though she had not heard the word in decades.

"I don't rightly know . . . You'd have to try in Saint-Rémy if there's any still there."

They had passed a signpost a little way back. Eight kilometres to Saint-Rémy. The old woman looked Gabriel up and down, concluding her inspection with the bandage and the crutch. Her conclusion was less than positive.

"Saint-Rémy, that's all I can think."

She was about to close the door when her curiosity was piqued by the cart, half hidden by Raoul. She craned her neck and squinted.

"Is that a dog you've got with you there?"

Raoul stood aside.

"Michel. He's in a bad way, too . . ."

The transfiguration was instantaneous, the old woman looked as though she would burst into tears there on her doorstep.

"My God . . ."

"I think his heart might be about to give out."

The old woman made the sign of the cross and bit her fist.

"Saint-Rémy is a bit of a trek . . ." said Raoul.

"Maybe you should . . . yes, you should go see Father Désiré."

"Is he a doctor?"

"He is a holy man."

"I'd prefer a doctor. Or a vet."

"Father Désiré doesn't practise medicine, but he performs miracles."

"A miracle would fit the bill . . ."

"You'll find him at Bérault chapel."

She pointed to a little path that branched off to the left.

"It's less than a kilometre from here."

## 50

A few of the locals, mostly farmers who happened to be passing, passed on such news as they had heard on the wireless to the prisoners and guards at the airfield, who were still waiting for orders.

This was how they learned that an armistice had been signed in Paris following threats by the Germans to raze the city. Someone had heard that the French Tricolour that had proudly fluttered from public buildings had been replaced with flags emblazoned with the swastika. That evening, they were told that, since news-papers had ceased publication, vehicles equipped with loudhailers were patrolling the streets of Paris, informing all residents that the city was now under German occupation.

They waited a second day, and a third and then finally, on Sunday afternoon, to general astonishment, some twenty trucks from the 29th Infantry Division arrived and parked up. The commanding officer, a colonel, introduced himself, saying that he had orders to take charge of the prisoners and transport them to Bonnerin.

For Fernand and his men, the mission was over.

After Capitaine Howsler confirmed that he had indeed been relieved of his duties, Fernand led his men away to a tent that was being dismantled by soldiers. He shook hands with his comrades, each of whom had his own plans. Some said they intended to catch a train back to Paris, which caused much laughter among those who intended to head further south. No-one spoke of re-enlisting, no-one knew who was in command now, their sole commander now was Fernand, who said "Right lads, I'll see you someday, and good luck to all of you."

He took Caporal-chef Bornier to one side.

"That order to execute a wounded prisoner . . . that was a bad business, wasn't it?"

Bornier bowed his head.

"It's funny," said Fernand, "when I give you an order, you usually fuck it up. But when you have to take the initiative, you usually get it right . . ."

Bornier looked up and grinned, he was happy, relieved.

Fernand clapped him on the back, shouldered his haversack, and set off down the road.

He felt grubby. There was nothing metaphorical about the feeling: it had been more than two days since he'd been able to wash properly, and he stank like a bear. He headed towards the Loire, confident he would find a sheltered spot where he could bathe, he had even found a sliver of soap in his bag. He took a narrow path that wound its way down to the river and stopped dead. The serenity of the Loire, of its sinuous meanders past low hills was enough to take his breath away.

He pulled off his shirt, kicked off his shoes and socks, and rolled his trousers up to his knees.

It was about five o'clock in the afternoon when Fernand reached the outskirts of Saint-Rémy-sur-Loire.

The reader will remember the state of the town, besieged as it was by the flood of refugees, where the few remaining public services were overwhelmed by demands. The night before, Loiseau, the sous-préfet, had left Montargis to make a tour of inspection:

the results were harrowing. This brisk, energetic man tirelessly ticked boxes as he redeployed civil servants, most of whom had not slept for four days, to those areas with the highest concentration of refugees. Earlier this morning, he had requisitioned a municipal garage in which to house social services, furnished with desks commandeered from the local primary school, where he had also found stacks of paper but no pencils.

Fernand had briefly considered offering to work for the town council, then thought better of it. Now, as he approached Bérault chapel (a sign indicated it was three kilometres away), his worries and disappointments began to fade as the image of Alice came into focus. How could he have allowed himself to be distracted from his worries about her health? Only a matter of days ago, he had been prepared to leap into a truck and rush off to find her, yet today he had dawdled on the road, and even taken the time to wash. He quickened his pace.

Slung over his shoulder, in his blue haversack, his copy of the *Thousand and One Nights* bobbed on a sea of hundred-franc notes.

## 51

Raoul Landrade had made his life more difficult by insisting on pushing rather than pulling the handcart, which veered this way and that, forcing him to execute all manner of contortions that further added to the exhaustion he was feeling, having hauled the rowing boat along the banks of the Loire.

"Why don't you pull it behind you," said Gabriel.

But Raoul adamantly refused; this way he could keep an eye on Michel. Not that there was anything to be done, the dog was dying, he did not stir, his huge head lolled on one side, his tongue protruded, his limbs were lifeless, his eyes glassy. The metallic squeal of the cart's iron wheels on the road got on their nerves. Raoul made the journey even longer, swerving to avoid a pothole here, a crater there, his contorted face so pale it looked as though it had been powdered with chalk.

Gabriel thought of offering to take over, but with his crutch it was impossible.

If Michel was in a bad way, Gabriel's wound was little better. Anyone else would have been annoyed that Raoul seemed more concerned about a dog he had known for two days rather than the comrade who had more or less been by his side throughout this war, but Gabriel took no offence. He had noticed a change in Raoul in recent days. It had started when he was given the letter, and though he had furiously ripped it up, it had left its mark. The questions it raised and the answers it promised had fractured the foundations on which Raoul had built his life. Gabriel had come to know him a little better; he knew Landrade was not holding up well.

As they approached Bérault chapel, Gabriel was fretfully wondering what use a priest would be when what he needed was a doctor, or better yet, a surgeon. He pictured himself with one leg, like those veterans of the Great War he had seen on the street corners of Dijon selling lottery tickets in order to survive.

Craning his neck to peer past Raoul's tense face, he could just see Michel's muzzle, he looked half-dead.

Such were their spirits when they came to the open gate of Bérault chapel. There was no sign.

They stopped and listened to the curious, chaotic hubbub of industry.

"Is this the place where they perform miracles?" Raoul asked. He was dubious. It looked like a Gypsy encampment.

"Yes, my brothers," came a voice, "this is the place!"

They glanced around to find the source of this clear but boyish exclamation and, looking up into the branches of the elm standing sentry next to the chapel door, saw a fluttering soutane they initially mistook for a crow. It was a priest. Sliding down a rope, he landed at their feet. He was young and smiling.

"Well now," he said, leaning over the cart, "there's a brave dog." Then, turning to Gabriel, "and a soldier who looks as though he is in need of the Lord's help."

No-one was expecting it, not even Gabriel: Raoul suddenly collapsed.

His comrade tried to catch him, but the crutch got in his way and Raoul's head struck a rock with a dull, disquieting thud.

"Lord God!" said Father Désiré. "Come unto me children of the Lord! To Heaven."

Alice and Cécile appeared.

The nun knelt down next to Raoul, lifted his head, checked the wound, then laid him down again.

"Alice, could you get the stretcher, please?"

Alice ran over to the truck. Meanwhile, as she took Raoul's pulse, Sister Cécile looked up at the trembling young man with the crutch.

"This man is exhausted . . . He's completely worn out," she said to Gabriel. "What about you, what's the matter with you?"

"I have a bullet wound in my leg . . ."

The nun narrowed her eyes and, with surprising swiftness, removed the bandage.

"It's not a pretty sight, I'll grant you . . ." (she palpated the sides of the wound) ". . . but we've still got time. Come and see the doctor in a little while."

Gabriel nodded, he glanced at the lifeless body of Raoul, then at the cart.

"Is there someone who can look after the dog?"

"We've only got one doctor," said Sister Cécile, "no vets."

This pronouncement had a marked effect on Gabriel; his features tensed, and he was opening his mouth to say something when Father Désiré interrupted.

"The Good Lord loves all His creatures, without exception. I am sure that our doctor will do the same. What do you say, Sister Cécile?"

The nun did not trouble to respond. Father Désiré turned to Gabriel.

"Take your time and get some rest, I shall look after the dog."

That said, he pushed the cart towards a military truck parked in the camp.

Alice reappeared with the makeshift stretcher – a length of

tarpaulin wound around two poles. Sister Cécile studied Alice's face; she was ashen.

"Are you alright?"

Alice tried to smile. "I'm fine."

"You stay here," said the nun, "I'll ask someone else. Philippe!"

The Belgian, who had been changing the oil on God's Chariot, strode over. Seconds later, he and the nun had rolled Raoul onto the stretcher and were hurriedly carrying him towards the field ambulance.

They had just left when Gabriel noticed that Alice was standing, mouth gaping, clutching her heart . . . She fell to her knees.

Everyone was falling, it was a sign of the times.

Tossing aside his crutch, he lifted her up, hoisted her into his arms and hobbled towards the truck. They looked like a couple of newlyweds heading for the marital bed.

Louise, who had witnessed the scene from afar, had been unable to help. It had all happened too quickly, and she had been looking after the younger children while another scene played out in a show that might have been titled "the twins against the rest of the world". It was not a situation she could leave unsupervised. To say nothing of the fact that the little girl was fast asleep in her arms and there was nowhere to set her down.

She watched as the little group reached the truck, the door opened, the stretcher disappeared inside, followed by Gabriel with Alice in his arms. There was a momentary confusion, then a hand pushed Gabriel away and the door slammed shut.

Gabriel found himself standing outside the truck with Philippe the Belgian and the handcart, which Father Désiré had left there, in which Michel lay dying.

Louise had been deeply moved at the sight of this young

man limping across the camp, cradling the woman who had been looking after her and her three children for the past two days.

She studied him.

He was staring at the dog and then, out of the blue, as though he had come to a decision, he furiously mounted the steps of the truck. He was about to pound on the door when it was flung open. It was the nun, armed with a syringe. She elbowed him aside – don't get under my feet. She raced down the steps, bent over the dog and, grabbing a handful of flesh, inserted the needle.

"He'll be fine now," she said. "They're hardy animals. Now get out of my way."

She elbowed Gabriel again and climbed back into the mobile ambulance, slamming the door behind her.

Gabriel leaned over; the dog looked dead. He laid a hand on Michel's side. He was sleeping.

The young man retraced his steps, picked up his crutch and the bandage that the nun had taken off, then shambled over to a stone bench near Louise where he did not so much sit as slump.

"May I?" said Louise.

Gabriel shuffled over a little and smiled, his crutch rested against her shoulder.

"Is it a boy or a girl?" he asked.

"A girl. Madeleine," said Louise. Then, to herself, in a hushed whisper, ". . . my God."

"Is something wrong?"

"No, no, everything is fine."

*Madeleine.* She had suddenly remembered Édouard Péricourt, the young soldier with the mutilated face who had rented the garret from her mother after the Great War. Madeleine had been his sister's name. Albert Maillard, Édouard's closest friend, had told her that Madeleine was a sweet, gentle young woman –

despite the fact that on the one occasion he had dined with the Péricourt family, he had come home depressed. Louise had even seen Madeleine once, though she did not know what had become of her. But Édouard always spoke of her as the one member of his family whom he truly loved.

"She's very pretty . . . little Madeleine."

Gabriel had been looking more at the mother than the child, but he could hardly say such a thing given the circumstances. But Louise was no fool, and she smiled as though he had addressed her directly.

"What is this place exactly?" said Gabriel, nodding to the rest of the camp.

"I don't think anyone knows exactly. It's like a refugee camp, but it's a chapel, it serves as a parish church for the village and as a meeting point for the local scout troop. I suppose it's an ecumenical camp."

"Is that why there are nuns?"

"No, Sister Cécile is the only nun. Father Désiré sort of commandeered her from the local authorities. He's blackmailed the local sous-préfet . . ."

"Is that how he got the field ambulance?"

"No, Father Désiré considers that the spoils of war. If only temporarily . . ."

She looked at the wound in Gabriel's leg.

"A bullet through the thigh," Gabriel said, following her gaze. "At first, everything was fine, but now it's turned septic . . ."

"I'm sure the doctor will take a look at it."

"So I was told. The nun looked at it and said it's not too serious. Easily said when it's not her leg that's oozing pus . . . But I'm not complaining. I'm more worried about my friend, this journey has worn him out completely."

"Have you come far?"

"Paris originally, then Orléans. What about you?"

"I think we've all come from much the same places."

A long silence ensued, during which they surveyed the hive of activity in the camp. Both of them shared a nebulous sense that they had arrived somewhere. There was something reassuring, something comforting about the bustle and the chaos of the camp that neither had felt in a long time. Louise thought about Monsieur Jules, she had been thinking about him a lot since her arrival. Had he managed to find a safe haven? She refused to believe that he was dead.

A question had been nagging at Gabriel ever since this young woman had come and sat next to him on the bench and he had watched her lean over the baby.

"Little Madeleine's papa . . . is he a soldier?"

"There is no papa."

As she said this, she smiled, and nothing about her expression suggested that this was bad news. Gabriel pensively continued to massage his leg.

"You really should go over to the field ambulance and wait to be seen," said Louise.

Gabriel nodded in agreement.

"Yes, you're right, but first . . . I don't suppose you know where I might get something to eat?"

Louise pointed to a man working the roasting spit next to the vegetable garden.

"Go and have a word with Monsieur Burnier. Oh, he'll grumble and say it's not dinner time, but he'll give you something to tide you over until then."

Gabriel flashed Louise a smile and set off into the heart of the bustling camp.

## 52

Gabriel was dreading the moment when he would have to climb the four metal steps into the medical officer's field surgery to have his leg examined. Sister Cécile had been reassuring, but being a nun, compassion was her métier. While such things probably happened, it was difficult to imagine a nun glancing at a wound and bluntly proposing amputation.

The more he feared the truth, the more his wound throbbed.

"What the bloody hell are you doing here?"

This was what the medical officer said by way of greeting. Gabriel was so startled that, for an instant, he completely forgot the pain.

"Is everyone from the Mayenberg here?"

The medical officer was the major with whom, a lifetime ago – time had slowed to a crawl since then – he used to play chess on the Maginot Line, the one who had assigned him to the Supply Corps.

"Looks like it . . . I've just been treating what's-his-name . . . you know, the con artist?"

He glanced through his files.

"Landrade, Raoul Landrade. He was at the Mayenberg too. Jesus, it's like the whole Maginot Line has moved south, it's a disaster."

As he prattled on, he pushed Gabriel onto the examination table, unwound the bandage and began cleaning the wound.

"I see you've given up asthma in favour of bullet in the leg. Seems a little reckless . . ."

"A German bullet . . ." Gabriel gritted his teeth, struggling to think of what to say next. "So, you've been here . . ."

The medical officer did not need him to finish the question, the first words were enough.

"What a shambles, I tell you. I've had four different postings in the past eight weeks. One look at the places I've been posted is enough to tell you why we're losing this fucking war. No-one knew what to do with me. I'm not saying I'm indispensable, that victory depends on me or anything, but I've got skills that could be useful, only no-one gives a shit!"

He paused and gestured vaguely around the camp.

"And now, here I am . . ."

Gabriel steeled himself against the pain.

"Does it hurt?"

"A little . . ."

The major seemed unconvinced.

"They sent a field hospital to this camp?" said Gabriel, gripping the bars of the bed.

Whenever he wanted to emphasise a point, the major would pause for a long moment. Gabriel was relieved he was not a surgeon.

"Father Désiré pulled some strings. He wanted a field ambulance, so he went looking for one. He requisitioned this ambulance, and I came with it. People say that when you're listening to Father Désiré, whatever he has decided always seems like the simplest solution, and I can vouch for that, it's absolutely true."

As he carried on cleaning the wound, the major shook his head as if to say "what a fucking mess".

"A complete fucking mess. You've got Belgians here, Luxembourgers, Dutch . . . Father Désiré says that foreign refugees have a harder time here in France. He started out welcoming one of them, then two, then three – I've no idea how many there are now, but it's a lot – I tell you, since yesterday, I haven't had a minute's rest. He's been pestering the local authorities to come and conduct a census. He claims these people have rights! We're in the middle of a war, for God's sake! Anyway, no-one would come. So, yesterday, he marched in and demanded to see the sous-préfet, and things went the way you might expect. The sous-préfet will personally visit the camp on Tuesday. So he's decided to hold an open-air mass. He's a queer fish, I can tell you."

"And so, you . . .?"

"Me . . .?" the doctor cut him short. He did not need to hear the question. "Colonel Beauserfeuil sent me here on secondment for a couple of days, but the way things are looking, I'll probably end up like you . . ."

"End up . . .?"

"A Nazi prisoner, obviously. Right, you can get up now."

He moved over to the table that served as a desk, sat down and studied Gabriel.

"You and I, we've always been prisoners, one way or another. First in the Mayenberg. Now here. The third time will probably be in a Nazi POW camp. I'd prefer the first two, but beggars can't be choosers."

Gabriel was still sitting on the examination table.

"What about my leg?"

"What do you mean, your leg? Oh, right, your leg . . ."

He stared at the document that lay open on the desk.

"It was no German bullet that you got in the leg, do you think I'm a complete moron?"

The medical officer had yet to give a prognosis. Gabriel sat and waited, but nothing came. Suddenly, he erupted.

"Alright, major, since you're so keen on the fucking truth, the bullet in my leg came from one of our own soldiers. Now, would you mind telling me whether I get to keep the fucking leg, or do we hack it off and feed it to the pigs?"

The doctor looked at him as though waking from a daydream. He was not outraged; he was a physician-philosopher.

"One: of course it was a French bullet, you're not telling me anything I don't know. Two: unfortunately, the pigs will have to find some other means of sustenance. Three: I've inserted a drain that will need to be changed every six hours. If you follow my instructions, by next week, you'll be able to walk to the nearest whorehouse. Four: do you fancy a game of chess this evening?"

That evening, the major lost two games; he was happy as a pig in shit.

It was late at night when Gabriel decided finally to go to bed. To join Raoul, he had to walk halfway across the camp. The most direct route passed by the chapel, which he had not yet been inside. Standing on the threshold, he paused: the nave, the transept and even the chancel were filled with cot beds, pallets and straw mattresses. Dozens of people, whole families, lay sleeping. Gabriel looked up. There were holes in the church roof; it was almost like sleeping under the stars. The atmosphere was not one of huddled masses. On the contrary, there was a sense of . . . Gabriel racked his brain.

". . . of harmony."

He turned around.

Father Désiré was standing next to him, his hands clasped behind his back, gazing at this sleeping congregation.

"So," said the priest, "how is the leg?"

"It'll mend, according to the major."

"He's a lost soul, but a fine doctor. You can believe him."

Gabriel asked after Alice.

"She's doing well. It was spectacular but not really serious. She needs to rest. Because the Lord still has need of her."

Gabriel felt relieved, but he was still worried about Raoul. Father Désiré obviously sensed this.

"Your friend is also doing well. He'll have a huge bump on his head, but coming through the war with only a contusion is a gift from the Good Lord."

Gabriel nodded to agreement. Lord or no Lord, he and Landrade had come through this war alive.

"On Tuesday," said Father Désiré, "to welcome the sous-préfet, we will celebrate mass. Oh, don't worry, it's not mandatory, you needn't feel obliged. 'Jesus said unto his apostles: "Follow not my path but your own, for it will lead you to me".'"

Father Désiré turned to wander away, covering his mouth to stifle a little laugh, his eye bright, like a little boy who has just said a naughty word.

"Sleep well, my son."

He accompanied this with a little sign of the cross.

And indeed, Gabriel had a peaceful night. He and Raoul had been billeted close to the pig troughs; it did not smell particularly pleasant, and the animals never seemed to sleep, they spent the night snuffling and grubbing, squealing and grunting. It should have been exhausting, except for two men in desperate need of sleep. Gabriel was unsurprised to find Michel lying next to Raoul. He stroked the dog's head; Michel was fast asleep and breathing evenly.

*

At first light, they were awake. Habits of war.

By the time Gabriel had hobbled on his crutch as far as the churchyard, Raoul was already holding a bowl of coffee in one hand, and patting Michel with the other.

"He's looking a lot better," said Gabriel.

Raoul was looking sullen.

"I don't think I'm going to stay here long."

This was bizarre. Where was he thinking of going? Paris was now on German time. Father Désiré had heard on the wireless that the French government had retreated to Bordeaux. There was nothing left to do but wait for the final unconditional surrender, and they could do that just as easily here as elsewhere.

Following Raoul's gaze, Gabriel saw Sister Cécile, chatting to Father Désiré by the church.

"She thinks Michel eats too much. Apparently, there's barely enough to feed the people so 'feeding a dog is not a priority'."

He drained his coffee bowl.

"I'm going for a shower, then I'll talk to the doc about getting something to treat Michel, after that, I'm off."

Gabriel was about to say something, but Raoul had already left. Michel lumbered after him. Gabriel headed off to have a word with Father Désiré to try and settle the matter. On the way, he bumped into Louise, who had just dropped the twins off at the nursery and picked up some coffee on her way back.

"How is the leg?"

"It'll be fighting fit for the next war, according to the major."

They sat down on a grave.

"Are you sure sitting here isn't bad luck?" said Gabriel.

"Father Désiré highly recommends it. He says that graves are filled with wisdom. It must be an ecumenical version of a sitz bath." Louise blushed at this image.

"I don't even know your name . . ."

Gabriel held out his hand.

"I'm Gabriel."

"I'm Louise."

He held her hand in his. It had to be a coincidence – girls called Louise are ten a penny . . . But Raoul had received the letter only three or four days ago, and it had come from somewhere local, because the adjudant-chef had handed it to him.

"Louise . . . Belmant?"

"Belmont," she said, surprised.

Gabriel was already on his feet.

I do not know how, but Louise understood.

"I'm just going to fetch someone . . . You wait here . . . Please . . ."

A few moments later, he returned with his comrade, to whom he had simply said: "Louise is here."

"Louise, allow me to introduce my friend, Raoul Landrade. I'll leave you to it . . ."

He limped away.

And that is what we will do, reader. Louise and Raoul need their privacy, and besides, we already know the story. We need only look upon the poignant scene. Raoul is sitting next to Louise, they have not yet uttered a word, he has rummaged in his pocket and exhumed a tiny scrap of paper, the one piece of the letter that he kept, her signature: Louise.

They had spent all day talking, moving from their seat only when Louise needed to tend to little Madeleine, but even then, the conversation continued, Raoul wanted to know everything about his mother. Hearing the story of her madness, her depression, was painful. Discovering that she had lived in Paris, only a stone's throw away, and that if the doctor had simply told him the truth he might have had a mother . . . Realising that Jeanne had never known that her son lived in Neuilly, with the family for whom she had worked as a maid. What was most frightening, most upsetting was knowing that the man who had abandoned him to the tender mercies of his monstrous wife was in fact his real father. And he had never lifted a finger to protect Raoul from her.

In mid-morning, having just returned from the supply run in God's Chariot, Father Désiré passed the spot where they were sitting, he paused, and from their entwined hands, their bowed faces and the tears Raoul clumsily tried to wipe away, he realised that something heart-breaking was happening.

"The Lord has placed you upon the same path," he said. "And whatever sorrow you may feel, remind yourself that He has acted wisely, for through sorrow you grow stronger."

He traced a cross in the air above their heads and continued on his way.

By midday, Raoul was holding the little bundle of Jeanne's letters, which Louise had miraculously managed to rescue from the debacle.

"Read them," she said.

"In a while," he said, still undecided.

Then, when they had asked each other a thousand questions, and the contours of the story became clearer, Raoul finally summoned his courage and unravelled the knot.

"No, stay," he said.

And he began to read.

*"April 5, 1905."*

It was almost seven o'clock and night was drawing in. Father Désiré had always insisted that dinner be served early. For the children, he claimed, "It is good for children to eat with their family, but they need their sleep, so let us set the table early." For all the new arrivals, dinner was the greatest surprise. There was no communal breakfast, everyone was free to do as they pleased, but dinner was a different matter.

"In a sense, it is our way of celebrating mass," Father Désiré would say.

At the appointed hour, families and small groups would gather around the flat gravestones and the few tables that were reserved for the youngest children and the oldest refugees. But no-one ate until Father Désiré had said the blessing. Everyone turned to face him while their spoons and forks gazed at the heavens. Gazing into the distance, he would say in a stentorian voice:

"Bless, O Lord, this moment of sharing. Fortify our bodies that we may better serve Thee. Fortify our souls with Thy Presence. Amen."

"Amen!"

They would begin to eat in silence, then would come the whispered conversations, which swelled to a rowdy mess hall din that delighted Father Désiré. He loved this moment. He liked to tailor his blessing to the events of the day, or even of the moment.

That evening, he said:

"O Lord, Thou who givest us food to nourish our bodies, feeds also our souls for it is through Thee that we find one another, to find that person, so close and yet so different, in whom we see ourselves reflected, and through Thee we are able to open our hearts to them, as Thou hast opened Thy heart to us. Amen."

"Amen!"

They began to eat.

Alice always greeted the blessing with a beatific gaze, as though overcome by the bounty of the Lord, the beauty of the moment, and the grace of Father Désiré.

But not this evening.

This evening, she had sat, hypnotised, staring at a mess of shadows by the church gate. Standing there was a bearded man in a grubby uniform, a blue haversack slung over his shoulder.

"Fernand!"

She leaped to her feet, brought her hands to her mouth and exclaimed:

"My God . . ."

"Amen!" said Father Désiré.

"Amen!" echoed the crowd.

# 53

"It's not the same," said Fernand. "Don't you get it? He's here, they're both here."

He was speaking in a whisper; the dormitory was crowded.

Alice hugged him to her. As he always did, he had laid a hand on her breast, her firm, heavy, welcoming, delicate, maternal, loving, silken breast – for Fernand, there were not words enough to describe Alice's breasts. At the first touch, he was reduced to tears. He asked his questions. How is your heart? Why are you here? Why do you insist on wearing yourself out? What exactly do you do here? Can't they find someone else to help? I'm sorry, but that priest might be many things, but I don't think he's a priest. We'll go back to Villeneuve and you can get some rest. No? But why not? etc.

Alice knew Fernand as well as if she had knitted him herself. Whenever he bombarded her with questions, it was not because he was disingenuous, the questions were important to him, and he expected answers, but they also conveyed his overpowering anxiety – he was a born worrier. Alice would patiently answer yes or no, but sooner or later this moment would come. He squeezed her breast (his hands were warm, winter and summer), it was very reassuring, and he said:

"It all started with the dustbin men, obviously it made me think of the *Thousand and One Nights*, about Persia, you know?"

Alice made a soft sound. To her, associating dustbin men to the *Thousand and One Nights* made no sense whatever.

Fernand told her his tale.

Far from reproaching him, Alice thought his story sounded like something out of a novel. An adventure worthy of the *Thousand and One Nights*. The realisation that Fernand was capable of doing such a thing so that he could make her dreams come true brought her to tears. Fernand thought she was distraught, he waited for her to castigate him but her only words were filled with love and passion; she lay on top of him, slid him inside her. Whether they made a sound would forever be a mystery; the makeshift dormitory was like the overcrowded houses of the poor: people heard everything but learned to say nothing.

They had finally found each other again. Usually, at this point, Fernand would roll over and start snoring, but that night he lay awake.

Alice realised that he had not told her everything.

"I have some of the money here with me. In my haversack. There's still about half a million francs."

Earlier, when he talked about the money, he had never said how much. He simply talked about a "bag of money", and Alice had imagined a purse. But if there was half a million francs in his blue haversack . . .

"And how much in the cellar back in Paris?" she said.

Fernand did not know; he had never counted it.

"I'd say . . . eight million, maybe ten . . ."

Alice was shocked.

"Yes, closer to ten million."

A large sum of money provokes surprise. A vast sum can seem shocking. But a sum of this magnitude . . .? Alice burst out laughing. Fernand put his hand over her mouth, but she could not stop, she buried her face in the makeshift pillow and mumbled I love you – not because of the money, but because of his sheer folly.

She straddled him again, slipped him inside her again, happily prepared to die of a heart attack, no time would be more fitting.

Afterwards, Fernand did not roll over and snore.

His tale, it seemed, was never-ending. To her it seemed as though he had lived three lives in the space of a week. What more was there for him to confess?

"Crimes, Alice, crimes."

She flinched. Had Fernand killed people? And so he recounted the tale of Cherche-Midi prison and the convoy to commuter buses that ended with a young man being shot in the head, an obdurate capitaine congratulating himself for doing his duty, and Fernand, with two fugitives in his gunsight, without the courage to pull the trigger.

"And the thing is, they're here," he said. "It's unbelievable. The minute I saw them eating dinner in the cemetery, I should have grabbed them both by the throat and arrested them in the name of the law, but I did nothing. They're fugitives, Alice, deserters, looters. Now it's all over. The war is over, and I'm done for."

Fernand was not sad, merely worried. It was not the escaped prisoners he was thinking about, but his cowardice, his spinelessness, his downfall.

When it came to his sense of duty, Alice could not placate Fernand as she had when he told her about the money; he was deaf to reason. Neither really managed to sleep. The cockcrow that woke everyone shortly before 5.00 a.m. (they had begged Father Désiré to put him on the spit, but in vain: "He is calling us to Lauds, my children, and Jesus is our 'rising sun'!") did not wake Alice and Fernand, since both were wide-eyed, gazing at the morning star. Alice turned to Fernand.

"My darling, I know that for some time now you've been attending mass in secret, I don't know why, and it is not my business, but I wonder whether it might not be sensible, even salutary, for you to go to confession . . ."

Fernand did not trouble to wonder how she knew – Alice knew everything, there was nothing surprising in that. No, what troubled him was the idea of making his confession to a priest like Father Désiré. They had spent part of the evening in the company of the priest, and Fernand had found him suspect.

"Suspect?"

"What I mean is . . ."

"The man is a saint, Fernand! It's not every day you get to make your confession to a saint, let me tell you . . ."

And so, by 5.30 a.m., Fernand was waiting outside Father Désiré's cell (the priest always rose early for Lauds). As soon as he saw him, Fernand said:

"Father, I need to make my confession, it's urgent."

Although the church had long since been stripped of its pews, its prie-dieux, even its altar, there was still a confessional. The only stick of furniture that still remained in the church was a conduit for sins.

Fernand told the priest everything, He was particularly troubled by the issue of the fugitives.

"But, what do you believe was your duty, my son?"

"It was my duty to arrest them, Father! That's why I . . . That's why the Lord put me here."

"The Good Lord put you there so that you could arrest them, not so you could kill them. If the Lord had wished it so, those two would be dead, believe me."

This logic left Fernand speechless.

"You acted according to your conscience, in other words, according to the will of the Almighty, you may go in peace."

"Is that all?" Fernand wanted to say.

"As for the money . . ." said Father Désiré. "You say you have it with you?"

"Not all of it, Father. Only a small part . . . It is stolen money."

This time it seemed as though Father Désiré was about to lose his temper.

"Not at all, my son, quite the reverse. In their panic and confusion, the authorities burned a large part of the wealth of this community, wealth that rightly belongs to everyone. You safeguarded a small part of it, that is all."

"When you put it like that . . . So, now I should give the money back."

"That depends. If you can be sure that the money will be used for the good of all, then return it. If not, you should keep the money and do good with it yourself."

Fernand emerged from the confessional in a daze. It was very curious: Father Désiré's approach to confession was like that of a defence barrister. But Fernand could not help but admit that he felt relieved.

## 54

Their long conversation had been a comfort to Louise and to Raoul. Louise felt that she had put something right, restored a measure of justice.

"Obviously, it's a little late for my mother . . ."

She had meant to say "Jeanne", but Jeanne had once again become her mother.

As for Raoul, in the space of a few short hours, he became a changed man. Gabriel, watching them from afar, witnessed this change, which was as spectacular as Jean Valjean's hair suddenly turning white during his trial at Arras. Raoul had been able to put words to what his life had been; Louise had given him the words. None of what had happened had been his fault. Far from being a disappointing child who was punished since he could not be sent away, he realised that he had been the victim of a bitter, twisted woman, and this was a great relief.

He felt a great anger towards his father. Here was a man who had abandoned him not once, but twice. The first time to the orphanage, the second to the tender mercies of his wife.

Moreover, what he had done to Louise had been profoundly cruel.

"Oh, no," said Louise, "not cruel. He never intended to hurt me. He couldn't help himself. He was fond of me . . . He must have been truly desperate to do such a thing."

Raoul nodded with unaccustomed gravity. Talking to Louise,

he felt as though he were finally entering a period of convalescence after the long affliction that had been his childhood.

Meanwhile, around them, a buzz was spreading through the camp. Everyone was excited at the mass to be celebrated for the visit of the sous-préfet because it would fall on a special day. The night before, "with a heavy heart", Maréchal Pétain had ordered that all fighting should cease; German troops had already crossed the Loire and would shortly arrive here. All in all, the populace of the little camp was doing what government authorities had done a year earlier: entrusting their future to God. But as the word spread, people felt increasingly that an open-air mass was not really appropriate to the gravity of the event, and so, on Monday it was decided to clear the nave, the transept and the chancel so that the mass could take place in the chapel.

Father Désiré was delighted by the enthusiasm with which his flock were preparing for the event. "May God bless you!" he said to anyone and everyone. The space was cleared so that there was room for everyone, with the congregation facing a raised table that would serve as an altar. The ancient stonework was washed and scrubbed, and, on Tuesday, Father Désiré suggested that there should be a procession before the mass. This initiative, which added to the solemnity of the occasion, was warmly welcomed. Since Désiré did not know a single hymn, he asked Alice and Sister Cécile to lead the procession and sing hymns that the congregation could join in with. Then he asked Philippe the Belgian to fashion a cross that he could carry, and Alice to sew a penitential robe from a white sheet.

At ten o'clock the following morning, when the sous-préfet arrived as expected, he paused in the garden to watch the procession. Leading the way, Sister Cécile was singing "Thou, O Lord, art the bread, broken and offered for our salvation, Thou O Lord art our deliverance, the risen Christ."

Behind her came Father Désiré dressed all in white, his head bowed, bent beneath the weight of the cross he carried. Désiré pictured himself as a bishop. As the Pope.

For the mass itself, Loiseau, the sous-préfet, was seated in the front row with Sister Cécile, stone-faced, on his left and, on his right, Alice, smiling beatifically, and next to her, Fernand.

Behind them sat Gabriel and next to him, Louise, with the baby in her arms and the twins at her feet. And Raoul, who had finally decided not to leave since it would serve no purpose. No-one thought it odd that he had brought Michel to the mass, and the dog sat next to him in silence like an ordinary parishioner.

"*Arse diem ridendo arma culpa bene sensa spina populi hominem furturi dignitate . . . Amen.*"

The assembled congregation were by now familiar with the curious rituals of Father Désiré, the gesture he made for them to stand or sit, the long screeds of "original Latin" and the strange gesticulations which were vaguely reminiscent of what they had sometimes seen priests do during the mass, though in a different order.

"*Pater pulvis malum audite vinci pector salute christi . . . Amen!*"

"Amen!"

On several occasions, Sister Cécile turned indignantly to the sous-préfet, only to find that Loiseau was enthralled by this unfamiliar liturgy which, though new to him, had been presented as the most ancient form of the mass.

Father Désiré quickly moved on to the sermon. This, together with confession, was what he most enjoyed about his role, the moment when his talent could be deployed in all its majesty.

"My dear brothers and sisters in Christ, let us thank the Lord our God –" he raised his arms to heaven and gazed up at the broken vault of the chapel, his face a mask of despair mingled with hope – "for bringing us together. Truly, Lord, we have called on Thee. Truly, Lord, we have implored Thee. Truly, Lord . . ." (Father Désiré had a proclivity for anaphora.)

Désiré was embarked on what would be a long and beautiful litany, but all eyes suddenly turned to the door of the chapel and the congregation began to disperse.

"Truly, Lord, Thou art come that Thy brethren might . . ."

There came the rumble of an engine. Several engines. Possibly trucks. Then the sound of voices outside.

"Truly, Lord, we have seen Thy celestial radiance pour o—"

Désiré fell silent.

Everyone was now staring at the three Nazi officers standing in the doorway while, from out in the cemetery, came the slamming of truck doors.

No-one knew what to do.

Loiseau, the sous-préfet, sighed and was about to get up and meet the enemy when Father Désiré's voice thundered:

"Truly, Lord, the enemy is at our door!"

The crowd turned to him once again. The Germans soldiers did not move, they stood, ramrod straight, arms clasped behind their backs.

Désiré picked up his bible and frantically thumbed through it.

"Brothers and sisters, let us remember the book of Exodus. Pharaoh arrived –" he pointed to the chapel door – "Pharaoh, the tyrannical and cruel, the pompous and depraved creature of Satan! And, Lo! Pharaoh did enslave and subjugate the children of Israel. And so the Lord did send unto them a saviour, a humble man, a man so racked with doubt that Thou didst send the plagues of Egypt that he might believe."

Father Désiré raised his hands to heaven.

"Oh, Lord Thou didst provoke the resipiscence in Pharaoh! But his soul remained black and evil. And, in his hatred, he pursued the children of Israel, for he longed to destroy them!"

Désiré's voice rumbled around the chapel like that of a prophet of doom.

"To be sole master of the world, that, O Lord, was Pharaoh's desire! So began the exodus of the children of Israel, they were seen on the roads and the byways fleeing the direful wrath of Pharaoh, they could be found, frightened, hiding here and there, trying desperately to elude his wrath! They could be seen walking ever onward, walking until they were exhausted in an exodus that seemed to them unending!"

Désiré paused for a long moment, he slowly scanned the congregation. At the back of the church, the soldiers had not moved a muscle, they stared at the priest, their eyes cold, calm and unwavering.

"And behold, Pharaoh drew nigh, so close was he that, without turning their heads, the Israelites could sense his baleful presence. And they were sore afraid. They had but two choices, to surrender or to die. The children of Israel were racked by despair. Should they turn and bow down before Pharaoh's ambition? Or forge on and be drowned in the Red Sea? It was then, Lord, that Thou didst make Thy will known. Thou didst come to the aid of the Israelites, for they had need of Thee. Thou didst divide the waters. By Thy grace, the children of Israel could flee! And when they had fled, O Lord, implacable but just, Thou didst close up the waters upon the Pharaoh, upon his chariots, and upon his horsemen."

Désiré spread his arms wide. He was smiling.

"We stand before you here, today, O Lord. We have steeled ourselves for this ordeal, but we know that Thou art with us, that our sacrifice will not be in vain, and that, sooner or later, Pharaoh will bow to Thy great will. Amen."

"Amen!"

As we can see, Father Désiré took a number of liberties with the biblical text, but his intention was plain, his meaning clear.

Désiré was about to lay down his life.

His homily at an end, he walked down the central aisle to the three officers who stood, framed in the doorway.

He held out his hands, slowed his pace. Then he stood in front of the man who was clearly the senior officer.

"Heil Hitler!" barked the officer, saluting.

Only then did the congregation realise that the three German officers did not understand a word of French.

This was why, by early afternoon, the table that had served as an altar was set out in the courtyard so that each of the refugees could present their papers to the German officer, who turned to Loiseau, the sous-préfet, on his right for a translation of various terms. Father Désiré, sitting on his left, peppered the proceedings with anecdotes which the sous-préfet tactfully summed up in three words.

First came the families with young children.

Louise appeared, flanked by the twins, cradling little Madeleine in her arms. Nodding to the boys, she told the story of the children's nursery in the town whose name she had forgotten, the mayor ordering an evacuation, the parents who had failed to collect their children. She seemed overcome.

The sous-préfet listened to a question from the German soldier.

"The officer is asking whether they had papers on them."

"No, nothing," said Louise.

Her voice trembled. The German officer was a man whose delicate face betrayed little, it was impossible to guess what he was thinking.

"And the baby?" asked Monsieur Loiseau.

Father Désiré burst out laughing.

"Ha! Ha! Ha! No, that's hers. The baby is hers."

Then he leaned over to the sous-préfet.

"Could you ask the officer whether he could make out new papers for the lady and her child, since she lost everything while fleeing Paris?"

The officer nodded and then beckoned the next family.

Louise would have collapsed if Father Désiré had not quickly risen from his seat and led her over to Gabriel to be looked after.

The parade lasted all day.

Everyone appeared before the makeshift desk.

When Fernand presented his papers, the officer asked, for no apparent reason, that they be translated word by word.

Gabriel and Raoul had no trouble explaining which unit they had served with. And how, as with so many other soldiers, force of circumstances had conspired to separate them from their unit – which was rather less true. In an instant, they were absolved, their names cleared.

At length, the officer closed the register, shook hands with the sous-préfet and the two men exchanged a few polite words. The officer glanced around, keen to say goodbye to Father Désiré, but no-one had seen him for several hours. When he could not be found, the Germans went on their way, having arranged to return the following morning when the camp would be dismantled and the refugees transferred elsewhere.

*

Many hours were spent searching for Father Désiré. But in vain. He was never seen again.

Late that night, Fernand noticed that his blue haversack had disappeared.

When apprised of the disappearance, Sister Cécile flew into a black rage, while Alice simply smiled.

"Monsieur Loiseau felt there was something fishy. He told me! The man's a charlatan, nothing more or less than an imposter!"

"I'm afraid so," said Alice, still beaming.

"You . . . you knew?"

Sister Cécile was outraged.

"Of course, I knew . . ."

"And you said nothing?"

Alice glanced around the camp, at all the people who had found refuge here.

"Pff! What does it matter whether or not he was a priest?" she said softly. "He was sent to us by the Good Lord."

# Epilogue

Let us begin with Monsieur Jules, since he vanished from our story quite some time ago. Fear not, he did not die in the bombing raid during which he and Louise were separated. He continued his journey south in fits and starts, and was in La Charité-sur-Loire when he learned of the armistice. So, he decided to retrace his steps, to go back to Paris. "Now they've finished with all this tomfoolery, I need to get back and re-open my restaurant," he would tell anyone prepared to listen. The odyssey of Monsieur Jules' journey back to Paris is another story, and one that was doubtless punctuated by picaresque adventures. He arrived home on July 27, 1940 and reopened La Petite Bohème two days later.

Louise married Gabriel in Paris on March 15, 1941. They had no children. Gabriel found a position as a maths teacher in a private school, and ten years later was appointed headmaster. Little Madeleine was the apple of his eye. Whether it was the cause or the consequence of his boundless love for her, she proved to be a gifted mathematician and, for many years, would be the youngest French woman ever to qualify as a teacher. Having been her teacher, Gabriel became her pupil when she was barely sixteen years old. When she left France to work for an American laboratory, Gabriel aged ten years overnight. He closely followed her career as much as his own skills permitted. He confessed to

Louise that he often read her papers though he did not understand them, as one might poems in a foreign tongue, for the sheer beauty of the music.

Louise, as one might imagine, did not return to her job at the primary school on the rue Damrémont, but devoted most of her time to little Madeleine. It became a tradition that they celebrated her birthday at La Petite Bohème. Monsieur Jules would make a sumptuous feast, and a cake the recipe for which, he promised the little girl, he would give her on his deathbed. On Madeleine's eighth birthday, Monsieur Jules was struck down by a heart attack. As the little girl sobbed next to his hospital bed, he reassured her that he was not about to die, because he had not yet given her the recipe. He was right. Nevertheless, when he came home, he was not the same man. He asked Louise if she wanted to take over the restaurant, and she did. She proved to be an excellent cook. As in Monsieur Jules' time, the place was never empty. The only change she made to the dining room was to remove the table at which the doctor had sat for almost twenty years and replace it with a jukebox.

Monsieur Jules died in 1959, surrounded, as they say, by his loved ones.

In 1980, at the age of seventy, Louise hung up her chef's toque. Gabriel had died the previous year, and her heart was no longer in her work. By then, Madeleine was living in a different galaxy, so Louise decided to sell up. These days, what had been La Petite Bohème is now a shoe shop.

The parents of the twins had been frantic. It became clear that, when she heard Germans were approaching, the woman running the nursery school had not waited for them to arrive, preferring to take to the road with the three children. The twins were two of the thousands of children brutally separated from their parents by the vagaries of the mass exodus from Paris to the south. Difficult as it is to imagine today, many were never reunited with their parents. In the months that followed, thousands of desperate pleas by fathers and mothers, hundreds of newspaper ads, some accompanied by photographs, expressed the torment and the agonies of remorse caused by these separations.

The twins were fortunate.

On the other hand, no-one from the little village ever claimed the little girl who had stayed with Louise. One can only imagine, though there is no proof, that tragedy struck the mother who had dropped her off at the nursery school that morning,

Raoul Landrade found it hard to deal with Louise's revelations about his past. Convinced that his sister Henriette had known everything and, out of cowardice, had kept the truth from him, he fell out with her.

Not quite knowing what to do with himself, he decided on a career in the army. "I don't see what else I'm good for," he told his sister Louise. While this might be fertile ground, given his penchant for wheeling and dealing, it was a bad choice though neither he nor she realised it. For someone who spent his life challenging authority (in the person of Germaine Thirion), a career in the army was ill-advised. He never rose through the ranks. But events conspired to restore his self-esteem. In the army, he rediscovered the camaraderie he had known with Gabriel. And when, in 1960, his comrades urged him to join the OAS in Algeria, he was all the more disposed to take up their cause since it meant defying Général de Gaulle, a convenient father figure against whom he could rebel. When Louise found out that Raoul was deeply involved in what was an illegal paramilitary organisation, she hugged him hard and said, "I'm happy that you're happy, but I can never see you again. I would be constantly wondering what blood you might have on your hands."

It was then that he finally saw Henriette again, and she welcomed him as though he had never been gone.

It was on the subject of Raoul that Madeleine rebelled against her mother for the first time. To her, he had always been a sort of generous, big-hearted uncle. From her earliest childhood, Raoul never visited without bringing a gift for her, he never tired of chatting to her, telling her his stories. Madeleine thought him devilishly handsome, he had saved her father's life, how could any little girl resist . . .

Once again, events – remember them – conspired to bring everyone together.

In November 1961, Raoul was killed during a violent skirmish between the OAS and the MPC, which supported de Gaulle's policies in Algeria (whose number, apparently, included the dim-witted, pig-headed Caporal-chef Bornier, who was as much a Gaullist as he was an alcoholic).

The subject of Raoul long remained a no-man's-land separating Louise and Madeleine, one into which they rarely ventured. From time to time, Madeleine would ask her father to tell her the story of the "taking of Tréguière bridge", which, to her ears, sounded like an episode from the Napoleonic wars.

A few short months after the armistice, Alice and Fernand also made their way back to Paris. They never touched the suitcase full of money they found, untouched, in the cellar when they got home.

Fernand, loath to become involved in the police operations conducted by the Vichy regime, managed to have himself reassigned to a junior administrative role in the republican mobile guard. He spent almost four years delivering mail to offices while he waited for his moment, which finally arrived on August 13, 1945, when he was among the leaders of the general strike of the gendarmerie, which was joined by the national police two days later. He fought alongside the French Forces of the Interior in the battle to liberate Paris and was killed on August 22, 1944, on the corner of the rue Saint-Placide (not far from Cherche-Midi prison).

Throughout her life, Alice would suffer from cardiac episodes, though this did not prevent her from living to the ripe old age of eighty-seven. Some months after Fernand's death, she cleared out the apartment and the cellar and moved to Sully-sur-Loire, where she cared for the sister of the man she had so dearly loved. In this, she did great good. She spent her vast fortune on good deeds, aid organisations and solidarity movements. She became a sort of benevolent Monseigneur Bienvenu to the people of Sully. She was responsible for the construction (and, until her death, the upkeep) of the magnificent buildings that comprised Saint Cécile orphanage. These days the buildings belong to a private bank, which uses them for conferences, seminars and that kind of thing. But most importantly, she was responsible for the buildings' famous gardens, and especially the magnificent "Great Kitchen Garden of Saint Cécile Orphanage", which attracts visitors from around the world.

This leaves only Désiré. I will tell you no tales, since almost nothing that people claim to know about him has ever been attested or confirmed. Following his absquatulation (if you cannot use this kind of word at the end of a novel, when can you?), the period 1940–45 offers, and I quote, "the only glimmer of certainty", according to the small handful of academic papers to explore the subject. It is an incontestable fact that, in 1940, Désiré joined the Résistance. Even more so than the war itself, the resistance afforded fertile ground for this extraordinary chameleon to assume all manner of identities. Désiré must have felt happy as a sandboy. There are alleged sightings of him later in various places at various times. The only proven fact is that one Giedrius Adem – a shameless anagram of Désiré Migaud – was the man who (in late '42 or early '43, I don't remember) masterminded the audacious escape of Philippe Gerbier from an SS firing range using a length of rope and a few smoke bombs. Traces of his work (or what appears to be his work) can be seen in various episodes during the Résistance. A number of historians are convinced (the photograph is somewhat blurry) that Désiré is the man marching next to Général de Gaulle down the Champs-Élysées on August 26, 1944. It seems perfectly possible. What is true of Désiré Migaud (or Migault, or Mignon, etc.) holds true of all great men: much is attributed to him. Meanwhile, we can but wait anxiously for the work of the dauntless historian now working on an exhaustive exploration (which, according to his publisher, contains "startling revelations") of what Roland Barthes called the "Désiré myth".

*Fontvielle, September 2019*

## As it should be . . .

When you come to the end, it is important to acknowledge express thanks; this I do with pleasure.

First and foremost, my thanks to Camille Cléret, whom I bombarded with questions and requests and who was invariably clear-sighted, relevant and responsive.

A small group of friends generously took the time to read the novel and offer useful comments. My thanks to Gérald Aubert and Camille Trumer, Jean-Daniel Baltassat, Jean-Paul Vormus, Catherine Bozorgan, Solène Chabanais, Florence Godfernaux and Nathalie Collard. My friend and partner-in-crime Thierry Depambour did a meticulous and astute reading of this novel which I found very useful; to him, I owe the closing scene in chapter 22, between the pigeon and the crows. Lastly, thanks to my editor, Véronique Ovaldé.

I owe a particular debt of gratitude to Jacky Tronel, to whom I owe the episode of the "prison exodus", a curious but entirely true incident. While obviously I have used poetic licence in retelling the event, a large column of military prisoners did set out in June 1940 (on June 12 from Cherche-Midi Prison and on June 10 from the Prison de la Santé) headed towards Avord, in the département of Cher. On June 15, six of these prisoners were executed for "mutiny, attempted escape or refusal to obey orders".

The following day, seven more were executed. Of the 1,865 prisoners who originally set out from Paris, 845 (more than 45.31 per cent) were missing when the column arrived at the prison camp in Gurs on June 21.

Details of this tragic incident can be found on the website of Jacky Tronel, a scrupulous historian.[1]

I have drawn many of the historical events recounted in the novel from two books penned by eye-witnesses: *Simple militant* by Maurice Jaquier, and *Le Radeau de la Méduse* by Léon Moussinac.

I came across the story of the burning of Banque de France bills in *Le Peuple du désastre* by Henri Amouroux. He claims the total exceeded three billion francs. The archives of the Banque de France corroborate the details of this curious incident.

The character of Désiré Migault owes a number of his fanciful ideas to the closing speech made by Maître Maurice Garçon barrister for the defence in the trial of 'les piqueuses d'Orsay' (four nurses charged with killing six of their patients in order to flee the German advance), which Pierre Assouline brought to my attention.

My sincere thanks to Jérôme Limorté for the Latin bromides uttered by the headmaster of Louise's school.

Some of the "news items" reported by Désiré in his radio broadcasts might seem utterly preposterous, but many of them are absolutely true . . .

The Mayenberg fort is a fiction largely inspired by the Hackenberg located in Veckring in Moselle, where I was given an

1 *Histoire pénitentiaire et justice militaire* – http://prisons-cherche-midi-mauzac.com/

invaluable guided tour by Bernard Leidwanger. Further details of the fort were supplied by the historian Robert Varoqui. Jacques Lambert and their publisher Terres Ardennaises.

A novel that uses the French exodus of June 1940 as its backdrop would have been all but impossible but for the invaluable historical books of Léon Werth (*33 jours*), Eric Alary (*L'Exode*), Pierre Miquel (*L'Exode*), François Fonvieille-Alquier (*Les Français dans la drôle de guerre*), Eric Roussel (*Le Naufrage*) and Jean Vidalenc (*L'Exode de mai-juin 1940*).

Among those whose works proved essential to me, I gratefully acknowledge Eric Alary, Bénédicte Vergez-Chaignon and Gilles Gauvin (*Les Français au quotidien, 1939–1940*), Marc Bloch (*L'Étrange défaite*), François Cochet (*Les Soldats de la drôle de guerre*), Jean-Louis Crémieux-Brilhac (*Les Français de l'an 40*), Karl-Heinz Frieser (*Le Mythe de la guerre éclair*), Ivan Jablonka (*Ni père, ni mère, Histoire des enfants de l'Assistance publique 1874–1939*), Jacques Lambert (*Les Ardennais dans la tourmente*), Jean-Yves Marie and Alain Hohnadel (*Hommes et ouvrages de la ligne Maginot*), Jean-Yves Mary (*Le Corridor des Panzers*), Jean-Pierre André-Ruetsch (*Tempête à l'est. L'infanterie berrichonne dans la campagne de France*), Michaël Séramour (*Les Troupes de forteresse en Lorraine et en Alsace* and *La Ligne Maginot. Ses casernes disparues*), Maurice Vaïsse (*Mai-juin 1940. Défaite française, victoire allemande sous l'oeil des historiens étrangers*), Dominique Veillon (*Vivre et survivre en France, 1939–1945*), Henri de Wailly (*L'Effondrement*) and, last but not least, Olivier Wieviorka and Jean Lopez (*Les Mythes de la Seconde Guerre mondiale*).

So much for books.

*

For digital sources, I once again turned to Gallica (BnF) and RetroNews, two outstanding databases maintained by the Bibliothèque nationale de France documenting daily newspapers of the period. I look forward to the newspapers of the post-war years being digitised . . .

I am grateful to Jean-Christophe Rutin for suggesting the cause of Louise's childlessness, to my friend Dr Bernard Giral for details of Gabriel's symptoms and to Marie-France Devouge and Stéphane André for the valuable information they provided on my visit to the War and Peace Museum in the Ardennes.

As always, in the course of my writing, certain words, phrases and images came to my mind which can be found in the text. These allusions come from Louis Aragon, Gérald Aubert, Michel Audiard, Honoré de Balzac, Charlotte Brontë, Dino Buzzati, Stephen Crane, Charles Dickens, Denis Diderot, Françoise Dolto, Roland Dorgelès, Fédor Dostoïevski, Albert Dupontel, Gustave Flaubert, Romain Gary, Guilleragues, Joseph Heller, Victor Hugo, Joseph Kessel, Carson McCullers, Jean-Patrick Manchette, Claude Moine, Paul Murray Kendall, Marcel Proust, François Rabelais, Restif de la Bretonne, Georges Simenon and Émile Zola.

So ends this trilogy of the interwar years, an adventure which, for me, began in 2012 and which, without Pascaline, would never have existed.

Like so many other things.

PIERRE LEMAITRE worked for many years as a teacher of litera-ture before becoming a novelist. He has thrice won the Crime Writers' Association International Dagger, most recently for *The Great Swindle*, the first volume in his between-the-wars historical trilogy, which also won the Prix Goncourt in 2013. It was made into a critically acclaimed film in 2017.

FRANK WYNNE is an award-winning writer and translator. His previous translations include works by Virginie Despentes, Javier Cercas and Michel Houellebecq. He chaired the jury of the 2022 Man Booker International. Most recently his translation of *The Art of Losing* won the 2022 Dublin Literary Award.